The Travellers

Praise for Ann Swinfen's Novels

The Anniversary
The Travellers
A Running Tide
The Testament of Mariam
Flood

'an absorbing and intricate tapestry of family history and private memories ... warm, generous, healing and hopeful'
Victoria Glendinning

'I very much admired the pace of the story. The changes of place and time and the echoes and repetitions – things lost and found, and meetings and partings'
Penelope Fitzgerald

'I enjoyed this serious, scrupulous novel ... a novel of character ... [and] a suspense story in which present and past mysteries are gradually explained'
Jessica Mann, *Sunday Telegraph*

'The author...has written a powerful new tale of passion and heartbreak...What a marvellous storyteller Ann Swinfen is – she has a wonderful ear for dialogue and she brings her characters vividly to life.'
Publishing News

'Her writing ...[paints] an amazingly detailed and vibrant picture of flesh and blood human beings, not only the symbols many of them have become...but real and believable and understandable.'
Helen Brown, *Courier and Advertiser*

'She writes with passion and the book, her fourth, is shot through with brilliant description and scholarship...[it] is a timely reminder of the harsh realities, and the daily humiliations, of the Roman occupation of First Century Israel. You can almost smell the dust and blood.'
Peter Rhodes, *Express and Star*

The Travellers

Ann Swinfen

Shakenoak Press

For my mother
Phyllis Pettit
with love

Chapter 1

The black leather-bound book was scuffed at the corners, and water-stained along the edges of the pages, some of which clung together, and had to be prised delicately apart. But the stains were old and brown. The book had lain for so long in the wooden trunk up under the eaves that it carried the scent now of dust and not of the waters of the great river which had, many years ago, nearly claimed it. As the old woman turned the pages a faint cloud of this dust rose from them, compounded of slowly disintegrating paper and the accumulating drift of the years.

Diary, 1936

Suppose, after all, we were to be called to account for our deeds in this world before some ultimate tribunal. The past made present, confronting us as it truly was – not as our flinching memories recall it – could prove appalling. But might there have been, even in our darkest acts, the seeds of redemption?

What if we could turn aside, walk through the unnoticed door into a hidden garden, and find there the past, ready to be lived again? Willing to be reshaped, fashioned from chaos into harmony and order? If the hurtling train of life could pause at the station, the hands of the clock stop.

If we could have another chance.

The old woman turned the pages slowly, reading the bold black script at random.

Diary, 1938

A man who will compromise his principles to save his skin – or, to put it in diplomatic language, to 'preserve peace for the nation' – makes a pact with the devil, be he never so assured of his own virtue and good faith.

I must find a way to send Eva and Sofia out of the country. The Nyilas party is gaining in strength day by day, and to please their masters in Germany they are already seeking out 'undesirables' by stealth. Eva's part-gypsy descent is no secret; they will hear of it soon enough. But I must stay and fight this thing, this creeping leprosy which is rotting the country in all its limbs.

If no man fights it, what is to become of us?

The woman lowered the book to her lap and gazed out of the window to where the waves broke on the rocky headland. Her hands were trembling. She had waited half a century to open this trunk of papers.

But one cannot go on running away for ever.

∽

Kate Milburn paused on the terrace, with the breakfast tray in her hands. Below her to the south the sloping lawn fell away steeply, bordered at its far edge by ornamental cherry trees, bosomy with pink flowers. The house stood apart from the old fishing village which lay below it, encircling the bay. On the left the bay was guarded by the long harbour breakwater, which extended the natural protection of the headland where the castle stood. Beyond the castle the shore turned sharply left at the end of the river estuary, and here a neat terrace of Victorian houses, built during Dunmouth's era of middle-class prosperity, faced the east breezes off the North Sea. The whole scene was spread out below her like a pictorial map, with a few toy fishing boats bobbing in the harbour, and the castle grounds a neat pocket handkerchief of green public park. By a trick of perspective, it looked as though she could toss a pebble on to the roof of the lifeboat station where it stood upriver from the harbour.

'Breakfast outside?' Tom stepped out of the French windows, pulling on his jacket. 'This is amazing weather for the beginning of May. Is it always like this in Dunmouth?'

Kate put the tray down with a clatter on the cast-iron table. She had found the table yesterday buried under a mound of rubbish in the shed and had spent the rest of the day scrubbing it clean.

'Sorry to disappoint you. Wait till November – or February, when the nights are so long and the wind from the Arctic lashes this coast. It's bad enough down in the village. Up here it will be like sailing a square-rigger round Cape Horn.'

'In that case we'd better enjoy it while the weather is good.'

He sat down and poured himself some coffee. As he cradled the cup between his hands he looked thoughtfully over the rim towards the village below. 'It's a pity we didn't have the chance to move here sooner. The children are too old to enjoy it now. It would have been great when they were still at the bucket-and-spade age. I could have taken them sailing. Now they don't seem to do anything but moan about leaving London.' Tom had never taken the children sailing. To the beach only under protest.

Kate avoided looking at him, and busied herself instead with spreading marmalade on her toast. She was unwilling to admit that she had not wanted to come back to Northumberland. Her shrinking reluctance was something she had always kept to herself, and she had never disabused him of the idea, built up during the twenty-three years of their marriage, that she was longing to return to this place far in the north-east, where her roots lay. When he had been promoted to general manager of Crossbow Computers for the northern half of the country, she had not wanted to take the edge off his triumph. The company office was located fifty miles inland at Banford, but he had declared that an hour's drive morning and evening was no problem, if it meant they could live at Dunmouth. Her reluctance, like so much else, lay unspoken between them.

Four months before they were due to move north he discovered that Craigfast House, the finest house in Dunmouth, was on the market. Built by an eighteenth-century merchant, it had beautiful proportions and a spectacular view over the estuary. For the last sixty years it had been shared by two sisters, and had declined with them into decrepitude.

Tom had bought the house without Kate's knowledge and announced the news with the air of giving her a present – an air both complacent and propitiating. Perhaps he felt some guilt that she had to give up her own job to move north, but his attitude implied that Craigfast House would more than compensate. The major repairs had been done before they moved in, but it was Tom's idea that they should carry out the finer details of restoration themselves whenever he could spare the time. Kate, faced with a house she had had no part in choosing, tried to reconcile herself to its isolation. Half-furnished, the house stood like an uneasy presence in their lives – beautiful but somehow soulless.

'I have to dash.' He gulped down the last of his coffee and got up, the second half of his toast in his hand. 'I'm sorry to have woken you up so early. I'll ring you from Manchester tonight.'

'It's all right.' She raised her face dutifully for his kiss, but he walked past her, his mind already absorbed by the day ahead. 'I like getting up this early when the weather is so glorious. I just need something to spur me on. Around here in hot weather the best of the day is the early morning. By noon a sea mist often drifts in. They call it the haar.'

'Sounds like a Viking word. I suppose this was one of the places the Vikings raided and then settled, wasn't it? Let Stephen and Roz make their own breakfast. You've been waiting on them too much since we moved up here. Pretend you're still a working mum.'

He spoke absently. The children had always been Kate's concern, and since they had reached their teens he had retreated even further from close contact with them.

'I might take Toby for a walk on the beach,' she said. 'Have a good trip, and I'll see you on Friday evening.'

Long after the sound of his car had disappeared over the hill, Kate sat staring into the distance where the sea appeared to curve upwards to meet the sky, her hands locked together between her knees.

❧

The plain wooden clock on the shelf in Magdolna Buvari's cottage chimed seven. József had already left for the fields half an hour before, and she had been lingering lazily over the last of her breakfast, breathing in the dark burnt chocolate smell of the coffee, and letting the last golden taste of Imre's honey linger on her tongue. It was going to be another blazing hot day, too hot to work. She gathered up the tablecloth by its corners and shook it outside on the beaten dirt where the chickens had scratched away the thin, dry grass. She folded the cloth carefully before laying it on the open shelf of the carved oak linen cupboard. The cloth was made of fine white cotton, embroidered in white with tiny stitches, edged and inset with hand-made lace. Her grandmother had made it when she was a girl, back during the last years of the first world war. It was to be part of her trousseau, prepared as an act of faith that her fiancé would come safely home again. So diligently had her grandmother laboured that now Magdolna could use the trousseau linen every day about the house.

Her mother had scorned such things as fripperies; her grandmother had treasured them for special occasions. But Magdolna believed in the loveliness of ordinary life. If you could not make the little daily business of living as beautiful as lay in your power, what was the point of the grand gesture or the special occasion? Her ambitions were not as high as her mother's had been, but then she had always suspected that her mother would have been difficult to live up to.

4

She washed the dishes in a white enamel bowl, somewhat chipped around the rim, then carried the water carefully outside and poured it tenderly into the earthenware pots and around the flowers in the patch beside the door. The geraniums were leggy, but already well into bloom, and the hibiscus was in bud. If the weather continued as dry as it had been, she would need to water everything at least twice a day. She walked down the sloping bank to the edge of the river and knelt to refill her bowl. Even the great river, seeded here with a cluster of islands, was low for late spring. The grey mud was showing along the shore, as if it were already August.

Magdolna watered her tomatoes and melons, and even brought a bowl of water for the apple tree. The water vanished into the hard greyish soil in a moment, leaving no trace of itself behind. Watering the apple tree was a futile gesture, she knew. In weather like this, if there was no blessing of rain to break the scorching days, the apples would be small and scabby when the time came to pick them.

She let the chickens out of their wicker hut, which stood on stone legs to discourage rats.

'Tyúk!' she called. 'Tyúk, tyúk!' and shook out a basketful of scraps for them.

They came sidling down the ramp with the dignity of plump matrons, one behind the other, the dominant hen leading. But when they reached the ground, they rushed about frantically, as if they had not seen food for a week, and the sun glinted on their bronze feathers. Magdolna smiled at them affectionately, and went to gather the eggs from the coop. There were five of them – good big fine-weather eggs. She placed them in a blue pottery bowl delicately painted with a leaping rim of fish, and put it in a cool corner of her whitewashed larder.

Only the floor to brush, then she could devise no more household tasks. She enjoyed the rhythmic swish of the bristles over the limestone flags, and prolonged the soothing job as long as she could, watching the glittering river through the open door and daydreaming about what she might make today. But she could put off work no longer. Propping the broom again the wall, and closing the door to keep the hens out, she crossed the strip of grass beyond the vegetable garden and opened the door of the barn.

જ

Toby galloped ahead of Kate towards the sea, starring the unmarked sand with his feathered paw prints. The beach was empty. At a quarter past six the sun was already fully up, glinting on the cockled waves where the river Dun met the North Sea – river current and tide jostling for supremacy. The sheen and sparkle of it dazzled her, robbing the scene of colour like a faded photograph, and when she closed her eyes the pattern of the waves danced red on the inside of her lids like memory. There was no one else about as early as this on a weekday morning. Behind her, back past the castle on the point, the harbour dozed briefly. The fishermen who had gone to sea the night before would be back soon, and there would be a brief flurry of activity before the quay and fish-sheds slumped back into idleness again.

When they had moved up from London a month ago, Toby had been terrified of the sea. An urban dog, wise in traffic, unmoved by road-drills or the howling sirens of ambulances and police cars, he had been dismayed by this moving edge to the solid ground, its insidious way of changing shape and location, its worrying undertone of sounds. But within days his Springer spaniel blood had asserted itself. He had become addicted to the water on his morning walks with Kate, and now she was concerned at his fearlessness as he leapt and paddled amongst the shallows, or breasted the waves, swimming outwards.

'Come here, Toby,' she would cry, her voice whipped carelessly away by the sea wind. 'Come back, you silly dog! There's nothing out there but Norway, and that's too far for you.'

He would turn his head, and pause, and finally swim back, but tolerantly, as if humouring a fearful child. He leapt back now through the shallows, straddled his feet and shook his lowered head so that the sea water flew out from his ears in a rainbow arc of drops.

On this abandoned beach you could become a child again, she thought, unseen from this end of Castle Terrace, whose prim Victorian fronts were set well back behind a railed, locked garden and a private road. In the centre of the row stood the house where she had spent her childhood. Beside the harbour and further back upriver around the curve of the bay, the old low-browed fishermen's cottages huddled together on the very edge of the water. Nothing but a narrow road separated their front doors from the iron rings where a few battered old boats were still tied, dragged up the pebbled beach above high water mark. Around them the women hung their washing, strung above the open boats like flags – jeans and knickers and school shirts flapping insolently above the bundled nets.

But here, around the corner where the tough pebbled beach gave way to silky sand, no one looked out from the early morning windows or peered between the trees of the Terrace garden. Kate pulled a long piece of seaweed, sturdy as a young tree, out of the flotsam at high-

6

water mark, and walked backwards along the beach, trailing it across the damp sand, sweeping abstract patterns in her wake. Quarrelsome gulls were racketing about overhead, and half a dozen sandpipers ran anxiously up and down at the very edge of the water, darting through the scraps of foam. Toby blundered back towards the sea into the midst of them, and scattered them to right and left. Buoyed up by an odd air of expectancy, Kate danced a few steps into the waves' edge. Her bare toes were laced with white foam, and the steel cold of the water sliced into her ankles.

She had walked further than usual this morning, leaving the village behind her as she passed the end of Castle Terrace. The last house, exuberantly turreted by some enthusiastic nineteenth-century builder, finished off the row with a flourish. She hadn't been on this far end of the beach. . . oh, for years. Never since she had been sent away to boarding-school at eleven. During the school holidays she had avoided this part of the shore. Then during her university days in London she had returned here less and less often to see her parents. And since her marriage it had become the practice for her parents to visit them in London rather than for Tom and Kate to make the long journey north with the children.

Beyond the last house, above the beach, there were only sand dunes, tussocked with the vicious marram grass that cut like knives. Here and there a clump of thrift or sea campion clung valiantly in a cupped hollow between the dunes. Behind the dunes, but hidden by them, lay a narrow road, pot-holed and little used. The main road running north up the coast lay further inland, beyond the strip of land that had once held the railway line, closed down and dismantled in the sixties. The old British Rail property had gradually been colonised by birch trees and elders, laburnums and rowans, with an undergrowth of broom and a tangled carpet of wild flowers. Rabbits had moved in, followed by foxes. There were hedgehogs. Blackbirds, thrushes and blue tits mingled with the sea birds from the beach and cliffs. A strip three hundred yards wide and nearly two miles long lay between the sea and the inland houses standing on the rising ground along the main road. It was a secret place, hidden unless you knew it was there. Even from the old road beside the dunes it was concealed by a heavily overgrown embankment. There were ways through to the sheltered little valley, for those who knew where to pull aside the brambles.

Kate turned again and looked ahead. The beach came to an abrupt end where a small rocky headland thrust out into deep water. Just this side of it, shifting sandbanks built up in the sea where the tide carried the sand in and dumped it in the lee of the headland, then in stormy weather scooped it away again. Level with the inner end of the headland, she knew, the old road swung inland in a curve for a short distance, away from the sea. The heavy sand dragged at her feet and she slowed to a stop. There was something about this place that disturbed her. She shivered suddenly, despite the warmth of the day, and shaded her eyes as she looked out towards the sandbanks. There were twenty or thirty seals out there, sunning themselves. Squinting into the low beams of the sun, she could see a big bull scratch himself with one flipper, then lumber to the edge of the water and flop clumsily in. She watched him reappear once or twice as he swam round the sandbank, then heave himself awkwardly back on to the sand where he had been lying before.

So absorbed was she in watching the seal that she found she had wandered on again without thinking, and was now almost at the foot of the headland. Toby was nowhere to be seen. She was suddenly afraid. There was something she ought to remember. Something that had happened here when she was a child. She tried to recall what had frightened her about this place, but could summon up nothing but the fear, and a kind of shrinking guilt.

'Toby!' she called, startled that her voice sounded so weak. 'Toby, come here! Good dog!'

A movement over by the rock pools at the foot of the cliff caught the corner of her eye and she turned and ran forward.

'Toby!'

It was indeed Toby, leaping delightedly about the edge of a deep rock pool, but he was not alone. An old woman was bent double over the pool, intent on the net she was using to fish cautiously in its depths. At the sound of Kate's voice she straightened and stood up, holding the net out in front of her. Something was wriggling inside it.

Panic swept over Kate, turning her cold and then hot again. Yet it was nothing but an old woman, out for an early morning walk like herself. Pottering about in the rock pools like a child. Perhaps she was a bit simple.

But there was nothing simple in the bright dark eyes the woman turned on Kate. Strands of unkempt grey hair whipped in the wind, giving her the look of a witch, and her bare feet, gnarled as driftwood, gripped the stones at the edge of the pool.

Kate backed away instinctively, and dropped her length of seaweed. Then good manners reasserted themselves.

'Good morning,' she said. 'I hope my dog isn't bothering you.'

There was a claw waving through the meshes of the net, and she saw now that it was a crab the woman had caught. Quite a large one, at least six inches across.

'Good morning,' the woman answered gravely, and even in those two words Kate could detect a faint foreign tinge. 'The dog, he is no trouble.'

The words came out slowly, as though she was reluctant to speak.

They stood hesitantly facing one another. Somehow Kate felt that the usual trite comments on the beauty of the day were inappropriate. The woman kept her eyes fixed calmly on Kate, but said nothing more. Kate whistled to Toby, then said awkwardly, as though she had to account for herself, 'I must be getting back to make breakfast for the children.'

The woman nodded briefly, then turned away. She dropped the crab into a galvanised bucket half-filled with damp seaweed, and bent again over the pool, as if she had forgotten Kate's existence. Kate began to retrace her steps towards the castle, oddly breathless, aware that her heart was racing. She was sure she had never seen the woman before, yet those dark eyes were compellingly familiar.

೮

It is dark. There is no moon, and the only light comes from a few pocket torches carried by the big boys. One, a great hulking fisher lad who already works the nets on his father's boat, is carrying a bundle of dry twigs tied together with tarred string. Kate can smell the tar, because the bundle is pushed up against her face. The boy has twisted her arm behind her back, and is hurrying her along. She tries to break free, but he jerks her arm higher, and she bites down on her bottom lip to stop herself crying out. She knows that if she makes the slightest sound of pain, they will torment her even more. In the dark she stumbles over the tussocks of grass on the dunes, and feels blood spring out and trickle down her legs. The boy jerks her upright again. He is breathing fast, with excitement and a kind of delight, and the rank smell of his sweat mingles with the smell of the tar. All around them the other boys and girls from the village crowd forward in silence. They are the bigger ones, all of them four or five years older than she, and she has spent much of her young life trying to keep out of their clutches.

೮

Kate found Stephen in the kitchen, surrounded by spilt cornflakes, toast crumbs and sticky knives.

'Sorry. I took Toby for a walk on the beach and I went further than I meant to. Did you manage to find everything?'

Stephen shrugged. 'No sweat.' He closed a textbook casually and shoved it into the huge black bag he used for books, sports gear, jazz and pop tapes, and almost everything else he had any interest in at the moment. Kate could barely lift it, but she poked it now with her toe.

'Is that still full of dirty socks and sweatshirts?'

'No. They're in my room.'

'Dumped on the floor?'

'Sure.'

'Not in the laundry basket in the bathroom?'

'Sorry!' he grinned at her cheekily. 'You and Dad did say I needed to concentrate all my energies on getting my A Levels.'

'That doesn't mean you can't stagger as far as the bathroom with your dirty clothes. After all,' she added dryly, 'I assume you do just occasionally cross the landing to the bathroom for other purposes.'

Stephen sidled toward the door. 'Sorry, Mum. Got to go. The bus leaves in five minutes.'

Kate shook herself out of the curiously detached mood brought on by her walk. 'Oh, no! Where's Roz? Has she had breakfast?' She sprang towards the hall.

'Roz! The bus goes in five minutes!'

The front door slammed behind Stephen.

Roz lay curled deep in her bedclothes, one thin arm flung out over her duvet. Kate shook her by the shoulder.

'Get up, lazy-bones, you're going to miss the bus!'

Roz groaned and turned over. A teenage novel with a salacious cover slid from the bedclothes to the floor.

'How late were you reading last night?' Kate could feel her irritation rising. 'Get up, will you? Surely you're old enough to get up in the morning on your own! What would you do if I was still working?'

Her younger daughter sat up slowly, rubbing her eyes. Kate looked at her with a mixture of affection and annoyance, in which the latter was rapidly gaining the upper hand.

'If you're downstairs in ten minutes flat, I'll drive you in. Any later, and you can catch the next bus and get a detention.'

A quarter of an hour later they were driving up the coast in Kate's Peugeot. The corporation bus followed a roundabout route through

10

several villages, and with reasonable luck they would reach the secondary school eight miles away in Charlborough just ahead of it.

'Thanks, Mum,' said Roz. She was cradling a bowl of her home-made muesli and spooning it up as they drove. She had been a vegetarian for three years now, and mistrusted most ready-made foods. At the beginning of every month she concocted a batch of this mixture – dried fruits and nuts and the flakes of various grains. By the end of the month she would complain that the amount left in the glass storage jar was lower than it should be. Kate knew that Stephen secretly helped himself to it when Roz wasn't around, but she hadn't betrayed him. He considered his younger sister's eating habits eccentric and ostentatious, and didn't want to be suspected of sharing her tastes.

'Orchestra this afternoon, isn't it?'

'Mmm.'

'When will you hear about the music camp in Wales?'

'Mr Elliot said, within the next two weeks.'

'Don't let thinking about it put you off your GCSEs.'

Roz looked at her pityingly. 'Of course not. I don't care that much. I'm only going if Angie and Bill and Sandy are accepted too.'

'I'm glad you've made friends here so quickly.'

Roz shrugged and pitched her bowl more or less accurately over on to the back seat. Then she pushed her hands into her pockets and stared moodily out of the window.

'They're all right, I guess. But I miss my mates from London. And there's so little to do in this place. It's hopeless trying to get to Charlborough by bus, and there's nothing in the village – no cinemas, no discos, not even a decent café.'

Kate chuckled. 'There's always the Castle Café.'

'Give us a break, Mum. It's antediluvian.'

'I remember when they first did it up. I came back for the summer holidays when I was fifteen, and it was transformed. Before that it was a fisherman's pub, all ancient dark wood and the smell of beer wafting out through the door. They'd wallpapered it with cream paper covered with red and blue zigzags, and filled it with Formica-topped tables and tubular steel chairs. There was an espresso coffee machine and a jukebox with rock-and-roll records. We thought we were in heaven. There really was nothing for teenagers before that. It must have been – what? –1963?'

'Have you been in there since we moved up here?' Roz asked, grinning.

'Can't say I have.'

'As I said. Antediluvian. It's *still* got the zigzag paper and the sixties furniture. And an ancient old espresso machine that mostly doesn't work. It's like a time capsule.'

'Really?' Kate laughed. 'I must go and have a look. I can't believe they haven't redecorated in over thirty years.'

'Granny's café is even more ancient.'

'That's true enough. Now that really is a time capsule.'

Kate's mother, Millicent Cartington, was one of a group of formidable matrons in the village who ran the bowling club, the bridge club and the WI. Since her teens, Kate had privately thought of them as the Dunmouth Mafia. They gathered every morning for coffee in the ancient and decorous tea-rooms behind Gamage and Simon's bakery, where the tables were still covered each morning with starched white cloths, and a generous selection of cream cakes arrived on a three-tier silver-plated cake stand. Woe betide any member of the public who unwittingly sat at one of the tables which had belonged to these powerful ladies for the last fifty years, or who dared to light a cigarette, although of course the tea-room did not demean itself to the extent of displaying a *No Smoking* notice.

'Look, there's the bus, just behind us.' Kate pulled in beside the school gate. 'You'll be in time.'

'Thanks, Mum.'

'I'm not prepared to do this every day, you know. You're really going to have to make more of an effort to get up in the morning.'

'Sure.' Roz was climbing out of the car with her bag and violin case, looking for her friends and not listening.

At the doctor's surgery in Sopron, the receptionist unlocked the front door and let in the first of the patients. The house was a modern one, painted a delicate lime green with white ornamental plasterwork framing the windows and roofed with fish-scale tiles of russet terracotta. In the waiting room it was cool and pleasant after the heat outside. The Austrian mother gave her name to the receptionist and settled down in a comfortable chair with her toddler on her lap. She had been driving over the border to attend Dr Rudnay's clinic from the time she had first found that she was pregnant. Treatment was far cheaper here than it was in Austria, and Dr Rudnay was an excellent doctor, particularly good with children. The drive took less than an hour, and she could do some shopping afterwards. The price of goods, too, was lower in Sopron.

12

In his consulting room István Rudnay glanced over the case files his nurse had put ready for him. It was going to be a busy day. Outside the window the acacias were in full leaf, shading the house from the sun. It was a pleasant enough spot, but he would rather be back in his grandmother's house, where he had grown up, with the river flowing past the end of the garden, promising adventure. As a boy he had always imagined that one day he would step into a boat of his own and go floating away down the river, borne by the current towards the distant sea. Instead, here he was, tied to his practice and his patients, and no more likely to follow his wild daydreams than he was to fly to the moon.

He sighed and pressed the button on the intercom. 'Show in the first patient, please, Miss Huszka.'

Kate drove home slowly. The weather was truly beautiful. The young leaves on the trees shone gold-green in the sun, and the sky was almost cloudless. Only out on the horizon did a low streak of cloud mark where the sky blurred into the sea. She savoured the drive, although she had meant what she said to Roz. She was not going to turn herself into the children's chauffeur. In London the whole family had got up at the same time, rushing to use the one bathroom, running up and down the narrow staircase in the small terrace house. Noises reverberated from room to room. If you sneezed in the fourth-floor attic bedroom, it could be heard in the basement kitchen. Breakfast had been a free-for-all, and the dishes were piled up in the sink for the evening as they all left together to catch their various tubes and buses. The house had been noisy and claustrophobic, but in her busy life she had had no time and no silences to be filled by her own sombre thoughts.

Kate had loved her work with dyslexic children. Helping them break through the invisible barriers that enclosed them was the most rewarding thing she had ever done in her life. But now she had stopped working she realised how tired she must have become recently. Despite the stresses of the move, and her ambivalent feelings about returning to Dunmouth, she had begun to feel, during the last weeks, that a certain tightness in her muscles was beginning to relax. She had thought she would enjoy being domestic for a while at least, and began to cosset the children – making their beds, picking up their dirty clothes from wherever they were strewn, doing the washing-up without assistance. After years of discipline, Stephen and Roz were taking advantage of it. Next month Beccy would be home from university for the summer,

13

after the first year of her degree in politics and law. Kate must impose some house rules again before then. It was difficult not to turn into a full-time house slave if you weren't working yourself.

Somehow it had seemed easier these last weeks just to drift around, doing the housework. Occasionally she astonished herself by falling asleep after lunch. Sitting down for a brief break with a book, she would find her eyelids drooping, then wake perhaps as much as an hour and a half later with a stiff neck and a dry mouth. Around her the big empty house seemed dead, its emptiness mockingly emphasised by the deep ticking of the grandfather clock. The loneliness and frustration of her life sometimes rose up like an engulfing tide around her and in these black moods her unease grew at the distance that had widened between herself and Tom. In London she had not allowed herself to think about it.

Perhaps she should try to find some teaching work in Charlborough; then she could go in with Stephen and Roz in the morning. If there wasn't a vacancy for a special needs teacher, perhaps she might be able to offer her original subjects, French and German. She turned left off the main road at the signpost to Dunmouth, and carried on past the end of the drive to Craigfast House. She might as well go into the village and do the shopping now.

Not that there is any chance of teaching until the autumn, she thought, as she parked the car by the harbour. And I need something now, to pull myself together.

The triple row of fishermen's cottages which had formed the original village had undergone some changes over the last couple of centuries. The first road, Harbour Walk, immediately facing the water, was still nearly intact – apart from the original cottages it held only the fishermen's church, two pubs and one larger house which had been converted into a residential home for the elderly. A glassed-in extension had been added to this on the seafront side, forming a lounge where the old people could sit all day overlooking the sea and the activity of the harbour.

The next parallel road, Fisher Gate, contained a few businesses – a bicycle repair shop, a Chinese takeaway, a fish and chip shop and a launderette – but the main shopping street was the third one, St Magnus Street. Here the ground floors of a group of buildings in the centre of the village held independent shops with flats above – butcher, newsagent, grocery, two bakeries, greengrocer – with a sprinkling of building societies and two banks. No supermarket had yet arrived. Having missed the earlier heedless building boom, when the old houses would have been knocked down without a second thought, the major chains were unlikely to try to set up shop here now. There was talk of an out-of-town hypermarket near Charlborough, and the local shopkeepers were already worried about the harm it might do to their businesses.

To the north of St Magnus Street the ground began to rise, and here roomy houses had been built by prosperous Victorians, looking out over the roofs of the fishermen's cottages towards the Dun. Nowadays, as when they were built, they were mostly occupied by people who worked in Charlborough, with a scattering of local professionals – doctors and solicitors, one chartered accountant. Dunmouth no longer had a large fishing fleet, as it had in its heyday. The dozen or so families still earning their living from fishing occupied the harbour-front cottages. The remaining cottages either stood empty or had been modernised with varying degrees of care and judgement.

As she walked back to the car along Jetty Lane with two heavy bags of groceries, Kate saw that someone seemed to be working on the derelict cottage at the corner of Harbour Walk and Jetty Lane. When they had first moved to Dunmouth she had noticed its continuing state of disrepair. There were slates missing from the roof, with a buddleia rooted in one of the gaps, and the front gutter dangled down at an angle across one of the windows. Like all of the oldest cottages on the foreshore it consisted of a single storey with a steeply pitched roof, where there was a loft which had provided storage space and a sleeping place for the children reached by a ladder. Downstairs there would be two rooms. One, the kitchen, combined all the functions of kitchen, dining room and sitting room, and in one corner would have a box bed for the parents. The other room, the parlour, always contained the best furniture, shiny with sticky varnish, with a fringed cloth on the mantelpiece, stiff photographs of husbands and sons lost at sea, and a ponderously ticking clock, wound every Saturday night. This parlour would be used to entertain the vicar or distant relatives. And, as the generations passed, the dead lay quietly here before burial.

Most of the cottages were modernised now. Dormer windows had been inserted into the upper storeys – where children had once groped in the dark spaces under the beams – and the loft space turned into bedrooms. Staircases had replaced the steep wooden ladders. Kitchens and bathrooms had been built out at the back. During the sixties and seventies, some of the old solid plank doors had been replaced by mock panelled ones with imitation bottle glass windows in them. This hideous practice had now been stopped by a preservation order.

Harbour Steps Cottage had never been modernised. Due to some legal tangle over an inheritance it had stood empty for nearly thirty years. On her infrequent visits Kate had watched its gradual slide into decay. It had once been a pretty cottage, larger than most and well proportioned, built out of the local grey sandstone with walls three feet thick and a roof of bluish Welsh slate.

She stopped to look. Surely the cottage had not collapsed so far that it was being demolished? No, there was a pile of new timber just inside the door. That suggested renovation. As she peered through the dusty glass of one of the windows, a woman came out of the door, brushing plaster dust off her overall. Her head was tied up in an old scarf, from which wisps of red hair escaped.

'Sorry,' said Kate, embarrassed at being caught out. 'How nosy of me!'

The woman smiled.

'Not at all. Everyone in Dunmouth is wondering whether I'm pulling down or shoring up. It's the latter, I promise you. I've just been clearing out the worst of the junk. The men are coming tomorrow to start on the roof, and they need room to move.'

'Are you going to live here?'

'I'm making a tiny flat upstairs. Downstairs I'm going to open a bookshop.'

'Wonderful! I hope you make a go of it.'

'Thanks.' The woman pulled off her scarf and shook out her hair. A billow of dust rose around her head, which she fanned away with her hand. She gave Kate a considering look.

'Don't I know you?'

'Perhaps.' Kate put down her bags of shopping and held out her hand. 'Kate Milburn. I was Kate Cartington when I used to live here.'

'Of course! Kate Cartington. I don't suppose you remember me – Linda Wilson. At primary school. I'm Linda Prescott now.'

Kate had a sudden sharp memory of ginger plaits and a freckled nose, one of those sudden cracks of memory that had opened recently on her dark forgotten childhood.

'Linda! But I thought you moved away years ago.'

'Oh we did, soon after you went away to school. My dad got a job as a foreman in a shipyard in Newcastle. Then he was made redundant and we went to Liverpool to try to find work, but he never had a job again.'

Linda's mum had died when she was small. There had only been Linda and her dad, living in one of the cottages further along the pebble beach. Dan Wilson had once had his own boat-building business, which had failed around the time Kate had started boarding-school.

'When did you move back?' asked Kate.

'End of February. And you? Are you just visiting?'

'No, my husband's company has just transferred him to Banford.' Kate spread her hands deprecatingly. 'We've bought Craigfast House.'

'Wow!' Linda raised her eyebrows and laughed. 'Look, could you use a cup of coffee? My mouth feels like an ash pit.'

↜

The old woman had cooked one of the crabs she had caught that morning. The other was still in the bucket amongst the seaweed, with a board on top to stop it escaping. She picked out the crab meat with care, and arranged half of it on a plate with lettuce and radishes from her garden. The other half she put in a basin and stored in her tiny Calor gas fridge. Filled with anticipation, her three cats wove round her ankles as she cracked the crab shell and put it into a pot to make stock, but her dog feigned indifference. He was sulking a little, because she had left him behind this morning and had come back with the scent of a strange dog on the hem of her skirt.

She took the plate outside and sat on the step in the sun. This afternoon she would look again at the papers in the trunk.

Chapter 2

'It was my great-aunt Winnie who left me the cottage,' said Linda, stirring her coffee. They were sitting at one of the less desirable tables in Gamage and Simon, where a draught swirled around their ankles every time someone opened the door. It was too early yet for Millicent and her friends, but they were taking no risks.

'After Dad's boat-building business failed and we moved away, I used to keep in touch with Auntie Winnie. Later on, I came to visit her from time to time. Not as often as I should. I sometimes wondered if I'd bump into you, but I never did.'

Kate lowered her eyes guiltily.

'I haven't often come back to Dunmouth,' she said. 'When did she die, your Auntie Winnie?'

'Oh, nearly five years ago. She left me everything. Dad died the year before, and I was all the family she had left. But the ownership of the cottage was sorted out only six months ago. It came to her from some distant relative.'

'What have you been doing all this time?' Kate asked. 'I've told you my news.'

'Well, when I left school in Liverpool I trained as a secretary, but I got bored after a bit, and started going to evening classes to take my A Levels. Then I did a couple of courses with the Open University – I was still working then, and it was pretty hard, trying to study and hold down a full-time job. I decided to chance my hand and give up my job so I could go to university full-time. They let me skip the first year, because of the OU courses I'd done, and I started at Liverpool University to read English when I was thirty-two.'

'Were you still living with your dad?'

'Yes. All we had was his dole money, and my grant, and the bit I managed to earn working behind a bar three nights a week. It was tough, but it was worth it. I loved every minute. And of course that was where I met Barry.'

'Your husband?'

'Yes. He was one of my lecturers. We got married the month after I graduated, and we had twelve great years together. He died of cancer just before Christmas.'

Kate's coffee slopped over as she put it down.

'Oh, Linda, I'm so sorry! I didn't realise.'

'How could you?' Linda paused and gazed into her cup. 'We heard about the cottage not long before he died, and we made up this daydream of moving here and opening a bookshop. We were only pretending – I suppose we always knew he had no real hope. But when I got the life insurance money, and the university pension, I thought, "Why not?" Barry and I would have loved doing it together, so I decided I'd do it anyway. For him. If that doesn't sound mawkish.'

Kate reached across and touched her arm. 'Of course it doesn't. And Harbour Steps Cottage will be perfect for a bookshop, though the upstairs will be small for a flat, even if it is just for one.'

'Oh, it won't just be for one!' Linda laughed. 'Didn't I tell you? I have two girls. Emma's nine, and Lucy's seven. We'll manage. It's no smaller than the flat Dad and I shared in Liverpool. I'm building a small extension at the back of the cottage – a kitchen on the ground floor, behind the shop, and a bathroom and a very small bedroom for me above. The rest of the upstairs is going to be two big rooms. One for the girls, with bunk beds and desks and plenty of room for their toys. The other will be a sitting room, with a table at one end. Though we'll probably eat in the kitchen most of the time.'

'The cottage must need a lot of repairs.'

'It isn't as bad as it looks. The old slates on the roof have to be rehung, but the structure is sound, even the floors. And the extension is almost finished. The girls and I are staying in a bed-and-breakfast place in St Magnus Street at the moment, but we can't wait to move in. Come and see the cottage when we've finished our coffee.'

She flashed Kate a sudden smile.

'It's so good to see you again. We always meant to write to each other, didn't we? But I suppose we were a bit too young to stick to it.'

'I'm a terrible letter-writer. Always guilt-ridden.' Kate smiled apologetically. 'I do rather envy you the bookshop. I'm at a complete loose end since we moved up here – really missing my job. I don't suppose you would like some help getting the shop set up? Purely volunteer effort, of course.'

'All assistance gratefully received. You are allowed to change your mind when you see how filthy it is.'

There was certainly a thick layer of plaster dust which had fallen like snow when Linda stripped off the ancient and ragged wallpaper that morning, but otherwise the cottage had been thoroughly cleared. The old roof had been stripped down to the beams. The extension was complete except for its roof tiles, with a tarpaulin providing temporary cover, although there were bare wires protruding from the walls, and the bathroom suite was lying on the floor, still swathed in brown paper.

'This fireplace has to be taken out so the firebricks at the back can be renewed and rebuilt,' said Linda. 'Apparently they're not safe and might be a fire hazard. I want to be able to light it in the winter.'

They were standing in the larger ground-floor room, where the fireplace was fitted with a small black range, less than two feet high, complete with a bread oven and a tank for hot water with a small brass tap.

'I suppose people must have been shorter in the days when this was installed,' said Kate, leaning over it. 'It would break my back if I had to cook on it. It's very pretty, though, with all this ornamental cast iron and brass-work, especially if you polish it up.'

'That's the idea.'

The room darkened suddenly as someone paused by the open door, and they both looked up.

'It's Dan Wilson's Linda, isn't it?' An elderly woman was peering into the gloom. 'I used to know your Auntie Winnie.' She stepped over the threshold and held out her hand uncertainly. 'Daisy Hennage.'

'Why, yes, Mrs Hennage, I remember you,' said Linda, taking her hand. 'And this is Kate Cartington. Kate Milburn now.'

The woman nodded shyly.

'I know Millicent Cartington, of course. I just wondered... Are you demolishing the cottage? Did you know that my grandparents used to live here?'

'I didn't know that.' Linda shook her head. 'But no, I'm renovating it, not demolishing it.'

'You won't be taking out the fireplace, then.'

'No. Repairing it.'

'Oh, I see.' Mrs Hennage looked embarrassed. 'It's silly of me, I know, but seventy-five years ago last Christmas, I dropped a ring down behind that mantel. You see...' She stepped over to the fireplace and ran a fingertip along a wide crack between the cast-iron mantelshelf and the wall.

'My granny had just given me a lovely ring for Christmas – one that had belonged to her granny before her. I was only eight, and the ring kept slipping off, so while we were playing Christmas games I put it on the mantel to be safe. But somehow I knocked it, and it slipped down between the fireplace and the wall. Nearly broke my heart, it did. I just thought, if you were taking out the old range, my ring might still be there. It probably wasn't worth much, but it was bonny, and it meant a lot to my granny. I've felt bad about it ever since.'

Linda explained about having to replace the crumbling firebricks.

'If the ring is there, I'm sure we'll find it. I promise I'll watch the workmen every moment while they're moving the range.'

'Bless you, lass,' said Mrs Hennage, smiling radiantly. 'It would be grand to have it back. Really grand.'

❧

Pécs, March 1919
My beloved,

I called today at your house, but your father would not allow me to enter. I think he suspects my intentions. How could an old man like that, past forty, understand what it is to be here in your own town, drunk on springtime and peace, knowing that on the other side of the door you are breathing this same breeze that has floated past my lips! 'You can wait,' he said, growling like a bear. 'You are young. You have all the time in the world.' But what do they know, these old men? They have not already squandered the new-minted coin of their youth on the battlefield. They do not know that for us, for our generation, every morning is a gift which we could barely have hoped for a year ago. We want to seize every morning, live each dazzling moment to the full, push away behind the barrier of the trees, cloudy with their new green, the memory of the friends who will never see these leaves, never breathe this intoxicating air, never touch again the hand of a beloved girl.

And all I wanted to do was to walk with you in the woods of Mecsek, your hand in mine, your black hair – your glorious gypsy hair – caught back demurely in its little gold net, like a panther in a cage, or the waters of the Danube confined behind a dam. Because I love to watch the fiery impatience of that hair, as it strives to break loose. Little secret tendrils creep out first, slipping beneath the gilded band around your brow. Then the net slides a fraction as you throw back your head and laugh, forgetting to be a lady, becoming my gypsy girl again. And then – ah, the joy of it! – the net falls away entirely, and I catch it up and confine it in the prison of my pocket. And the waterfall of beauty breaks free and flows down your back to your tiny waist. And

21

I bury my face in it and it smells of the wind and the grass when I ride on the great Alföld, mile upon mile of the endless plain.

Darling girl, I am in pain, just because I cannot walk with you under the trees. Will we ever win him over, this bear of a father? I have bribed one of the servants at the concert hall to smuggle this letter into your violin case. When I watch you from my box tonight I will know you have read it. And when you lift your bow to play the Mendelssohn, I alone in the audience will know that the gold net is really imprisoned in my pocket and your hair is flowing as free as the wild horses of the puszta. I kiss your lips, my love, my Eva, my girl of the paradise from which I am banned. Your lips are as red as the paprika of Kalocsa, but as sweet as the summer apricots ripening on the trees of Kecskemét.

Your slave, in pain and loneliness,
Zsigmond

The letter was very creased, and worn away along the folds, so that the old woman had to handle it with great care. It was one of the oldest papers that had been stored in the trunk, and clearly had been read many times, and carried about until the paper – which was beautiful, hand-laid and creamy in colour, with an embossed crest at the top – had developed a sheen where it had been fingered or had rubbed against the lining of a pocket. The writing was big and bold, sprawling across the page with the urgency of the writer to commit his words to paper. The ink must have been of excellent quality, for it was still as black as when the words had first been written, and had not faded to the soft brown of age. The young man's eagerness and desire leapt out from the letter still.

The diary had been started in the same year, and although the writing was recognisably the same it was more contained, more sober. In talking to himself upon the page, the writer had proceeded more slowly, although from time to time the writing would take on a more hurried quality, the letters becoming smaller and more broken. Towards the end of the final diary, years later, the words pressed close to each other like refugees huddling together for warmth. Perhaps it had become difficult to obtain the fine leather-bound books he had favoured, or perhaps he had known that the last diary would come to an end and would pass out of his hands.

She laid the letter gently back into the cardboard box with the others and picked up the photograph album. Near the beginning was a picture of a large country house standing in parkland. An open motor car was parked at the foot of the curving steps that led up to the front door, and some young people were clustered around it holding tennis racquets. The men wore blazers and the women cloche hats – their figures were as flat as ironing boards. On the opposite page was a studio photograph of a beautiful young woman in evening dress, holding a violin. She had roses in her hair, and her lips were slightly parted. The modest décolletage of the dress revealed that she, by contrast, had a rounded and feminine figure, and the hands holding the violin were not fine-boned and slender, but the strong, well-shaped hands of the professional violinist. The photograph had been hand-tinted, in the fashion of the time, and the lovely sensuous mouth was clearly defined against the translucent skin. The old woman laid her age-spotted hand against the photograph and brushed the cheek delicately, as if she could touch the young woman herself.

ഏ

It is a desperate night here in the isolated cottage on the headland, where the breakers lash the rocks. The November darkness has closed in earlier than usual because of the storm, and the two women huddle together over a small fire of driftwood. One woman is in her forties, but looks older, and she is ill now, her breath rasping and difficult. Her daughter is in her twenties, but she too is marked by privations and drawn with concern. Her mother's breathing rattles in her chest.

'I must get a doctor, Mama. You cannot go on like this.'

'Don't worry.' The mother tries to smile, and begins to cough instead.

'I must go. I must.'

The mother puts out a hand, imploring. 'They will be waiting for you again. They will throw stones. Look at yourself. That gash on your forehead hasn't even begun to heal.'

Involuntarily the daughter touches her forehead. 'I won't let them stop me this time. And on such a night – surely they won't be waiting? They will be safe at home, not concerning themselves with us.'

Making up her mind, she takes an old coat from a hook on the back of the door and pulls it on. She ties up her head in a scarf and touches her mother's cheek lightly.

'Lock the door after me, and you'll be quite safe.'

The mother follows her to the door and watches fearfully as she draws the bolts and slowly opens the door on the black night. A wedge of light falls out into the darkness beyond, and the daughter catches her breath. That was foolish of her. She should have dimmed the lamp first. For a moment only, she stands silhouetted in the doorway, and then a heavy lump of rock flies past her ear, striking the older woman behind her. With a soft cry she slides to the ground. Outside, voices are raised in a shout of triumph, mingled with cries of hate: 'Dirty bitches! We'll get you!'

⁓

The weather had turned cloudy again, and cool, more like a normal English May. Tom telephoned from Manchester on Friday evening to say he would not be able to make it home for the weekend.

'Sorry. I have to meet these people in the council again at eight o'clock on Monday morning, and I'm going to fit in a briefing session with our project manager on Saturday. It really isn't worth coming home late on Saturday night and then driving straight back on Sunday.'

'No, of course not,' said Kate, swallowing her disappointment and trying to sound cheerful. For the last two weeks they had been planning to spend this weekend redecorating their own bedroom. With a big south-facing window opening on to a wrought-iron balcony it had panoramic views, but the wallpaper was covered with voluptuous roses in a particularly nauseating shade of maroon, on a background which had once been cream but had now darkened, like old varnish on an oil painting, to a dreary brown. The Hapgood sisters had used this room as an upstairs sitting room, and must have covered the walls with large paintings, which now showed like ghosts in rectangles of less faded paper. Across the walls the dark shapes of the roses seemed to Kate to crawl like spiders towards these brighter patches. The paint on the woodwork was dark brown and so old that it had turned dull and flaky. If you ran your hand along the window frame a powdery cascade fluttered to the floor, which was still uncarpeted.

'You'll be back Monday evening then, will you?' said Kate, as casually as she could.

'Should be. I might just have to stay over till Tuesday. Definitely no longer than that.'

Anyone else, Kate thought disconsolately as she replaced the receiver, might have suspected another woman in Tom's life, but she knew that the other woman in their marriage was the job.

Once, Tom had been like any other young executive – keen to rise in his career, but expecting to work normal office hours. Evenings and weekends had been spent with Kate and his growing family, and when he closed the office door he closed his mind to the concerns of Crossbow Computers. Things had changed over the last four or five years. As he rose into top management, the job had consumed more and

24

more of his life. It seemed to her that as unemployment rose during the recession, those still in jobs worked longer and longer hours.

Nowadays, Tom was never home before nine in the evening, and left again – at the latest – by half-past seven the following morning. Every night he brought home a fat briefcase full of papers, which he worked on until sleep rolled over him where he sat in his chair. Then Kate would carefully move the folder that was about to slip from his hand, turn off the lamp, and tiptoe off to bed. An hour or two later he would stumble upstairs and roll into bed beside her, complaining irritably that she shouldn't have let him doze off, he needed to finish reading the report... and would plunge into sleep again before the sentence was finished.

She worried about his health. When they had first met, he was on the university tennis team and spent his weekends sailing. Now he seemed to regard the few minutes it took to walk to and from his car each day as a segment of wasted time. His talk about sailing, on the morning he left for Manchester, was no more than lip-service to an abandoned dream.

Once or twice she had said, 'For heaven's sake, Tom, give it a rest! The world won't come to an end if you don't brief yourself for seven meetings tomorrow. Can't you delegate some of this?'

He would smile enigmatically and pretend to listen, but she knew that in his heart he was impervious to her appeals. Work had somehow become a drug which both excited and soothed him. She could not put her finger on the reason for it, did not think that she was in any way to blame, or the children. The frantic pressure seemed to come from that other world, where the pursuit of successful business deals had replaced the atavistic male need to display prowess as a hunter.

Kate spent a gloomy weekend. She had no energy even to walk Toby, but let him out into the drizzly garden instead. Roz was spending the weekend with her friend Angie in Charlborough, and Stephen had suddenly been seized by panic over his A Levels, and refused to stir from his room except for frequent raids on the fridge. On Sunday afternoon Beccy phoned – 'Just for a chat,' she said, but it soon became clear that she had spent all her money again and was angling for further funds. Kate tried to be strong.

'You know we discussed all this before you went up to university last autumn, darling. We are giving you well over the equivalent of a full grant, and you said you could easily budget on that.'

'I know, Mum, but I've had extra expenses. I have to pay my share when we all go to the pub, don't I? And the last telephone bill for our flat was horrendous. It wasn't me that was making all the long

25

calls, or Pam – Debbie's family is in Ireland, and Neil calls his girlfriend in London every single night – but we agreed we would split the phone bill four ways right at the start, and it's difficult to go back on that now. And then the microwave blew up and we had to get a new one. That cost us over £200.'

Kate bit back the desire to point out that when she had been a student she had managed to survive without either a telephone or a microwave.

'I didn't want to ask you for more money,' said Beccy virtuously, 'but I've taken out the maximum student loan and they won't let me have any more.'

'Oh, Beccy! You *promised* you wouldn't take out a loan. We don't want you to get into debt.'

'Well, I just had to, Mum,' said Beccy icily. 'What do you want me to do, go on the streets?'

I suppose it is our fault, thought Kate, as she hung up, having promised to transfer £300 to Beccy's bank account on Monday morning. We have made life too easy for them, and they expect to have the same comforts in student life as they have at home.

Stephen grudgingly agreed to emerge from his room long enough to eat dinner on Sunday evening when Kate's parents came up from their house on Castle Terrace, but he retreated as soon as the table was cleared.

'Come on, Katie,' said Howard. 'We'll give you a hand with the washing up. You're looking a bit down tonight.'

Kate tried to shake off her gloom. 'Just my awful family,' she said ruefully. 'Tom working himself into the ground, Roz moaning about missing London, Stephen refusing to help with anything around the house because of his exams, and now Beccy running out of money again.'

'You should discipline them better,' said Millicent crisply, tying on an apron and filling the sink with hot suds. 'No, don't put the dishes in the dishwasher, Howard. It doesn't do the job properly. I'll wash, you dry, and Kate can put away. She's the only one who knows where anything goes in this new house.'

Her husband and daughter knew better than to argue with her.

'Now *I* would never have let you get away with the nonsense you put up with from your children,' said Millicent, efficiently soaping and rinsing the glasses and the cutlery. 'Tell Beccy she must manage on the money she has until the end of term. She will just have to learn to do without things.'

'Apparently they have all these bills for the flat...'

26

'They should have budgeted properly, and put money aside for the bills.'

'We'll have a really serious talk with her over the summer,' said Kate weakly.

'Settling in, are you?' asked Howard, firmly turning the subject. His years as a headmaster had taught him diplomacy. 'We heard you met up with Linda again.'

Kate laughed. 'Nothing ever remains a secret for long in Dunmouth, does it? I really admire all she's done – taking a degree in her thirties, setting up this bookshop. She's been so courageous after losing her husband.'

'That's Dan Wilson's daughter for you. He was a grand chap.'

Millicent gave a dismissive toss of her head, which her family knew well.

'I hope you aren't going to get mixed up with the fisher folk, Kate.'

Kate took a deep breath and held it. She could feel the flush of anger rising up her neck, but she concentrated on stacking the plates in the oak dresser which had come with the house. When she turned around again she had herself under control. Howard winked at her.

'Speaking of secrets,' she said, 'I had an odd experience on the beach the other day. I was right down at the far end of the sandy beach, near the headland, and this terrible feeling swept over me, but I couldn't exactly remember... Did I have some sort of accident there when I was a child?'

Her parents exchanged a quick glance. She saw her mother's back stiffen, and her father turned away, busy with the tea-towel. They did not answer her.

'Wasn't there an old cottage there?' she went on, suddenly recalling. 'Is it still standing?'

Millicent cut across her, ignoring what she had said. 'When did you say Beccy would be coming home for the summer? Perhaps she should get a job, so she'll have some money of her own for next year. I'll ask around. Something nice and professional, like a dentist's receptionist, or helping in the library.'

Kate recognised this technique of her mother's. She would get no answer to her questions, which only made her the more curious. There *had* been a cottage there once, but the memory of it was also clouded by a sense of unease. She couldn't remember seeing anything of it the other morning, but then she had been concerned with finding Toby, and disconcerted by her meeting with the odd, barefoot old woman fishing for crabs in the rock pool.

27

Howard and Millicent lingered after dinner in the half-furnished drawing room until Kate ached with weariness, longing for them to leave. The weekend felt as though it had gone on for ever. She saw her mother out to the car at last with relief. Glancing surreptitiously at her watch, she was surprised to find it was only half-past ten. Her father lingered on the doorstep, turning his hat in his hand.

'That cottage, Katie,' he said, speaking in a low voice, with his face turned away from the car, 'I wouldn't press your mother about that. There was a bad business went on there during the war. I only heard about it after I was demobbed. It was one of the young fishermen who was the ringleader, though somehow Millicent got caught up in it.'

'But Mum is always so snobbish about the fisher folk!'

'Ah well, I think that episode might have something to do with it. Scared her, I think. Not that I ever really got to the bottom of it. Best to leave well alone.'

'But, Dad, why should that give *me* such a nightmarish feeling? I wasn't born till three years after the war. You're telling me I'm psychic?'

'You probably heard something about it when you were a child. You know how children have their own folklore and like to scare each other with frightening stories.' To Kate, he sounded evasive.

She shook her head. 'I don't know... It seemed more immediate than that. But I'm probably just imagining things.' She looked at him steadily. 'Just answer my simple question, will you? Is that cottage still there?'

'Yes, I believe so. I haven't been along that far since my hip began to give me trouble.'

'And does anyone live there?'

'Some old woman, I believe. A bit of a recluse, so I've heard.'

An old, grey-haired woman, thought Kate, with eyes as bright and fearless as a herring gull, and long bony feet, brown with sun and sea-spray.

⌘

Tom returned home on Tuesday evening, and when he set out for work on Wednesday he was feeling pleased with what he had achieved in Manchester. It was a big project, worth £8 million, and things could have gone disastrously wrong if he hadn't intervened himself. Young John Lindan, the project manager, was able and hard-working, but he lacked the seniority to put pressure on some of the consultants who had been brought in to carry out part of the system design, with the result that the milestones had begun to slip. Tom had worked out a new project plan, agreed it with the council, and explained in no uncertain terms to the consultants that he would be invoking the penalty clauses in their contracts if they failed to meet a single one of the revised deadlines.

The road he took every day to Banford turned away from the river and the sea within five minutes, and ten minutes later had topped the rising ground behind Dunmouth and dropped down to the inland plain behind. He had hoped, when they moved north, that he would be able to enjoy their nearness to the sea, but so far he had hardly seen it. He wanted to take up sailing again, first enjoyed during childhood holidays on the Isle of Wight and followed up enthusiastically at university (often when he should have been attending lectures). There was a tiny marina at one end of Dunmouth harbour. And between the castle and the beginning of Castle Terrace, just beyond the Castle Café, two local lads had recently started up a water sports centre in a refurbished redundant fish-shed. They hired out boats, surfboards and jet bikes to a few locals, and to visitors who came from Charlborough and other nearby towns. At the first opportunity, he promised himself, he would hire a dinghy and take Kate out sailing – something she had never done, despite growing up in Dunmouth.

She had looked at him sardonically when he had teased her about this.

'You have to understand, Dunmouth has always been a working fishing port. Serious business. Men only. When I was a child, trippers in sailing dinghies would *not* have been welcome, particularly not female ones.'

Banford was a dreary town, Tom thought, as he entered the city limits. Its centre had been torn down and rebuilt in the sixties and seventies, and the office blocks and unimaginative shopping malls put up at that time were now disintegrating – bits of concrete flaking off, metal window frames buckling out of true, paint shabby and not maintained because the buildings could not last much longer. One office building had been sheathed in scaffolding more than two years ago, Tom had heard. Then the owners had run out of money. The scaffolding still stood, neglected and rusty, while pedestrians picked their way awkwardly around it.

Here on the outskirts, Banford was pleasanter. Concentric rings of thirties semi-detached houses surrounded the desecrated centre, each house with its substantial front garden. The local soil was favourable to roses, and when Tom had visited the town last summer these gardens had been a lush tangle of roses of every variety and hue. It was still too early for the roses this year, but the hedges were clipped, and the lawns tidy. It must have been a cosy sort of town once, he reflected. A bit claustrophobic, perhaps, an inland, inward-looking town, a mite complacent. But you knew where you were with Banford. Safe, decent, reliable. Though current crime statistics showed that life here was changing. Tom pulled his BMW into the senior executive space in the office car park, and locked the door carefully.

⁓

'Is that you, István?' his sister asked. She always began her telephone conversations with him in this way. The need for care, for reassurance, was the legacy of a childhood spent in terrifying times.

'Magdolna? How are you? How's József? And my scamp of a nephew?'

'We're all fine.' He could hear the sound of cheerful voices and clinking glasses behind her. She must be ringing, as usual, from the village inn. 'András skinned both knees when he fell off his bike on the way to school yesterday. Went about all day without washing them, so I had to pick out the bits of grit when he came home. It must have been very painful, but he just bit his lip and said he could be as brave as his grandfather.'

There was something about her tone, something in the way she spoke of their father, that alerted him, but he went carefully.

'I'm looking forward to my long weekend with you.'

'Ye-es.' She drew the word out. 'There's something I want to show you, something József and I have found.' Her voice was tight with caution.

'Yes?' He sounded casual, relaxed.

'Yes.' She paused, and he could hear her hurried breathing. 'I think perhaps Mama must have hidden it. At the end.'

His interest quickened, but he kept his voice easy.

'Where did you find it?'

'You know that I'm getting that new kiln? Large enough to fire my bigger pieces, so I don't have to risk sending them away?'

'Yes, you told me about it last time I was down, and showed me the picture in the catalogue.'

'Well, it's arrived, and József thought the wooden floor wouldn't be strong enough to take the weight. He decided to build a concrete base for it, and that meant taking up one end of the floor.'

'So that's where you found...it? Under the floor of the barn you use for your workshop?'

30

'Mmm.'

'Sounds interesting. You can tell me all about it when I arrive. I should be with you by seven tomorrow evening.' He was intrigued. Magdolna must be very excited about her find, whatever it was, or she would never have rung him. She distrusted the privacy of telephone lines, suspecting that even today, in times of freedom, the Ávó might still be tapping them. She probably did not want to be overheard by neighbours in the bar either.

'We're looking forward to seeing you. András wants you to go fishing with him.'

After she had rung off, István tapped his desk thoughtfully with his brass paperknife. That reference to their father had seemed deliberate. Something Mama had hidden in 1956... He felt a sudden spurt of excitement. On his desk stood a photograph of his parents, laughing, dishevelled, in military boots and camouflage trousers, taken a few months after he had been born. For years he had had to conceal it, but now it was framed and in full view.

What could his sister and her husband have unearthed?

On Thursday morning Kate woke early and lay watching a silvery band of light probing between the curtains and falling across the chair where her clothes lay folded. Cautiously she raised herself on her elbow and looked at the clock. A quarter to six. Tom was breathing heavily, lying deeply asleep and sprawled half across her part of the bed. She drew the edge of her nightdress carefully from under his arm. He looked exhausted, but had laughed at her suggestion, last night, that he might take a day off on Friday or Monday, to make up for the time spent working in Manchester the previous weekend.

She felt restless and knew she wouldn't fall asleep again. With infinite care she slipped out of bed without waking Tom, and carried her clothes to the bathroom to shower and dress. In less than half an hour she was walking a delighted Toby past the water sports centre. All the curtains were drawn in the houses along Castle Terrace, and she noticed that the sign on the railings around the private terrace garden had been repainted. NO CYCLING, it said sternly. NO BALL GAMES. PRIVATE.

It was a breathtaking morning. The sky, still pale in the early light, was cloudless, and its colour was deepening from the fragile luminescence of a bubble, minute by minute, to the sturdy blue of a robin's egg. At the edge of the dunes Kate removed her trainers and tied the laces together so she could hang them round her neck. She picked her way wincingly through the marram grass and reflected that her feet were an unattractive putty white. They might be more shapely than those of the old woman she had seen, but they lacked that wonderful natural mahogany colour.

She wandered down to the water's edge and tested it with her toes. It still felt arctic. Perhaps if the sun shone all day it might warm a little by the afternoon, but there would be no swimming in it for weeks yet. As usual Toby was teasing the sandpipers and flinging himself with enthusiasm into the moderate breakers which were coiling over on to the shore this morning. In his tightly waved liver and white pelt he seemed impervious to the cold. Further along the beach three gulls were fighting over a dead fish at high-water mark, shrieking with fury and making vicious jabs at each other with their beaks. Linda had been saying only the day before that the gull population was increasing alarmingly along this stretch of the coast, having multiplied by a factor of ten in recent years. Kate remembered reading about resorts on the south coast where the gulls had been attacking children and grabbing food out of their hands. She hoped Toby would keep away from the gulls, who looked more than a match for him.

Something had been nagging at her all week, drawing her to this part of the beach, where the last curve of ochre sand swept up and around the foot of the rocky headland. She had been busy helping Linda every day at Harbour Steps Cottage, and her walks with the dog had been necessarily brief, but the image of the woman standing so securely on the edge of the rock pool lingered in her mind. Her father's inconclusive remarks about the cottage had made her more curious than satisfied, and the *frisson* of distress that seemed to be associated with the place merely goaded her on, as she had often been goaded in the past by challenges she set herself – to walk along a narrow fence or climb a dangerous tree and, later, to drive a more powerful car than she was used to or venture out on to the battlements of a crumbling castle despite a sickening sense of vertigo.

It was with almost such a sense of vertigo that she caught sight of the old woman again. This time she had her skirts tucked up and was wading around the large rocks which formed the base of the headland. Once again she was carrying a bucket (blue plastic this time), but no net, and she seemed to be gathering seaweed. Remembering the icy cold of the water on her toes a moment before, Kate shuddered at the thought of the grip of the waves on the woman's calves. It was a wonder she was not seized with cramp. Here, so far away from help, she might collapse and drown. As Kate drew nearer to the distinctive figure, she realised that the woman was not as old as she had supposed at first, perhaps a few years older than her own mother, which would put her in her early seventies. She looked less wild and witch-like today. Her hair was tucked back neatly into a bun, and that simple change gave her at once an air of dignity. A large black dog, mostly Labrador, was climbing stolidly up the tumbled rocks above her. Toby rushed ahead towards the woman, recognising her from their previous encounter. Always affable and curious, he would want to make friends with the other dog as well, a character trait which had brought him trouble on many occasions in London parks.

Kate quickened her step, ready to intervene if a dog fight should break out. But the black dog squatted down placidly on a cushion of bladder-wrack and sniffed noses calmly enough with Toby. Now she was only a few yards away Kate could see that the other dog was heavily greyed around the muzzle, and had legs a little bowed with age. The woman straightened slowly, easing her back, and looked up. Kate smiled.

'It seems our dogs have made friends! I'm afraid Toby always believes that everyone will love him, and sometimes he gets a nasty shock.'

'Ákos is very good at reading character. He understands when the intentions are good.'

Kate drew a little nearer.

'I'm fascinated by what you are doing. Is that seaweed edible? I've heard that some of them are, but I wouldn't know which was which.'

'This is the sea-lettuce.'

The woman held up a wide streamer of seaweed, with ruffled edges. Its colour was a glorious uninhibited bright green, like the flesh of a newly cut lime.

'Do you eat it raw or cooked?'

'Raw, it is like a salad vegetable. Very good. But with this I will make soup, together with onions, and thickened with barley. Many of the seaweeds can be eaten.'

She waded in from the water. Close to she was as tall as Kate, and might once have been taller. Kate fingered the seaweed.

'It's beautiful. But then so are lots of vegetables, don't you think? Whenever I cut a purple cabbage in half, I can hardly bear to go on and chop it up. The cross-section of a purple cabbage is one of the most beautiful things in nature – yet you never come across a sonnet written to a cabbage, do you?'

The woman gave a low chuckle.

33

'A sonnet to the purple cabbage – now that is an idea I like.'

'My name is Kate Milburn,' said Kate, dropping the seaweed back into the bucket and holding out her hand. 'As our dogs have introduced themselves, perhaps we should do the same.'

The woman shifted the bucket to her left hand and took Kate's hand in hers.

'Sofia Niklai.' She continued to hold Kate's hand as she studied her. 'Until we met the other morning, I do not think I have seen you about. You have come to live here, yes?'

'I lived here as a child, but not for years now. My husband and I have just moved north from London with his job. We've bought Craigfast House.'

The woman gently released Kate's hand and shook her head.

'I never go up there. Mostly I live here by the sea. I can get all I need in the village. I have hardly been out of Dunmouth for more than forty years.'

She seemed about to say something else, then stopped herself. The dogs had wandered down from the rocks and were companionably investigating the fringe of fragile dried weed and broken shells which marked the furthest line of high water.

'I suppose I ought to be getting back,' said Kate regretfully. 'All my family were asleep when I came out, but they'll be wanting breakfast soon. Perhaps we'll meet again. I hope so.'

For a moment Sofia hesitated, then she gave a smile.

'Come to see me some time, when you wish, and I will show you how to make a soup from seaweed.'

'Where do you live?'

Kate looked about, but could see no sign of the cottage which was supposed to be nearby.

Sofia pointed. 'Do you see that line of trees, just back from the rocks of the headland? That is the wind-break I have planted round my cottage. The winds used to be terrible, but now that the trees have grown it is sheltered. Beyond there you will find me.'

'I will come,' said Kate.

Chapter 3

'You will be very careful, won't you?' said Linda for the third time.

She and Kate were kneeling on either side of the fireplace in the bookshop, watching anxiously as two cheery and nonchalant workmen began to prise the entire cast-iron framework away from the wall. They had already dismantled the range, which now lay strewn about the floor in disconsolate heaps. There was the screech of metal on metal as one of the crowbars slipped, and a large chunk of plaster fell out of the wall, showering them all with dust. Kate wiped her face with the back of her hand, and tried to breathe without inhaling the dust. One of the men began to cough.

'Don't worry, missus,' said the other, taking out a large red handkerchief and blowing his nose. 'You can't beat these old fireplaces for strength. You could drive over this with a steamroller and not see a scratch on it.'

'My old man,' said his partner, leaning his weight on the crowbar again, 'reckons that when he was my age he was taking out three or four of these a week and sending them off for scrap metal. Nowadays, he can't find hardly any to put back in houses, now people are wanting them again. Says if he'd just stored them away in them days, he'd be a millionaire now.'

'It doesn't bear thinking about,' said Kate sympathetically, as, with a shudder and an avalanche of plaster and soot, the fire-surround finally parted company with the wall. The men lifted it between them and staggered across the room to lean it against the wall opposite.

'Watch out, now, missus. That'll be mucky in there.'

The mass of debris in the dark hole was disgusting. There were three or four bodies of birds in various stages of decay, the skeleton of what might have been a rat, and several bucketfuls of greasy soot, still clinging together with the deposits of ancient cooking.

Linda took one look, then got to her feet and went to fetch the two pairs of heavy rubber gloves they had used while disinfecting the old fish-smoking shed at the back of the cottage, which she was planning to use as a storeroom. Kate was too impatient to wait for the gloves. She began to stir the mess gingerly with a stick before Linda came back. Promising lumps proved to be deceptive, falling apart into small heaps of soot as she poked them.

'Here, put these on. Those carcasses are probably riddled with germs.'

'I'm not touching anything,' said Kate, then contradicted herself by leaning forward and gently prodding with one finger. 'Wait a minute! I think this might be it.'

The two workmen, who had grabbed the opportunity for a quick cigarette while these crazy women combed through the ancient filth behind the fire, came back from the door and leaned over Linda's shoulder. Kate delicately lifted something between her finger and thumb, and blew the dirt away from it.

'That must be it!' said Linda delightedly.

Dirty as it was, they could all see that it was a ring, a heavy gold ring, chased with a pattern of spirals and set with a dark stone. Kate licked a finger on her clean hand and rubbed the stone free of dirt. A sudden glint of rich purple caught the light from the window.

'An amethyst, I think,' she said. 'Not hugely valuable, I don't suppose, but it's a very attractive ring. Mrs Hennage will be so pleased. Imagine getting it back after seventy-five years!'

All four of them beamed at each other, as if the survival of the ring had been their own personal achievement.

István decided to walk from the railway station to the village. The distance was less than two miles and it was a beautiful evening, balmy and still. The intense heat of recent weeks had slackened a little, and there had even been a brief shower of rain that morning, which had refreshed the trees and given the fields of maize a dull sheen in place of the weary dustiness that had covered them before. He had left his car for repairs at the garage in Sopron, where he would collect it on Tuesday morning before surgery. This was the first time in five years that he had made the journey to Szentmargit by train, and he felt relaxed but eager for fresh air and exercise.

Grasping his small suitcase in his hand he looked about him as he came out of the station. It had been built, back in the nineteenth century, for the convenience of the manor house rather than the village, so weekend guests arriving from Vienna or Budapest to attend balls and shooting parties could alight here, to be met by carriages and driven off to the golden-ochre house which he could just make out in the distance beyond the trees.

He set off resolutely along the road, noticing that it was in an even worse state of repair than it had been on his last visit. Within five minutes he was passing the vast wrought-iron gates of the manor, which towered above his head. Nowadays they were permanently wedged open. Weeds were matted thickly about their base, and strands of columbine climbed up the convenient scrolls, twining about the bearded heads and lascivious limbs of fauns and trumpeting out their delicate white blooms between the scabs of rust. A fresh sign indicated that visitors were admitted between the hours of 10 a.m. and 1 p.m., and between 2 p.m. and 5 p.m. Magdolna had told him that the Ministry of Tourism had recently opened the building. He wondered who would want to come to visit it. Cut off by marshland on two sides, and by the river and forest on the other two, the area was remote and backward. The only access was by this single road and the station where few trains stopped.

Even in its decay the house was beautiful. As a boy he had often climbed in through broken windows and played there, racing along the panelled corridors, and venturing – with some nervousness – across the vast floor of the ballroom crowned by its baroque plasterwork ceiling. In those days he had never seen any room of a size to compare with it, and it appeared more menacing than open spaces under a wide sky. He knew that every single movable object had been stripped from the house – the valuables by the Germans, who had used it as an SS headquarters during the second world war, and later by the Russians, who had taken, indiscriminately, objects of no worth whatsoever. The only remaining furnishings (if they could be called that) were the huge cast-iron or porcelain stoves built into the corners of each room, eight or ten feet high and heavily decorated. Their survival had been ensured by their enormous weight and unwieldiness.

When he was about ten he had found the way into the inner web of hidden corridors from which, in the old days, an army of servants had fuelled and cleaned these stoves, completely out of sight of the family and their guests. The service door had been concealed behind panelling in the kitchen, so that even from the working end of the house it had been hidden away. He had wandered there for hours, until his pocket torch had grown dim and he had had some moments of blind terror, thinking that he might never escape again. The smell of that secret place had stayed with him – a warm smokiness, as if the great stoves had only just gone out. There in the warren of service corridors a few objects had still remained, undiscovered by either Germans or

Russians. There had been several candle lamps, set down by the last servants to have worked here. There were dirty shovels and buckets, used for carrying ashes, and one basket of logs, still waiting to be burned, dry as tinder. In one corner he had found an old and worthless one pengö coin and just inside the door which led back to the outside world an old pair of cracked leather slippers, worn by some long-dead stove attendant, creeping about behind the tapestried walls while on the other side music had played for balls or confident men with whiskers had sat over their glasses of brandy, plotting moves in the endless chess game of politics.

So at least he had imagined it. He realised that such scenes might have reflected the past of the house in the eighteenth and nineteenth centuries, but he knew very well that the events it had witnessed throughout the last eighty or ninety years had been very different. He wondered what the official guides in their uniforms, with their bright impersonal smiles, told the tourists.

Beyond the ruined garden of the house the road ran through an arm of the woods; then the village farmland opened out. Fields of sunflowers yearned westwards, towards the last light of the evening. The maize was still small, held back, he thought, by the lack of rain. He could see the river now, and before it the village. There were no buildings here less than a hundred years old. Even collectivisation had not brought the vast barns found in the richer parts of the country. The houses were small and squat, sitting down like broody hens in haphazard groups with roads of beaten earth between them. The metalled road, on which he made his way down the sloping ground, petered out in front of the church with its onion-shaped dome, which lay at the near end of the village, beside the square and opposite the Blue Heron, the village *csárda*.

Some of the cottages were thatched with reeds gathered from one of the islands in the river, which had provided local people with roofing material for centuries. Others had shingles, cut by the village carpenter from wood gathered in the nearby forest. What the houses lacked in sophistication of architecture they made up for in the shades of their colour-washed walls. The same golden ochre, peeling on the mansion house, glowed freshly here, and deep rose red, citrus yellow, umber, mint green and pale shell pink were jumbled together in a riot of colour he could almost taste. Strange, how he had run about here as a child, never noticing it. Now, whenever he returned, the sight of all that joyous affirmation lifted his heart. The fields might be poor, the river dangerous and the marshes a forbidding barrier, but the village asserted itself with all the vigour of the wild, hypnotic gypsy dance, the *csárdás*.

Their grandparents' house – Magdolna's house now – was painted a rose pink. Not the bright colour of the newly opened flower, but softly faded, like a bloom of late summer about to shed its petals. His sister had retained the old thatched roof for the warmth it provided, although it needed more frequent repairs than the wooden shingle roofs. He could see her now, standing before the house and silhouetted against the brightness of the river. A small, compact woman, not beautiful, but serene, somewhat withdrawn inside her own imaginative world. She would not walk up the slope to greet him. He saw her shade her eyes against the low rays of the setting sun and wait for him.

'Good,' she said, when he reached her. 'It is good to have you home again.' Then she reached out her arms and hugged him warmly.

ॐ

Beccy turned up unexpectedly in Dunmouth a day early, having been given a lift with friends part of the way and having hitched the rest. It was Friday lunchtime, and she found Kate about to leave the house for the bookshop.

'Lovely to see you, darling,' said Kate. 'Do you want to have a shower and crash out on your bed, or do you want to come with me?'

Beccy had admired her room, newly decorated by Kate. It had seemed thoroughly depressing on her one previous flying visit to Craigfast House. Now she had planted herself on a kitchen chair and looked disconcerted as Kate turned towards the door.

'Why are you rushing off? Can't you stay for a cup of tea and a natter? I've only just *arrived*.'

'I know, and I'd love to, but I promised Linda I'd go back this afternoon and help. She's opening tomorrow and half the stock hasn't even been unpacked yet.'

'What on earth are you talking about?'

'Linda. My friend Linda from primary school. Who's done up Harbour Steps Cottage and is opening it as a bookshop. Tomorrow. Darling, I wrote and told you every single thing about it.'

'Oh, yes,' said Beccy vaguely, who had a blurred memory of half reading a letter from her mother, then throwing it aside when friends collected her to go to the pub one evening. She couldn't remember what she had done with the letter, which had arrived about a fortnight ago. She rather thought she had never finished reading it.

'So what is it you're going to be doing? Unpacking books and putting them on shelves?'

39

'That's it. We could natter while we do it, if you come too. And there will almost certainly be a cup of tea.'

Beccy had been hoping to have her mother to herself before Stephen and Roz came home from school, but she agreed, somewhat ungraciously, to come down to the bookshop and help.

They found Linda kneeling on the floor surrounded by cardboard boxes, some still tightly bound with plastic tape, others open, with piles of gleaming new books glimpsed within. She was holding a sheaf of invoices in one hand and pushing back her cascade of red hair with the other. There was a young man with her, quite a personable young man, holding a stiff new reporter's notebook and looking at her hopefully.

'We'll be featuring the opening of the bookshop in tomorrow's *Dunmouth and Welbank Herald*,' he was saying. 'It should help to get you off to a good start. And the photographer will be here soon.'

Linda looked around wildly. The cottage resembled a cross between a car boot sale and the aftermath of a hurricane.

'This is Chris Harding,' Linda said to Kate. 'He's in his first week as a junior reporter on the *Herald*.'

'How do you do,' said Kate, shaking his hand. 'This is my daughter, Beccy.' She glanced at the heaps of crumpled brown paper and the unopened boxes. 'I don't think you can take a picture yet, do you? Unless you want to wait until we've finished.'

'We could photograph the front of the shop, if you like, instead of the inside. Your sign and the lettering on the windows look really good.'

'I'll need to finish doing the window displays,' said Linda, but more calmly.

'I could help with that,' said Beccy, noticeably reviving in the presence of Chris. 'Show me which books you want to use and I'll arrange them.'

'While you do that I'll go round to the jewellers,' said Kate, 'and pick up Mrs Hennage's ring. Then we can give it to her this evening.'

Beccy, who had been told the story of the ring on the way down into the village, repeated it to Chris. His face lit up.

'That's fantastic. We could do a feature on that. "Lost Ring Found After 75 Years!" We'll get a picture, too. Tell you what – why don't you have a presentation of the ring as part of your opening ceremony tomorrow? Then as well as this week's preview article about the shop opening, we could do a follow-up featuring the opening itself and telling the story of the ring.'

Kate could see that Linda was too tired and worried to be able stand up to this enthusiastic young man's energy. She laid a restraining hand on his arm.

'Mrs Hennage is quite an elderly lady, you know, and not very robust. I don't think you should think of putting her through a lot of publicity. At first we were simply going to hand the ring back when we found it, but we decided to get the jeweller to clean and polish it, and check that the setting of the stone is quite secure. He's putting it in a pretty ring box for her as well, and we're just going to take it round to her this evening. No drama. No fuss.'

He really was quite a nice young man. He capitulated at once, but asked if he might come along that evening. 'I promise I won't harass her. I'll just get the details – the names of the family, the date the ring was lost and so on. And –' he grinned wickedly – 'people aren't as averse as you might think to having their pictures in the paper. I'll ask her if I can send the photographer round to take a picture.'

In return for getting his way, at least partially, Chris rolled up his sleeves and helped them unpack the books, put them on the shelves, and clear away the debris. Later, when they were all sitting in Linda's newly completed kitchen, he told them about himself. Mainly, Kate suspected, for Beccy's benefit.

'I've just finished a diploma in media studies. I *think* the exams went all right.' He touched the wooden table, laughing. 'I was lucky enough to land the job with the *Herald* a couple of months ago and they wanted me to start straight after my exams, because they have two people going on holiday next week. So here I am.'

'It must be great to be finished with exams,' Beccy groaned. 'I've got two more years to go. Uni is great, but exams are the pits.'

'Of course, the *Herald* is just a start,' said Chris. 'I want to join a national paper eventually. But it has a good reputation as a stepping stone. People reckon you've been trained well if you start at the *Herald*.' He drained his mug of tea. 'Yes, thanks, some more would be great. Awfully thirsty work, unpacking books! Of course, there's another reason why I'm glad I got the Dunmouth job.' He paused.

'What's that?' Beccy asked, on cue.

'I did a degree in east European studies before I did the diploma, and I got very interested in a Hungarian woman poet who is supposed to live somewhere around here. She writes mostly in Hungarian, publishing in magazines run by exiles – though now that eastern Europe has opened up she's starting to be published in Hungary itself. Hungarian wasn't one of my languages, but I've read her work in translation, and the few things she's done in English. I suddenly made

41

the connection after the *Herald* offered me the job. Nobody has ever been able to do an interview with her, and I thought if I could pull that off, it would really make the big boys sit up and take notice.'

'Terrific!' said Beccy, enthusiastically.

'Mmm.' Linda's mind was still on tomorrow's opening.

But Kate felt a sudden instinctive surge of alarm, seeing in her mind's eye a slender, upright figure wading towards her out of the sea, with her hands overflowing with the beautiful ruffles of the sea-lettuce.

❧

The ceremony of presenting Mrs Hennage with her ring took place at seven o'clock that evening. Linda's two children, Emma and Lucy, had arrived home from primary school and been taken round to a friend's house for tea. Kate and Beccy walked down the hill again after Stephen and Roz got back from Charlborough. Beccy seemed more willing to come with her mother this time.

'I thought you had a steady boyfriend already,' said Kate delicately, as they reached Mrs Hennage's house, one of the modernised cottages in Fisher Gate. 'Jerry, isn't he called?'

Beccy smiled blandly. 'Do him good to learn he can't take me for granted,' she said.

Mrs Hennage welcomed the addition of the young people to the party, producing two more glasses of dark, sweet sherry, and passing round home-made cheese straws. She answered Chris's questions and agreed imperturbably to having a photograph taken. When Linda handed her the black velvet ring box, however, she became very quiet, and sat down in a chair by the window. Her hands, caressing the box, were trembling. She fumbled over the catch and when the lid sprang open and the ring was revealed, gleaming against the white satin lining, she groped in her sleeve for a handkerchief. They had all been watching her eagerly, but now turned away, a little abashed.

'I'm sorry,' said Mrs Hennage. 'It's very silly of me. But I can't tell you what this means to me. So many of my family and friends gone, and now this little bit of my childhood coming back to me. Bless you, both of you, my dears.'

Later, when they were standing outside the front door of the cottage, Chris said he must rush off to the office. Friday was their busy night, with the *Herald* coming out on Saturday, and though he had filed his story about the bookshop opening he was needed as general dogsbody until midnight at least.

'I'll see you all at the grand opening tomorrow,' he called, as he started off down the street at a fast lope.

Linda left to fetch her daughters and Kate and Beccy started the climb up the hill. Beccy drew her mother's arm through her own and glanced over her shoulder at the red bars of the sunset lying across the sky upriver.

'Red sky at night, sailor's delight. You know, I think I might find this summer in Dunmouth quite tolerable after all.'

๑

After dinner István, Magdolna and József sat outside on a wooden bench, with their backs to the sun-warmed wall of the house and their faces to the river. József had brought out glasses and a bottle of Tokay, and they sipped the fine sweet wine in a contented silence which did not require conversation. From the rough meadow behind the village they could hear András and his friends kicking a football, and from the open window of a neighbouring house came the sound of a radio programme playing gypsy music. István could make out, as well as the fiddles and a small drum, the sound of a cimbalon. They were playing the plangent, repetitive refrains of the *lassu*, which brought to his mind the tragedy of old battles and lost sons and lovers. The air was still heavy with the heat of the day, but a faint breeze seemed to rise off the river as if it were exhaling long slow breaths.

'You will be glad to have Anna back,' said István, holding out his glass for József to refill. 'When the law faculty closes for the summer.'

'She may not come home,' said József. He was a slow, quiet man, with a pipe usually held in the corner of his mouth, unlit. 'She thinks she will get a job and stay on for the summer in Budapest. There's a lot of confusion over student grants, with the change of government this spring. She wants to be sure that she can complete her studies, and she knows we can't give her much. Magdolna's work may be highly praised by the critics, but the galleries keep three-quarters of the selling price of her pieces for themselves.'

Both men smiled fondly at Magdolna, who was sitting between them. There was a smear of whitish clay on her cheekbone which neither of them had mentioned. It gave her round, serene face a slightly rakish air.

'If I can help at all,' said István, 'I hope you'll let me. Now that László has finished his studies, I have no one else to spend my money on, apart from your two.'

43

'No, no.' Magdolna patted his knee. 'It is not a serious matter yet. Anna is very independent and does not want to be a burden to us. Odd, isn't it, that we had our education paid for, under the communist regime? It is one of the penalties of freedom, I suppose. Now the students are free to say whatever they like, but they may need to earn the money to pay for their own education.'

'Well, it's the same for us farmers,' József pointed out. 'It used to be that the Soviets took all our produce and paid us badly for it – or paid us by so kindly stationing their garrisons here. Now we are producing more than ever, but they have no money to pay, so we have to compete with the West. There is good and bad in everything.'

The music coming from the other house had changed. The gypsies had moved on to the second part of the performance, the *friss*, with its strong martial rhythms that made you want to tap your feet in time to the beat.

'More good than bad,' said István firmly. 'A little financial tightening of belts will do the country no harm. It's a small price to pay. What I don't like is the way some of the old Party members have been resurfacing, wolves dressed in sheep's clothing – pretending that what we need is their brand of "socialism": the "good old days" when the State took care of everything, including what we were allowed to think and say.'

'Now, now,' said Magdolna soothingly, 'you don't have to convince us. Relax a little now that you are home. You're looking tired. You've been overworking.'

'Not too much. But I do wish I could stay longer than Tuesday.'

'You will come for your month's holiday later on, won't you?'

'Try to keep me away!' István laughed and stretched out his long legs. 'Now then, when are you going to tell me about what you found under the barn floor?'

His sister and brother-in-law exchanged glances, then József got up and went into the house. He returned with a black metal box, about two feet long, a foot wide and a foot high. It had been padlocked, but the lock had been prised open with some tool, and the bright metal shone through the black paint where it had been scratched and dented. József laid the box on István's lap and sat down again beside his wife.

When István lifted the lid, he saw, in the light falling from the window, that the box contained mainly papers – letters, notebooks, newspaper cuttings and pamphlets. There was also a small leather jewellery case. He opened this first. It contained a heavy fob watch on a triple interlinked chain in three kinds of gold.

'It is Papa's watch,' said Magdolna. 'Grandmama never knew what had become of it. She thought the soldiers had stolen it. But Mama must have had it all the time, and kept it secret.'

'Perhaps Papa hid it himself.'

'No, no. Some of those papers are later, from the time after he was taken away. The earrings are Mama's too. I remember her wearing them, and I was only two years old when he was taken, so all these things must have been put there later by Mama.' Magdolna clasped her hands tightly together, but her face was calm. 'Look at the locket hanging on the watch chain.'

István inserted his thumbnail in the tiny catch and opened the locket. It was about two inches high, with a delicate frame and glass on both sides. Under the glass on the left lay a curl of black hair. On the right there was the photograph of a beautiful young woman, with dark hair piled up on her head in an old-fashioned style. Her lips were slightly parted and curled in a secret smile.

'It isn't Mama,' said Magdolna.

'No.' István gazed at the photograph, then raised his eyes and looked out over the river, where the outlines of the islands had blurred into the river with the nightfall. He could hear the musicians change tempo again. With a swoop and a heart-stopping leap of melody that never failed to move him they plunged into the *csárdás*.

'No. It must be his wife.'

Silence fell over them. They knew very well that their father had had a wife. That he had lost her, but did not know if she was alive or dead, so he had never been free to marry their mother, although they had lived together as man and wife for seven years. Living rough in the woods, in a partisan camp, their mother had cared nothing for the conventions. But later, when they were children in Szentmargit, Magdolna and István had felt it keenly.

'What are the other papers? Is this Papa's underground newspaper?'

'Yes. And the issues Mama produced after he was gone. The cuttings are from government papers – during the war, Nazi papers, and afterwards, Stalinist ones. They are reports of sabotage and revenge taken, or demonstrations put down. I suppose they must be operations our parents were involved in.'

István fingered the yellowed newsprint abstractedly. It was all so long ago. The Nazis were gone. Stalin was dead and reviled even by his own country. He caught sight of a picture of tanks in Heroes Square in Budapest. The date on the paper was November 1956. It must be one of the last cuttings.

45

'And these other things? What are they?'

'A few letters from friends. A few our parents wrote to each other when they were apart – which wasn't often. Those brown school notebooks are a diary Papa kept. It starts at the end of 1938 and goes on to 1948, just a day before they came for him.'

'I would like to read that.' István felt a sudden bitter yearning, which he had not experienced for years, but which used to seize him often when he was young. He had been four when his father was taken away and he retained only a few hazy memories of him. All his life it had itched like an unhealed scar. As a child he would make up stories of how his father would come back. István would be running across the village square and suddenly a tall man would appear from the woods below the great house. They would know each other at once, and his father would catch him up in his arms, and then they would walk down to Grandmama's house, striding along together. For a long time he had clung on to this dream. Sometimes people did come back from the gulags. But gradually, as he had grown up, the dream had faded, and he came to accept that he would never know his father.

'There's something else,' said Magdolna, 'and I don't know what to do about it.' She got up and went into the house.

István raised an eyebrow at József, who had remained silent all this while.

'She will explain,' he said. 'She is very troubled about it.'

Magdolna came back with another letter, which she had set aside. It was newer than the others, a blue airmail envelope with slanting red lines printed round the edge. It was addressed to their father, care of the priest in the village, and it was dated October, 1956.

'It's from his daughter,' said Magdolna, who could not contain herself long enough for him to read the letter. 'She says they have tried repeatedly to reach him since the end of the war, but their letters must have gone astray. She thought she would try again, because this time the letter might get through – and of course, it did.'

'So they did survive, after all.'

'Yes. But her mother, Papa's wife, was dead by then. She asks him to write. Do you think Mama could have replied? There would have been so little time after this arrived.'

'Probably not. Surely she would have said something to Grandmama, even if we were too young to understand.' But István was not sure. The dangerous life she led had made his mother very secretive.

'But what do you think we should do? There is an address. Do you think we should write?'

46

'Madji, this letter is thirty-eight years old! Surely she won't still be at the same address. Will she even be alive? She was much older than us – she was nearly twenty before the war.'

Magdolna looked at him, serene now. He knew she had made up her mind.

'She is our sister. Of course we must try.'

The last chord of the *csárdás* fell upon the air, then the lamenting melody which brought the dancers back to reality.

'Very well,' he said, 'we will write. But let's wait until I come for the summer holiday. Then we can think very carefully what we want to say.'

Lying awake that night in the room he shared with András, István wondered how to compose such a letter. It would be best, he thought, not to reveal the relationship. He could say that the letter had come into their hands... He tossed restlessly. He was high above the floor in the ancient carved bedstead, lying upon a goose-feather bed with nothing over him but one of the lace-trimmed dowry sheets. The weather had grown ominously hot again after nightfall, and there were distant rumbles of thunder in the sky, though no rain. András was asleep on the wooden truckle bed which usually lived underneath the high bed when he had his bedroom to himself. His breathing was steady and contented. István had promised to spend Saturday morning fishing with him in a stream that ran down from the manor into the river, where there was a good chance of a catch.

István wished Magdolna had not found the box. He wished she had not decided they must write this letter to their missing sister. The world was changed now. Hungary was changed. Let the past bury its dead – wasn't that the saying? Nothing they could do now could alter the past, and the future would be better kept clean of its taint. Behind his carefully constructed barriers, his life was now secure and inviolable.

But he wanted to read the diaries.

ఞ

Linda had given Beccy a job in the bookshop. This had led to a row with Millicent, whose friend Helen's daughter Maggie ran an exclusive ladies' dress shop in Fisher Gate. Millicent, it was understood, had been to a great deal of trouble to persuade Maggie to take Beccy on for six days a week, at £1.75 an hour. Beccy had told her grandmother – rudely – that 'exclusive' meant that nobody wanted to buy any of the frumpy old frocks stocked there, and that Maggie could keep her sweatshop wages. She was going to work at the bookshop four and a half days a week (extra hours if she wanted them) for a legal wage (amount not revealed) doing something she would enjoy, in congenial company, where customers actually came in to buy.

Millicent considered that all of this was Kate's fault, and was barely speaking to either of them. Kate was worried that Linda might have felt obliged to give Beccy a job, and couldn't afford the wages, though she secretly sympathised with Beccy, having been forced to share many trips to and from boarding-school with Maggie in their young days – an attempt to throw them together which had singularly failed. Stephen and Roz were jealous that Beccy would be earning real money before they had even broken up for the school holidays, and threatened to go back to London to stay with friends for the summer and work in McDonald's.

The launch of the bookshop had been a great success. Balloons and competitions brought in the children. A draw for a bottle of champagne was won by old Mr Fairclough, an avowed teetotaller, who insisted that it should be sent to the elderly people in Seaview Home. This had aroused the interest of the residents. The more mobile of them had made their way round the corner to the shop during the following days and raided the paperback detective fiction shelves. The local library had placed a large order, to test the shop's speed and efficiency, and the article in the *Herald* had attracted attention over a wide area. A young schoolmaster from Charlborough High, who had just published his second historical novel, offered to come and do a reading at a wine and cheese evening.

With all this going on, Kate's walks with Toby had been much curtailed and she had not yet kept her promise to visit Sofia in her cottage, although they had met several times on the beach and always stopped to speak. Kate had even met Sofia one evening at the corner shop run by an Indian family, which stayed open until 10 p.m. She rushed in to buy dried dill for a fish pie she was making for dinner and found Sofia with a long shopping list, talking to Mr Shiraz about his family as they worked their way slowly through her purchases. Sofia insisted that Kate should be served first.

'Come, my dear, you are in a rush – as always! I do my shopping once a month, and this I like to take time over. Mr Shiraz and I understand each other very well.'

'I wondered why I hadn't met you in the shops before.'

'I do not like the act of shopping. It makes me very impatient. So I plan it like a general, and come when things are quiet and I can shop like a duchess, with all the attention for myself!'

More than a week after the bookshop had opened, Tom had one of his particularly early starts, and Stephen and Roz were on study leave – which meant they would not get up till ten at the earliest. Kate made her way down to the village at seven o'clock with Toby trotting obediently to heel. She paused at Harbour Steps Books to admire the new window display, which she had helped to set up the previous afternoon, and then crossed over the street to the lifeboat station. Every time she had passed by this way, on foot or in the car, she had told herself that she must stop and read the memorial to the Dunmouth lifeboat, lost in 1978. She stood before it now, with the old fishermen's cottages sleeping behind her. In front the harbour lay flat as glass except where a pair of swans with their three small grey-brown cygnets cruised imperiously, setting up five identical Vs of wash that spread out and lapped in minuscule waves on the pebbles below the old beached rowing boats.

The plaque was made of bronze, and was screwed into one of the outside walls of the lifeboat station. It had been paid for by public subscription, raised in Dunmouth, Welbank and Charlborough, which had also provided a relief fund for the families of those lost.

IN HONOURED MEMORY OF THE CREW
OF THE ROYAL NATIONAL LIFEBOAT 'ALICE'
STATIONED AT DUNMOUTH
WHICH FOUNDERED WITH THE LOSS OF ALL HANDS,
IN A GALE IN THE DUN ESTUARY
ON 23RD DECEMBER 1978,
WHILE RESPONDING TO A CALL FROM THE
DUTCH MERCHANT SHIP 'CARA' WHICH WAS
ADRIFT IN THE NORTH SEA

EDWARD STANNARD	ROLAND HENNAGE
JOHN LOCKLEY	JOHN D. LOCKLEY
JAMES WATSON	GEORGE WILSON
ROBERT DALE	MATTHEW YOUNG

George Wilson was Linda's uncle. Roland Hennage was Mrs Hennage's middle son. The younger John Lockley had been in her class at primary school – his dad had been a lifeboat man even then. Hardly a fisher family in Dunmouth had gone unmarked by the lifeboat tragedy, with the loss of husband or son, brother or cousin. The modern lifeboat was now moored just offshore. Too large to be kept in the old building, which held a smaller back-up boat, the *Sara Belle* had safety devices and modern technology which might have saved those men, had they been available sixteen years ago.

'Looking at the memorial, are you?'

A cracked voice behind her made her jump. She turned and saw a weatherbeaten old man, bent with arthritis, standing at the door of the cottage opposite, Barometer Cottage, which had a barometer mounted beside the front door in its own stone case. Above the barometer the date 1859 was inscribed, and it had served the local fishing community well until the advent of more sophisticated weather forecasting. The older men swore by it still.

The man rolled a brown-stained cigarette to the corner of his mouth and pointed towards the plaque. His hand trembled slightly.

'Edward Stannard. That was my only son. Coxswain, he was, of the *Alice*. They awarded him a medal after he was gone, for conspicuous bravery. Wouldn't bring him back, would it?' He glowered at her, removed the cigarette and spat into the gutter.

'Had to bring up his son myself, didn't I? No medals nor plaques don't put food on the table, do they?'

Kate felt uncomfortable under this glowering eye. 'I thought there was a relief fund, wasn't there?' she asked hesitantly.

'Lot a good that was. Government should have done more. Instead of taking in all these wogs and foreigners and giving them food and houses at our expense. My nephew took over as coxswain. Stannards have always been coxswains in Dunmouth. Nearly lost two years later, he was. What do the government care?'

He glared at her again, then stumped back into the cottage and slammed the door. Kate turned back to the plaque. Whatever the old man said, the courage of those men was undiminished, lost in a gale on the estuary answering a desperate cry for help. Drifting in the North Sea. How forlorn it sounded. She had never heard whether the crew of the *Cara* had been saved by someone else. Had they, too, all perished? The estuary looked as innocent as an ornamental lake this morning, yet she knew it had never yielded up the bodies of three of those who had died. Gently she ran her finger over the raised letters that spelled out Johnny Lockley's name. He hadn't been a very clever boy, but he had always been kind, and protective towards the smaller children. Somewhere out there he was still lost at sea.

She pulled herself together, and marched Toby briskly along the harbour wall, past the Castle, the café and the water sports centre, and started up the long stretch of the sandy beach towards the headland.

There was no sign of Sofia about this morning, and when she reached the end of the beach she hesitated. The line of trees Sofia had pointed out stood back a little from the base of the headland. The cottage must lie in the loop of land where the old road turned inland before swinging out towards the sea again and wandering on to its eventual junction with the main road more than a mile further along the coast. The ground in front of Kate was covered with rough grass, not so vicious as the marram grass of the dunes, but some other tough variety that could tolerate salt spray and sandy soil. The ground rose a little towards the trees, lifting itself away from the beach.

At first Kate could see no signs of habitation, then Toby ran ahead and began to sniff around some bushes, disappearing from view round the side of them. Following, Kate found that beyond the windbreak of trees there was a stone wall about six feet high and roughly built. The cottage must lie behind this. Toby had now found a crude wooden gate and was sniffing eagerly at the gap below it. His tail was wagging enthusiastically, and from behind the gate the sound of another dog could be heard, making small yelps of welcome. Ákos must be there, recognising Toby's scent.

Kate hesitated. The gate and the wall had a forbidding appearance. Then she saw that to the right of the gate an old ship's bell had been hung up, with a rope dangling down from it, and a wooden sign, neatly lettered, said 'Please Ring.' She pulled the rope and a sweet clear note rang out, surprisingly deep.

She could hear footsteps now, on a path, then Sofia's voice speaking to Ákos. There was the sound of bolts being drawn back, and the gate opened inwards.

'Kate, my dear, I hoped it would be you. Come in.'

Kate stepped forward, over the stone threshold of the gateway, with Toby rushing ahead of her. Then she stopped dead. Her eyes, accustomed to the grey stone houses of Dunmouth, to the sea and the sand, and the dull colours of the dunes, were momentarily confused by the sight. The garden inside was as vivid as an Indian embroidery. The sun, not long risen, seemed already to have soaked into earth and stones here. Huge bushes of lavender were interspersed with the white trumpets of nicotiana already in bloom, and a creamy yellow rose, densely flowered, clambered through a plum tree. Just inside the gate, Kate brushed against a clump of sweet cicely, and at once the scent of honey and aniseed rose around her. Scarlet poppies spilled over exuberantly on to the path, scattering their petals on her bare feet. Flowers, herbs, vegetables and fruits were crowded together, cascading over each other in a miraculous abundance.

There were beehives, and the bees were busy about the honeysuckle and thyme, burrowed into the foxgloves and wandered drunkenly over the lavender. A goat was staked out on a lawn as green as glass. There were espaliered fruit trees against the walls, with young

51

apples and pears just beginning to form. The air was rich with the scent of the flowers, but underneath it there ran the sharp aroma of the nearby sea. In the centre of this astonishing Eden stood a small grey stone cottage, but it too was smothered with climbing plants – more honeysuckle and ceanothus holding up its blue spikes and clematis montana so covered with blooms that no leaves could be seen.

'Oh, Sofia, I cannot believe this! Why didn't you tell me?'

Sofia smiled awkwardly. 'Welcome to my home,' she said.

Chapter 4

The weather continued to veer from damp and chilly to an almost Mediterranean heat. Stephen and Roz suffered from it most, alternately shivering and sweating through their exams. Due to shortage of funds, the school could not afford to turn on the heating during the summer term.

'In any case,' the headmaster pointed out patiently to an irate PTA meeting early in June, 'even if we switched on the system, by the time it warmed up we'd probably be in the midst of a heat wave again.'

It was the hot days that were the worst, as Roz complained bitterly to her mother and Beccy. 'At least when it's cold you can put on an extra jersey. When it's hot, the exam hall feels like the hottest tropical house at Kew.'

The new secondary school at Charlborough had been built at the enthusiastic start of the seventies, before the oil crisis, and its design was a permanent nightmare. The main assembly hall, where the exams were held, had a wall of sheer glass, two storeys high and facing south. There were no windows which could be opened.

As soon as his exams were over, Stephen refused stubbornly to go to school, although various activities had been organised to keep the leavers entertained.

'I'll go back for the leavers' party, and maybe for a couple of other things, but you're not going to catch me trailing round on worthy trips to the council offices in Charlborough or factories in Banford. I can do that for all the rest of my life. Right now I'm going to sleep.'

And sleep he did, falling into bed at nine in the evening to the pounding rhythms of his pop CDs, which sent him to sleep – blessedly for the rest of the household – within half an hour. Beccy, if she was at home, would creep in and turn off his stereo system. Otherwise Kate, more nervous of waking him, would slip into the bedroom where he lay sprawled on top of his duvet in a pair of boxer shorts, looking like a drowned man. She was always afraid of pressing the wrong button on the stereo and increasing the decibels instead of extinguishing them, but nothing disturbed him. He would come down the next day about two in the afternoon and make himself a huge meal out of bowls of cereal, bacon and egg, and peanut butter sandwiches. Then he would fall asleep again in a deckchair on the lawn until it was time for dinner.

Watching the way Stephen wandered about the house like a sleepwalker, Kate realised how much strain his A Levels had caused him. He had been sarcastic and offhand about them all year, but that had been a protective mechanism. Now he was abstracted, and seemed deaf when members of his family spoke to him. This maddened Roz, whose exams continued nearly two weeks after his and who resented his freedom.

'At least you'll soon have the music camp,' said Kate consolingly, over tea in the garden. 'With all your friends from Charlborough and Catherine from your old school.'

'It's only in grotty old Wales,' said Roz resentfully. 'Who wants to go to Wales? It rains all the time.'

'Might be a nice change,' said Beccy, who was larding her arms with lotion after an injudicious sunbathing session on the beach during her lunch break from the bookshop.

Roz looked at her crossly, then turned to her mother. 'How come Stephen can go on a cycling tour of France, when I have to go to Wales, to a place that's only a kind of school anyway?'

'What?' said Kate, startled. This was news to her.

Roz looked pleased. 'You mean you haven't said he can go to France? He's just having me on, then?'

'Stephen?'

Stephen said nothing.

'Stephen,' said Kate, 'what is this about going to France?'

He must have heard the slight sharpening of her tone, because he rolled over on the grass and opened his eyes.

'Yeah, well, Mick and I thought we'd do a cheap holiday biking round France and maybe get some work picking grapes or something.'

'They don't pick grapes till nearly autumn,' said Beccy witheringly.

'Well, something,' he returned equably. 'We can get a lift down to Kent with Mick's cousin, who has a four-wheeler that'll hold our gear. Then it's pretty cheap to cross by ferry with a bike, if you choose one of the unpopular sailing times. I've got a bit saved up. It won't cost you and Dad a penny.'

Kate looked at him gloomily. He was eighteen, which made him nominally an adult, though he didn't look it, with his knobbly knees and his fair complexion. He still only shaved every three days, and he was incapable of switching on a washing machine or – it seemed – of making his bed. Was he really old enough to be let loose in a foreign country? And his friend Mick was no better. They would probably be mugged, or run out of money and demand to be rescued from the middle of the Rhône valley. But at his age he couldn't exactly be forbidden to go.

When at last the dinner was cleared that evening, and Kate and Tom had a few rare minutes alone together over a cup of coffee before he started work on the inevitable pile of papers, she put it to him.

'I don't think we can stop him,' said Tom. 'Time he found his feet anyway. It will probably do him good – to take some responsibility for himself. You know you've been molly-coddling him and Roz both since we've been here. He'll be off to university in the autumn. We have to get used to the idea that he's growing up, like Beccy.'

'She's always had more sense of responsibility.'

'Well, she's the eldest. And you are always telling me girls are more grown-up for their age.'

He put down his empty cup, and reached for his briefcase.

'Just a minute, Tom, before you start. Are we planning to have a holiday ourselves? Beccy wants to work all summer, and perhaps go somewhere in September, so she could mind the house and look after Toby, if we wanted to go off before that. We haven't had a holiday in four years.'

Tom looked at her doubtfully.

'I'm not sure, Kate. It's early days still in this new job.'

'Tom,' she said, somewhat desperately, 'I am really worried about your health. You're working far too hard and one of these days it's going to catch up with you.' She smiled, to take the sting out of the words, and adopted a mock pedagogic tone. 'Surely good management is all about being able to delegate?'

Tom sighed.

'Oh, all right. Find out some details about a holiday, then. I'm not promising anything, mind. France would be good. Not too far to get back if there's an emergency.'

With that she had to be satisfied.

It was a mechanical problem, however, rather than Kate's urging, which forced a holiday on Tom, albeit a brief one. In the middle of one of the hottest spells of summer weather yet, the air conditioning plant in Crossbow Computers' Banford office failed. A building of almost the latest design, Crossbow House was dependent on its computer-controlled heating and cooling system. All the windows, triple glazed to exclude the sounds and traffic fumes from the streets outside, were sealed into their frames. The air was recirculated on a regular cycle, though the system did not draw in fresh air from outside. The employees' Health and Safety Group had had a meeting with Tom just the week before to put forward their complaints about the high incidence of respiratory illness amongst the staff, and to float the idea that Crossbow House might be subject to sick building syndrome.

With the air conditioning off and the recirculating pump stopped, the building on that Friday morning grew hotter and hotter, and the air more and more difficult to breathe. Several people in the finance office began to complain of severe headaches. A young typist who was an asthma sufferer collapsed and had to be given first aid, then sent up to the accident and emergency department at Banford General.

Tom decided he could take no further risks with the health of his staff, and sent everyone home at eleven o'clock. When the last person had left, apart from the security guards who were making their rounds before locking the building, Tom sat slumped in his office, sticky with sweat and exhausted. He seriously wondered whether he could summon the energy to walk as far as the car park and drive home. He held his head in his hands. It was throbbing. Suddenly the whole endless round of his life seemed futile beyond belief. He shut his eyes and imagined sailing in a stiff breeze over a cool green sea, with Kate in a sun-dress, laughing and trailing her hand in the water.

He sat up. It was impossible for him to work here in the office. Just this one time he would take the rest of the day off and go home. With a sudden surge of cheerfulness he threw into his briefcase the papers he would need to read before Monday and reached for the phone.

Kate was astonished, and then concerned.

'Are you sure you're all right?'

'I'm fine. It's just the building that's intolerable. As I said, I've had to send everyone home. I'm starting back now myself. Pack us a picnic, will you? I'll be home by half-past twelve.'

'Right.' Kate's voice rose a little, joyfully. 'Oh, Tom, that will be lovely.'

As he drove back towards Dunmouth and the sea, Tom caught himself whistling and grinned. Today was the day to hire a dinghy and take Kate out sailing. There was hardly any wind here inland, but there should be a bit more movement in the air over the estuary. Enough to make some headway without scaring her.

At the head office of Crossbow Computers in London, an old friend of Tom's who had heard a whisper of disturbing news searched in his office directory for the number of Tom's direct line in Banford. He held the receiver to his ear for five minutes while the telephone rang and rang in the empty office. No one answered.

୭

The dinghies supplied by Dunmouth Water Sports were very light and skittish, quite unlike the clinker-built wooden dinghy Tom had sailed in his youth, and he was glad the breeze was so gentle. Kate had stowed a plastic box of sandwiches, a bag of fruit and a thermos of tea under the foredeck, and then had submissively obeyed his orders, even when he grew a little rattled about the unfamiliar rigging and was somewhat curt with her.

At last, however, they stood offshore in a light north-westerly breeze, and Tom set a course northwards past the sandy beach and the headland, explaining the principle of tacking and reaching, and enumerating the various lines and the parts of the sail.

'Of course this is a very small jib,' he said. 'Hardly makes any difference. I believe they do sometimes use a larger jib on this class of boat, but I expect those people at the sports centre don't want to run any risks when they're hiring boats out.'

The young man, Harry, who had supplied the boat and who was one of the two partners in the business, had taken the trouble to ask Tom a few searching questions about his knowledge and experience of sailing.

'Stan – that's my mate – is more into speedboats and jet bikes,' he said, 'but me, I'd surfboard any day. Nearest thing to flying, I reckon.'

'Not so good when there are two of you, though.' Tom grinned. 'I haven't tried one of those things, and I don't intend to, not on these waters. I might just venture out on a nice quiet reservoir.'

'You ought to have a go, seriously,' Harry urged. 'A lotta middle-aged businessmen taking it up. Keeps them fit. Impresses the birds.'

Kate was snorting with suppressed laughter as they ran the dinghy down the slipway.

'That put us both firmly in our place, didn't it? Better get your middle-aged muscles toned up if you want to pull in the birds.'

Tom had tipped her amiably over in the shallows and she had retaliated. By the time they pulled away from the shore, their clothes

57

had nearly dried, so hot was the sun. As they drew level with the headland, Kate caught sight of Sofia probing amongst the bladder-wrack for mussels, and waved. Sofia raised one hand solemnly and let it fall.

'Who was that? Friend of yours?'

'Sofia. The old lady who lives in the cottage by the headland. I told you about her.'

Kate, however, had not told him everything. The secret of the wonderful garden she hugged to herself. Whenever she came away from it, out into the drab world of every day, she felt as though she must have dreamed it, and expected, on returning, to find it had vanished, like a palace conjured up by a genie in *The Arabian Nights*. She had also said nothing about her suspicion that Sofia might be the reclusive poet whose whereabouts the young reporter Chris was so assiduously seeking. If Sofia wanted to remain private, Kate was going to respect her wishes.

Yesterday when she had been visiting the cottage, Sofia had handed her an old photograph album.

'You have told me of your family. Here is mine. This is all I have left.'

Kate examined the old photographs with interest. Sofia had lived in a beautiful house, built in the eighteenth-century baroque style, and her parents had been a handsome couple. Her father was dashing in a hussar's uniform in the early pictures, with a thick moustache and dark, sad eyes. Her mother seemed hardly more than a young girl herself, holding the young Sofia. She wore rather old-fashioned clothes, with tight waists and long full skirts, when the other young women who appeared from time to time – house guests, tennis players – had begun to wear the straight, revealing dresses of the flapper era.

One photograph in particular caught Kate's attention. It showed a summer-house in a clearing in a wood. The structure was painted white, with absurd latticework, and a pagoda-like roof crowned with a metal dragon. Sofia's father – older now, and shorn of his moustache – stood with one foot on the bottom step and his hand resting on one of the delicate ribbed wooden pillars which supported the roof. There was something compelling about this picture that drew her back to it again and again. Beyond the dainty white building the forest diminished into darkness.

Sofia had offered very little information about herself, but Kate took the photograph album as an invitation to venture a few questions.

'Is this where you lived with your parents?'

'Yes. In the north-west of Hungary. Not far from the Austrian border. In a region called Szigetköz, lying between the Danube and the Mosoni-Duna. It was a very beautiful and secret place. My father was forced to fight in the Austrian army in the first world war. You know about this? Probably not. No one here understands about the position of Hungary. We were yoked to Austria under the Hapsburgs, but all true Magyars wanted to be free and independent. In the last century we tried to break away from the Austrian Empire. During the revolutionary time of 1848 our people were spurred on by the poetry of Sándor Petöfi, but we were defeated. Hungary tried to stay out of the first world war, but again Austria was too strong for us.'

'But your father was all right? I mean, he wasn't injured?'

Sofia looked at her broodingly.

'I do not think that anyone who fought in that war was "all right", as you say. Certainly it made him determined to keep Hungary independent and neutral in the future. He met my mother shortly after the war. She was a professional violinist, and he heard her play in a concert in Budapest. After that he followed her everywhere, while her father tried to keep him away.'

She smiled.

'My mother, Eva, was the child of a gypsy mother and a Magyar father. When his wife died, my grandfather undertook the education of his little seven-year-old daughter himself, and he found she had a wonderful gift for music, inherited from her mother, who came of the musician class of gypsies. These are a special group, you understand. They scorn the artisan gypsies who live like vagabonds. The musician caste are the aristocrats – or they were in the past.'

She spread her hands apologetically. 'Of course, I do not know how it is today. My grandfather had his daughter trained by the best masters, and forced her to practise and practise for hours every day, until her fingers bled and she cried from the pain in her shoulders and arms. Nowadays this would not be permitted, no? But that is how you make a musician. Like Mozart's father, my grandfather wanted to live through her glory, and of course her earnings. But Eva had also inherited some of the gypsies' wildness. One night, after a concert in Pécs, when she was just seventeen, she gave her father the slip and ran away with her lover, taking nothing but her violin. In spite of her father's cruel regime, she loved her music. They married in Budapest, and I was born a year later. She never saw her father again. He disowned her, but I do not think she minded.'

She paused, looking inwards.

59

'The year they married was 1919, in the middle of a time when there was another attempt to make Hungary free and democratic, under the leadership of Count Mihály Károlyi. It was not all noble and good, you understand, this Chrysanthemum Revolution – too many foolish things were done, like disbanding the army through an idealistic belief in peace, when the French, the Serbians and the Romanians were all marching on Hungary from different directions. And at the end, when Béla Kun tried to throw in Hungary's lot with the new Bolshevik state in Russia, everything turned sour. But for my parents' generation, who remembered the early hopeful days, it seemed a door had opened briefly, only to be slammed shut in their faces. And then the White Terror came, under Horthy, with its mass killings of peasants and workers and Jews and anyone who spoke up for democracy.'

Sofia sank into silence again, and Kate did not feel she could probe any further.

Now, seeing the figure amongst the rocks on the waterline, Kate was struck as never before by the extraordinary contrast between what Sofia's life must once have been and what it was now. What had become of her parents? How had she fetched up, of all places, in Dunmouth? The album of photographs had stopped abruptly when Sofia was probably in her late teens, a pretty girl, but not as remarkable looking as Eva had been.

'Kate, pay attention,' said Tom, irritably, 'I don't think you're listening. I asked whether you would like to take the tiller for a while.'

She pulled her mind with difficulty back to the boat.

'I'd love to.' She was pleased, really pleased, that he had come home early and suggested this outing. She must not spoil it for him. 'Let's just have our lunch first. You'll manage to steer and eat at the same time, but I'll have to concentrate and hold on with both hands. I hope I won't turn the boat over!'

'Capsize it,' said Tom. 'OK, pass me a sandwich then. I wish you'd brought beer instead of tea.'

On shore Sofia watched them gliding smoothly northwards, and could detect at once when Kate had taken over the tiller, as the boat dipped and hesitated, then moved forward awkwardly, like a bird with a damaged wing. That must be the husband with her in the boat. It was curious that he should be here now, in the middle of the day, sailing with his wife out on to the North Sea. According to Kate he was obsessed with work, hardly aware of his family, his mind always turned towards that inland city where he worked. This boat trip seemed a good sign. She had taken, inexplicably, to Kate.

After so many years of living on her own and talking only to her animals, she had found it difficult at first to cope with Kate's shy friendliness. But there was something about the younger woman that seemed to call out to her – an aura of loneliness and unhappiness that bore little relation to the surface appearance of her life as a fulfilled wife and mother, with a large house and a successful husband. Kate herself seemed only half aware of her need. She talked about being bored without a job, and of the partial relief from boredom afforded by helping to set up the bookshop. Yet underneath the polite English façade, Sofia sensed strong emotions and a deep loneliness. Her initial invitation to the cottage had been made on the spur of the moment, and immediately regretted. Before Kate's first visit she had dreaded it as an intrusion into her perfect self-contained solitude. Now, to her surprise, she found that she welcomed the visits.

The cottage felt blessedly cool after the heat on the foreshore. Sofia made herself a tisane of peppermint sweetened with honey, and sank into one of the sagging, threadbare armchairs which had been here when they had bought the neglected house from an old man during the war. Sofia had retained these old chairs because they were comfortable and they were too large for her to move out. Covered with bright shawls they now looked like a pair of magpies' nests on either side of the fireplace.

The photograph album was still lying on the table beside the chair, where Kate had laid it down yesterday. Sofia picked it up and turned the pages over. Until she had dragged out the old wooden trunk, she had not realised that Eva had brought any photographs with her. All these years they had been lying there. Little by little she had been examining them, but the process was disturbing, stirring up the muddy sediment of discarded memories. Interspersed amongst the photographs were programmes for Eva's concerts, fewer after her marriage, but always at famous halls in Budapest, Vienna or Prague – even as far as Paris and London. There were a few postcards, including some of the Lido at Venice. Sofia could remember that holiday, spent in northern Italy when she was about seven. But it was to the photographs of the house and her parents that she kept returning.

She had gone back to her father's diaries, but instead of reading them chronologically she found herself dipping into them for reminders of times she could remember herself, curious to see what different light might be shed on events by her father's perspective. She turned over the pages now until she found an entry which corresponded to the postcards of Venice.

Diary, Venice, July 1927

    Today was spent amongst the glories of Venice, admiring the architecture of palazzo and chiesa, and introducing Sofia to masterpieces by Giorgione, Bellini and Titian. I am afraid the child was hardly impressed. However, eating magnificent Italian ices amongst the pigeons in the Piazza di San Marco was the true high point of the day for her. As for Eva, she loves the painters of the Rinascimento, but not, she says, in such hot weather. I was forced to concede victory to the fairer sex without too much regret, and enjoyed the gliding trip by gondola amongst the hidden waterways, behind the great buildings which are the public face of the city, and under the lines of washing strung across the back canals. Here the women tie their small children on long reins to the iron railings, to protect them from a sudden tumble into the water, while the older boys (some no older than Sofia) swim like eels amongst the striped mooring posts and steps slimy with weed. The smell of these canals is not agreeable in the heat of summer, but a strong Turkish cigarette soon takes care of that, while the rest of the senses are ravished. Even the shrill cries of the women from window to window, calling to their neighbours across the canal, have a native music in this most musical of languages.

    On returning to our hotel at the Lido in the early evening I found a letter from cousin Gábor. He says that the effects of the Prime Minister's decree of last autumn, restoring the upper house of feudal magnates, are working further mischief. Our liberal colleagues have been rendered almost powerless. The composition of the upper house, with its great hereditary landholders, its ecclesiastical barons, and a few Horthy placemen from amongst our own country gentry, ensures the reactionary authoritarianism of the regime. There have been one or two unpleasant anti-Semitic incidents in Budapest, he says, and the appeals of industrial workers and farm labourers for a return to pre-war conditions are treated with contempt. At least I can do whatever I am able on my own estate. The háztáji I have made over to each of the peasants according to family size do provide sufficient land for growing vegetables and keeping some stock, enough for the household's needs. The other fields above the village furnish some arable land. If I had none but myself to consider, I would follow the lead of Tolstoy and share out the whole of my land amongst them, but I cannot see that to copy his example and pauperise my family would be the act of a decent man. As it is, Jenö complains that the estate is now

62

too small to be viable, and he can no longer manage it profitably. He grieves for the days when his grandfather managed it for mine, and regards me as a dangerous lunatic!

❧

It did not take Kate long to grasp the basic principles of handling the dinghy, and the outing – which she had agreed to simply out of pleasure at spending some time with Tom – began to take on its own excitement. The tiller under her hand was not a dead piece of varnished wood, but quivered and throbbed with life. The sheet, a length of faded blue rope, linked her to every whim of the breeze as it filled the sail. The slightest shift in strength or direction ran down the nerves and muscles of her arm, so that she felt herself slipping into a union with the boat, no longer woman and object, but some mingled creature like the centaurs of mythology.

Ahead and to their right the sea stretched open and inviting, unmarked by any sail or ship. The swell was slight, but here and there, due to some freak of current and tide, or a sudden breathing of the wind, small whitecaps would break and curve over, their undersides green and glittering, their crests white with blown surf. Out here amongst them, it was easy to see why they were called white horses. The foam leapt and ran down the curve of the breakers with the same graceful yet powerful line as a horse's mane flowing over the arch of its neck. Somewhere out there, where the colour of the sea deepened to purple grey on the edge of sight, lay the sea lanes to Scandinavia. The wide expanse of sea, the sky stretching cloudless and high, filled Kate with a sense of buoyant freedom. Away from the land she felt weightless, as though she could float away down those sea lanes without a backward glance.

As the boat rounded the far end of the promontory and headed up the coast, she saw that the seal colony was occupying a different sandbank today, further out from the shore. They were unperturbed by the sailing boat, although she had seen them plunge in panic into the sea when one of the new jet bikes roared past, with the sound of its engine bouncing and reverberating off the rocks. She sailed as close to the sandbank as Tom would allow her, warning that they might run aground. The big bull seal, whom Kate supposed to be the patriarch of the colony, lifted his head once and gazed at them steadily. He shifted his great body, heaving it awkwardly round so that he could view them more easily, then he lowered his head again, satisfied that they posed no threat.

Kate was reluctant to hand back the tiller to Tom.

'Can't I carry on a bit longer?'

'We need to be starting back now. Once the tide turns, the combination of the river current and the ebb tide is very powerful. There isn't enough wind to carry us back across it, and it would be a long hard row.'

'I could go on steering, couldn't I?'

'No, not this first time. The wind has shifted, and it'll be coming from directly astern. That makes it quite difficult to avoid gybing, so I'll take her back.'

'Gybing?'

The technical explanation took them back past the headland. If only, Kate thought, the rest of our life together could be as straightforward as this. Out at sea here we've been at ease with each other again. We've been able to talk without the furtive hidden meanings behind the words. If only...

'Have you enjoyed it?' asked Tom.

'Brilliant! I'm converted. You were right, and all the old fishermen of my childhood were wrong.'

୨

István had taken the box containing his parents' papers back with him to Sopron after his weekend in Szentmargit. He wanted to look through them quietly, and had persuaded Magdolna that they should not decide what action to take until he had considered everything carefully.

At first he was too busy to spend time on them. The continuing heat wave was causing problems in the little town. Children stayed outside too long playing, and came home with painful sunburn. The group of expectant mothers who attended his pre-natal clinic were showing signs of heat exhaustion. Although his Austrian patients who came over the border were generally wealthy, and could afford the comforts wealth can buy, many of the local Hungarian women were still at work far into the late stages of pregnancy. Their families needed the money, and he had to exercise his persuasive skills to curb the damage they were doing to themselves. Like most of his fellow citizens, these women welcomed freedom from the occupying Russian troops and the growing sense of liberation in the new democracy. But money was very short and unemployment – once avoided by over manning in communist state industries – was now rising at an alarming rate.

Some of the old people, too, were finding the heat trying, especially those with heart conditions or breathing difficulties. All of these problems, in addition to the usual casework of his practice, left him little time to himself. His young partner, Endre Wolff, had excellent qualifications but little experience. He had been in Sopron just six months, and the patients still felt safer with Dr Rudnay, who had looked after them for twenty-four years.

Today, however, he had left Endre in charge of the baby clinic. The younger doctor was quite capable of administering injections and it would give him an opportunity to get to know some of the patients better. During István's summer holiday Endre would have to take charge, with assistance from the usual locum, a semi-retired lady doctor from Budapest who liked to spend a month every summer in Sopron, walking in the wooded hills during her free time.

The whole ground floor of the house was given over to the practice, but upstairs István had his own flat, which László had shared with him until he had left home six years ago for Pannonhalma. István lived a pared-down life here. He had come to Sopron with his baby son after Maria's death. In his first weeks of grief and anger, he had destroyed everything that reminded him of her, ruthlessly burning her clothes and tearing up letters and photographs. Her few pieces of humble jewellery he had given to Magdolna to put away, with the unformed notion that one day László might want them for his wife. It was years now since László's boyhood clothes and toys had been passed on to András. The bed in his room was kept made up, but he had not slept in it for years. Alone in the flat, István lived like an ascetic bachelor, as though he had never had a wife and child. It suited him this way.

The big airy sitting room had windows opening on to a wooden balcony overlooking the garden. These were flung open now, letting in a little movement of air, as István sorted the papers on his modern table of pale polished fruitwood. In the box the papers had been jumbled together in no sort of order. He made four piles: the cheap school notebooks filled with his father's writing, which seemed to form a sort of diary; a few letters; copies of his father's underground newspaper, *Freedom!*; and miscellaneous cuttings from official newspapers. The other items from the box, like the watch and the jewellery case, he had left with Magdolna.

The last of the four piles was the least interesting. All the cuttings referred to partisan activities of one kind or another, either during the Nazi regime or in the first few years of the Russian occupation. As they had been cut from propaganda publications, the reports were almost certainly distorted, but they did give hints of considerable partisan activity in the area around Győr, some twenty-five kilometres south-east of Szentmargit, where his father's group had mainly operated.

The copies of *Freedom!* were cyclostyled in purple ink on thin, greyish paper, and were undated, although they were numbered. The sequence ran from number one to number ninety-seven, with only one, number fifteen, missing. It was impossible to say with certainty at what dates the individual copies had been printed, but in looking through them István found references to successful operations which seemed to have some links with the items from the newspapers. He thought that with a little time and patience it might be possible to date them by using these cross-references. He knew that his father had started the paper in 1941 as a forum for democratic but clandestine opinion during the regime of the Nazi puppet government. The declared purpose of the paper had been to serve as a rallying cry for a free and democratic Hungary, which would shake off the yoke of foreign, Germanic rule – a rule which had started with the Hapsburg Empire and extended to the Third Reich. After the war, his father had continued the newspaper intermittently as a voice of protest against the invading forces of Soviet Russia until he had been arrested and taken away. The irony of being liberated from Hitler by the troops of Stalin had not been lost on István's father, as could be seen in the cartoons he himself had drawn for the paper. His mother had carried on publishing *Freedom!* until restrictions on life had become a little easier after the downfall of the butcherous Rákosi in the spring of 1956 – a time when it had seemed at last that the hopes of a brighter future might be realised.

The letters were a miscellaneous lot. There were one or two from his father to his mother, but during their seven years together they had rarely been separated for more than a few days. István scanned a few of the letters at random. One, dated 11 April 1945, caught his eye. It had been sent by hand, a week after the last German troops had left Hungary, and addressed to his father via the priest of the Church of Szent Margit in the village. The priest, a courageous protector of the partisans, had later been executed as an enemy of the state after one of Rákosi's show trials in the early fifties. Inside, the letter was addressed to 'Lancelot', his father's partisan code name.

I was greatly relieved to receive word that you'd reached home safely and that the gunshot wounds to your chest and side are healing. You ask me if I can help you to fill in the blanks in the story of that terrible night in December last year, since your memory is confused. Not all the

66

details are clear, but this is what I have been able to piece together. Some of it, I am sure, you remember.

Early in the evening you were with Wallenberg when word was brought that the Arrow Cross were planning raids on several of the Jewish safe houses outside the ghetto. You set out with fifty of the simplified Schutzpasses that he had managed to have printed earlier that day. You were intending to hand them out in three of the houses where Jewish families without Swedish papers had taken refuge in the last few days. As you yourself remembered, you managed to reach two of the houses without difficulty. On your way to the third, in Deák Ferenc Utca, not far from the Danube, you were seized by one of the Arrow Cross bands who were roaming the streets during those last days while the Nazis still held Budapest.

You'll remember that the forced marches of the Jews had been stopped on 24 November, and there were no transport wagons left to ship them to the labour camps – by then the retreating Germans were using the wagons to carry off all our heavy machinery and raw materials they could lay their hands on. The Arrow Cross were rounding up Jews and anyone else they didn't take a fancy to. After they had stripped them of any valuables they shot them and dumped the bodies in the Danube.

As you hadn't reached the last house, you were still carrying some of the Schutzpasses (we found a few in your pockets later). This marked you out as a 'Jew-lover' in their terms, so they kicked you around for a bit. We found someone who'd seen you lying in the road, being kicked in the head and kidneys by a crowd of the Greenshirts. Much of the bruising must have happened then. Maybe they got tired of beating you. Or maybe they saw some other victim. They shot you and threw what they thought was your dead body into the river. Our witness didn't try to save you, because she thought you were dead, but she did send word back to Wallenberg, who raised hell with the authorities. They weren't in a mood to pay attention, because by then they must have realised it was only a matter of days before the Russians drove them out.

You remember what a terrible winter it was. The river was half frozen, with borders of ice building up around Margaret Island and lumps of the stuff floating downriver from higher up. It was the freezing water that saved you, as it saved quite a few others. Your wounds were frozen, the flow of blood staunched by the ice. The shock of the cold water must have revived you, and you managed to swim near to the bank just opposite my building. I knew that anyone shot by the Arrow Cross had to be a friend, so I pulled off my shoes and jumped in to get

67

you. A couple of my friends gave me a hand to pull you out. It was just as well because I couldn't have held on to you much longer. Cold! I don't think I've ever known the meaning of the word before! Despite the shortages I've always been shaped like a tub of lard, and that probably helped me, but I don't know how you survived. Though as I've said, I've heard since about a lot of other cases where the freezing waters saved victims of the Arrow Cross bullets. Perhaps it was our Danube protecting her own against those vermin, those Nazi Hungarians who would eat their own mothers if it suited them. We carried you back here to my parents' apartment, stripped you and wrapped you up in blankets, and got a decent doctor to come and dig out the bullets. You regained consciousness on the third day, and the rest of the story you know. Copies of Freedom! *have reached us here in Budapest. If you need distributors, you know where to find us.*

Your friend,
Ferenc Kalla

István laid the letter down on the table. The calm, matter-of-fact way in which it narrated the story of the attempted murder of his father by the Nyílas – the Arrow Cross – left him numb. The terror of those weeks when Nazis and Stalinists had fought over Budapest must have paralysed people's normal feelings, so all that mattered was the bare fact of survival. The letter had been written nearly fifty years ago, and Hungary had undergone occupation, police brutality, Stalinist terror, civil war and the slow path to freedom during the intervening years. Yet people *had* survived. He wondered what had been the fate of Ferenc Kalla. The address on the letter he recognised as being in one of the elegant eighteenth- and nineteenth-century blocks overlooking the Danube on the Pest side of the city.

Much had been made, in recent months, of confiscated apartments in Budapest being returned to their rightful owners after half a century of neglect, and of the difficulty the private owners were now having in trying to repair broken pipes and shattered roof tiles. He knew many such homes himself from his student days in Budapest and more recent visits – homes where electric wires in cracked and perished insulation hung in loops from ceilings, toilets would not flush and damp patches spread green tentacles across bedroom walls. Outside, the buildings were still beautiful, adorned with plaster scrollwork and caryatids, with balconies and doors of delicate wrought iron portraying beasts and fruits and ancient gods.

Searching his memory, he thought that the address on the letter was one of the apartment buildings just down river from Petőfi Square

68

– after the Belvárosi Templom, the oldest church in the city, but before Freedom Bridge, Szabadság Híd. Despite the bombing of the bridge during the struggle for the city between the Nazis and the Soviets, many of the buildings along that stretch had survived. Might this Ferenc Kalla have survived also? From the reference to his parents, it sounded as though he might have been one of the student partisans. István folded the letter and returned it to its envelope. He thought he might make a few discreet enquiries.

॰

After they had returned the dinghy safely to the water sports centre, Tom said he was so hot that he needed to replenish the household supply of beer. While he went to the off-licence, Kate looked in at the bookshop. Apart from a customer turning over the pages of cookery books, it was quiet. The two downstairs rooms of the cottage, which now formed the shop, had been painted a soft green, with white woodwork and bookcases. On the dark moss-green carpet a few wicker chairs were scattered amongst the bookcases, so that customers could sit down and browse in comfort. Tom had viewed these with amusement during the launch party, his only visit to Harbour Steps Books.

'I'm not sure those chairs are a good idea. People will come in and read the books here instead of buying them to take home. She'll lose business.'

Kate had shaken her head impatiently.

'The whole idea is to make it as homey as possible, so people will come in and spend time here. Linda wants them to be sure about a book before buying it. She isn't going to hustle them into making a wrong choice. They're more likely to come back if they're happy with what they buy. She's going to offer them a free cup of coffee or tea if they spend a long time browsing. And look, she's made this corner for the children.'

She pulled him over to a Wendy house and a group of miniature Windsor chairs arranged around a low table.

'The children's books are here for them to look at, or else they can play while their parents are looking.'

Tom shook his head and laughed.

'All very cosy.'

Kate felt a spurt of annoyance at the patronising tone in his voice.

69

'Not everybody is out to milk their customers of every last penny, like Crossbow Computers,' she began crossly, but fortunately they were interrupted by Chris with a wine bottle in each hand, eager to top up their glasses.

Coming in now, she saw that Linda and Beccy were behind the counter looking at some sheets of paper Chris was flourishing in front of them.

'Look at this, Mum,' said Beccy. 'I never would have believed such things could have gone on in Dunmouth!'

'What is it?' asked Kate.

'I thought I'd have a look through the newspaper archives, Mrs Milburn,' said Chris. 'To see if I could find anything interesting that I could use for a new feature I've suggested to the editor. You know: "Twenty Years Ago Today" or "Fifty Years Ago in Dunmouth", that kind of thing.'

He passed the photocopied items across to her. The first was dated December 1940.

Foreign Occupants of Dunmouth Cottage

Our reporter has learned that an isolated cottage just outside Dunmouth, formerly owned by the late George Hadham, retired fisherman, is now occupied by two foreign women of unknown nationality.

ARP warden Albert Gresham reports that on several occasions lights have been seen showing at the cottage, which faces directly on to the North Sea.

Says Albert, 'I knocked on the door to tell the women to douse their lights, but they refused to open to door to me and I was obliged to shout through the letterbox.'

The younger woman has been seen occasionally in the village, and is said to speak with a strong foreign accent. The older woman was spotted when the cottage was first occupied.

'We don't want foreigners in Dunmouth,' says Edward Stannard, fisherman. 'Who knows where they come from?'

Dunmouth police are understood to have said that they have received no internment order for the women.

In the margin, someone had scrawled 'German?'

'Is this handwriting new or old?' asked Kate, pointing to it.

'Old,' said Chris. 'That's what the story is implying, isn't it? All that about being foreign, and internment, and showing lights, and not letting the ARP man in – it's suggesting in so many words that they're German spies.'

Kate laid the sheet of paper down on the counter beside the till.

'There were the craziest stories going around during the war,' said Linda. 'I remember Dad talking about it. Especially in the coastal towns and villages. Some of the German Jewish refugees had a terrible time; people thought they were Nazis because they were German.'

'Yes,' said Kate slowly. 'I remember friends of ours from Kent saying that some people who lived in a converted windmill were suspected of being spies – they "spoke funny", and it was alleged that the sails of the windmill had been fixed to point the way to London for the German bombers. Of course, the Luftwaffe would hardly have needed a barely visible windmill in order to find London.'

'Were they foreign?' asked Chris, intrigued.

Kate laughed. 'No. They came from Liverpool. To the local people in Kent, I suppose that sounded foreign. Remember, this was more than fifty years ago – no universal TV watching in those days, to familiarise us all with each other's ways of speaking.'

'Well,' said Chris, 'it sounds as though the rumours went on circulating, and had a nasty outcome. I found this in one of the issues for November 1944. The war was nearly over by then. You wouldn't think people would still have been neurotic about spies. It must refer to the same women, and I haven't found anything else in between, though I may have missed something.'

He passed the second sheet to Kate.

Fatal Accident in Dunmouth

A woman died yesterday in Charlborough Hospital as the result of pneumonia and head injuries. The woman was admitted two days ago, already suffering from an advanced case of pneumonia, and having received a severe blow to the head, it is believed from a stone being thrown at her.

The woman's daughter, who lives with her at a cottage near Dunmouth, alleged that a large stone was thrown at her as she tried to leave the cottage to fetch medical help for her mother. Missing her, the stone struck the older woman on the temple and rendered her unconscious.

Police say that as it has not been possible to identify the alleged assailants, they will not be making any arrests.

Beccy was rereading the article over Kate's shoulder.

'Isn't that awful? You can see what happened. Those women were attacked, because of the German spy rumour, and the police just weren't going to bother following it up. And one of them *died*.'

There were tears in Beccy's eyes. The tone of the article was brutally offhand, Kate thought. It was almost as though the reporter had said, under his breath: 'And good riddance too.'

'I wonder which cottage it means,' said Linda thoughtfully.

'And what became of the other woman,' said Beccy. 'Do you suppose they drove her out, or killed her as well?'

Kate said nothing. 'A bad business' had gone on at the cottage during the war, her father had said, and her mother had somehow been caught up in it.

She suspected that she knew what had become of the younger woman.

Chapter 5

'Not a gîte,' Tom said firmly. 'If we're having a holiday, let's make it a *holiday*. And as it's the first one without any of the children, we'll push the boat out and stay in a decent hotel.'

Kate had managed at last to pin him down to the second and third weeks in August. She, too, was conscious that this would be their first holiday without the children since Beccy's birth nineteen years ago. She supposed she ought to feel liberated, but the thought came over her like a cloud that the family was breaking apart. A few years ago it had seemed as though it would go on for ever, the five of them – laughing, bickering, doing things together. Or at least that was how it had been, in the times before Tom had become so obsessed by his job. The change had been so gradual that she could not put a finger on when it had started. Briefly, during the two hours they had spent sailing the dinghy, Kate thought they had recaptured the old intimacy and warmth, but since then the silent space between them had opened up again.

Once they had been a close family, with a lot of shared interests but enough differences between them that they did not crowd each other too much. Roz was the only one who was musical. Beccy shared her mother's flair for languages, but was caught up in what the family called her Causes – Friends of the Earth, dolphin sponsorship, campaigns to help the Third World. She planned to use her languages working for an international charity. Stephen had been a late developer, more concerned with football and cricket than with any serious thoughts about his future – until two years ago. Then, on entering the sixth form, he declared that he was dropping his plan to do arts subjects at A Level and switching to physics, maths and chemistry instead. Kate had no idea what had induced this change, but knew it had entailed hours of extra work catching up in subjects he had appeared to have no interest in before.

With the rational side of her mind she knew all three children were growing up and away from their parents. And of course the shape of the family had been altered as soon as Beccy had gone away to university last autumn. But she had never previously thought how rapidly the changes would come. In little more than two years they would all be away, at least during term time. Already they were focused outward, feeling the pull of the wider world.

When Tom had specified France for their holiday, she had thought at once of the gîte in Brittany where they had spent five or six happy summers when the children were small. It would probably be booked up, but they might find somewhere else nearby. But when Tom reminded her that this would be their first holiday alone without the children, she felt her heart sinking. Somehow she could not face the places they had known as a family – the *crêperies*, the 'spinner of glass' in Dinan, or the *hypermarché* just outside Guingamp, which the children always insisted on visiting immediately in order to spend large portions of their holiday money on supplies of delicious and cheap French chocolate.

Was this what people meant when they spoke of the 'empty nest' syndrome? A feeling almost of bereavement as the children departed? Laughing at herself, but ruefully, she went to the travel agent in Charlborough and booked one week in the best hotel in Avignon, followed by one week at what the travel agent recommended as an extremely grand resort on the Mediterranean coast.

'It used to be one of the places most favoured by the British aristocracy before the first world war,' he explained. 'There are four luxurious Edwardian hotels, overlooking the sea. They have all been restored within the last five years, retaining the period atmosphere but with modern plumbing and other facilities. They are only available for private clients – no package tours. The local business consortium there is aiming to keep everything very upmarket and exclusive. And because they haven't been discovered yet by the Americans or the Japanese the prices are very reasonable for what you get.'

Kate had blenched a little at these reasonable prices, but Tom had been very definite about the kind of hotel he had in mind and how much he expected to pay, so she docilely made out the cheque for the deposit and arranged to collect the tickets and other documents the following week when she paid the balance.

Roz was to leave the next day for her music camp, and Stephen the day after for his cycling holiday. Kate found Roz sitting in the middle of her room that evening looking despairingly round at the clothes spread all over her bed and chairs, dangling from hangers hooked over the picture rail and spilling out of her drawers.

'Oh,' said Kate.

'I *can't* get everything into my squashy bag, Mum,' wailed Roz. 'That's all we're allowed to take, apart from our instruments and music cases. And I don't know what to take and what to leave behind. I just know I won't have the right clothes.' She looked near to tears.

Kate remembered how vital it was at sixteen to have the right clothes, to fit in with the rest of the crowd. She gave the problem her consideration.

'Well, you're obviously going to need underwear and night things and sponge bag and make-up,' she said, swiftly gathering these up and clearing a space for them on the bed. 'I'll bet they won't mind if you take a shoulder bag. Don't take a handbag, take your big canvas shoulder bag instead. That will hold all of these things, plus some reading matter and a purse and so on.'

She perched on a corner of Roz's desk and considered the problem of outer clothes. She had no more idea than Roz what the required dress would be.

'Jeans and T-shirts,' she muttered, 'and a sweatshirt or jersey if it turns cold. There's a concert on the last night, isn't there?'

'Yes. In Aberystwyth.'

'Better take your black skirt and white blouse, then.'

Kate considered. Roz's bag would certainly not hold everything she had spread out.

'Why not plan on mix and match co-ordinates? You know – all those articles in women's magazines advising you "how to travel light and still ring the changes!" You've got a lot of things with green in them. Let's lay out those and see what outfits you could make up.'

Privately Kate suspected that the jeans and the concert clothes were the only things Roz would wear for the entire time, but her daughter greeted the idea with a cry of delight.

'That's brilliant, Mum! Here, give us those red trousers. I won't need those.'

She began folding clothes and stuffing them back into drawers.

'Hey, would you like to hear my new CD?'

'Mmm. Been spending your money before you go away?'

'It was a bargain classic – they're reissuing old recordings from the pre-war years of some of the famous musicians back then. They have some process for taking out the scratches and background noise and cleaning up the recording for the CD. Sandy did explain it. He's into all that stuff, but I wasn't really listening.'

Roz slid the disk into the CD player, unplugged the earphones and plugged in the loudspeakers.

'I think it's pretty fabulous, particularly when you think it was recorded in 1923. And it only cost £6.99.'

'I suppose they don't have to pay large royalties – or any – on a recording as old as that. What is it?'

'Violin music, of course. Starts with the Mendelssohn.'

Roz pressed the play button and the fiery, passionate music filled the room. Kate felt humbled, as she always did, that a composer so young could have achieved so much. It made her feel inadequate, with a wasted life behind her. She paused in her packing of Roz's bag. The violin had a supreme tone, and the player had power and tenderness and lyric intensity. The Mendelssohn concerto was followed by the Bruch, with its soaring lyrical passages. Kate sat quietly on Roz's bed listening, her hands clasped loosely around her drawn-up knees and her eyes half closed. Before the next piece began, she pressed the pause button.

'That is simply wonderful. Who is it?'

'I hadn't heard of her before, though the programme notes say she was very famous for a time, a child prodigy like Yehudi Menuhin. And it's rather sad. That was a Guarneri she was playing – one of the best. Apparently it was lost or destroyed in the war.'

'But who was she? Such power – I didn't realise it was a woman.'

Roz stuck out her lip. 'Women can be powerful players too, Mum.'

'Yes, I do realise, darling. But there can't have been many then.'

'She was a Hungarian. Part-gypsy, apparently. Perhaps that's where the power and the...wildness comes from.'

Roz pressed the button to spring out the deck and handed the little silver disk to her mother.

'She was called Eva Tabor.'

The following day after Roz had left, Stephen mooched gloomily around the house. Kate suspected that he had slightly lost his nerve over the cycling holiday in France, but restrained herself from saying anything. In the middle of the afternoon he slouched into the kitchen, where she was stirring a pan on the stove.

'Making dinner already? Isn't it a bit early?'

'No, I'm baking a double batch of flapjack. Half of it is for you to take with you. It keeps for ever, and it will stop you starving if you find yourselves a long way from cafés and civilisation.'

'Brilliant! Of course, we're meant to be cooking for ourselves. Mick's bringing a camping stove and some pans. But I'm not much good at cooking.'

'So I've noticed. Pass me over those two greased baking sheets, will you?'

She began to scrape the mixture into the tins, pressing it into the corners and levelling the surface with the back of her wooden spoon. As she leaned down to put them in the oven, Stephen seized the saucepan and began scraping up the bits and licking them off the spoon. Kate hid her smile as she washed her sticky hands and put the kettle on.

'Tea?'

'Mmm, yes please.' Stephen peered at the pan, then abandoned it in the sink.

'Water in it. To soak. First lesson in cooking.'

Stephen ran the tap, and with his back to her said, 'Remember old Benjy? He was mad on flapjack. Used to steal it off the table if we left any lying around.'

Benjy had been Toby's predecessor, a mongrel of very mixed ancestry, who had died seven years before.

'Poor old Benjy! He was always hungry. It was probably a memory from his deprived puppyhood, before the animal shelter took him in. What made you think of him?'

'Oh, I don't know. Flapjack always reminds me of him. But then, he was sort of my dog, wasn't he? I kind of miss him.'

Kate was startled by this. It was true that Benjy had attached himself particularly to Stephen, as Toby had attached himself to her, but she hadn't suspected that Stephen was still missing his dog.

'You could always have had another dog, you know.'

'In our house in London? You've got to be joking, Mum. And now it's too late. I couldn't have a dog at university, could I?'

'No, I'm sure they wouldn't allow one in the halls of residence.'

Kate lifted the kettle and began making the tea, then checked on the flapjack in the oven. It was easy to overcook it.

'I suppose if you rented a private flat after first year you might be able to have a dog, though most landlords ban pets. And you'd have to keep going back between lectures to take him for a walk.'

'Oh, I know it isn't really on.' Stephen slumped into a chair and cradled his mug of tea. 'Actually, I'm not particularly looking forward to university.'

Kate poured her own tea, then lifted the flapjack out of the oven and checked the clock. It needed to cool for five minutes before being scored across. She sat down opposite him.

'University can be a bit intimidating before you start,' she said, recalling her own mixture of elation and dread. 'But you do have the freshers' week, which we never had. That gives you time to find your way around before you have to start the term properly.'

Stephen raised a face taut with worry.

'I don't think I'm good enough. What if my A-Level grades aren't high enough? What if I can't cope with the work when I get there?'

'I'm sure you're good enough, and you'll probably find everyone else feels the same way. Just concentrate on doing your best without overdoing things, and I'm sure you'll be fine.'

She reached across and squeezed his hand.

'Remember, it doesn't matter a hoot in the long run. Look at Linda. She never went to university when she was young, then had a wonderful time going when she was older. Keep it at the back of your mind that this isn't your one and only chance. But give it your best for a year anyway.'

He smiled at her, a little shamefaced.

'Thanks, Mum. I just don't want to let you both down.'

'Of course you won't.'

She got up and began to score the warm flapjack into squares.

'Hey, can we have some now – out of the *family* half, I mean, not out of mine?'

She laughed.

'Get a plate, then.'

The next day, after Stephen had departed with Mick and his cousin – the bicycles slung about with bulging panniers and carriers – the house seemed worryingly empty. It was no emptier than when Stephen and Roz were at school and Beccy away, but the very walls seemed to hold the knowledge they would not return in the evening. There was a hollowness to the sound of Kate's feet on the floorboards, and when she flung open the window in the bedroom the sound echoed as if the house were unfurnished. Toby followed her everywhere, as though he felt the difference too.

Beccy was going to see a play at the Charlborough theatre that evening with Chris.

'It starts at seven, so we're going straight in after I finish at the bookshop. I won't bother to come home. We'll have a bite of tea in the theatre café. Then Chris is taking me out to dinner after the play at this fabulous new Turkish restaurant that's just opened in Charlborough. They say the food is fantastic.'

'Ah,' said Kate, who had never been to a Turkish restaurant. 'Very nice.' She remembered how she and Tom had loved visiting new and unusual restaurants in their early days together. Money was tight, and a meal out always seemed a terrible extravagance, so they would live frugally for days before, in order to justify it to themselves. A lingering guilt stayed with her still, especially after some grand business occasion which she had not even particularly enjoyed. Beccy's generation did not seem to suffer from the same guilts. She tried to remember when Tom had last taken her out for a meal, just the two of them. Not since they had left London. And not for a long time before that, if the truth were told. Money was no longer a problem, but now there was never time to do things together. And it was almost as if they avoided each other when he was at home – they seemed to have run out of things to say. This evening she would eat alone again, as Tom planned to work late at the office. The big Manchester project, he claimed, needed his personal attention again.

Viewing the blank desert of a day stretching ahead of her, Kate decided to visit Sofia, whom she hadn't seen for nearly a week while she had been organising Roz and Stephen to go away. After lunch she packed up some of the flapjack in a plastic box and called to Toby.

As always, Kate was soothed by Sofia's garden. They sat in the shifting, dappled shade of one of the apple trees on a couple of ancient wicker chairs that sighed and whispered with every movement. Sofia had made fresh lemonade, and they sipped tall cool glasses of it and nibbled at Kate's flapjack.

'The bees are going mad,' said Kate dreamily. Opposite her a tall clump of fennel was alive with Sofia's own bees, and wild bees, and hover flies. They swarmed in from every direction to crowd and jostle each other on the flat yellow umbels.

'They look like dozens of little helicopters all trying to land on one pad.'

She could smell the spicy scent from where she sat, mixed with the aniseed of the sweet cicely beside her chair. Its white flowers were finished now, replaced by clusters of shiny, crisp, black seed pods. Kate plucked one and bit into it absentmindedly. The flavour of liquorice spread over her tongue. It was warm and sheltered in the garden, but its nearness to the sea meant that there was always a faint stirring in the air. The breeze must find its way over the sheltering wall and drop down to play around the trees like a boy climbing into a forbidden orchard to steal apples. She closed her eyes and felt this hint of a breeze brush her eyelids like the faint touch of a warm finger.

'It is so peaceful here,' she murmured sleepily. 'So safe.'

'Yes,' said Sofia. 'Perhaps too safe?'

Her voice held a slight note of interrogation and suddenly Kate was reminded of the newspaper stories Chris had found in the archives of the *Dunmouth and Welbank Herald*. Impossible to think that this place could ever have been the scene of such a violent and fatal attack. Yet what other cottage near Dunmouth could have been occupied by two foreign women back during the war years? It was conceivable that, in those days of suspicion and paranoia about Nazi spies, Sofia and her mother might have been taken for Germans. She had discovered that Sofia spoke German as fluently as Hungarian, coming as she did from the region that bordered on Austria, where almost everyone was bilingual. Kate tried to push away the thoughts of that terrible scene which had taken shape in her mind ever since reading the account, and another more detailed article Chris had found later. The dark, bitterly cold night, the sick woman, the crowd of young people from the village bent on playing their part in the war, led by a fisherman called Edward Stannard who had been declared unfit for war service, the rank hatred welling up, the fear of the trapped women. And somewhere in the crowd – her mother.

She opened her eyes abruptly.

'When did you have the wall built, Sofia? You said it wasn't always here.'

'No, it wasn't always here. And I built it myself, very slowly. It took about three years. When?' She paused thoughtfully. 'It was thirty years ago. At the beginning of the sixties.'

'You built it to protect the garden? To keep the wind out?'

Sofia looked at her steadily.

'Yes. To keep the wind out.'

They lapsed into silence again. But after pouring out more lemonade, Sofia said, 'I have been thinking about the past a great deal lately. I have been thinking that I ought to go back.'

'Back? Back to Hungary?'

'Yes. We left in such haste, you understand.' She laced her fingers together, and Kate could see how taut her hands were.

'I have always felt that there was unfinished business there. In my heart I carry a kind of guilt, to have run away like that. I would not go back to live, but somehow, before I grow too old, too feeble to travel, I need to see...'

Kate thought, suddenly: Yet to me she seems to grow younger and younger. When I first saw her, she looked like an old woman. Now – she is so vigorous, so alive, she doesn't seem much older than I am.

'I suppose you couldn't have gone back before. Under the communists, I mean.'

'No. In 1956 – which you will barely remember, you must have been a child – in 1956 it seemed that the Russians would be driven out and democracy established. Later, when the tanks rolled into Budapest and the slaughter began, I knew I could not go back unless, some day, Hungary gained her freedom from the terror and dictatorship that spread out from the Soviet state.'

She broke off and reached down to fondle Ákos's ears.

'I never knew what happened to my father, you see. He managed to smuggle my mother and me out on a boat going down the Danube to Romania, but he felt he had to stay behind and fight the Nazi collaborators who were springing up in Hungary.' She sighed. 'I do not even know if he survived the war.'

'Don't you think you should go? Just to try to find peace of mind?' Kate looked around the garden, at the chickens scratching in their wired-in enclosure, at the goat waiting to be milked within the next hour. 'Of course, the garden and the animals – you're worried about them. But... perhaps we could help? Beccy and Chris are going to be around all summer, and Chris grew up on a farm.'

'The young man who works on the newspaper?'

'Yes. Of course, I realise nowadays the farmers all use milking machines, but he could probably learn to milk the goat, couldn't he? And chickens are easy enough. The bees would look after themselves, wouldn't they, at this time of year?'

'Oh yes. But it would be sad for Ákos and the cats to be alone in an empty house.'

'You know, Chris might be glad to move into the house for a couple of weeks. He's always moaning about how cramped and dingy his digs are.' Kate laughed. 'I think he's been hinting for me to take him in while Roz and Stephen are away!'

'I do not think I could do this, Kate. I do not even know this young man.'

'Would you like me to bring him to meet you? Then you could see how you feel about it.'

Suddenly Kate was smitten by the recollection that Chris was searching for Sofia, if she was indeed his mysterious poet. He hadn't spoken of it for weeks and she had forgotten about it. Perhaps she shouldn't have made the suggestion.

81

'Besides...' said Sofia.

'Yes?'

'Well, you will think me very foolish, an old woman like me, but I am... afraid. Yes, that is truly the word, I am *afraid* to travel so far. I have scarcely left Dunmouth since I came here as a very young woman. I did go once to Paris, three years ago. Just for a weekend, for a conference. Mr Shiraz and his family looked after the animals then, but it was nothing, only three days. And everything was arranged for me. I took the bus to Charlborough, and the train from there to London. After that, I was looked after like a fragile parcel.'

She gave one of her rare laughs, deep and musical.

Kate, who almost never asked her a direct question, felt emboldened. 'This conference – was it in connection with your poetry?'

Sofia shot her a penetrating look.

'Now where did you discover this? I have never spoken about it.'

'No,' Kate agreed, 'you never have. But this same Chris, with whom Beccy has become so very friendly – he took a degree in east European studies. He mentioned on the day I first met him that he was trying to discover the whereabouts of a famous Hungarian woman poet who lived as a recluse near Dunmouth. He didn't mention her name, but I can't believe there can be another cultured Hungarian woman living like a recluse off the fruits of the sea and of a paradise garden, hidden away behind a high wall – not *both* of you in the neighbourhood of Dunmouth.'

'No,' said Sofia. Her eyes were dancing. 'Perhaps not. Like you, I believe that this is unlikely.'

'Should you mind Chris finding you? Maybe it was a silly suggestion.'

'What is he like, this young man?'

'A very good sort of boy, I think. He wants to be a success as a journalist, one has to be aware of that. But he is sensitive and tactful. I think, if he wrote about you, he wouldn't publish anything you didn't approve of. I believe he would respect your privacy.'

'Well, perhaps I will agree to see him, Kate. Let me think about it for a little. But although that might solve the problem of the animals and the garden, it does not solve the problem of my fear. I tell myself it is stupid. I want to go, and yet I am afraid. Our escape, you see, was very frightening. The ship was overloaded, full of Austrian Jews escaping after the Anschluss. Near the end of our journey, in Romania, the ship foundered. Twenty or thirty people were drowned – no one was sure how many. We survived, but lost many of our belongings.'

She shivered, and wrapped her arms around herself.

'It is difficult to shut that out of my mind – the terror during the journey, the stories the Jews told, the dark water closing over my head. For years now I have been able to pull down a shutter over it, but ever since I began to think about returning – just to discover what happened, nothing else – the memory has been growing in me, more and more of it coming back. I did not even open the trunk containing my father's papers until a few weeks ago. Those photographs I showed you? I did not even know we had brought those out with us. Studying the papers – mostly my father's diaries and a few letters – and looking at the photographs, that part of my past has suddenly come alive again. Can I explain this properly? It is not as though I am simply remembering it. It is as though I am living it again.'

'If Tom and I weren't going to France, I'd come with you,' said Kate, thinking of this strange, remote country which had never truly entered her consciousness before she had met Sofia. 'But Stephen and Roz will be home soon after we're due back and I'll be swamped with domestic duties. And if we left it till the autumn, Beccy and Chris are talking about going off somewhere together, after he has earned some holiday entitlement.'

'No, you must not think of it,' said Sofia briskly. 'How free the young are now, are they not? In my youth, a girl who went on holiday with a young man would have had her reputation ruined for ever. Nowadays it is quite normal. Even a recluse learns about such things!'

❧

'I thought we might have a small dinner party the day after tomorrow,' Kate said to Tom that evening.

'What? Who?' He sounded surprised. 'People from Crossbow?'

'No. I haven't met any of your colleagues from Bamford. I want to invite two people from the village. Linda, who runs the bookshop, and Sofia, the old lady I told you about.'

'What, some sort of hen party? Or do you want me to bring some unattached men to even out the numbers?'

'No, I don't think so. I don't see it as that sort of party.' Kate paused. 'You've met Linda already. You know she's lost her husband just recently. I think a pairing off of the sexes would be very insensitive. I thought we would just make it family, and the two of them, and perhaps Beccy's friend Chris, unless he's working late at the paper.'

Tom grunted. He was reading the weekly project report from Manchester.

'You will be here, won't you?' she insisted. 'The day after tomorrow. Could you manage to be home by eight, just this once?'

'Oh, all right.'

'Put it in your diary, then.'

He jotted down a note and settled back to his report. The deadlines were only just being met and the whole project made him uneasy. Also, he was finding it difficult to concentrate – for weeks he had been plagued by headaches. Reading glasses prescribed by the optician were not providing any help.

Linda and Sofia both accepted the invitation to dinner. Chris would be tied up at work.

'Five of us,' Kate said to Beccy. 'I think we'll eat in the dining room for the first time in this house. We could eat in the kitchen, but this way I can shut the chaos away out of sight!'

As Sofia had so much seafood in her normal diet, Kate decided against it for the dinner. A chilled watercress soup, because of the hot weather, duck in a wine sauce and home-made sorbet, she thought. All fairly easy to prepare in the short time available.

On the evening of the dinner Linda and Sofia walked up the hill together. With Beccy's help, Kate had everything ready in good time, and the four women sat down in the drawing room with pre-dinner drinks. The antique mahogany table in the dining room glowed a deep red, reflecting the flames of the candles in the heavy silver candelabra. Kate had arranged yellow roses from the garden in small cut-glass vases in front of each place and folded yellow cotton napkins into fans tucked into the wine goblets. The white wine was chilling, the red wine breathing on the sideboard, and pyramids of fruit stood at each end of the Louis XV serving table. She had flung open the french windows in the drawing room and the evening breeze rising up the hill from the sea billowed the long curtains of white voile so that they lifted and spun like girls in white dresses.

At half-past eight, she took the duck out of the oven to relax, and moved the sorbet from the freezer to the fridge. At ten to nine, she put the softened sorbet back in the freezer, wrapped the duck in foil and returned it to a low oven. At nine she phoned Crossbow, but no one answered Tom's direct line. At half-past nine, at Beccy's suggestion, they started their meal. The duck had dried up. The sorbet was studded with fragments of ice crystals. Politely and awkwardly the four women made their way through the ruined meal.

At a quarter to eleven, Beccy drove Linda and Sofia home in Kate's car. When she returned they washed up in silence. At midnight, Tom arrived home.

Kate was reading in bed.

'It was our dinner party tonight,' she said quietly. 'What happened to you?'

'Oh, was it?' Tom tugged at his tie. 'Well, you didn't need me, did you? I sent for the Manchester project team and we spent the evening going through the plan and assessing the work still to be done.'

Kate laid aside her book and switched out her light. Her anger had dried up. Nothing was left but emptiness.

The drought at Szentmargit continued, and the unyielding heat of midsummer. In her barn workshop Magdolna straightened her throbbing back and looked about her, bemused. She was always like this after a day totally absorbed in her work. She came back to the everyday world slowly, unsure of the time, unsure even of the season. Her intense concentration while she was working on one of her figures deafened her and dulled her sense of heat and cold. The earthy scent of wet clay and the faintly metallic hint of ceramic glazes filled her nose and lingered on her tongue, but above all her sight was focused – partly inwards on the vision, partly outwards as the power of the vision flowed down her arms and into her fingertips.

The barn was poorly heated by a portable paraffin stove, except when additional warmth was given off by one of the kilns. In winter time József would come in to find the stove burnt out and ice forming in the buckets of water. Magdolna's hands would be blue with cold, but she was aware of nothing but her fingers working, making tangible the ideas which crowded her mind. Then he would refill and relight the stove. Moving with soft sounds to bring her gradually back to him, until she looked up at him wide-eyed like a child suddenly woken. He would take her hands and gently rub the warmth back into them, and together they would stare down at the fingers, suddenly stiff and chapped with cold, now that the driving force had been withdrawn.

Not that it was cold today. The heat wave which had begun several weeks ago had continued unabated and the farmers, amongst them József, were worried. Unless it rained soon the maize would remain shrivelled on the cob and the sunflowers – already stunted and poor-looking – would be useless for making oil. At first the excessive heat had drained Magdolna of energy. She had completed very little work over the last month. The finding of the box hidden by her mother had also unsettled her, awakening memories she had tried to bury. But a few days ago she had suddenly woken from sleep with clear ideas for three studies in her head, and now she was working as if possessed, trying to make up for lost time. She had been leaning over her worktable at the same angle far too long, hours probably, and now that she had become aware of her surroundings the pain at the base of her back was acute. She flexed her spine with a groan, pressing her hands into the small of her back and leaving grey smears of clay on her dress.

It was András who came to fetch her this evening, not József.

'Papa said to tell you that he will be late tonight,' he said, perching on the rim of a barrel in which clay was packed, wrapped in damp cloth. 'He and Gyula and Uncle Imre are trying to fix up some kind of irrigation system for the cornfields. Uncle Imre has brought back a pump and a kind of spray from Györ. It's supposed to throw water in a big arc and spin round. Uncle Imre says it will cover half a field at a time, then you shift it to the other half. They're joining all their hoses together with some fixings he bought, so they can run one long hose down to the river for the water. It'll be super if it works.' He said 'super' in English, not Hungarian. British and American television had reached a few houses in Szentmargit, though not his own, and the children were learning fast.

Magdolna laughed, her backache forgotten. József's brother Imre was mad for inventions and gadgets. Brushing up his thick moustache with the back of his hand, he would pace around the walnut tree in the middle of the village square, the favourite gathering place in the evenings, and harangue the other men about all the wonders of the new technology that would transform their farming. As most of the farmers found it difficult even to afford enough petrol to run one tractor they treated his ideas with a certain amount of mocking amusement, but all the same they respected his ingenuity.

After the years of forced collectivisation on the land, stubbornly resented by the   farmers, the Kádár government had allowed the peasants ownership of their *háztáji* or household plots for growing vegetables for the family, for keeping a cow, a pig, a few chickens. These little plots, less than an acre, were poor recompense for the land, ten or twelve times as much, they had been compelled to hand over to the collective. Yet the *háztáji*, cultivated by the village families for themselves, yielded far more than the state or collective farms. Now most of the land around Szentmargit had been handed back to the peasants, but few of the men had the means to develop their farming methods.

86

Szentmargit had always been a farm village, as far back as anyone could trace. Owned originally by the great family in the manor and worked by the villagers – who paid rent for their land in produce and in labour on the manor farm – the fields around the village had been given unencumbered to the peasants by the young count after the first world war. Until 1946 the Szentmargit families had regarded this land as their own, until it was taken into government control and they were told they were 'kulaks' – landed peasants, a species as despised by the Stalinist government as the bourgeoisie.

József and Imre and the others had regained their land during these last few years, but they had no experience of being private farmers except on their *háztáji*. They had no capital, their machinery was poor and rusting, their tractors decrepit. They could hope for little help from a government which – though expressing itself willing – was desperately short of money in this new, competitive, capitalist world. Magdolna suspected that it would be farmers like Imre who would save the system if anyone could. Otherwise there was the danger of foreigners, most likely Austrians, buying up the land, whole villages even. A few bad harvests and many of the farmers would be tempted to give up the unequal struggle and pocket the hard currency, closing their minds against what it might mean for the future. With Imre in Szentmargit, the village's chances were better than most.

'Come,' she said to András, ruffling his hair. 'We will not wait for your father to come home. We'll put a picnic in a basket and take it out to the fields. I should like to see this wonderful machine which is going to irrigate the crops from the Danube. Do you think they will let me borrow it for my vegetable plot?'

'Oh, Mama!' said András. 'It's huge! It would water our house and two on each side. What can we have for our picnic?'

'There is some cold bierwurst, and we'll take bread and tomatoes.'

'And cake? Is there some cake?'

'Yes, I think there might be some cake.' Magdolna tidied her workplace quickly, and closed the barn door. It was twilight already.

'Papa did say...' András began hesitantly.

'Yes, what did Papa say?'

'He said that when we got the harvest money, we could go to Győr and buy me some trainers. There's a shop that has real Reeboks.'

'Must they be Reeboks?'

'Of *course*. *All* the boys in my class are getting Reeboks, when the harvest money comes in.'

'Mrs Milburn?' said the voice on the telephone. It was familiar, but she could not place it.

'Yes? Speaking,' said Kate, coming in a little breathless from the climb up the hill from the village, where she had been paying a visit to Harbour Steps Books.

'Oh, good evening. It's Lawrence Elliot here. Rosalind's violin teacher.'

'Good evening, Mr Elliot. I thought you had gone to the music camp with the children.'

'Yes, I have. I mean, I'm ringing from Wales.' He paused, then cleared his throat. 'I've been meaning to speak to you for some weeks. About Rosalind.'

'Is there a problem?' said Kate, sitting down suddenly. She knew how much Roz's music meant to her, even though she assumed the pose of indifference expected by her teenage peer group.

'Oh no, nothing like that!' He laughed. 'Well, I suppose some people might see it as a problem, but I'm sure you won't. You do realise, don't you, that's she's very good? Exceptional, in fact.'

'Well, I... none of us knows much about music.'

'Exceptional,' he repeated firmly. 'It is high time to be making decisions about her future. She should really be thinking about starting at music college now, this coming year, without wasting any more time.'

'But her A Levels...'

'Bother her A Levels. We're talking about a violinist who will soon be of concert standard. Musicians of her calibre have to concentrate their talents. There's no room for anything else.'

Kate began to pleat the fabric of her skirt with her free hand. Why had the man sprung this on her without warning, over the telephone?

As if he could read her thoughts, he said, apologetically, 'I'm sorry to ring you up like this, instead of talking it over with you face to face, but we've had Sir Oswald Kirkwood here today.'

'At the music camp!'

'Yes. He sometimes pays us a visit, if we let him know that we have some special talent. He came from London just to hear Rosalind.'

Kate swallowed. 'And?'

'He wants her to start at the college in the autumn. I told him that money probably wouldn't be a problem, but they would be willing to offer a scholarship if there is any difficulty. I just wanted to warn you, because he's writing to you straight away.'

'I don't suppose Roz is there, is she? Could I speak to her?'

'No, I've rung while the students are having their dinner, but I'll get her to phone you from the office when they finish.'

'Thank you,' said Kate faintly.

'Goodbye,' he said. 'And, Mrs Milburn...?'

'Yes?'

'Sir Oswald thinks she is *outstanding*. The most promising young violinist he has heard in twenty years, he said. I think we all owe it to her to give her this chance.'

Kate replaced the receiver feeling stunned.

For once Beccy was home by seven, as Chris was busy writing up a story for the newspaper. Tom had phoned yet again to say he would be late, and Kate did not mention Lawrence Elliot's phone call, knowing she had no hope of securing his full attention while he was still in the office.

'Let's have omelettes in the kitchen, Mum,' said Beccy, 'as it's just the two of us. I'll make them. You lay the table and then relax with a glass of that white wine I put in the fridge yesterday. There's nearly half a bottle left. Pour me some too.'

'I'll cook, darling. You've been at work all day.'

'I'm fine. You look bushed.'

So with a glass of wine in her hand and her elbows amongst the knives and forks, Kate told her about the phone call from Wales.

'But that's brilliant!' said Beccy, stirring mushrooms in butter in a small pan, and then whisking the eggs. 'Of course you'll let her go.'

'I suppose we'll have to.' Kate rotated her glass thoughtfully, watching the wine rise around the sides in a golden wave. 'But she's very young to go away on her own to London. And music is such a chancy career. I would be happier if she did her A Levels. That would always give her something to fall back on if she doesn't make the grade as a soloist.'

'If she doesn't make the grade as a soloist she can always be an orchestral violinist.'

'It's an awful life. All that travelling and living out of suitcases. No chance of a proper home. I don't suppose it's very well paid, either.'

Beccy slid her mother's omelette on to a warmed plate and passed it to her.

'Here, you start while it's hot.' She turned back to the stove. 'I suppose being an orchestral player means you have all the disadvantages of the life of a soloist without the fame and fortune, but you are making wonderful music all the time, and that's what Roz really wants to do.'

'Are you sure? This is a lovely omelette.'

'Thanks. I practically live on them at college.'

Beccy sat down opposite her mother and began to eat ravenously.

'Roz and I had a late-night heart-to-heart a couple of days before she went off. These last few months she's really begun to care about her music, I gathered. Apparently Lawrence Elliot is a brilliant teacher. I can't imagine why he's stuck in Charlborough instead of setting up in London.'

'He's one of the founders of the Charlborough Festival of the Arts,' said Kate. 'It will be its fifth year this autumn. He's dedicated to the idea of sponsoring the arts in the provinces, instead of concentrating everything in London. There's no need for him to move there – his students come to him up here.'

'Well, anyway – Roz thinks her playing has come on tremendously under him, and she told me that she was dreading the sixth form, and having to concentrate so much time on working for her A Levels. If they think she's ready for music college now, it's probably the best thing for her. Musicians are rather special, after all, aren't they? I mean, for lots of careers it's better to be a bit older, and gain some experience, but musicians have to seize the moment.'

'I don't really know enough about music. But I suppose it isn't as if she's an infant prodigy. I can't approve of putting really young children on the concert platform. That must do more harm than good, ruining any chance of a normal, happy life.'

'But isn't that just the point? They aren't normal. They're specially gifted, not like the rest of us poor mortals. Is there anything for pud?' Beccy pushed back her chair and looked around hopefully.

'Let's have some fruit. There's a bowl of peaches and grapes behind you on the dresser.'

Kate traced a spiral pattern on the tablecloth with the tip of her spoon.

'Musicians may not be normal, as you say, but I still think they deserve the chance of happiness.'

'I bet Roz will find her main happiness in music.' Beccy held out the bowl. 'Like a peach?'

They had cleared and washed up before Roz telephoned. Beccy sat at the kitchen table drinking a cup of tea as Kate talked to Roz on the kitchen phone.

'Can I, Mum?' asked Roz without preamble. 'Oh, *please*! It's the most incredible opportunity.'

'What exactly does the course involve?' said Kate cautiously.

'Violin would be the main thing – hours of tuition and practice every day. Just think of it! Being able to concentrate on violin instead of having it pushed into the evenings after I'm tired with swotting for A Levels. I'd keep up flute and piano as well. They like you to have more than one instrument. Then there'd be harmony and composition and background stuff, you know, lives of composers and all that. I wouldn't be in the main choir, that's for the real singers. But they have a sort of second-string choir which is just for people who like to sing but aren't specially good, like me. Think of it, Mum! All that music!'

She was bubbling over with high spirits. Kate couldn't stop herself smiling at the sheer joy in her daughter's voice.

'What about living arrangements?' she managed to cut in at last.

'Oh, there are college hostels for anyone under eighteen. After that they have college-approved digs, or some people get flats.'

Kate started adding up the cost of a flat for Roz in central London. Tom had sunk every penny of capital into buying Craigfast House, and any surplus income since they had come north had gone towards redecoration.

'But...!' Roz interrupted her thoughts dramatically. 'Sir Oswald thinks I might have started on my concert career by then.' Her voice cracked with excitement. 'Mum, he said I might make the Proms by the year after next!'

Kate could not believe this was happening. Her youngest. Still – in spite of appearances – mentally tagged as 'the baby' in the back of her mind. Launching out soon on a career that would take her far out of the reach of her family. But she could not blight her daughter's happiness.

'It's wonderful, darling. Just wonderful. I'm still feeling stunned. Beccy's here, would you like a word with her?'

'Yes please. Is Dad there?'

'Not yet. I'll tell him as soon as he gets home. He'll be so excited for you. Here's Beccy. Goodbye, darling. I'm so *thrilled*! And so *proud* of you.'

Tom did not come home until midnight. By then Beccy was in bed and Kate was sitting in an armchair dozing over a book. She blinked at him sleepily in the subdued light from her lamp. He looked pale, she thought.

'Have you eaten?' she asked.

'I had some sandwiches,' he said curtly. He went into the kitchen and came back with a glass of beer. He stood looking out of the french windows with his back to her. Beyond him she could see the lights of a ship moving up the Dun. He was tense and irritable, and she decided at once not to tell him about Roz's extraordinary news until the next morning. It would be dismissed with a shrug and an indifferent 'Oh yes?' Somehow she felt she could not face that. His lack of interest in his daughter's achievement would tarnish it.

Tom began to pace around the room, picking things up and putting them down again without looking at them. She could read every gesture, every movement of his taut body, the way he had avoided looking directly at her since he had come in. There is something he doesn't want to say to me, but feels he must, she thought, and was suddenly afraid. She started up from her chair, heading towards the door and bed, hoping to forestall him. Instead it seem to galvanise him into action. He set down his glass on the piano and came towards her, seizing her wrists in his hands.

'Kate, I'm sorry.' There was a curious look in his eye. A kind of shamefaced relief.

No, she thought, no.

'There's a crisis at work. The major outside consultants working on the Manchester project have gone into receivership. All their papers are impounded at the moment, including everything relating to our project. It's reached the point where it will be very difficult for someone else to take over. We'll have to backtrack and start one whole module from scratch. The client will hold us to the penalty clause, there's no hoping they won't. That means every week or part week we're late delivering the completed system we'll be penalised £15,000. I'll have to take charge personally. I can't rely on the project manager. There's no way we can have our holiday in France. You'll have to cancel it.'

Kate snatched her wrists away from him. A huge anger began to swell inside her, and she realised that it had been building there for weeks, like a hidden disease. It wasn't the loss of the holiday that upset her − or only as a symptom of something else. For a moment he had truly frightened her. She had believed that something other than his job had come between them. She thought of her worries over Stephen, of Roz's success, of her own empty and aimless days. And there was that odd look, as though he was secretly pleased.

'People just don't matter to you any more, do they, Tom?' she shouted. 'There's no blood left in your veins, just electronic messages. All you care about is balance sheets and bloody project plans and...' As he opened his mouth to speak, she waved her arms frantically to cut him off. 'You might as well not have a family. The children need you. I need you. But what do you care? Your clients are the only thing in the world that matters. Family life is nothing beside the glistening reality of the project plan.'

She threw open the door, then stopped and said tightly, 'I wouldn't want to go to France with you any more. You would be about as congenial as a company report. I'll go into Charlborough tomorrow and change the bookings. I'm going to Hungary instead.'

Chapter 6

'I cannot agree to this, Kate.' Sofia paused with her hands over a large bowl, her fingers stained purple.

Kate, sitting opposite her as they bottled the dessert gooseberries, which had ripened with a rush in the hot weather, was finding Sofia remarkably stubborn.

'It's very simple. Tom and I are *not* going to France. The travel agent wouldn't agree to refund the money at this late stage, but he was willing to swap the flights. I've got tickets for the two of us, flying from Edinburgh to Amsterdam, and then from Amsterdam to Budapest. That seemed more sensible than trailing down to Heathrow, and there was space on both flights. The only return flight I could get was three weeks later. *Please*, Sofia,' she added cunningly. 'My original holiday has been ruined and I was so looking forward to it. I don't want to go abroad on my own, and I'm wild to see Hungary.'

Sofia said nothing, but began again to nip the tops and tails off the gooseberries between her thumbnail and the tip of her finger. At last she said, 'But it is not simply the flights. There will be hotels, meals...'

'No problem. Luckily the travel agent had another client who was desperate to visit this new upmarket resort on the Côte d'Azur, so he's taken our hotel booking for the second week. And the agent is pretty sure the week at the Avignon hotel can be re-sold too. So I've booked you and me in at the Marriott Hotel in Budapest for the first three days. I expect it will be like any of these American hotel chains – identical wherever in the world you are. But it overlooks the Danube and it's within walking distance of everything interesting. Then I've booked the next two days at a hotel in Győr. That seemed to be the nearest town to your old home. After that, I thought we could play it by ear – find somewhere truly Hungarian to stay. I've used up the balance of the money I'd paid in advance for the French holiday to hire a car for the whole of the time after we leave Budapest. That way we'll be free to move about as we like, without having to book ahead everywhere.'

Sofia looked stunned at all this organising.

'You would not mind, to drive in Hungary? They drive on the right, you know.'

'Yes.' Kate laughed. 'I do know. It will be all right. I've ordered a Peugeot like mine, so it will be quite familiar, apart from the left-hand drive. When we used to go to France years ago with the children I drove sometimes. It will be easy.'

Privately she felt a chill in her stomach at the thought of it, but she smiled bravely. It would be the first bit that would be the worst, driving out of Budapest. Large, unknown cities were always confusing, and she wasn't sure whether the road signs in eastern Europe would be recognisable. Once they were out in the country she was sure she would be able to cope. She had already studied the route in the European road atlas, and the drive from Budapest to Győr looked simple enough.

'Please, Sofia,' she said again, scooping up another handful of gooseberries. 'It would be wonderful. You want to go, but don't want to go alone. I've lost my holiday, and would love to visit Hungary. I can't speak Hungarian, and you can. It's the obvious answer.'

'I cannot allow you to pay,' said Sofia stiffly, getting up and tipping the gooseberries into a colander. She ran the tap over them, shaking and stirring them with her fingers to rinse off bits of leaf and stalk.

'The point about the money,' said Kate, 'is that if we don't spend it on going to Hungary it will just be thrown away.'

'Well...'

'Good, that's settled then,' said Kate hastily. 'Now, you do have a passport, don't you? You said you'd been to France about three years ago.' A sudden thought struck her. 'You didn't go on a visitor's passport, did you? I'm sure Hungary requires a full passport.'

Sofia began to pack the gooseberries into Kilner jars.

'I have a full passport,' she said guardedly. 'But once we are in Hungary, you must allow me to pay my share of everything.'

'Of course,' Kate agreed blithely, intending no such thing. She had no idea how Sofia derived her income, if indeed she had anything apart from the basic pension. Even a published poet, writing in Hungarian, was unlikely to earn anything visible to the naked eye from her writing. If they could just reach Hungary, any further battles about paying could be sorted out there.

'When did you say the tickets are for?'

'Monday. I thought perhaps I could bring Beccy and Chris round this evening to meet you. Chris would be happy to live in your cottage and look after the animals, if that would help. He even likes gardening

– unlike most young men of his age! Would it be all right for us to come? About seven?'

Sofia poured the sugar from the scales into a pan and added water from a measuring jug. Crossing the kitchen and taking up a wooden spoon, Kate began to stir the syrup for her. She saw that Sofia was flushed, and not just with the heat of the stove.

'I'm sorry,' she said contritely. 'I've rushed you. Stupid of me. You'd only just begun to talk about going back, not thought it through. And I come crashing in with my two left feet, bossing you about. It just seemed such a chance, as I had to use the travel money anyway.'

'No, no.' Sofia washed her hands under the sink tap, scrubbing in vain at the fruit stains on her fingers. 'You were right. Left to myself, I would never have had the courage to make the decision. Together, we will do this. Bring the young people this evening.'

Following days of indecision, István had decided to ring his niece Anna, Magdolna's daughter. The discovery of his parents' papers had, he found, disturbed him profoundly. After the time of terror which had marked his early childhood, life in his grandparents' house had been peaceful and secure. The Rudnays had been briefly in great danger after the armed Russian invasion in 1956, but as the regime became less totalitarian their lives became easier. When he grew older István learned to shut his mind to the past and concentrate on his studies. His determination to become a doctor, he realised years later, was the one tangible legacy of that fearful time.

He married at twenty-two and he and Maria lived very happily for four years, in one and a half rooms near the hospital in Budapest where he had his first job. Their joy in the birth of László was not at all clouded by the near impossibility of feeding two of them on István's salary, without the addition of a third.

One bitter January when László was three months old, István had returned tired from a long day in the casualty department to find the tiny flat empty and the stove unlit.

'Old Kati says there will be meat at the butcher's shop today,' Maria had said at breakfast. 'I'm going to see if I can buy some chops.'

'You'll have to queue at least two hours.'

'It doesn't matter. I'll carry László in the sling and we'll have a walk in the park afterwards. The fresh air will be good for him.'

But it was dark now, and they should have been home hours before. István checked with old Kati on the ground floor and the Hermanns on the floor above, but no one had seen Maria. With growing anxiety he lit the wood stove which she had left ready laid, and started to make potato soup for supper.

When the doorbell rang, part of his mind was already prepared.

A policeman, as young as himself, stood on the landing outside. He looked pale and sick, and for a moment István thought he had come looking for medical help. He was holding a dirty white bundle to which, inexplicably, fragments of leaf and dry grass were clinging.

'Dr Rudnay?' The young policeman swallowed with difficulty.

'Yes?'

'I'm very sorry. I'm afraid I have bad news for you.'

Maria had slipped on the icy pavement and fallen in front of a heavy lorry which could not stop. István was required to come and identify the body.

He had felt no pain then. Only numb disbelief.

'But she was fine this morning,' he said stupidly. 'She just went to the butcher's shop and for a walk in the park.' Somehow it seemed important to establish these facts. Maria would be back at any moment.

The policeman reached in his pocket and brought out a squashed package wrapped in brown paper and blood-stained.

'She had this in her basket,' he said. 'Nothing else. It's two lamb chops.'

István took the package, looked at it, then thrust it back at the policeman, shaking his head.

They stood staring at each other, locked into the impossibility of speech. Then the dirty bundle in the curve of the policeman's arm stirred and a thin wail rose from it. István recoiled with shock as the other man held the bundle out to him.

'He was thrown clear. A passer-by found him lying safely under some bushes beside the pavement. He seems to be fine. We had him at the station while we sorted the paperwork and traced you. He's probably hungry.'

Reluctantly, István took the bundle. From within the shawl two eyes looked up at him watchfully. A small fist worked its way out and pounded the air between them.

'László,' he said.

After the funeral, István decided he could not go back to his job in the casualty department. Any day he might be confronted with another young woman like Maria, who could not be saved.

'I became a doctor because I wanted to heal people,' he said to Magdolna, when he arrived in Szentmargit with the baby, needing the help that only she could give. 'Our facilities at the hospital are so poor, there is almost nothing we can do for the serious cases. That isn't my kind of medicine. I want to be a family doctor. I want to know the whole family. I want to bring babies into the world, and help mothers to rear healthy children, and give labourers some ease for their bad backs. And with the old people, I want to sit and hold their hands as they slip away quietly in their own beds. Does that sound foolish and sentimental?'

Magdolna, who had recently finished her studies under Margit Kovacs and returned to live with their grandparents, knew that her brother was neither foolish nor sentimental.

'I think it's a very good plan. If you are a family doctor you can practise from your house, so you are always there for László. We will find you a good nurse-housekeeper. I wish you could come back here to Szentmargit, but old Dr Krautz retired last month, and the new doctor isn't much older than you. You will have to find somewhere else – but, please, not too far away.'

In the end he had set up his practice in Sopron, which was much further from Szentmargit than he had intended, but he had not, on the whole, regretted it. Although he would have liked to be nearer his family, Sopron was a good place to work. Not large and impersonal like Budapest, or even Györ, but still a town of fairly respectable size, which allowed him to introduce preventive medicine clinics long before they became fashionable. The local people soon recognised the skill and kindness that lay behind his quiet manner. He also found himself treating the visitors sent to Sopron to convalesce. Famous for its healthy climate, it lay amongst woods on the edge of the mountains rising to the Austrian border.

When these visiting patients turned out to be – as they often did – high Party officials on privileged rest cures, István treated them impersonally and held his tongue, though the recollection of his own origins underlined the irony of the situation. There were others, though: sickly children, factory workers trying to rebuild their lives after accidents, frail old people hoping to regain a little strength. As the country began to recover and readjust its politics, there were more of the latter kind of patient, and fewer of the former. Nowadays there were no Party bosses. István wondered sometimes what had become of them all. Had they fled to Russia? If so, they must be having a very thin time. Some, of course, had re-emerged in politics, wearing different colours and swearing their conversion to democracy.

István's own life was undergoing subtle changes. His education finished, László was gone, working in the south in a village near Mohács, not far from the border with the former Yugoslavia. It might even be possible for István to move back now to Szentmargit. Magdolna said that the village doctor was thinking of retiring early, as his own health was not good. But István was proud of what he had created in Sopron. He thought he would probably stay here.

What he had not bargained for was this sudden re-emergence of his past. First his frightened boyhood and then the brief, happy years with Maria had been closed away in the locked rooms of his mind, and he did not want to revisit them. He knew that if he began to probe too deeply into his parents' lives, the old pain and terror would be reawoken. Already his sleep was troubled, and he found himself, from time to time, not attending properly to his work. Yet, despite this, the old longing to know his father seized him. His mother he could remember quite clearly. He was twelve when she died, and she was only thirty-two. It astonished him to think of it now. He had already outlived her by nearly eighteen years. He could summon up her face, almost catch the sound of her voice in his ears. But his father had been taken away too early.

He was going through the papers very slowly. Partly this was because he was busy with the practice just now, in the last few days before he left to spend his summer holiday with Magdolna and her family. Partly it was because he was half-fearful of what he might find, or of what effect his discoveries might have on him. One of the most tantalising items so far had been the letter from the man called Ferenc Kalla, who had rescued his father from the freezing Danube after he had been shot and dumped by the Arrow Cross in those last terrible days of 1944. At that time the Russians were moving in on Budapest, pounding it mercilessly with heavy artillery, and the departing Germans and the local Fascists were looting and killing indiscriminately.

He himself had been a few months old then and living in the partisan camp in the woods between Sopron and Szentmargit. He knew that he had been born in the camp, in a rough hut of brushwood, and as there was no doctor or nurse, or even another woman partisan apart from his mother, he had been delivered by one of the men who had been a shepherd before the war and reckoned that a human baby was not that different from a lamb.

His father had been away from the camp at the time, but István had heard his grandmother tell the story. When his father returned from blowing up a railway line used by the Germans for bringing war

99

supplies into Hungary and found himself the father of a lusty, squalling son, he had insisted on setting off at once to have the child christened.

'So if he brings the Boche down on us with his yelling, at least his soul will be saved when they bayonet him.'

Many of the partisans were communists and thought the idea of getting the baby christened was crazy, but his father, though not a churchgoer, was in his way a deeply religious man. István's parents had walked the twenty kilometres to Szentmargit to hold the christening by night in the village church, in a ceremony performed by the selfsame priest to whom the letter from Ferenc Kalla had later been addressed. When he was told this story as a boy, István had been quite caught up by the romance of himself as a newborn baby appearing from the forest and then disappearing again. It made him think of King Arthur, one of his boyhood heroes. Later, when he realised that his mother had given birth, then risen from her brushwood bed two days later to walk twenty kilometres to the church and twenty kilometres back, he realised who was the real heroine of the story.

All these thoughts were going through his mind now as he telephoned Anna at her student hostel.

'All I would like you to do,' he said, 'is to try to discover who lives at that address now. See if you can find out anything about this Ferenc Kalla or his family. He describes it in his letter as his parents' flat, so he was probably quite young – younger than your grandfather.'

'It's fascinating, Uncle István.' Anna's clear, cool voice came down the phone from Budapest. She was uninvolved. For her this was like a story out of a history book. Her distant tone jarred slightly with István.

'Yes, well, if Ferenc Kalla hadn't saved your grandfather's life, Magdolna would never have been born and you wouldn't exist, young lady.'

'No,' said Anna thoughtfully. 'I suppose I wouldn't. I'll certainly do what I can.'

'If he was, let's say, twenty at the time, he'd only be seventy now.'

'Mmm. Well, of course it is fifty years. He may not have survived at all.'

She made it sound like a millennium. István felt suddenly tired and old.

'If you do find out anything, just let me know, will you? I don't want your mother upset until we have something definite to go on.'

'Absolute discretion promised. It'll be rather good practice in a way. For when I'm a lawyer and have to direct investigations.' She sounded half joking, half serious. 'When are you going home?'

Like Magdolna, she regarded Szentmargit as his real home.

'I'll be with your parents from the second of August. They'll miss you this summer. So will I.'

'I'll try to manage at least one weekend while you're there. Bye for now. Got to go. Someone else is waiting to use the phone.'

'Goodbye, Anna. And thank you.'

As they walked along high water mark, their feet crunching in the dried bladder-wrack, Kate wondered how much she ought to say to Chris. He and Beccy were a little behind her, following absent-mindedly while they talked of their own affairs. All she had told them so far was that she was going on holiday abroad with Sofia, who needed someone to look after her animals while she was away.

Beccy had been unsurprised by the collapse of her parents' planned holiday. She had shrugged and said, 'Well, what did you expect? Crossbow Computers has to come first always in our lives, doesn't it?'

There was a harsh note in her daughter's voice and Kate suddenly realised that she was not alone in her bitterness at what the greedy corporate demands were doing to Tom and to the family. She had tried – contrary to her own earlier reactions – to make excuses for him, but Beccy was having none of it.

'You go off and have a holiday with your friend and let him stew,' she advised. 'Maybe if you aren't here all the time providing support and comfort he'll realise how much you matter. At the moment he treats you as though you're of no account at all.'

Kate was stung. Yet this was how she had been feeling herself – resentful, ignored and lonely. She made up her mind to enjoy the holiday with Sofia and to sort matters out with Tom when she returned, when she would be in a calmer frame of mind and the crisis with his project would have resolved itself, either well or badly.

The day had been a little overcast and twilight was setting in early. Ahead of them she could make out a faint glow marking the position of the cottage. She had not previously visited it in the evening, and it seemed more isolated than ever after the long walk up the darkening beach. The lower windows were screened by the wall, and as they drew nearer she realised that the light from one of these windows was catching the leaves of the Bramley apple tree from below. In the chancy in-between light the leaves glowed silver, like an olive tree caught by some Mediterranean breeze. Kate decided that she would simply introduce Chris to Sofia, and make no further comment. She had no idea whether Sofia wrote under her own name, or even whether she was indeed the poet he was seeking. Apart from her teasing smiles she had never admitted to Kate that she was.

As usual, the bell at the gate triggered a volley of barking from Ákos, but Sofia came at once and drew back the bolts. Ákos threw himself upon Kate with delight, but growled a little in his throat at the other two, despite Sofia's remonstrances. Chris knelt at the gateway, not attempting to go forward until the dog had inspected him thoroughly and allowed himself finally to be caressed.

When they were all seated indoors with coffee (not one of Sofia's curious herbal tisanes, as Kate had feared) Ákos flung himself down at Chris's feet, with his chin on Chris's trainers, damp as they were from crossing the beach. Beccy was trying to persuade Midnight, one of the cats, to jump on to her lap, but he was reserving judgement.

'You understand dogs, Mr Harding, I can see,' said Sofia. 'But are you are happy in the company of chickens and goats?'

'Please call me Chris.' He smiled at her as he fondled Ákos's ears. 'At home I had my own laying hens from the age of five. But I've never kept a goat. You'll need to show me exactly how to milk her and what other care she needs. Most animals seem to like me, though.'

As if to prove this, Midnight turned his back on Beccy's blandishments and leapt into Chris's lap. He turned around two or three times, then settled himself. A steady purring rumbled across the room.

Beccy laughed. 'Totally rejected!' She spread her hands in mock despair. 'I yield to your greater charms.'

Sofia and Chris began to discuss the care of the animals and the garden, and Kate leaned back a little sleepily in her chair. The cottage was warm after the cool breeze off the sea as they had come along the beach. She had slept little during the last few nights, since the quarrel with Tom. Beccy joined in the conversation from time to time, but Kate was content to let it flow around her, wondering with a curious, floating detachment what she would be doing a week from now, what scenes would be lying before her, what voices sounding around her.

'Come,' said Sofia, 'I will show you around the cottage now, and then tomorrow afternoon, if you are free, you shall come and have a lesson in milking the goat.'

'I'll come for the morning milking as well, if I may,' said Chris, getting up slowly and lifting Midnight with great gentleness down into the chair.

'At five o'clock?'

'I'm farm born and bred.' He laughed. 'No problem.'

Beccy and Kate followed them out of the sitting room. They went first into the kitchen, the only other room Kate had seen. Sofia pointed out the stop-cock and explained the Calor gas appliances.

'I am afraid there is no electricity, although there is mains water and drains,' said Sofia. 'Two years ago they tried to persuade me again to have the electricity, but it was going to cost me far too much. There is no other house nearby, you see, so I would have had to pay for the cable to be run out from the end of Castle Terrace. But I manage very well with oil lamps.'

'I think they're lovely,' said Beccy. 'It's such a soft light, it makes you realise how harsh electric light bulbs really are.'

'The oil for the lamps is kept here.' Sofia opened the door to her large, walk-in larder. 'Most things are stored here, except for garden tools and animal feed, which I keep in the lean-to at the back of the goat's shed. This is the bathroom, behind the kitchen. That's everything on the ground floor.'

Upstairs under sloping ceilings were two bedrooms – one clearly Sofia's, one unoccupied, with the bed not made up. This must have been her mother's bedroom, Kate thought.

'I will put sheets on the bed here,' Sofia said to Chris. 'Then you will have plenty of room to spread your belongings about without my things getting in your way. Be sure to keep this skylight over the stairs closed. If you open it, it never seems to shut again properly, and the rain comes in.'

As the others started back down the stairs again, Kate went to the window of the empty bedroom. The two upstairs rooms each had a dormer window facing east, towards the sea. Here you were high enough to see over the garden wall, and looking out from the darkened room, now that Sofia had carried the oil lamp downstairs, Kate could see the water lying like a scarf of pale grey silk beyond the rocks of the headland. A ship was making its stately way back from the sea, heading in to the Dun. Its lights laid shimmering bands of gold on the water, but the night was so still that it seemed to glide as effortlessly as a swan up the river. Two booming hoots sounded out, and Kate suddenly remembered how she would kneel up in bed as a child, in the house in Castle Terrace, and watch the ships moving on the water, and listen to the cry of the gulls, like lost ghosts at twilight.

All that time Sofia must have been living here, she thought, and sometimes looking out at the same ships passing and hearing the same gulls. How strange that so many years should pass before we met, and now I feel as though I have known her all my life.

'Kate,' Sofia called from below, 'why are you hiding in the dark? Come. I am going to make more coffee.'

Later, when they had left the cottage and walked back along the beach which felt so much longer in the dark, Chris said, 'She is, isn't she?'

'Is what?'

'Sofia Tabor, the poet.'

'You've never told us the poet's name, you know, Chris,' said Kate.

'Yes, he has, Mum.'

'Well, he hasn't told me anyway.'

'An oversight,' said Chris apologetically. 'But of course Sofia Niklai must be Sofia Tabor. Perhaps Tabor was her maiden name.'

'She's never been married,' said Kate. 'But I'm sure that you're right. It must be her pen-name. I've never asked her straight out, but she hasn't exactly denied it.'

'I won't rush things with her, Mrs Milburn, I promise. After you come back from your holiday, if she will let me do an interview, fine. If not... Well, I'll just have to wait a little longer.'

'She's a wonderful person, isn't she?' said Beccy. 'The more I see of her, the more I realise why you like her so much, Mum. It's difficult to put your finger on exactly, but I think it's her dignity and her humour. It's an unusual combination.'

As they began the long climb up the hill to Craigfast House, they stopped talking, saving their breath. Something that had been said niggled at the back of Kate's mind, but she could not think what it was.

The house was in darkness when they reached it. As none of them had eaten since lunchtime, Kate proposed pasta, and the other two agreed hungrily. While she chopped onions and Beccy laid the table, Chris told them about more of his discoveries in the archives.

'You know how it is – if you meet an unfamiliar word, suddenly you see it everywhere. It's the same with this. Once you find something curious in the archives, you keep coming across related items. That cottage is one of the oldest in Dunmouth. There used to be a whole cluster of cottages there, almost a separate hamlet, mostly built in the fifteenth and sixteenth centuries. Then in the 1840s, the cottagers were forced out to make way for the new railway. The cottages were all pulled down except that one, because it stood on the other side of the road, nearer the sea.'

'Is that why the road is there, then?' asked Kate, interested. 'I've always wondered. It used to curve inland and then peter out. The bit that goes on along the coast and joins up with the main road was only built after the railway was shut down in the sixties.'

'Yes, odd, isn't it? They pulled down all those houses, some of which had stood for four hundred years, and built a railway which lasted barely a hundred.'

'They probably thought they were building something that would last for ever,' said Beccy. 'The railway, I mean.'

'Scary, that's what it is.'

'A bit like the Russian Revolution,' said Kate.

They looked at her blankly.

'Well, the Bolsheviks thought they were setting up a new world order. And a few years ago we would never have believed it could collapse so soon. Yet it barely lasted a single lifetime.'

'I see what you mean,' said Chris. 'As I said, scary. I mean, it makes you feel as if nothing is safe, nothing will endure. When I was a kid, I thought everything just went on the same for ever. I might grow up and do things and come home like a conquering hero, but home would always be there, and my mum and dad would always be there, and my old dog. I suppose the first time I realised that you can't hold on to the world was when my dog died.'

Kate thought of Stephen and Benjy. How fragile that safe childhood world is, she thought. Yet she could remember so little of her own childhood. It lay shrouded behind more recent memories, except when something leapt out at her, as the memory of watching the ships had done this evening, or that strange sensation of fear she had felt the very first time she had walked near the headland, the day she had met Sofia.

'I found something else about the cottage,' said Chris. 'Much more recent. In the late fifties – I think it was 1958 – there was a fire there. The article said that arson was suspected, but no one was charged. It makes you wonder.'

'Wonder what?' asked Beccy.

'Whether the locals were still harassing her, more than ten years after the war. Of course I didn't mention anything while we were there. I didn't want to upset her. It wasn't the cottage itself that was burnt, but some outbuilding. Do you remember anything about it, Mrs Milburn? Or were you too young?'

Fire.

'No,' said Kate shortly. 'As you say, I was far too young. Come on, this is ready. Let's eat it before it goes cold. There's more white wine in the fridge, Beccy.'

❧

Fire.

There is so little at first. Just a golden thread running along the edge of a plank. Pretty, like the spangles on the dress of a circus acrobat. Sparks fall from this golden thread in ones and twos, slowly arcing down to the ground, gleaming for a moment and then winking out. Innocent as sparklers at a Guy Fawkes party. Then the thread of fire widens to a ribbon, and the sparks fall in clusters, and linger amongst the tufts of grass. There is a smell like Daddy's bonfire – sharp and smoky and exciting.

She realises that the boy has let go of her arm and she rubs it tenderly with the other hand. The pain runs up from her bruised wrist, where she can see red marks on her skin lit up by the fire, and there are stabs in her elbow and her shoulder. He has twisted it so badly, it feels as though her shoulder has come out of its socket. Staring hypnotised at the fire, she rubs and rubs at the pain.

The flames have run up other planks now and are reaching across to join up with each other in a wide curtain of red and yellow and orange. If she closes her eyes she can see the pattern of the flames dancing on the inside of her eyelids. She realises that the others have run off, and that before they did there was a shout from somewhere.

Suddenly there is a terrible howl, a cry of pure terror.

It is a dog. It must be a dog, and it is on the other side of the sheet of flame. The howls come again, rising in pitch.

❧

'Mum, I said, "Shall I get the phone?"' said Beccy.

'What? Oh, sorry, no. I'll go. Linda said she would ring me this evening. She was going to try to get me some guidebooks for Hungary.'

'That's right, she was waiting for the supplier to ring her back when I left this afternoon.' Beccy looked at her mother. 'Are you all right?'

'Fine,' said Kate. 'Just not concentrating.'

❧

106

The evening before they were due to leave for Hungary, Kate carried a large empty suitcase down to the cottage. They had realised at the last moment that Sofia possessed nothing suitable to hold her clothes for three weeks' holiday. On her short trip to Paris she had managed with an overnight case. The other luggage stored away under the roof beams in the attic of the cottage consisted of ancient pigskin suitcases, almost impossible to lift when empty and smelling of mustiness. Kate had found a large lightweight case which could be towed on its own wheels if necessary. Chris had promised to carry it along to the bookshop the next day after morning milking. Kate would collect both Sofia and the case there at ten, and drive to Edinburgh airport in time for the plane to Amsterdam.

Chris had moved into the spare room of the cottage the day before and seemed to be in his element, so much so that Kate wondered whether his professed plan to work on a London newspaper would really suit him. Sofia had greeted him with a meal of mussel soup followed by devilled crab and a dessert of raspberries with goat's milk yoghurt. Compared with the grey flannel meat and frozen chips he was allegedly served at his digs, he had declared this to be ambrosial fare. Kate could see him already calculating how he might move in permanently.

When she delivered the suitcase she found Sofia agitated about the following day's journey. She had every reason to be, thought Kate. After escaping as a young woman from Fascist search parties on the eve of war, to be returning as an elderly exile after so many years must be disturbing. However, Chris was very good with her, chattering away and bullying her gently to get on with her packing.

When she reached the village again, Kate did not at once turn up the hill towards home. Instead she walked along the harbour front, where the men were getting ready to put to sea, loading empty fish-boxes into seven boats. Six of these had 'Dunmouth' painted on their sterns and on either side of their bows. One came from a home-port about twenty miles south along the coast. She recalled that one of the fishing families had another branch there. The men must have called in at Dunmouth and would be going out tonight with the rest of the local fleet. She spoke to one or two of the fishermen she knew, and they responded with a nod and an 'Evening, missus.'

The smell of the fish which never left the harbour, the tarred ropes, the rhythmic tinny ring of metal rigging slapping in the wind, the bulky figures moving under the dim harbour lamps in their thick jerseys and bright orange dungarees – all these were part of the real Dunmouth which, in spite of everything, she realised she loved. She remembered how she and Linda had hung about when the fishing fleet was putting to sea – twenty or thirty boats in those days. They would perch on a pair of mooring bollards, perilously near the steep drop into the harbour but quite unconcerned, swinging their legs and watching critically. As a shipwright's daughter, Linda considered herself an expert and would point out the weak points in those built elsewhere. Dan Wilson's boats had always had a little more elegance, a combination of strength and grace, that even Kate could spot. There were two of them here still, for a good fishing vessel lasts many years, and the men of Dunmouth could not afford fancy new boats with unnecessary luxuries, although even the old ones were fitted up with better communications and safety devices than in her childhood. One boat, the *Merry Day*, a sad grey vessel with peeling paint and sagging decks, lay in darkness at the far end of the harbour breakwater. No one was taking the *Merry Day* to sea tonight, perhaps never again.

From the fishermen's church, just beyond the lifeboat station and Barometer Cottage, the bell for evening service began to ring. The men climbed out of their boats, not hurrying, and made their way along Harbour Walk towards it. They were not particularly reverent. One or two spat in the gutter. Another group was arguing raucously about the availability of a certain barmaid in Charlborough. But as they crossed the threshold into the church they wiped their clumsy boots on the mat, and those wearing greasy knitted hats pulled them off.

On an impulse, Kate followed them and slipped in at the back. The service was quite short, as busy fishermen expected. The hymns all had a nautical theme and safe, familiar tunes that did not require any vocal gymnastics. There was the same sort of congregation as Kate remembered from the past. The men standing together to the right of the aisle. To the left, their womenfolk. It was a tiny congregation nowadays, but the men wore the same expression. Not self-confident. Men whose daily lives were spent at the mercy of sea and storms knew their limitations. It was more a look of acceptance, a fatalism, perhaps, that they would be ready when their time came, but until then they would give the old sea as good as they got. The women – the wives, mothers, girlfriends – wore a different look. They were less resigned. How terrible it must be, Kate thought, to send your man out week after week, never knowing if he will come home at the end of it.

The rector spoke the final prayer, for the safe return of the fleet, and for all ships on the sea, and they filed out to the sound of the same old wheezy organ. Kate was surprised to see, amongst the men, the old man from Barometer Cottage who had spoken to her so rudely some weeks ago. He had not struck her as a churchgoer. But then, he was one who had survived to enjoy a quiet retirement. Perhaps he had something to give thanks for after all.

Out in the street people became talkative again. A few of the women greeted Kate by name. She noticed a very pretty girl, not more than eighteen and heavily pregnant, clinging to the arm of one of the young fishermen. Her face was tight with apprehension, but he was embarrassed by her and tried to shrug her off. It would not do to be seen going soft with his wife in front of his mates.

As the families dispersed to their houses for an evening meal before the men set out, Kate walked further along the road past the church, to a group of three houses, a little larger than the others on the harbour front. She had always liked these houses and she realised now – never having thought about it before – that they were Georgian. Well-proportioned if small, with their high ceilings and pretty bow windows. Probably these had belonged to the aristocracy of the old fishing village, the families who owned more than one boat and employed other men, or who were fish-merchants trading inland. A narrow, cobbled lane ran behind these houses, called Fish Lane, and there were old fish-sheds there, where the boxes and barrels had once been loaded on to horse-drawn carts from the stables which opened into the same lane. From here the fish would be hauled to Charlborough, Welbank and even further afield, perhaps as far away as Banford. When the railway came, the fish-carts only needed to make the journey to Dunmouth station. Now the station was gone, and so were the working horses. The small catch now landed at Dunmouth was loaded on to refrigerated vans and whisked away almost as soon as it had been unloaded from the boats.

For a time when Kate was younger someone had tried to run the old working stable in Fish Lane as a riding school. She had had lessons there herself, and remembered riding on the hill above Craigfast House, where the gardens petered out into rough grass and scrub. The riding school must have failed after she had gone away, because the old stables had been standing empty and derelict for years now.

The last house in the group of three was her favourite. As well as the delicate bow windows it had a semicircular fan-light above the door with a fine tracery of carved wooden glazing bars. At the time the house was built such a fan-light must have been a sign of real status in the community. The front door was generously wide, and in its centre had a very large, faceted brass knob, rather tarnished at the moment, she noticed. Then she saw that an estate agent's sign was leaning drunkenly over the side wall next to the opening which led into Fish

Lane. The house was for sale, and looked as though it had been for some time. Tendrils of Russian vine and bindweed had wreathed themselves around the sign and looked well established. There were no curtains at the windows and the whole place was in darkness. It was a much smaller house than Craigfast, but Kate recalled that in her girlhood this was the house she had dreamed of owning. It probably had four bedrooms, and the garden was not very large, though spacious compared with the scrap of yard they had owned in London. Altogether it had a more kindly look than the grand house up on the hill.

The church clock began to strike. Kate craned to check her watch in the light from the street lamp. Eight o'clock already. She must get back home and finish her packing. Her heart gave a lurch. This time tomorrow she would be nearing Budapest.

ço

The morning drive to Edinburgh airport was easy: they went by back roads and allowed plenty of time. Kate felt elated. The scenery northwards up the coast and over the border was beautiful; at some moments the road allowed glimpses of the sea, at others it swooped above hidden valleys with small farms and ancient fields girded with dry-stone walls, then crossed high moorland with nothing but a few sheep and curlews amongst the scrub. They saw few cars and no lorries.

When they set out, Sofia sat beside Kate tensed forward in her seat, her hands gripping her knees. She had found it difficult to fasten her seat belt, and Kate realised with a shock that she had probably hardly ever ridden in a private car since she had come to Dunmouth. She made rare visits to Charlborough, but they were by bus. The thought of all this strangeness, of Sofia whisked away from her solitary life by the sea to the busy hum of international airports and jet travel, added to the dreamlike quality of this whole adventure.

They left the car in the secure car park and were ferried to the airport in a jolting minibus by a cheerful driver who whistled as the hard seats banged up and down. The traffic at the Newbridge roundabout held them up for several minutes.

'Awful lot of traffic, isn't there?' said Kate.

'Och, this is no' bad. Ye should see it in the rush hour.'

As soon as the lights changed, the bus shot forward, nearly throwing Kate into the aisle.

'Aye,' he resumed, swinging on to the road to the airport. 'Before they put the lights in, ye couldnae get across from the Edinburgh end in under half an hour in the mornings.'

He helped them unload their suitcases from the bus, and Kate thought that (despite the discomfort of the non-existent suspension) it was a good service. They had had sole use of the bus.

'Now, I've a note of your return flight. Ye'll be picked up yon.' He pointed round the curve of the service road to the far side. 'If we're no here, ring this number and we'll be straight over to fetch ye.' He gave Kate a business card, and went whistling off, with the bus clanking and rattling around him.

They bought magazines and checked their luggage in, then went to have tea and cakes at a table overlooking the runway.

'Our last food in England,' said Kate. 'Scotland, I mean.'

'This is very good,' said Sofia, biting into a Danish pastry.

'They're supposed to be locally baked. What is the food like in Hungary?'

'Nowadays, I do not know. When I was a girl... Well, the true Hungarian food is quite rich and heavy, with lots of paprika. It is necessary to understand paprika to appreciate Hungarian food. There are many different kinds, many different flavours. But of course, because of the Hapsburg Empire, there was also much Austrian influence. A lot of dumplings.'

Kate made a face.

'It all sounds very heavy for this hot weather.'

'If it is hot here, it will be much worse in central Europe! But the Austrians also brought their cakes to Hungary. Very beautiful, very light. These you will enjoy. But you may not be able to get tea. Unless everything is changed.'

Kate, who had had the same fear, did not admit that she had packed a box of tea bags in her case.

'They must be starting to cater more for the tourists now, I suppose. At least in the big towns.'

There was a click from the loudspeaker above their heads.

'Air UK Flight 0818 for Amsterdam now boarding at gate 4.'

'That's us,' said Kate, draining her teacup and gathering up her handbag and shoulder bag.

Sofia stood up calmly and smoothed down her skirt.

'Let us go,' she said.

111

Chapter 7

By the time they boarded the KLM flight from Amsterdam to Budapest, after scurrying across Schipol airport with little time to spare, Sofia began to feel like an experienced traveller. She had been dreading the flights more than she allowed Kate to suspect. Her only previous experience of flying – on the trip to Paris three years before – had been unnerving. They hit a freak thunderstorm on the outward flight, which threw the plane about with sickening jolts and sudden drops. On the return journey the pilot discovered technical trouble after he taxied out on to the runway. They returned to the loading bay, sat in the plane for half an hour without explanation, and were then unloaded and put on to another flight three hours later. Her innate fear of flying had been made much worse by these mishaps, and she did not want to repeat the experience. But the new determination which had driven her to confront the papers in the trunk, and then contemplate a return to Hungary, forced her to take hold of her courage.

Kate was turning over the pages of the in-flight magazine, *Holland Herald*. She seemed tired, as though the strain of the last few days and the long drive to Edinburgh airport had taken their toll. Sofia looked out of the window. They were passing over a rolling field of white cloud, mounded like whipped cream, with the horizontal rays of the descending sun laying a pink glow over the west-facing contours. Although Kate had said little about Tom's abandonment of their shared holiday in France, Sofia had gathered enough to realise that she was distressed and angry about it. The two women were travelling into an uncertain time ahead. Sofia was both excited and dismayed at the thought of seeing Hungary again, and she felt she was not sufficiently calm and in command of herself to be much help to Kate. Perhaps, she thought, we would have been better to have gone for a true holiday to some impersonal place. We do not know each other well enough to cope with the difficulties which may lie ahead.

'Dinner, Madam?' The air stewardess was proffering a tray.

'Oh, yes, thank you.' Sofia was startled out of her thoughts, and hastily pulled down the table from the back of the seat in front of her.

'Madam?'

Kate stuffed the magazine into the net pocket and took her tray from the girl.

'Looks quite nice,' she said, inspecting a colourful array of dishes and starting on the smoked salmon and salad.

The stewardess returned with hot rolls and individual bottles of wine, and they progressed to Cajun chicken with rice, and Dutch cheese.

'It's just as well they feed you quite reasonably on international flights these days,' said Kate, pouring out the last of her white wine and sipping it. On the Air UK flight they had been given tea with open sandwiches, scones, clotted cream and jam. 'By the time we reach the hotel in Budapest it will be nearly eleven, what with the difference in the clocks. I suppose we could always get room service, but we'll be too late for the restaurant.'

'I'm not used to being looked after like this,' said Sofia. 'It's quite a novelty. Look, they've given us strawberries and cream for dessert.'

They ate for a while in silence, but Kate was thinking ahead.

'The travel agent assured me that there would be a minibus to take us from the airport to the hotel. I hope we can find it all right. Thank heavens you speak Hungarian! I'm not used to travelling in a country where I don't speak the language. My French and German will usually see me through any western European country. I wonder if we will find many people in Hungary who speak either of them – or English, for that matter.'

'In the western part of the country they will surely still speak German. Austria is so near. In Budapest, I don't know. Because of the long years of Russian occupation most people probably learned Russian.'

Kate ripped open the packet containing a cloth soaked in eau de cologne and dabbed her face and hands.

'From what I've seen of it, Hungarian looks an impossible language. It isn't related to any of the other European languages except Finnish, is it?'

Sofia smiled. 'Like any language, it doesn't seem difficult if you grow up speaking it. I suppose you could say that it is a microcosm of our history. We Magyars brought it with us from the east when the Turul bird led us to our promised land.'

'The what?'

'The Turul bird. A huge mythical bird who flew ahead of the wandering tribes until he brought us to the *puszta*, where there were rich wide plains of grass for our horses, and good lands for us to plant crops for ourselves. The tradition says that we arrived in 896 AD, and in 1896 there were great festivities for the millennium. The very first metro in mainland Europe was built, and the parliament building, and the cathedral of St Stephen.'

Kate dived into her bag for the guidebook.

'I think I saw a picture of that bird somewhere.' She flipped over the pages. 'Yes, here you are.'

She held up a picture of Szabadság Híd, Freedom Bridge. On the pinnacle of each of its great supporting cast-iron towers was a bronze statue of a huge bird with wings outstretched, both soaring and protective. Sofia took the book from her and looked at the picture hungrily.

'So the Freedom Bridge is still there. I wasn't sure. So much was destroyed when the Germans and the Russians fought over Budapest.'

'Most of the bridges were blown up by the retreating Germans, but they were restored. There's something here about the millennium,' said Kate, pointing. 'It says the domes of both the parliament building and the cathedral were built 96 metres high, to commemorate the settlement of the Magyars in the country now known to outsiders as "Hungary". That's a very fine building, the parliament.'

'It was inspired by Westminster, did you know? The Hungarians have always felt a special affection for the British.'

'Look, it says there that the Chain Bridge was designed by an English engineer and built by a Scot.'

'You see?'

Kate sat back again. 'We English haven't been very good friends in recent times, though, have we? When Hungary appealed to us for help in 1956 we sat back and did nothing, too absorbed in our squabbles over Suez. And I was reading some Hungarian history in the first part of that book. It seems to me that we didn't try hard enough to help Hungary get back the parts of the country taken away by the Trianon Treaty after the first world war.'

'Yes, two-thirds of the country was given to Czechoslovakia, Yugoslavia and Romania,' said Sofia. 'Then when we got a little bit back, when I was a girl, it was only by making concessions to Hitler. It was the start of his clever campaign to entrap our leaders.'

The stewardess came round to collect their trays, and then the duty-free trolley was pushed along the aisle, which put a stop to conversation. Soon afterwards they landed at Vienna. It was half-past eight and twilight, so they could see little, although as they glided down

114

towards the earth there was a glimpse of the Danube reflecting the lights of the city. After half an hour they were airborne again.

The flight from Vienna to Budapest seemed to take no time at all. As they were fastening their seat belts for the descent to Ferihegy airport, Sofia said, 'While we are in Budapest, I think we should be tourists. We are here on holiday, and you must see some of the beauties of the city. But there is one bit of business I must try to do.'

'What's that?'

Sofia opened her handbag, and unzipped an inner pocket.

'This,' she said, handing Kate a creased sheet of paper, on which the beautiful italic handwriting had faded to a pale brown. At the top of the sheet were some printed words which looked like the name of a shop, and an address.

'What is it?'

Sofia took back the paper and stared out of the window.

'A few weeks before we fled from Hungary, my mother took her violin to Budapest for a small repair. She always went to the same place – a family of Jewish instrument makers and repairers who had a business near the Opera House in Pest. Then we left very suddenly from our own home in the country, because my father managed to arrange passage for us on a Polish boat travelling from Vienna to Romania. He rowed us out himself to join the ship. There was no chance to collect the violin, and my mother thought she had left the receipt at home with Papa. Later, after we reached London and unpacked, she discovered that she still had it. Of course, many of the Jews were killed by the Germans and by the Arrow Cross, and much of the city was bombed and destroyed by artillery fire. There is almost no hope that it will still be there, but I will not rest happy unless I try to find it.'

She smiled sadly.

'The instrument business dated back to the sixteenth century, before the Turks came, but it isn't likely to have survived both the Germans and the Russians in this century.'

When they emerged from the aeroplane at Ferihegy the building seemed grim as an army barracks, and quite deserted, although it was not yet ten o'clock. There was just one immigration officer on duty at passport control – a good-looking young woman who was painfully methodical. She scrutinised each passport, held the inside pages up to the light as if checking for forgeries, and stared balefully first at the photograph and then at the person proffering the passport before final stamping it and motioning to the next person. The queue of tired travellers shuffled slowly forward. A large American businessman just ahead of Kate and Sofia was grumbling loudly about the delay to an elderly Japanese couple.

'Time they got their act together if they want to attract outside investment and tourism. You wouldn't see this kind of hold-up at any airport in the US of A, no siree. She's making like we're some kind of criminals.'

Considering, thought Kate, that they are so recently out from under the heel of the Russian military, it's not surprising they're still a bit like communist border guards.

The American was now laying down the law about transport from the airport to the hotels in central Budapest.

'Naw, naw,' he was asserting. 'You don't want to take one of those bus things. Take a limo. They're so desperate for hard currency here, it's cheap.'

Irritated, Kate murmured to Sofia, 'I'm going to change some money at the *bureau de change* over there. I couldn't get any small denominations from the travel agent. If they speak English, I'll find out whether the buses are still running as late as this.'

The woman at the *bureau de change* was helpful, and spoke English. She pointed out that at the adjacent counter tickets for the bus could be bought at a standard price of 600 forints each, to any hotel in Budapest. Certainly the buses would run until the last flight of the night landed. Kate returned triumphant and flourished the tickets at Sofia. They were now at the head of the queue for passport control. Kate noticed that Sofia was very tense, with fine beads of sweat on her upper lip. Would there be any trouble over the fact that Sofia had been born in Hungary, but held a British passport? She urged the older woman ahead of her. If there should be any difficulties, she didn't want to find herself processed through and Sofia left behind.

The passport official seemed to take longer than ever with Sofia's passport, turning over every page, scrutinising the photograph. Once she closed the passport and seemed about to hand it back, then she opened it for a further look. Kate could feel sweat gathering on her own back and trickling down the groove of her spine. At last Sofia was waved through, and Kate received only cursory attention. As they collected their luggage and a smiling customs man indicated that they might pass on, Kate noted with some satisfaction that the loud American was having all his handsome cases thoroughly searched.

They passed through a door and were suddenly hit by colour and sound. After the grim concrete bunker on the other side of the barrier, this seemed a different world. Dozens of people were milling about –

new arrivals and locals who had come to meet them. There were all the usual airport conveniences – a café, a bar, a kiosk selling magazines and postcards, another *bureau de change*, comfortable chairs and low tables, and a desk for the airport buses.

'It is like stepping from the communist past into the new Hungary,' murmured Sofia, 'but I am not sure yet whether one is free to say that.'

A man with a clipboard was talking to the people clustered about the bus desk, checking destinations and asking them to take a seat until their bus was called.

'It seems very efficient,' said Kate as they sat down after telling him their hotel.

Within five minutes he was back.

'Atrium Hyatt, Marriott, Forum,' he called. 'This way, please.' He repeated himself in French, German and Hungarian.

They followed him out of the door into the night, and at last Kate began to feel that she had really arrived in Hungary. A smart white bus was parked beside the pavement. Along the side it said obscurely, in red-painted script, '...a légi utasok földi szállítoja...' However, below this, sturdy black letters announced cheerfully: 'Airport Minibus'. As they pulled away from the terminal buildings, Kate noticed that the large American, now with the small Japanese couple in tow, was arguing with a taxi driver.

She wished that it was not so dark. She could see nothing of the city but strings of lights defining the edges of the road, and the chiaroscuro of traffic travelling both ways. The driver had switched on the radio and a man's voice spoke continuously. It sounded monotonous, with little music in the speech. She wondered whether Hungarian always sounded so flat.

'What is he saying?' she asked Sofia, who was sitting beside her mesmerised, staring past the driver at the light glowing on the radio.

Sofia smiled. 'Forgive me. It is so strange to me, you see, to hear my language spoken again.'

'Is it something interesting?'

Sofia's smiled broadened.

'It is the football results.'

❧

Kate was so tired when they reached their hotel room that she fell into bed without even inspecting the night-time view from their window.

Waking the next morning, deeply rested but indolent, she saw that Sofia was already sitting up in her bed reading.

'Good morning,' said Kate, stretching luxuriously. She crossed to the window and drew back the curtains to catch her first sight of Budapest. To her delight there was a small balcony beyond the french windows and there, seven storeys below, was the Danube. It was only eight o'clock, but already traffic was busy on the river. Elegant cruise ships and huge lumbering barges were moving in both directions. Pleasure cruisers of every kind were moored along the bank below, and on one she could see a girl in a bright red skirt washing down the deck with a bucket and mop.

Across the river the cliffs of Buda rose high above the flat plain of Pest, here where their hotel stood. To the right these were crowned by the castle and by a spire she thought might be the Mátyás Church. To the left the statue of a woman holding aloft a plume in both hands dominated the skyline, while below her the statue of St Gellért, who first converted the heathen Magyars and was martyred for his pains, marked the steep slope where he was rolled down the cliff in a spiked barrel. Overhead the sky was clear and blue, but there was a faint haze over the river which reminded Kate of the haar lying over the Dun. Along the promenade below people were hurrying to work, and trams clanked up and down between the promenade and the river.

'It's wonderful!' she cried. 'Have you seen the view?'

'I peeped round the curtain while you were still asleep,' said Sofia. 'Shall we go down to breakfast?'

They breakfasted outside on the terrace above the promenade. Here they had a closer view of the yellow and white trams which moved with great deliberation along the riverside track, stopping frequently. The sides of the trams carried advertising, like buses at home – familiar names like Old Spice, Air France and Burger King. (Burger King? thought Kate. Oh, dear.) There were a few local promotions as well, but on the whole it was the names of big non-Hungarian companies which passed before the eyes of those strolling on the promenade.

Breakfast was excellent. There were the usual cereals and cooked breakfasts that could be found in any western European hotel, but what struck Kate were the pyramids and silver dishes of gleaming fruit, piled up lavishly – strawberries, blackberries, bananas, four kinds of melon, sliced oranges, grapefruit, peaches, grapes, apples, every kind of fruit imaginable. Greedily she piled her plate full and sat in the sun nibbling at it and watching the first river cruises of the day getting under way.

She wondered whether the same abundance of food existed for the ordinary Hungarian.

As they were sitting over the last of their breakfast, Kate took out of her pocket the handful of small coins she had been given the evening before at the airport and examined them.

'This is pretty, isn't it?' she said, holding up the gold-coloured five-forint piece. 'Is that a heron, do you suppose?'

Sofia took the coin and turned it over in the palm of her hand. 'Yes. We'll see many herons in western Hungary. My part of the country is famous for them.'

'Would you like to look for your musical instrument shop first today?' Kate asked.

'No, no. Today we must do as all the tourists do and go to Castle Hill. It is obligatory to see the Mátyás Church and the Fishermen's Bastion. We can decide whether we want to look inside the castle. It is not very old.'

'Shall we take a taxi?'

'Certainly not. You see how close the Chain Bridge is? Just there? We walk across that and take the funicular from Clark Adam Ter to the top of the cliff.' Her face clouded suddenly. 'I hope the funicular is still there. It was a great treat when I was a child.'

'Yes, it is,' Kate hastened to reassure her. 'I've seen it in the guidebook.' She popped the last piece of Galia melon in her mouth and savoured its cool sweetness against the roof of her mouth. A tall man walking along the promenade just below their table caught her eye.

'Hungary may be short of hard currency,' she said, 'but people look healthy and well dressed. And there are plenty of private cars – you can see them whizzing along on the other side of the river.'

'Yes,' said Sofia, her eyes following the same man, who was dressed in a neat grey suit like any London businessman and carrying a smart leather briefcase. He was followed by two teenagers of indeterminate sex with close-cropped heads, wearing jeans and outsize T-shirts. They were speaking Hungarian, so they were certainly not tourists. They wandered past with their arms twined around each other and their hands tucked into each other's hip pockets. Already Sofia was finding Budapest disorientating. Partly so familiar with its main landmarks from her girlhood, and partly as alien as another planet. 'Yes, they look quite prosperous. Certainly as prosperous as England. We must keep our eyes open and see if there are any beggars.'

'Heavens!' cried Kate. 'What is that noise?'

A terrible monotonous twanging sound had started up, a little further along the promenade. Just past a lady displaying her

119

embroidered tablecloths for sale, and a youth setting out a table covered with postcards, sat an old man with a stringed instrument on his lap, from which he was producing the most unmusical cacophony Kate had ever heard from a street musician.

'A zither player,' said Sofia. 'I suspect that he is tone deaf.'

'I think I prefer beggars,' said Kate.

The apartment block looked much as it must have done a hundred years ago, István thought, but shabbier. This was the address he had found on the letter sent to his father early in 1945, and like this whole row of houses it had escaped serious damage during the battle for possession of Budapest, although there was a row of bullet holes like a dotted line underscoring one of the first-floor windows. Those had been made by a machine-gun, not artillery, he thought, and might even be a relic of the 1956 uprising and not the second world war.

Originally these fine houses overlooking the Danube would have been occupied by middle-class professional families during the eighteenth and nineteenth centuries. In the early twentieth century they had been divided into large flats – one or at most two on each floor. Then during the communist regime many had been subdivided, and he had no idea whether the flat he was seeking would be one of these. Anna's discreet enquiries had quickly revealed that a Ferenc Kalla did still live at the same address. It might be a coincidence – the name was not unusual. This might be a son or some other relative, but if so at least that would be a point of contact with the man who had rescued his father from the ice of the Danube, nursed him back to health and sent him home.

The building had been painted – many years ago – a warm cinnamon, which had bleached in the sun, not unpleasingly, so that it looked like faded autumn leaves. In places some of the stucco had fallen off, revealing brick beneath, but the original finish was designed to look like stone. There was elaborate plaster scrollwork outlining every window, once painted white but now weathered to cream, and the front door was protected by a wrought-iron grille depicting dolphins and mermaids intertwined with wave-like scrolls. Perhaps the original owner of the building had been a merchant trading on the Danube in the days of the Hapsburg Empire. On either side of the doorway voluptuous caryatids supported a monumental lintel. István tapped one of these figures on the foot with his fingernail. They were carved from real stone, a sure sign of wealth.

Now, however, there were ugly wires trailing across the façade of the building, some looping up to a telephone pole on the other side of the pavement, some disappearing underground. These must be electric cables. The insulation was cracked and dangerous-looking. Although the weather had been hot and dry now for weeks, there were green stains down one corner of the building where the plumbing was defective. In other words, it was a typical example of a fine old Pest building – architecturally superb, but desperately in need of expensive renovation.

On the right of the door was a mismatched array of doorbells, most of which had metal holders for cards next to them. The cards were handwritten or typed, some ancient, faded and water-stained, others more recent. Next to the bell numbered 7, a neatly typed card read KALLA FERENC.

István hesitated before ringing. The old doubts assailed him again – did he really want to stir up that long-dead past? His childhood had been haunted by nightmares, and during the last few weeks, since Magdolna had discovered the tin box, they had returned to plague him again. If he went ahead now he was allowing a breach to open up in his carefully constructed defences. Moreover, had he the right to arrive, unannounced, at the home of this old man – supposing it was indeed his father's rescuer – and inflict the same terrible memories on him? Many people in Hungary wanted nothing so much as to put their past behind them, either because it was too painful to live with, or because reminders of it might cast a blight over the changed persona they had subsequently assumed. For all he knew, Ferenc Kalla might have been a dedicated communist in the days of the partisans. Many of those who had fought against the Nazis had welcomed the Russians with open arms. During the Stalinist regime some had flourished and risen to positions of great power and influence, while others had been purged. Some who had been communists had recanted only within recent years with the downfall of the Soviet Union. Kalla might belong to any of these groups. Or he might just be a frail old man who wanted to be left alone.

With his hand already raised to the bell, István wondered whether he should telephone first. It was only a step to the Marriott Hotel, back past the Petőfi statue and the curious London bus someone had set up serving Douwe Egbert coffee. There would be public telephones in the hotel lobby. He could ring from there. When he had passed the terrace of the hotel a few moments before he had seen the guests breakfasting, a mixed group of Hungarian and foreign businessmen interspersed with the tourists who were beginning to find their way back to Budapest.

Even while he was thinking of finding a telephone, he heard footsteps coming down the stairs inside the building. Feeling foolish, and not wanting to be caught standing like this, hesitating in front of the door, he pressed the bell for flat number 7. A young woman, smartly dressed and clearly on her way to work, came out of the building and smiled at him as she let the heavy door swing closed behind her. As she walked away, her high heels tapping on the pavement, the intercom box crackled and a faint voice said, 'Yes?'

'Mr Kalla? This is Dr István Rudnay from Sopron. I wonder if I might speak to you?'

István had decided in advance that he would simply introduce himself as a doctor from Sopron – his professional status normally allayed any suspicions from strangers. He would wait until he had sized up Ferenc Kalla before he introduced his father's name.

'Come up,' said the voice on the intercom, and there was a loud click as the bolt on the door was released.

István pushed open the door and stepped into the hallway, cool after the street outside, where another day of soaring temperatures was already building up. An elegant curved stone staircase with wrought-iron balustrades led to the upper floors. He counted off the flats as he ascended. Number 7 was on the third floor, overlooking the Danube. He thought of Ferenc and his friends struggling up these stairs with his father's inert body on that bitter day in December, Ferenc's clothes dripping and freezing, blood from his father's wounds staining the pale stone of the stairs.

Before he reached it, the door of flat number 7 opened. As he drew nearer and his eyes grew more accustomed to the dim light in the hallway, he felt partly relieved and partly disappointed. A stocky, vigorous, middle-aged man was holding the door open to him. He wore heavy horn-rimmed glasses, and his thick dark hair was just beginning to show a faint sprinkling of grey.

'Mr Kalla?' said István, holding out his hand, 'Good morning. It's kind of you to see me. I am István Rudnay.'

The man took his hand, shook it and drew him into the flat. He was staring intently, disconcertingly, at István, still holding him by the hand.

'It's uncanny,' he said, shaking his head. 'Forgive me.' He released István's hand at last, but continued to stare. 'I could have believed, for a moment there... Rudnay, did you say? You cannot be... You must be... Juliska's boy?'

As the funicular clanked almost vertically up the cliff face, carrying them from the level of the river to the top of Castle Hill in Buda, Kate looked eagerly out of the grubby windows at the widening panorama of Pest in front of and below her on the far side of the Danube. Away to the right she could see their hotel. In two places the track of the funicular was crossed by decorative cast-iron bridges carrying the footpath which wandered through the trees on either side. Eighty forints each for the ride seemed a small price to pay for such a treat. About 50p, she reckoned. Sofia, beside her, was gazing about with all the eagerness she must have felt when she was brought here as a child by her parents. The other passengers were a mix of foreign tourists and locals. Kate supposed the people of Budapest must use the funicular all the time to avoid the climb up the long winding road around the houses that dotted the wooded slope up to the top of the hill.

'It's lovely, isn't it,' she said as they clambered out at the high-level stop. 'I can see why you adored it as a child. Now which way? Oh, look, there is another Turul bird.'

Sofia set off purposefully to the right, towards the spire of the Mátyás Church, which they could see above the trees. There was a promenade along the cliff edge, and looking out over the tops of horse chestnut trees growing lower down the slope they could see the parliament building further upriver, and the wooded outline of Margaret Island, blurred a little by the lingering mist. The chestnuts were covered with pale green, unripe conkers, and amongst them were a few Spanish chestnuts with their much smaller, spikier nuts. The berries on the rowans were already bright orange. The promenade widened out into a pretty paved area, where a woman selling her embroideries had taken refuge from the heat under a huge willow. She proffered her work diffidently, and Kate wondered how many women had been forced to start selling in the streets since capitalism had come to the country. The tablecloths and blouses were covered with beautiful work, but there was no indication of prices and she felt daunted by the thought of bargaining. It would seem, somehow, as though you were trying to devalue the woman's skill. Sofia was striding on ahead as she lingered, but then a group of prosperous-looking Japanese tourists stopped to admire the embroidery and Kate felt she could slip away without being offensive.

Tom had always ridiculed this shyness and vulnerability she displayed when confronted by street pedlars.

'Don't be stupid, Kate,' he would say in irritation. 'They're all just con-artists, trying to sell you something made in Korea – at a one thousand per cent profit.'

But Kate knew, she *knew*, that the woman had spent hours during the winter months labouring over the exquisite stitchery, and she felt something like shame as she turned and hurried after Sofia.

It was when they were admiring the Trinity column – set up to give thanks for the end of the plague early in the eighteenth century – that Sofia gave a sudden start and looked for the first time shocked and disorientated. She had been prepared for modern hotels beside the Danube, and the heavy traffic on the main roads, but not for changes here, in the very heart of ancient Buda.

'What is that!' she cried.

Next to the Mátyás Church, with its delicate pale stone and its charmingly comic roof covered with tawny ceramic tiles, stood something in vulgar plate glass, which seemed to have half devoured a much more ancient building, parts of which extended from the fatal grasp of the modern structure like the thrashing limbs of a victim at the moment of being swallowed by a shark.

'My God!' said Kate. 'Just a minute.' She riffled through her guidebook. 'It's the Hilton Hotel,' she said in a subdued voice. 'Built in 1976, incorporating parts of the mediaeval monastery and eighteenth-century seminary.'

'How could they?' said Sofia. There were tears in her eyes. 'I know the Turks turned the Mátyás Church into a mosque when they ruled us, but to let that desecration be built, less than twenty years ago...'

'I suppose they thought it would bring the tourists, and they needed Western currency. It says here that it is famous for the way it reflects the church in its multiple windows.'

'There is a moral in that, I'm afraid.'

Kate fanned herself with the guidebook. 'I'm going to treat us to an ice. Look, they're only 40 forints! Then we'll give some money to that nice old man playing the hurdy-gurdy over there and inspect the Fishermen's Bastion, which looks as though it has come straight from the set of a Walt Disney film.'

'You are insulting,' said Sofia, 'one of the patriotic monuments of my country, built at the height of nineteenth-century taste.' She studied the sign on the ice-cream stall. 'Hmm. Pistachio and vanilla for me, please.'

She cheered up as they climbed the Bastion for further views over the Danube.

'I knew the ice-cream sellers would speak English,' she said.

For Kate the best part of the visit to the square beside the Mátyás Church was the eye-to-eye view from the Fishermen's Bastion of the great bronze equestrian statue of King Stephen I.

'Look,' she said. 'He's wearing both a crown and a halo. That's an unusual combination.'

'He was an unusual man, István... Stephen,' said Sofia. 'King and saint. I will tell you about him some day. We still possess his crown, nearly a thousand years old. The royal treasure was carried off to America after the war, but it was returned at last, after more than thirty years.'

The interior of the Mátyás Church was a disappointment. Its repeated transformations from church to mosque to church again, from its mediaeval origins to its nineteenth-century and post-war restorations, had robbed it of its dignity. Sofia explained that it had a special significance as the coronation church, but Kate muttered under her breath that it reminded her of a tattooed lady.

After leaving the church they wandered away into a maze of little streets in the heart of old Buda, and found themselves virtually alone. This was how Kate had imagined the old city might be. She was entranced by the small but elegant houses painted in muted shades of green and pink and ochre, with steeply sloping slate or tile roofs from which crescent windows peered out like heavy-lidded eyes. The roads were cobbled. Here and there small squares and triangles of grass set off the architecture, which was on a comfortable human scale.

'You are very fond of arches, aren't you?' said Kate. 'You Hungarians? I love the way the arched openings break up the severity of the straight lines. What do you suppose is through here?'

They went through an arch into a dim paved entrance, beyond which another arch opened on to a cobbled courtyard between pale cream walls, where bushes and trees in tubs cast a pattern of shadows. A tabby kitten was curled up in the shade of a bulbous terracotta pot holding a lemon tree.

'Perhaps it's a private house,' Kate said, retreating. And then as her eyes adjusted to the shadowed vestibule between the two arches she saw that it contained a small collection of gravestones.

'That's Hebrew,' she said, peering more closely at the lettering. 'Oh, of course. The Jews of Budapest... But these gravestones are very old, I think.'

She knew of Raoul Wallenberg, who had saved a hundred thousand Jews from the Nazi butchers during the last desperate days of the Third Reich in Budapest. But it was only now, standing here in this

125

ancient place, that she felt the knowledge as a shock, as a living awareness of the tyrannies of East and West meeting in this city – and of their victims.

'Yes,' said Sofia. 'I think they are very old. You were remembering the Jews of Budapest murdered by Eichmann during the last war.'

'But they would have had no gravestones.'

'No. They would have had no gravestones.'

≫

'You are so like your father,' said Ferenc, 'so like Lancelot, that I could not believe my eyes. You must be much the same age as he was then, I suppose.'

'I'll be fifty this autumn.'

'He would have been about forty-five or six when I first met him, but of course he was not looking his best!'

'I don't understand. You're surely much too young yourself...'

'I'm sixty-five. I was just fifteen when we pulled your father out of the river. Many of the partisans were youngsters like me. You have to remember that Hitler had forced all Hungarian men of fighting age to be drafted into his armies in January 1942. Some of them went into hiding and later joined the resistance, but lots of us were under age. I was strong for my years – it's a good thing I was, or I would never have been able to pull your father out of the water. When I spotted him he was struggling through the floating ice, trying to reach the edge of the river where more ice was forming around the boat jetties. But almost as soon as I caught hold of him he passed out again and then he was a dead weight. He was a tall, slender-built man, but he was being dragged down by his waterlogged clothes.'

They were sitting in Ferenc's comfortable but shabby apartment, drinking coffee and looking out of the window which opened on to a tiny balcony.

'Don't stand on it!' Ferenc had warned. 'It isn't safe.'

On the promenade below them a boy was walking his dog, and two elegant women were heading towards the shops in Váci Utca.

'But you called me "Juliska's boy". How did you know my mother?'

'I suppose you wouldn't have been told about those days. Better for the children not to know, of course.'

István looked at him. Ferenc was only fifteen years older than he was, but what a crucial and dangerous difference in age that was.

'More coffee?' Ferenc refilled their cups. They were, István noticed, fine Herend china.

'We sent Lancelot back via a chain of partisan helpers once he was well enough to travel. It was dangerous, I can tell you! The Germans and the Russians were shooting the city to pieces, and heaven help any Hungarian who happened to get caught in the middle. I knew roughly where he was going, and his code name – I never knew his given name, not even later on. After he sent word and I wrote that letter back, things began to get a bit hot for me in Budapest. The Russians were here by then, but I wasn't a Russian lover any more than a Nazi lover. I'd been very impressed by your father – both his active service and his underground newspaper. Word got through to us, you know. So with three friends I decided to try to get through to the area where he was operating, west of Györ. Two of us made it.'

He smiled reminiscently, and István realised that he had been mistaken in thinking he might reawaken painful memories. Ferenc was an old soldier, and recalled his exploits with the same pride and detachment as many old soldiers, somehow managing to dissociate his personal feelings from the horrors of warfare.

'I lived in the camp with your parents and the others, and I've carried you around on my shoulders many a time. Bright little kid, you were. Started talking very young. After the Russian army had driven the Germans out, most of the partisan groups disbanded and went home, but Lancelot didn't trust the Russians. We stayed together, mainly producing and distributing *Freedom!*, which was campaigning for Hungary to get the same kind of post-war deal as Austria – partition between the four occupying powers – but nothing was going to shake the stranglehold the Russians had on us. It became clear pretty quickly that Rákosi was going to be a puppet of the Kremlin. What none of us realised was that he was going to out-Stalin Stalin himself in his ferocity.'

'But just a minute.' István tried to stem the flow of reminiscence. 'After the war we went to live with my mother's parents in Szentmargit. We didn't stay on at the camp in the woods. My sister was born there, in the village.'

'That's right!' Ferenc grinned and took a deep gulp of his coffee. 'Little... wait a minute, it'll come to me... Magdolna, wasn't it?'

'Yes.'

'And... she's all right, is she?'

István recognised the polite way of asking whether someone had survived the purges of the post-war years.

'She's fine. She's married to a farmer and has two children – a girl studying law here in Budapest and a boy still at school.'

'Wonderful, wonderful.' Ferenc's eyes were moist, and he blew his nose discreetly. 'It means a lot to me that you children survived.'

He tucked his handkerchief back into his breast pocket.

'Yes, you're quite right. After the war we moved our base of operations to Szentmargit for a couple of years. Your family lived there, all perfectly legitimate, and many of the others from the group – those who hadn't been killed during the war – came from the village or the surrounding area. Nominally, I worked for one of the local shopkeepers, but I continued to be the courier carrying copies of the newspaper to Budapest for distribution. My parents were living in this flat. They never meddled in politics, and they didn't know that I did, so my cover was fairly safe.'

'So what happened in the end?'

'Someone betrayed us. I was here when it happened, but we knew who it was. He was a communist – always had been, quite openly during the war. He left the group after the war, but he had seen copies of *Freedom!* condemning the communist regime in Hungary and calling for an uprising to set the country free. The Ávó and the NKVD were wild to get hold of your father, and this fellow probably got a fat reward for betraying him.'

He smiled grimly into his empty cup.

'He didn't have much time to enjoy it, though.'

István looked at him steadily, waiting.

'Yes. We took care of him. He was shot while he was buying flowers at the market in Györ.'

'Who did it?'

For the first time Ferenc looked uncomfortable.

'We keep names secret after operations.'

'I need to know. It was forty-six years ago. No one can hurt her now. It was, wasn't it? It was my mother?'

'Yes. It was Juliska. The man had betrayed your father to the gulags. It was justice.'

On Wednesday, Kate and Sofia decided they would explore the centre of Pest at a leisurely pace on foot, starting at Vörösmarty Tér and visiting the Basilica of St Stephen before trying to find the instrument shop in one of the back streets behind the opera house. It was on the steps of the Basilica that they saw their one and only beggar in

128

Budapest. A frail old woman in decent black stood apologetically at the side of the steps with a hesitant hand extended. Kate felt a sudden, overpowering rush of pity and shame. She had never felt very strongly about the beggars she had seen on the streets when they had lived in London. There they seemed to fall into two main categories: the true down-and-outs – filthy, red-eyed and torpid – and young runaways living rough. She always wanted to reason with the youngsters and say, 'For heaven's sake, go home!' But she never did. A friend who had once tried to speak kindly to a pretty girl of about fourteen had been met with a torrent of abuse and foul language.

The woman on the steps of the Basilica was of a different type altogether. She might have been anyone's granny – threadbare but clean, with patched shoes and her white hair twisted into a neat bun. As Kate dropped some coins into the outstretched hand, lowering her eyes in embarrassment, she noticed that the woman's fingers were dreadfully swollen and distorted with arthritis. If her hands had remained undamaged she would probably have been selling embroidery, like the women around the hotels and beside the Mátyás Church. Sofia had paused at the top of the steps and was looking at Kate and the old woman with a curious expression on her face. When Kate caught her up, she said:

'It is sad, is it not, that freedom, when it has come at last, has not been good for everyone.'

'Do you think she would have been better off under communism?'

Sofia shook her head. 'Who can say?'

Inside the church it was cool and peaceful after the heat and the traffic outside. Kate found this interior much more to her taste than the Mátyás Church – ornate, indeed, but with a certain restrained dignity. Her eyes were drawn again and again to the great dome overhead, through whose arched windows the sun flooded the church, lightening the effect of the marble and gilding. Turning to the left from the high altar she caught sight of a huge painting of the crucifixion on the wall. She had never much cared for crucifixes of any kind, but this painting was eerily compelling. Wherever you walked within sight of it, the twisted body of Christ seemed to turn towards you, forcing your eyes back to the image of pain, the knotted muscles standing out from the arms as they bore the weight of the body – the head bowed, it appeared, in defeat. Kate shuddered, and walked back to the door and the sunlight.

Sofia joined her a few moments later and they descended the steps soberly, each occupied with her thoughts. The old woman was still there, and she gave Kate a tentative smile. Kate smiled back.

In their search for the instrument shop they started from the Opera in Andrássy Út. This fine street, also constructed for the millennium, stretched in a straight line from Deák Tér to Heroes' Square far away out of sight, at the entrance to Városliget, the great green lung of the city, with its museum and art gallery, its zoo and Gundel's restaurant, and its acres of parkland and paths and lake. The street, lined by elegant buildings dating from the last decades of the nineteenth century, was as fine as any boulevard in Paris. They found the Opera without difficulty, just a short walk from the Basilica, but here Sofia faltered.

'I remember the shop being two or three blocks over, behind the Opera, but I am not sure... If we walk in that direction, perhaps I will recognise the street.'

'We could ask,' Kate suggested sensibly, but Sofia seemed curiously reluctant. Perhaps, Kate thought, she does not want to hear the answer. She knew these people who owned the shop. She does not want to hear that they were driven away on one of the death marches, when as many people died on the way to the border as died in the concentration camps when they arrived.

For twenty minutes they wandered up and down the streets without any success. Sofia was beginning to look very tired and dispirited. At last Kate noticed a woman in her early twenties coming towards them, with a toddler in a pushchair. She was far too young to have any memories which might disturb Sofia. Kate drew the receipt gently out of Sofia's hand and approached the young woman. With smiles and gestures she indicated that she was trying to find the shop. The woman peered at the faded paper in puzzlement, then her face cleared. She took Kate's arm and led her back to the corner they had just passed. Beyond the next crossroads stood a building which looked older than those which lined Andrássy Út, more like the houses in the back streets of the Castle quarter in Buda which they had seen the day before. It was painted a faded salmon pink and looked rather shabby. This, her gestures clearly indicated, was the place they were seeking. Over the door the name 'Stern' could be read even from this distance.

The shop occupied the ground floor and first floor of the building. Above were flats. As they entered, an old-fashioned bell tinkled somewhere in the back, but the shop was deserted. As Kate's eyes grew accustomed to the dark interior she began to make out instruments hanging on the wall – violins, violas, cellos and a single

130

double bass. Beyond them in a hand-carved rack was a complete set of recorders, from sopranino to bass. A glass-topped counter held wind instruments while several stands of dark varnished wood against the walls were filled with rows and rows of sheet music and albums. Behind the counter an open doorway was screened by a hanging strip curtain of lace. Then, as a young man brushed through it, Kate realised that it was not lace but paper, skilfully made like a child's string of folded cut-paper dolls holding hands, though this cut-work was so fine it was almost an art form in itself.

The young man was smiling and clearly asking if he could help them. Sofia stepped hesitantly forward and addressed him in Hungarian, then switched to English for Kate's benefit. He responded in heavily accented but perfectly clear English.

'An instrument left in our care many years ago, you say? And you have the receipt? It is possible it may be in the vaults. How long ago?'

'1938,' said Sofia, passing him the piece of paper.

He blinked. If this sounded to him like the time of the Ark, he was too polite to show it.

'I will fetch my grandfather,' he said. 'If you would wait one moment, please.'

He disappeared through the paper curtain and they could hear his feet going up a staircase at the back of the building. In a tense silence they waited for his return. Kate turned over the sheet music. It would be fun to buy something for Roz here, but she was so ignorant. She didn't know what Roz already had, or what would be suitable. She gave up and went to study the row of clarinets in the glass case. Sofia was staring out of the window.

Sofia is bored and impatient and tries to conceal it by gazing out of the window. Mama is taking for ever talking to the young man in Stern's, who is quite handsome in a dark, passionate, Jewish way. While they talk about the small repair to the bridge and the regular check Stern's gives Mama's violin, Sofia is planning what she will buy when they go shopping. Now she is eighteen, she wants some clothes that are smarter and more fashionable than anything she can buy in Győr, which is a provincial backwater. Sofia has only recently begun to take an interest in clothes since she left school. There she has been a little too earnest, a little too much of the budding scholar for her parents' tastes. For Mama, music is the centre of life, second only to her love for her husband; Papa is interested in social and agricultural reform, and talks far into the night with his political cronies, and neither of them has Sofia's passionate interest in books. Once or twice they have suggested, in an oblique way, that she should do something more active with her life now that she has left school, but she dreams away the hours reading in her room or – when the weather is fine – in the little Chinoiserie pavilion which stands in the clearing in the woods.

At last the business is concluded and Mama puts the receipt in her handbag.

'I will collect it in two weeks' time, then,' she says, giving the violin a farewell stroke. 'My next concert is in Vienna in just over a month.'

At the mention of Vienna, the young man looks suddenly disconcerted and opens his mouth as if to say something, but thinks better of it. He comes round the counter to open the door for them, and shakes hands as they leave.

'Goodbye, and thank you, Madam. Goodbye, Miss Niklai.'

'Goodbye, Jakob,' says Mama as they step out into the sunny street.

'At last!' cries Sofia, with a skip of impatience. 'Can we go and do our shopping now?'

'Of course,' says Mama, suddenly as pleased as Sofia at the prospect of the Budapest shops. She is, after all, only thirty-six, and is still more beautiful than her young daughter.

That evening, when they return to their hotel laden with parcels and pleasantly tired, there is a telegram waiting for them at the reception desk.

'It is from Papa. He wants us to return home at once and not wait for the weekend.'

'Whatever can be the matter?' wonders Sofia.

Her mother suddenly looks grey and tired.

The curtain of paper lace was swept aside and the young man returned with a much older one, stooped but bright of eye, who was holding Sofia's receipt delicately, as though it might crumble away. Kate noticed that the fingers of his right hand were damaged in some way. They seemed to be twisted out of shape. He bowed formally to Sofia and Kate.

'Can I help you, Madam? You have shown my grandson this receipt.' He cleared his throat. 'You realise that it refers to a transaction made many, many years ago.'

'Yes,' said Sofia. 'I realise that. My mother was never able to collect the violin because my father sent us out of the country. This is the first time I have returned.' She gripped the counter as if to steady herself, and the younger man, standing watchful behind his grandfather, hurried to bring her a chair.

'Thank you.' She smiled at him wanly. 'I know the likelihood that the violin is still in your possession is very remote, but I felt I must try. And in order to establish my credentials, I have my passport here, and I have also brought my mother's old passport, from before the war.'

She opened her handbag and began to search in it. Kate was surprised. She had thought of Sofia as vague and unworldly. Bringing the old passport with her showed remarkable shrewdness and foresight. The old man turned aside and murmured something in Hungarian to his grandson, who slipped away into the back of the shop. Once again Kate could hear his feet on a staircase, this time going downwards.

Sofia laid the documents on the counter: her own crisp new passport and a faded old document, dog-eared and, it seemed, water-stained. The old man opened this passport and looked at the photograph inside. Kate leaned over Sofia's shoulder to see. The photograph showed a woman who was clearly the same as the lovely young woman with the violin in Sofia's photograph album, but older and dressed in ordinary street clothes instead of evening dress. The suit jacket had padded shoulders, and showed a blouse beneath it with a neat Peter Pan collar.

'Eva Tabor,' the old man breathed, not as if he was reading the name from the passport, but as if he had recognised her. Indeed, Kate could see that the name on the passport was 'Eva Niklai'.

He looked up and seemed almost unable to speak, but at last he said, 'You are Eva Tabor's daughter?'

The grandson had reappeared behind the curtain, Kate saw, but he seemed shy of coming into the shop.

'Yes,' said Sofia. Her voice too was unsteady. 'I am Eva Tabor's daughter Sofia. And I believe I have met you before, Jakob Stern, when we left the violin here.'

'I remember,' he said. 'An impatient daughter, eager to hurry away to more interesting shops!'

Sofia smiled. 'I was eighteen, and just out of school. But...'

'The Guarneri?'

133

He hesitated, his eyes filled with faraway thoughts. 'After the Germans came, we knew, we in the Jewish community, that we would not remain safe for long. My father and I stored all the instruments in the vaults below the shop, and a friend who was a builder had his men brick up the entrance and plaster over it. The work wasn't done long before we were ordered to close the shop, and we were forced to leave the flat upstairs and move to the ghetto.'

Sofia stretched out her hand to him instinctively, and he touched it briefly with his maimed one.

'We Jews in Budapest were left alone longer than those in most of the countries occupied by the Nazis, but when Eichmann came in the spring of 1944 he was determined to wipe out every Jew in Hungary.'

He drew in his breath sharply.

'Raoul Wallenberg... he saved so many... and the first time the SS tried to round up my family, he managed to save us. We lived in the ghetto for some months after that. But later we were taken.'

He laid the receipt down on the counter, and his hands were trembling.

'Because I was young and strong, I was sent to the forced labour battalion, and the rest of the family was driven away on the march to the Austrian border, the death march. It was winter. There was no food, no water, and no protection from the ice and snow. At night they lay in the open by the roadside, and each morning fewer continued the march. The bodies were left there, where they had died in the night. My mother and sisters died before they reached the border. I met up with my father when the slave labourers were marched to join the others, and we were all herded together in a wooden shed at Hegyeshalom. My father died later, in the camp. They kept us working until we became too weak, and when he developed flu he knew he would be sent to the gas chamber. Before they took him, he made me promise, if I survived, to come back and carry on the business. It has been in our family for four hundred years.'

'I remember. But... Jakob... your hand?'

'I was tortured in the camp,' he said briefly. 'They broke the bones of my hand, one by one. My friends did what they could to set it, but it mended like this.' He laughed grimly. 'Not much good for an instrument maker, is it?'

'But you came back, after the war?'

'Yes. The building had been looted, but they had not found the entrance to the vaults. All our tools were there, and our seasoned timber. And the instruments.' He looked over his shoulder. 'Tamás?'

The young man came through into the shop carrying a viol and laid it on the counter. Jakob Stern fumbled with the catche. raised the lid. Kate caught sight of the warm copper glow of poli wood as he lifted out the violin and laid it in Sofia's hands.

'The Guarneri,' he said.

Chapter 8

ᴗ next day, Thursday, was their last in Budapest, but Kate and Sofia found it difficult to get up in the morning, feeling both ₁hysically and emotionally drained after the previous day's discoveries. They had stayed to have lunch with Jakob Stern and his grandson Tamás, in the flat on the second floor above the instrument shop. Tamás's young wife Sarah was perhaps a little taken aback when two strange women arrived in her home, but on learning Sofia's identity and hearing the full story of the Guarneri kept hidden in the vaults all these years she welcomed them warmly and set about making a rich *gulyás* with salad. Tamás was sent out to buy fresh bread and fruit, and the five of them sat down very companionably to lunch.

Sarah spoke little English and the conversation slipped more and more into Hungarian. Kate did not mind. This was part of Sofia's story, and she had merely a walk-on part in it. She fed the baby in his high-chair while Sarah served them, and attended only dreamily to the bits of the discussion she could understand. From the moment the young woman in the street had pointed out the Sterns' shop to them, it had seemed inevitable that Sofia should find her mother's violin, against all the odds. Nothing, Kate felt, would surprise her in this country, which seemed every minute to grow more extraordinary. With her rational mind she understood the horror that had been experienced here, experienced by this very family, but this was outweighed by the charm of the people, the grace of the buildings, the majestic flow of the Danube through the heart of the country.

'Of course the Guarneri has not lain untouched all these years,' Jakob explained. 'As soon as we opened the vault again – myself and Mischa Kocsis, who was the only one of our craftsmen I was able to find again during the first year after the war – we set about caring for the instruments. They were in surprisingly good condition. The cellar of this building has always been cool and dry, that is why we were able to use it to store instruments. Sealing the only entrance had kept out any damp that might have got in during those war years.'

He paused to hold out his glass to Tamás for more wine.

'Most of the instruments were our own stock, of course. which had been left here for repair when we closed down reclaimed in the next year or two. Finally we were left with just mother's violin and a flute of no great value. The flute is there still.

'You are a very honourable man, Jakob,' said Sofia, 'to h kept that violin so long and so faithfully, when you knew how much was worth.'

He shrugged. 'To have betrayed your mother's trust would have been to behave no better than the Nazis, who looted all the treasures they could lay their hands on. And while the Russians had their troops stationed here I would never have risked allowing even a whisper of its existence to creep out. But during these last three or four years – now that we have a democratic government, and contact again with the West – I have thought of trying to discover through people within the music world whether your mother's heirs could be traced. It was rumoured at the time of the Anschluss that she had fled to France, but no one knew where. And when she did not reappear on the concert platform after the war, we all feared the worst.'

'She died in 1944,' said Sofia.

The old man made a grieving noise in his throat and Kate lowered her eyes.

'Ah, that is sad. She must have been so young – just in her early forties, yes? Such gifts, to be lost to the world!'

He turned to Kate. 'She could wring the heart in your breast with her music, or lift you to a transport of joy beyond this earth. My father took me first to hear her play here in Budapest when I was five years old, and I vowed I would become a violinist. Alas, I had not the talent! In the camp, when things were very bad, I used to close my eyes and hear her playing inside my head.'

'I have heard a recording of her playing the Mendelssohn and Bruch violin concertos,' said Kate. 'I know exactly how you must have felt. Such power and tenderness at the same time.'

'A record of Eva Tabor? But surely... her recordings were made so long ago, before the war...'

'It's recently been reissued on CD. My daughter Roz bought it – she is studying violin.'

'But this is wonderful,' said Jakob. He drew out his card-case and gave Kate his business card. 'When you are back home again, would you send me the details of the CD? I used to own every recording she made, but like everything else we had in the ghetto they were lost.'

~ate, tucking the card away in her bag. She
, gift, and any others she could find of Eva's

, the table over hand-made local chocolates, and
, Budapest and the state of the country under the
,hers drifted more and more into speaking Hungarian
,oticing it.
,our o'clock in the afternoon by the time they left. Tamás
,d to the shop and Kate had helped Sarah with the dishes
, baby had been taken away for his afternoon nap. They left the
,der people to talk, sitting inside the half-shuttered window, and
,king quietly.

Tamás offered to drive them back to their hotel, but Sofia refused, saying that she had taken up enough of the Sterns' time. The Guarneri was left behind to be checked thoroughly; she would collect it when they returned to Budapest on the last day of the holiday, before catching their flight home. Jakob said that he would also see to the export papers, and sort out any difficulties there might be.

'As the violin has always been the property of your family, I don't think there will be any problem,' he said, 'but perhaps you would give me a phone number where I can reach you in, let us say, ten days' time, so that I can speak to you if I need to.'

Sofia explained that they had not yet booked a hotel after their visit to Györ, but promised to ring him instead.

Before they were halfway back to the hotel, Kate was regretting that they had refused the lift. The hot pavements made her shoes too tight and her feet were throbbing. Sofia was silent and abstracted, and Kate herself felt exhausted by the day's events. Back at the hotel at last she took a cold shower and then lay down to ease her feet. Sofia had fallen asleep on her bed and, although Kate tried to read the guidebook, she found herself sinking down into the pillows as if she had not slept for a week.

At dinner she felt giddy and slightly sick, as she always did after sleeping in the daytime, so she was irritated when a gypsy band importuned them while they were eating out on the terrace. Their playing was barely adequate and seemed an anticlimax to the strange events of the day. Sofia sent them off sharply, refused to pay for their unwanted music.

When they went up to their room just before ten o'clock, Kate tried to telephone home. Her anger with Tom had faded since they had arrived in Hungary, and she felt slightly shamed by the intensity of her feelings when he had abandoned their holiday together. She ought to check that everything was all right in her absence, that Beccy and Tom were coping without her. But although the phone rang and rang, no one answered. Beccy must be out with Chris, she thought, and Tom not back from the office yet, or else away in Manchester or London.

And now here it was Thursday morning, and neither of them had any energy to do anything on their last day in Budapest.

'I know what we should do,' said Kate, spreading honey on a piece of toast as she watched a hydrofoil heading up the Danube for Bratislava and Vienna. 'I think we should take a boat trip. I couldn't walk *anywhere* this morning, but I don't want to waste today.'

'Yes,' said Sofia with a smile. 'That is an excellent idea!'

As the small pleasure steamer puttered gently upriver, Kate knew they had made the right choice. From the water you had a new perspective on the city, and could appreciate how high the cliffs on the Buda side towered above the river, making them the natural site for a citadel. Franz Josef, last of the great Hapsburg emperors, had had the gates of the citadel blown up as a symbolic gesture. 'A good emperor,' he said, 'has no need of a citadel.' His wife, Queen-Empress Elisabeth, Sissy, was still recalled with affection by the Hungarians. She had learned the language and spent much of her time in the country, pursuing her favourite pastime of hunting in the woods – lover of Hungary and (it was whispered) of a certain Hungarian count.

The commentary on the boat trip, however, was romantic to the point of silliness. The guide spoke of Buda as the man and Pest as the woman, embracing each other across the river. He pursued this analogy relentlessly, and Kate let her mind drift, admiring the parliament building, even more impressive from the boat, with its reflected dome and perfect symmetries upside down in the river at its feet. At Margaret Island they decided to disembark and return by a later boat. There were gardens and lawns here, and couples holding hands under the trees. They lunched at an open-air café under a canopy of weeping willows beside the river, where it was difficult to believe you were in the centre of a busy European capital city.

At two o'clock they caught a return boat, where they were served a wine cup with chunks of oranges and strawberries floating in it, and then everyone was given the 'magical water of youth' in tiny handle-less ceramic pots about an inch high. Laughing, Kate drank hers down – it was chilled mineral water – and handed the cup back to the girl in national costume.

'Please,' said the girl, smiling and shaking her head, 'it is for you to keep. To remember Budapest.'

Sofia sipped at hers.

'I could certainly benefit from the water of youth!'

'You don't need it,' said Kate. 'You are looking younger every day. Your native air must be good for you.'

Carefully she wrapped her scarf around her tiny cup, which was copper-coloured, and Sofia's, which was deep blue, and stowed them in her bag.

'I shall treasure this,' she said.

After they returned to the hotel they indulged themselves with tea and magnificent Hungarian cakes – as many as they could eat for 375 forints.

'I have been promising myself this since we arrived,' said Sofia. 'When I was a child, a visit to Budapest always meant cakes at Café Gerbeaud, and I do believe these are just as good.'

'They're wonderful!' said Kate. 'So light, you can be really greedy. I've had *three*. My children would go quite mad here, especially Stephen. He eats like a ravening wolf but never puts on an ounce of fat. I do hope he and Mick are managing all right in France.'

Sofia decided to rest until dinner, because of the long drive the next day, but Kate felt refreshed and said she would stroll past the elegant shops she had glimpsed only briefly in Váci Utca. She set out from the hotel feeling a little nervous. It was the first time she had been on her own, without a Hungarian-speaker to rescue her from any difficulties, but soon she was absorbed into an international crowd, enjoying the inexpensive pleasure of window-shopping.

Many of the shops were truly Hungarian, although the American chains had begun to gain a foothold, and she was amused to see a tiny branch of Marks and Spencer. In a food shop she bought hand-made chocolates for her parents, and then wandered into a gallery displaying paintings, carvings and ceramics. A landscape in pastel caught her eye. It showed the *puszta*, with high grasses bowed by the wind all in one flowing curve and – just hinted at by fluid shapes in browns – a group of galloping horses on the skyline. The price was very low, less than £100, but she hesitated at the thought of trying to struggle with it on the plane going back.

As she turned away from the painting she noticed a smaller room opening off the main gallery, subtly lit and displaying a few ceramic figures. There was no one else in the room, and Kate went from figure to figure, astonished by what she saw. The figures were vigorous, original and full of passion. Each one was clearly unique, but there was a kind of family relationship between them, and though there could not have been more than a dozen of them they created a powerful and consistent world of their own.

Most of the figures were three or four feet tall, and displayed on tall plinths so that their heads were on a level with the viewer's eyes. The forms were deceptively simple, the clothes falling in long loose curves which formed a continuous line for the eye, uniting arm, hand and skirt, the curve of a back flowing into the angle of a shepherd's crook or a swineherd's horn. A mother held her child nestled against her shoulder, her hand delicately cupping the back of the vulnerable head. The bodies of woman and baby locked together in one poignant whole. In a shadowy corner an old woman in rough peasant dress sitting on a stool was stretched out in a spasm of grief which held her whole body – from the top of her head and the hands pressed between her knees, to the battered shoes – in one tense arc of agony, taut as a strung bow.

Some of the figures had coloured glazes. A young bridal pair were wreathed about with flowered garlands and decked in bright peasant costume, although the detail which caught Kate's eye was their tightly clasped hands, half hidden by the girl's apron. But it was the monochrome figures which affected her most powerfully. Some, like the old woman, were the dull colour of unglazed brownish clay, as if the woman herself were part of the soil, living only to suffer this terrible pain before she sank back into the earth again. Some of the figures – like the cowherd raising the horn to summon his flock – were terracotta, the glaze glowing with a dull sheen.

She was so absorbed that at first she did not notice the high relief plaques on the walls. Most of these were the same glazed terracotta as the cowherd, and very large – four or five feet across. The technical problems of making them so large had been solved by constructing them in separate parts for the separate figures, which then fitted together, like a jigsaw, into a harmonious whole. Kate particularly liked a group of shepherds with their sheep. Both men and beasts had long, anxious faces, and as she looked from one to the other she realised that, by exchanging horns for hats, the faces could be interchanged. She laughed aloud in delight.

A man had come into the room behind her, unnoticed. He smiled at her. Something about her must have betrayed her nationality, for he addressed her in English.

'It is a good joke, is it not?'

'It's lovely! All of them,' Kate gestured around the room. 'What wonderful talent – he's a genius. Such a range of emotion, such skill hiding under a cloak of simplicity. They're the most beautiful ceramics I've ever seen.'

'The artist – it's a woman. She studied under Margit Kovacs, our most famous ceramicist, but many of us think this artist has sometimes even greater skill, though no one can deny the wonder of Kovacs's work. Have you seen her museum in Szentendre?'

'No. I've only been in Hungary three days.'

'You should go.'

'I can't imagine anything could be better than these.' She looked longingly at the mother and child. The price was high. These were the most expensive items in the gallery. She could afford it, but it would be an extravagance. Also, it would be even more difficult to carry back on the plane than a painting. She peered at the signature scratched into the clay at the base of the figure. It looked like M Buvari.

Kate sighed. 'When we come back to Budapest before we leave, I shall have to see if I could manage to carry one home. It would be sacrilege to risk damaging it.'

'I am sure it would be packed very carefully for you.' He smiled again and gave a little formal bow before going back into the main gallery, leaving her alone with the figures.

త

The start of the journey on Friday was a nightmare. The hired car (a Peugeot, as Kate had specified) was delivered to the hotel, and apart from the left-hand drive looked familiar enough. They had studied the map of Budapest carefully the night before, and had worked out that their route lay over the Elizabeth Bridge, which was just downriver from their hotel, then along Hegyalja Út to Budaörsi Út, where Kate hoped she would be able to pick up signposts to Vienna, Lake Balaton and the M1.

Everything went well until they had crossed the Danube. In her eagerness to make an early start, Kate had not given sufficient thought to the morning rush-hour traffic. Despite rural driving years ago in France, she found herself in the wrong lane on the busy highway, and was carried away inexorably on to a sliproad which landed her in a commercial district of Buda thronged with cars. There was nowhere to stop and nowhere to turn.

Kate felt herself growing hotter and hotter, her hands slippery on the wheel. She crouched forward, trying to read the unpronounceable Hungarian street names, and being hooted at when she dithered at crossroads, uncertain which way to turn. Sofia sat trustingly beside her, with her eyes closed and her head back, apparently dozing after their early start. At last, however, Kate's tension must have communicated itself to her and she opened her eyes and looked around.

'I'm sorry,' said Kate, pushing her hair out of her eyes with one damp hand. 'I seem to have lost us. I have no idea where we are or which way we ought to be going, and I can't stop.'

Sofia became brisk.

'Look, pull in there.'

'It's a bus stop.'

'I know, but there isn't a bus nearby. I'll ask that woman who's waiting there.'

Kate pulled in, glancing around fearfully for traffic policemen, while Sofia conducted a brief conversation with the woman at the bus stop.

'Good,' said Sofia, sitting back in her seat. 'Can you pull out again into the road? Then you need to be ready to turn left. It is the third turn on the left, she says. Then we go about 500 metres to a main road with a traffic light. Turn right and that will take us straight on to the M1.'

The woman's directions were faultless, and in a few minutes they were moving rapidly along the M1 into the suburbs of Buda. There was another bad moment when the M7 led off to Balaton, but Kate managed to stay on the M1, following the signs which now promised Györ as well as Vienna. Budapest drifted away behind them, and they found themselves at last out in the countryside.

'It's very dry, isn't it?' said Kate, as dust swirled from the fields across the road. There were vast landscapes of sunflowers on either side of them, but the heads sagged wearily on their stems, and the petals looked bleached in the sun.

'Yes, I was speaking to a couple from Miskolc while you were signing the forms for the car. He is a wholesale dealer in farm products – is that how you would say it in English? The first few years after the end of communism have been good, but this year everyone is worried about the harvest. There has been so much hot sun and so little rain this year that the corn and the sunflowers are very poor, and unless there is rain soon the grapes will fail too.'

'That would be a great pity, when the country is trying so hard to survive financially. But even with the effects of the drought those fields are spectacular – like a great gold tapestry!'

The rest of the drive to Györ was easy. The M1 seemed to turn into the E75 and then the E60 without explanation, but caused them no problems. Near a place called Tatabánya Kate suddenly spotted another huge Turul bird high on a hill, looking down at them.

'Look!' she cried, taking one hand off the wheel to point.

'Ah, yes,' said Sofia contentedly. 'The Turul bird is leading us on still, and watching over us. Is he bringing us to our promised land? To our heart's desire?'

Kate glanced sideways at her. Sofia was looking at her quizzically. Kate turned back to the road. To her heart's desire?

After that they were quiet, Kate concentrating on her driving and the scenery, Sofia on something she was writing in a small notebook she had taken out of her bag. At last they found themselves in the outskirts of Györ. The man at hotel reception had helpfully drawn them a sketch map, showing the route from the motorway to their hotel in Györ. This time Kate did not get lost, as Sofia read out the directions from the map, but the traffic was heavy, with lorries rushing at top speed, clattering and banging over the poorly made road and hemming Kate in on all sides. It was with relief that she parked, shaking a little, in the area in front of the hotel reserved for guests.

The hotel was not prepossessing. It had a grim, institutional look, despite a new reception desk in highly varnished wood and some monstrous plants in pots dotted about the small entrance hall. It was much worse upstairs. The lifts could have come from a factory, and the dark, windowless hallways were so narrow that two people meeting had to shuffle past each other sideways. Their room was poky and airless, and felt as though the heat had been accumulating in it for the whole of the long, hot summer. Kate soon found out why. After struggling with the rusted catch on the dirty window, she managed to force it open on to a 'balcony' which looked as though it had been fashioned from a tin tray. She was hit by a blast of noise from the inner ring road below, where all the lorries which had been chasing her before had now congregated and were playing dodgems up and down the worst stretch of urban road in Hungary. The window let in a slight breeze, but the noise was intolerable.

'Oh dear,' said Sofia. 'I think this must be some left-over institution from the communist regime. Do you suppose the plumbing works?'

It did – although the water ran brown – and they were able to wash off the stickiness of their journey, but Kate was suspicious of the electric sockets, which sagged perilously from the crumbling plaster of the walls.

144

'Let's go out,' said Kate. 'I'm sure outdoors will be much better. Parts of Györ are supposed to be quite pretty. I didn't realise, somehow, that it would be such a big, noisy town.'

It did not take them long to find their way to the river, and the old town, where there were one or two streets of baroque houses. They dutifully visited the Cathedral and admired the amazing mediaeval gold reliquary in the chapel of St László. Even more remarkable than the beauty of the work, one of the world's greatest mediaeval treasures, was the fact that it had survived both German and Russian occupations and was still here in Györ. Kate opened her mouth to mention this to Sofia, but she seemed abstracted, and it came to Kate suddenly that they were now very much on Sofia's home ground. Györ had been the nearest town to her childhood village, and she had probably attended services in this very cathedral in her youth. When they came out again from the dim interior, still cloudy from the incense of a recent service, and stepped into the sun, Sofia emerged from her pensive mood.

'Come,' she said, as they started down the hill again, 'I am going to treat you to cakes in the best *káféház* in Györ. I noticed that it was still in business as we came from the hotel. I suspect the evening meal there will not be of the highest standard, so I suggest we fortify ourselves.'

On the way to the *káféház* they passed through the flower market. Kate remembered overhearing a kindly American woman on the boat to Margaret Island talking to her companion, who was Australian.

'This is such a poor country,' she had said, in tones of the deepest compassion.

The Australian had agreed, commenting that the clothes she had seen in the shops were made of shoddy materials. Kate had nearly turned round and taken issue with them, but on reflection held her tongue. She thought the Hungarians looked prosperous and happy, and seeing the people of Györ now, strolling about the flower market, strengthened her view. There were buckets full of gladioli and roses and Michaelmas daisies, there were pots of stephanotis and jasmine crowded together on the wooden stalls under gaily flowered awnings. They passed old women who had slipped out in apron and slippers to buy a bunch of flowers and chat to friends behind the stalls. A young man came towards them with an armload of red roses. Surely, thought Kate, a country cannot be poor, either materially or spiritually, where the people find the money to buy flowers for one another?

✍

István had driven down to Szentmargit early, leaving Budapest before seven. As his BMW bumped down the road to the village it was nearly lunchtime. In the fields on the left just before the village he was surprised to see a spray of water arching across the sky. As the curve of water paused at the highest point of the trajectory, the rays of sun were netted by the drops, turning them into diamonds flashing through every colour of the spectrum. Then it sank below the level of the bushes lining the road, only to rise again, slowly, majestically. The field was full of maize, and István noticed that it looked markedly plumper than the maize he had passed on the drive from Budapest. Suddenly he laughed. He remembered that Magdolna had written to him about Imre's latest invention. Well, at least it appeared to be bearing fruit, literally. The other men in the village sometimes thought Imre quite mad, but this success would have raised his stock considerably.

Just past the church the road widened out into a broad area of beaten earth surrounded by houses – the village square. On the south side, nearest the church, stood the Trinity column, like those in so many villages in the country raised by survivors of the plague. It was not as fine as the one in Sopron – perhaps the most beautiful in all Hungary – but for István it had the lovely familiarity of home.

In the centre of the square stood a huge walnut tree, whose broad branches provided welcome shade for the circular wooden bench built round its base, and for half a dozen tables which spilled out from the village *csárda*, the Blue Heron, during fine weather. Around the remaining sides of the square were grouped the few village shops and one or two private houses. István parked his car in front of the inn. As he opened the door, letting the outside air into the car's air-conditioned interior, the heat hit him as if he had walked into one of Budapest's thermal baths. Sweat sprang out on his face, and he wiped it away with his handkerchief, calling and nodding to friends seated at the tables, where they were resting from their work in the fields with a midday drink.

Inside the inn it was cooler. István bought a bottle of the best Tokay from Mihály behind the bar, and exchanged news. He always liked to bring József a bottle when he came on a visit, and he preferred to give his custom to the village rather than to an impersonal shop in Sopron or Budapest.

'I saw the new irrigation system as I drove in,' he said.

Mihály winked at him. 'Imre's done us proud this time. There's probably some regulation about taking water from the Danube without a permit, but nobody much bothers us down here. It's no bad thing to

146

be tucked away behind our woods and marshes. Too difficult for the interfering bureaucrats to bother with.'

Yes, thought István, as he started the car again to drive down the last bit of bumpy village street to Magdolna's house. That was probably why my father and his group operated successfully from here for so long. And he probably would never have been found, if he hadn't been betrayed by that bastard.

Until Ferenc Kalla had told him the story of his father's arrest, he had known nothing of the details. Juliska had managed to get word to Ferenc to lie low in Budapest, and afterwards he had remained there, acting as the agent for distributing *Freedom!* in the capital until 1956. Like Juliska he had been active in the uprising that year, but unlike her he had managed to escape arrest after the arrival of Soviet troops. No other members of the group had been arrested with István's father eight years earlier in 1948. Ferenc believed that Lancelot had probably been tortured by the Ávó for information, but must have held out against it, since no one else was seized. The original betrayer, Ferenc thought, had most likely intended to sell his information bit by bit, but had been prevented because of his swift execution by Juliska.

'You have to understand,' Ferenc had explained, seeing the younger man's distress, 'that your mother was only carrying out the regular practice of the partisan bands. Everyone knew that betrayal meant death. The fellow merely showed his arrogance, strolling about in public like that, when it was well known to many people that he was the traitor. Your father was deeply loved and honoured. Everyone expected the group to exact justice for his death.'

'Did my father die then? Soon after he was arrested? For years Magdolna and I hoped he might return from the gulags.'

'No, he survived long enough to be shipped off to Russia. We had spies in the government service who saw the papers. Didn't your mother ever talk to you about it?'

'She was always very secretive, my mother.'

He thought about it. As a child he had resented her secrecy, and as an adult had felt she had deprived the two of them of the usual intimacy between mother and children, but now he began to see that the secrecy had been a way of protecting them. Protecting them against questioning, and perhaps also protecting their innocence against the fearful world that surrounded them.

At the end of the road down from the village he stopped the car and sat studying the house thoughtfully. No one was about at the moment, and the house with its rosy walls slumbered like a contented cat on the river bank, encircled by its vegetable garden and fruit trees. It was hard to imagine a more peaceful scene. Yet it had known very different times.

છ

The night is very dark. Moonless. István has woken up and stares around the room. He can hear the soft breathing of his little sister in her cot. He listens. Then he hears again the noise that woke him – a dog barking up in the middle of the village. It barks frantically, angry and frightened. He knows which dog it is – Géza, the innkeeper's dog, who spends the night in the yard at the side of the inn, tied to a long rope attached to his kennel. Géza barks again, and then there is a sudden agonised yelp, as if someone has kicked him.

In the bedroom next door he hears his father get out of bed. Mama is away. Often one or both of his parents are away. It has always been like this, even more when they lived in the woods than now, when they live with Grandpa and Grandmama in the village. Papa is moving around, opening and shutting drawers and cupboards, getting dressed. It feels like the middle of the night. István climbs out of bed and pads in his bare feet over the cold bare boards and small rugs to the window. As he does so he can hear Grandpa's voice at the door of his parents' room, just a rumble, no words. He lifts the curtain and peeps out.

There is a heavy blanket of snow over everything. Even the edges of the Danube are frozen, and snow lies on top of the ice, so that it is difficult to tell where the garden ends and the river begins. The night is not quite as dark as he thought when the curtain was drawn. There is a thin crescent of new moon, casting a faint silvery light over the snow, and István makes a quick wish: Please may I get skates for Christmas? It is only two weeks till Christmas. Will God have time?

Papa comes in the door of the bedroom. He is fully dressed, with a greatcoat and boots, and his winter cap with the fur lining and the earflaps.

'Out of bed, István? Come, you'll get cold.' He folds back the feather bed invitingly and István climbs back into the cosy nest. Papa kisses him and then goes over to the cot and drops a kiss on the forehead of the sleeping Magdolna.

'Are you going away?' István whispers.

'Just for a little. Hush now, and go to sleep.'

But the moment his father is out of the room, István skips across to the window again. He expects to see his father emerge from the front door and then slip away to the left, skirting round the village to the fields, as he has done before when he has left in the night. But before the door opens a large black car glides round the corner from the village street and stops in front of the house. The snow muffles its arrival, so that it seems to appear silently and as if by magic. But the next moment a great wave of noise rises up and engulfs István. Four men jump out of the car, shouting. Two run round the back of the house, the other two start to pound on the door. All the dogs in the village begin to bark, and the donkey next door brays frantically. The light from the moon gleams on something in the men's hands. Revolvers, thinks István, who is familiar with guns, and he is suddenly sick and afraid.

The door opens and Papa steps out, quite calm and quiet, and speaks to the shouting men in a low voice. The men grab him and drag him away from the door. One of them strikes Papa on the side of the head and he falls to his knees in the snow. The other man pushes Papa over, kicks him, and then fumbles with his clothes. He waves Papa's gun in his face. The other two men have come back round the house and now they run in the front door, and István can hear feet thundering up the stairs. The door of his room is thrown open and one of the men comes in. He shrinks against the window, but the man ignores him, pulling his bed apart, tearing the clothes out of the cupboard.

Magdolna wakes up and begins to cry. The man turns and prods about in her cot. Grandmama is at the door now, in her dressing-gown and with her hair falling in a grey plait over her shoulder. Very quietly she says to the man: 'There is nothing here but the children, as you can see. Must you frighten them so?'

The man shrugs and does not speak, but he goes out. Grandmama looks across at István.

'Go back to bed now. I'll come back in a minute and see to the baby.'

She closes the door.

But István cannot move. Frozen in terror he looks out again at the scene below. The first two men are pushing Papa into the car. There is something dark running down his face, as he raises it briefly towards the window where István is watching. Then all of the men climb into the car, and it drives away.

Gradually, the village dogs stop barking.

৵

Sitting now in his car on the place where the black car parked that night, István found he was gripping the wheel until his knuckles showed white. His teeth were clenched together, and he was shivering, despite the heat of the day. He forced himself to relax.

But the thought came to him, as it always did these days: If his father had not stopped to kiss his children goodbye, would he have had time to escape?

'Uncle István,' called András, coming across from the brook with his fishing rod over his shoulder, 'why are you sitting there in your car? Mama's in her studio, but we'll call her in half an hour for lunch. I'm starving, aren't you?'

๛

The village inn at Szentmargit looked charming, Kate thought. It was painted a soft lime green, against which the wisteria, trained around the windows and over a trellis, made darker patterns of leaf and shadow. There were window-boxes overflowing with pink geraniums, and a scatter of tables in front under a walnut tree where some men were drinking beer – farmers, by the look of them, in faded dungarees and dusty work boots. The square was no more than flattened earth, but the village looked well kept and the men smiled and nodded affably as they climbed out of the car.

'This certainly seems better than that grim institution in Győr,' said Kate. 'I kept expecting a female warder to come round with a bunch of clanking keys at her waist to lock us up if we didn't conform.'

Sofia looked about her in satisfaction. 'The Blue Heron was always a decent clean place, but it seems much improved. It never used to be so pretty. I was a little doubtful when we telephoned for the rooms, but I think I need not have worried.' She laughed suddenly. 'Look.'

She pointed to a curious platform fixed to the roof of the inn, which was covered with what appeared to be a pile of sticks.

'What's that?' asked Kate, puzzled. Then she had her answer. A large heron came lazily flapping from the direction of the marshes they had passed a little way back to the east. A frog dangled from its mouth, and it landed with awkward grace on the platform, like a film in slow motion.

'There are many herons and storks here in the Szigetköz, because of the marshes,' said Sofia. 'The herons have nested on the inn for years. For centuries, if you believe village tradition. As long as they remain, the superstition goes, the village will be safe.'

Kate wondered whether this had proved true over recent years, and speculated about what they would discover in this place. Sofia was bright-eyed and excited, and for the last miles, since they had turned off the main road, had been pointing out landmarks like an eager child. It was good to see her so happy. Kate hoped, whatever they might find here, that she would not be hurt.

As if Sofia could read her thoughts, she said, 'It was right to come.'

They walked towards the door of the inn.

'I needed to confront the past in order to be at peace with the present, and with whatever future I have left. Good or bad, it will put my mind at rest to know. Not to be any longer in the cloud of ignorance.'

The Blue Heron proved to be as pleasant inside as out. It was very old. The door lintels were low and the rooms a little bowed, but it was spotless. They each had a separate room. Kate insisted Sofia should have what was clearly the best room in the inn, on the first floor, whose wide wooden bed had elaborate carved head and foot boards. Her own room was one floor higher, a sloping attic room with beams she would need to dodge and a sagging brass bedstead piled with feather beds to compensate for the dip in the springs. The windows were smaller than Sofia's large one overlooking the square, but there were two of them, one on to the square, where she could see the onion dome of the church rising beyond the walnut tree, and one at the far end of the long narrow room, which looked across village rooftops to a rose-red house beside the river. Beyond it she saw a cluster of islands riding on the sparkling waters of the Danube, and beyond the islands she could just make out the top of a large ship moving along the deeper water of the shipping lane.

Her heart leapt up. It was a perfect room. A room to be alone in, but contented. The light flooded in from the south-facing window over the square, while the other end of the room, with its wider view, was cool and shadowed. The floor was of wide old oak boards, glowing with years of waxing. There was a small rag rug beside the bed, and another in front of the basin. The rugs had faded to a soft pink and green. The bedlinen, blindingly white where the sun fell across it, was hand-embroidered and inset with lace. An old carved cupboard was wedged in under the uneven ceiling. Kate ran her fingers over the carving, which depicted apples and pears twined about with leaves and blossom. The cupboard stood at the shadowy end of the room, but her exploring fingers found, down in the far corner of one door panel, a harvest mouse with cupped ears alert and tail coiled around a clump of wild flowers.

151

I love this, Kate thought exultantly, I love it. In Budapest Hungary had already begun to weave a spell for her, but here, in this crooked room up under the eaves she knew that something important was happening her. She was filled with expectancy, like a child on the eve of a party. Dunmouth, her family, the troubled undertow to her life that had seemed always to be tugging at her there, had all fallen away. The very air of this place was exhilarating. The heat which, in the city, had been almost too much for her, was lifted here by the breeze coming off the river and stirring the curtains as she stood looking out of the far window. She could see a boy with a fishing rod, and a man in a dark city suit, and a small woman who came out of a door and hugged the man. Then they disappeared from her view, hidden by the house. There was a soft tap at her door.

'Kate?' called Sofia. 'Are you ready for lunch?'

Kate ran across the room and opened the door.

'Sorry to be so long, but isn't this lovely? Oh, Sofia, what a wonderful place.'

And she threw her arms around Sofia and hugged her.

The next morning they decided to visit Sofia's old home. They had spent a quiet time the day before, partly resting – during the heat of the afternoon – and partly sitting at one of the tables outside the Blue Heron sipping wine and watching village life going on around them, while the village – covertly and politely – inspected them. They were the only guests at the inn. It served mainly as the village bar and café and only had occasional visitors – officials from the agriculture ministry or the waterway inspection board. Few outsiders came to Szentmargit, so Kate and Sofia were naturally an object of some curiosity.

The square was the centre of village life. Women coming to the shops stopped and gossiped, children rode their bicycles round and round its perimeter, and at regular intervals – at lunchtime, in the evening – the men would gather there to drink and exchange views on the state of the crops and the weather.

After breakfast Sofia checked that the manor would be on view that morning and was assured that it would be, every day, at least until the end of September.

'After that,' said Mihály, the innkeeper, speaking in German for Kate's benefit, 'no doubt they will decide.'

'Decide what?'

'Whether to continue to open. This is the first season, and not many people have come. We are away from the regular tourist routes here, you understand? Unless some of the tour companies put the manor house on their itineraries, the authorities may decide it isn't worth spending the money to staff it and keep it repaired. It's not like the Esterházy palace at Fertöd, where people will come because of the associations with Haydn.'

'What will become of the house if they close it again?' asked Sofia.

Mihály shrugged. 'Who knows? I do not think they would pull it down. But there isn't much money in the country for old buildings. What there is will go to the famous ones, the ones in Budapest.' There was a note of scorn in his voice, the scorn of the provincial for the pretensions of the capital. 'But if they do not keep the manor sound, it will eventually fall down.'

'That would be a pity,' said Kate, looking up from her camera, in which she had been fitting a new film. 'Surely visitors to the house would bring money and employment to the village?'

'I would not mind more business at the Blue Heron.' Mihály laughed as he put away the glasses he had been polishing. 'But I wouldn't like to see Szentmargit overrun with coaches and tourists.'

Kate thought of the tourists who flocked to the châteaux of the Loire, and the surrounding souvenir kiosks, litter and noise. 'Oh no!' she agreed fervently. 'That would spoil it altogether.'

'You have come to see the house?' asked Mihály politely. Clearly he was very curious about them.

'Partly,' said Kate, as Sofia did not answer. 'Partly just to have a peaceful holiday.'

Mihály seemed reassured.

'Fresh trout for dinner tonight. My wife will cook it for you, Hungarian style.'

'With paprika?' asked Kate, teasing.

'Of course!'

They set off on the walk up the hill past the church to the gates of the manor. Sofia was quiet and Kate did not disturb her thoughts. She took a few photographs of the village from the rising road, and one of the lovely, neglected gates to the manor. Sofia made a slight sound of protest at their rusty state and Kate touched her arm.

'Are you sure you want to see it? It may be very sad.'

'Yes, of course,' said Sofia firmly. 'But that does not mean that I have to be pleased about everything I see.'

The house was painted the yellow-ochre Kate had learned was called 'Esterházy yellow' because of that family's fondness for decorating their great houses in the colour. As they drew nearer they could see that the outer fabric of the building was crumbling.

'I don't believe it can have been painted since we left,' said Sofia, looking at a peeling patch to the right of the front door.

'You and your mother left in 1938, didn't you? What about your father?'

'I don't know. We received two letters from him via an exiles' network in London during 1939. At that time he was still living here. After that, nothing. We sent letters to him, of course, but I don't believe he ever received them. The letters we did have from him gave no indication he had heard from us. He was still asking if we had arrived safely.'

'But surely then, before the war, your letters should have reached him?'

'It couldn't be counted on. The Horthy regime was always oppressive and grew worse when the "Regent", as he called himself, tried to appease Hitler. They would have regarded my father as a known subversive. I expect all letters to him were confiscated and scrutinised.'

'That's horrible,' said Kate. She felt a moment of chill, then shook herself.

'Is this where we pay? It seems to be 100 forints.'

She paid for both of them and they joined one Hungarian and three Austrians who were waiting for the next guided tour. The Hungarian, it appeared, was a schoolteacher from Győr who was planning to bring a school party to visit the house during the autumn term.

'This was once a fine house,' she explained to Sofia. 'The family who lived here, the Niklais, were a very ancient family of this region. They distinguished themselves in the heroic siege of Szigetvár which halted the Turkish advance in 1564. The infidels won the battle, but they lost 25,000 men to our 2,500, and that was the start of their long decline. And in the rising of 1848 the Niklais led the demand in this area for independence from Austria. The very last count, Count Zsigmond Niklai, joined the resistance during the war. That was when the Nazis took over the building. And of course they stripped it of all its treasures.'

Kate, sitting on a low bench and tying the compulsory grey felt slippers over her shoes, thought that Sofia had very quickly learned the

154

answers to some of her questions about her father, but she seemed reluctant to talk to the teacher. Kate looked up.

'What became of Count Zsigmond,' she asked. 'Did he die in the war?'

The teacher glanced at her in surprise, as if she had just noticed her for the first time.

'I'm afraid I have no idea, but perhaps the guide will tell us.'

The guide was a cheerful, plump girl about Beccy's age, probably a student doing a holiday job. She led them, shuffling in their clumsy slippers, from the imposing entrance hall to the even more imposing grand drawing room. She began to rattle off facts and figures – dates, the dimensions of the room, the number of rooms in the house.

'We never counted them,' Sofia muttered.

The guide explained how all the furniture, tapestries, paintings, silver, china and other treasures had been looted by the Germans.

'We have now just a few pieces. You will see a dining table and chairs of the appropriate period in the dining room.'

'Couldn't you demand them back?' asked Kate.

'Excuse me?'

'The treasures that were looted by the Germans. Why don't you demand them back?'

The girl looked nervous. 'It is very long ago, you understand. Fifty years. The Germans are the friends of Hungary now...'

Ah, thought Kate, I see.

'We are now entering the private salon of the Countess,' the girl gabbled on, hurrying them ahead, so that one of the Austrians stumbled over his awkward felt slippers.

'Here we have put some photographs of the Niklai family. This is Count Ferenc Niklai in a photograph taken about 1900. Notice his formidable whiskers!' The visitors laughed politely. 'And here is the last family to live here, Count Zsigmond, his wife Eva Tabor, the famous violinist, and their little girl.'

Kate craned forward to look at the family seated on a garden bench under a flowering tree of some sort. Sofia, aged about fourteen, sat between her parents with a puppy on her lap. Kate looked around and saw that Sofia had retreated to the window and was staring out at the garden. She had turned rather white. Perhaps it would have been better not to come. Or at least to have waited for a few days, until she had grown accustomed to being back here near her old home.

To divert attention from the photographs of the Niklai family, Kate asked, 'What are those huge, ornate cylinders in the corner of each room?'

The Austrians and the schoolteacher looked amused, but the girl smiled patiently. She was used to the ignorance of the British and Americans.

'These are the wood-burning stoves. There is one in every room, some made of cast iron – mostly the ones in the main rooms downstairs. Upstairs, in the bedrooms, they are a little smaller, and many are made of ceramic.'

Kate laid her hand on the cool side of the great cream-coloured pillar, which rose above her head to a height of about ten feet. It was deeply moulded in a pattern of fruit and flowers similar to the carved cupboard in her bedroom at the inn, and in places it still bore traces of gilding where the pattern had once been picked out. At the top it narrowed to what she supposed was a disguised chimney, which disappeared through the ceiling.

'But I don't understand. There's no opening. How could you light a fire in it?'

The guide tapped the wall beside the stove. It echoed hollowly.

'Most stoves in ordinary homes, of course, they have a door for the fire. Behind the wall here there is a door, but it is concealed from the sight of the rooms. The stoves were stoked and cleaned from behind.'

Kate looked along the wall. 'But there is no door.'

'Not here, no. Not into the family part of the house. Behind all the walls there is a network of little corridors and stairs, so the servants could carry in the fuel and attend to the stoves without disturbing the family. Come, now we go upstairs to the bedrooms, then down again to view the library and ballroom.'

As the others, including Sofia, moved away, Kate lingered with her hand still on the stove, thinking of the servants scurrying about behind the walls like a secret army of mice. If a servant lad was careless and dropped a bucket of ashes, would he have been heard in here? And could the servants overhear what was going on in these rooms as they made their way all over the house, just on the other side of the wall? The thought of those interdependent yet separate lives going on was curiously unsettling.

They were taken through four of the bedrooms upstairs. In the last one Sofia walked over to the window and stood gazing out as the guide explained that this room had once been lined with French tapestries which had depicted events from Greek mythology. Kate joined Sofia at the window.

'Was this your room?' she asked softly.

Sofia nodded.

'Look,' she said. 'You can just catch a glimpse of the village and the river there, where the ground dips and there is a gap in the trees. You can see more in winter, after the leaves have fallen. I used to stand here and wonder what it would be like to play with the children in the village. My parents were quite liberal for their time, I suppose, but they would never have dreamt of allowing me to associate with the children down there. Sometimes I would watch them playing ball or running about together. You can see a corner of the village square in winter. About the only time I mixed with them was when the Danube froze, and my parents and I would go skating, along with half the village, when work was finished.'

'Were you a very lonely child?'

'Yes, I must have been, I realise now. At the time I never questioned it. I knew all the village people by name, of course. Many of them worked for my father, and I would go with my nurse or my mother to buy things in the village. There used to be a wonderful pastry shop kept by a Turkish family. Visits there were always a treat. I'm sad to see that has vanished.' She gave a little rueful smile. 'I was a great reader as a child, and I always had a dog. I would go exploring in the woods sometimes.'

'Was that your dog in the picture?'

Sofia turned away.

'Yes. That was Bárat. I had to leave him behind when we left in 1938. He knew something was wrong. He followed us down to the river and when we climbed into the rowing boat he tried to follow. My father ordered him home, but he sat on the shore and howled as we rowed away, out to the ship in the main channel. My father was afraid he would give us away. I never knew what became of him.'

Kate touched her hand lightly, but the guide was urging them back downstairs to admire the library (empty, although the bookshelves were still intact) and the ballroom, the one room in the house to have been restored to its former glory. There was a magnificent painted ceiling of voluptuous nymphs riding on dolphins. The walls had been repainted in their original colours of cream and duck-egg blue, with all the riotous mouldings, the cornices and the plasterwork around the windows re-gilded.

'I never liked this room,' said Sofia with distaste. 'I hated those fat women, as I called them. I suppose they embarrassed me, baring their breasts like that. I was a modest child.'

After they had shed their felt slippers and come out again into the sunshine, Sofia said she would not walk around the grounds. She preferred to go back to the hotel and sit quietly until lunchtime, but she urged Kate to stay and explore the garden, which was gradually being restored, and the woods, which always used to be full of pretty walks. Kate agreed. Sofia might want some time to herself to come to terms with seeing the forlorn shell of her home.

'The summerhouse you admired in the photograph is down in that direction,' said Sofia. She indicated the dip in the ground which Kate recognised from the view out of the bedroom.

Kate set off in the opposite direction from the Austrian family and the schoolteacher, who were talking animatedly as they went towards a formal garden where small box hedges had been replanted but not yet trimmed to shape. Following an overgrown path heading the way Sofia had pointed, Kate found herself under the welcome shade of the mixed woods which at one time would have been carefully managed, the undergrowth kept down and dead trees cleared away. Now it was wilder, but not totally neglected, and after ten minutes' walking she found herself at the edge of the clearing she recognised from the photograph. Ahead of her was the summerhouse, a little shabby, some of its railings broken, but still lovely. The metal dragon sat slightly askew on the peak of the roof, and his tail spiralled in an elegant curve towards the sky.

She had a strange feeling, as though she was stepping into the photograph which had so attracted her. The printed image seemed to melt into the scene before her, and she crossed the grassy clearing dreamily, scarcely hearing the birds around her in the trees, or the sound of her skirt brushing the long grass. Finding herself in this place, she felt the barrier between image and reality dissolve. The illusion, the sense of déjà vu, swept over her as she saw the man from the photograph come out of the summerhouse and hesitate on the steps with one hand on the ornate railing. Then she shook her head, amused at her fanciful thoughts. The man was familiar, but he was not Zsigmond Niklai. He was the man she had met in the gallery in Budapest.

Chapter 9

István shaded his eyes against the sun. He could see the outline of a woman's figure at the edge of the clearing, but whether she was old or young, known or strange, he could not tell. She was a black silhouette, rimmed about with the dazzling midday summer sun. She stepped forward and addressed him hesitantly in German.

'How strange, but I think we have met before.'

She came to the bottom of the steps, tilting her head a little to look up at him. He could make her out more clearly now that he was no longer looking directly into the sun, but his vision still swam with stars and explosions of light.

'You are the gallery owner, aren't you? From Váci Utca?'

She looked suddenly embarrassed, put out by his continued silence. She was a few years younger than he, slim, brown-haired. Pleasant-looking, with intelligent eyes and lines of worry about her eyebrows. He stared at her nonplussed. What was she talking about? A gallery owner? Then he remembered. He had spoken to a woman in the gallery in Budapest a couple of days ago. He had taken no particular notice of what she looked like. What had struck him was her total absorption in Magdolna's work. He recognised her now. He had addressed her in English because her clothes had that indefinable English air – well cut but understated, not as elegant as French clothes nor as outrageous as the multicoloured outfits the Americans were wearing this year. Her German was good, very good, but there was a lightness in the guttural sounds that told him she was indeed English.

'Forgive me!' He jumped down the last few steps to the ground. 'You took me by surprise. We did indeed meet in the gallery, but I am not the owner. I was just a visitor like yourself.'

He did not choose to tell her he was the brother of the artist whose work she had been admiring. When he was in Budapest he always visited the gallery, to check that Magdolna's work was being displayed properly, and to grind his teeth a little at the high prices the gallery was charging, compared with the little they paid her.

What was this woman doing here? The gallery was strictly forbidden to give out Magdolna's address. She shrank from publicity and the whole family closed ranks protectively around her. How had this woman found her out? But the next moment he thought that perhaps he had done her an injustice.

'I'm still hoping to go back and buy one of those figures before we leave. Aren't they wonderful? I've never seen anything like them before, even when we lived in London and we had all the galleries there to visit.'

She smiled without guile.

'What a coincidence, meeting you again! I've fallen in love with your beautiful village. My friend and I are planning to spend some time here. You do live here, don't you?'

'I grew up here,' he said, switching to English. 'But now I have a practice in Sopron. I am a family doctor there. István Rudnay.' He held out his hand.

'Kate Milburn.' She took his hand in a firm grasp. 'Are you here on holiday too?'

'Yes, I always stay with my sister and her family for a month in the summer.'

Kate glanced at her watch.

'I must be getting back. My friend will be waiting at the inn for lunch. It was nice meeting you again.' She turned to head towards the main gate of the manor house.

'The pleasure is mine. But if you are going back to the village you don't need to follow the road. It's in very bad condition, uncomfortable for walking. If you will allow me, I can show you a path down through the woods behind the summerhouse. It is much quicker and very pleasant under the trees.'

Kate hesitated only for a moment. Then she smiled and turned with him into the wood. He held back some low-growing branches at the far end of the clearing and beyond them a fairly well-defined path led between great, widely spaced oaks and some younger trees, silver birches and rowans, which had insinuated themselves between the older ones.

'I thought the house and grounds had been deserted for years and were only just starting to be renovated,' said Kate, 'but this path seems well used.'

'People from the village sometimes use it as a short-cut between the fields near the village and the other land beyond the manor gardens, over there.' He pointed back in the direction from which they had come.

160

'Does all the land belong to the people in the village now?'

'Yes, except for the gardens immediately around the house. The last count gave much of his land to the villagers between the wars. Then the communist regime forced them to hand it over to the local collective farm. Now we've got it back again.' He laughed. 'I think even the politicians have come to understand that a man farms best the soil he owns himself. My brother-in-law is a farmer. These fields just ahead of us belong to him and his brother.'

They came out of the edge of the woods beside a field of maize. Over to the left was another of sunflowers, and further away, wheat.

'Goodness, they have an irrigation system,' said Kate. 'I kept thinking, all the way from Budapest, how dry and parched the fields looked. But these are in much better heart.'

'It has been a terrible summer. Good for the tourists, perhaps, but hardly a drop of rain for the farmers. The irrigation system is really a sort of giant lawn-sprinkler that József's brother has rigged up, but it does seem to be making a difference.'

They dodged, laughing, through the drops from the sprinkler and rejoined the road just in front of the church.

'I know where I am now,' said Kate. 'Thank you for showing me the way.'

'It was a pleasure. Perhaps we will meet again while you are staying in Szentmargit.' He bowed briefly, smiled, and walked briskly away through the village.

๛

Sofia had recovered her composure.

'The house was not so very different from what I had pictured to myself,' she said to Kate as they sat over the last of their lunch under the walnut tree in the village square. 'Seeing the photographs upset me for a moment. Until then, you know, I could quite put myself at a distance from it, as if the house had nothing to do with me. Then the photograph of us all... And to see Bárat again. Foolish, isn't it? How you give your heart to animals, when you know it must be broken? That picture would have been taken in 1934 – when he was a puppy. I suppose my parents already knew that dangerous things were happening in Germany, but for me life was going on just as it always had. I was away at boarding-school in Switzerland by then, of course. Quite happy, on the whole, but I only really felt alive when I came home to Hungary.'

161

She broke off, sipping her coffee. 'How fortunate it is that we can't see into the future.'

She poured them each a second cup and sat stirring it thoughtfully.

'I had a curious experience after I left you,' said Kate. 'Do you remember the picture you had, of your father on the steps of the summer-house?'

'Yes. You were very interested in it.'

'I don't know why. Something about the delicate structure with the dark trees behind, and your father...' She could not say what had so moved her about that picture of Zsigmond Niklai.

'I went looking for the summer-house where you said, and I found it.'

'It is still standing?'

'Oh, yes.' Kate was puzzled by this. 'I think someone must have been looking after it. You would expect a building that is mainly wood to have fallen down by now, wouldn't you? Anyway, as I came out from under the trees into the sunlight of the clearing, there was a man coming down the steps of the summer-house, and for a moment I felt I had stepped into that photograph. He looked so like your father. The next minute I realised that I had met him before, in the gallery with the ceramics I told you about.'

'Strange you should meet him here.'

'Isn't it? It appears he's a doctor from Sopron, and he's spending his summer holiday with his sister, who lives in the village. He said he grew up here himself. He showed me a way back to the village through the woods from the summer-house.'

Sofia smiled. 'Ah yes, I remember that path.'

Suddenly Kate recalled the little scene she had witnessed from her bedroom window yesterday – the boy, the man in the city suit, and the woman throwing her arms around him. She had thought they were husband and wife, but now she realised that it must have been Dr Rudnay and his sister, who was married to a farmer in the village. When they had met this morning he was wearing jeans and a white T-shirt, and she had not connected him with the man in the suit, who looked so out of place in Szentmargit.

When the worst of the midday heat was over, István agreed to go fishing with András. Their favourite stream ran down from the gardens of the Niklai manor house – where it formed the central feature of the water garden – and wandered between the fields until it joined the Danube a little way upriver from the Buvaris' house. Willows grew along its banks, ancient pollarded trees which had provided the villagers with withies for centuries. There were several deep pools under the trailing branches where, with a bit of luck, trout might be taken.

The canopy of leaves provided welcome shade from the heat of the sun, which was still uncomfortable, even though it was now declining in the afternoon sky. They had brought three-legged stools with them from the house, and made themselves comfortable under a large willow, with sandwiches and drinks to hand – fizzy lemonade for András and beer for István. They debated wedging the bottles in the water to keep cool, but the stream was warm on their dipping fingers, running sluggishly under the sun. They laid out their lines.

András was a good companion for a fishing trip, thought István. He had a great capacity for stillness, and would sit by the hour dreamily watching the float bobbing and the movement of the stream through the rushes along the shore. A moorhen had its nest opposite them, and was busy taking its chicks on their first swimming expeditions, never more than a metre or two from the nest up stream or down and then back again. How mysterious children are, he thought. One minute so adult, the next reverting to babyhood. Playing football with his friends András was as noisy and boisterous as any of them, but now, sitting quietly beside his uncle, he was as silent and absorbed as a grown man.

His own son László had been a mystery to him. István, struggling when László was young to be both father and mother to him, had thought they were as close as a father and son could well be. Despite the fact that he was also trying to build up his practice in Sopron, he spent every available minute with László. Always, at the back of his mind, was his own sense of loss, his feeling that without a father he himself had been somehow incomplete, diminished. Yet he could never remember having with László the easy companionship he knew with András. Perhaps with László he had tried too hard, while with András he had never felt the need to try, so that their friendship, more important even than kinship, had grown and strengthened naturally.

As he had reached adolescence, László withdrew more and more into himself, actively cutting himself off from his father. Did I smother him? István wondered. Did I somehow drive him away through loving and needing him too much? Because I did need him, do need him. More, it seems, than he ever needed me.

A sharp sighed escaped him involuntarily, András looked across at him.

'Are you tired, Uncle István? Do you want to go home?'

'No, no, not at all. I was just thinking.'

'About work?' András knew that this often made his mother distracted, and his uncle was like his mother in many ways.

'Something like that. Do you want to stay by this pool, or do you want to try that smaller one, further up above the alders?'

'Let's stay here. I've seen one whopper down there by that rock.' András pointed. 'He just doesn't seem hungry.'

'We'll have to be patient, then.'

They lapsed back into silence.

István was still puzzled by the two women staying at the Blue Heron. Visitors to the village were rare. What had brought them here? On their walk down through the woods to the village, Kate Milburn had made no further reference to Magdolna or her work. If she was here in search of the artist, surely she would have tried to find out more from him?

Then there was her companion – a tall, gaunt woman, reserved and dignified. He was sure he had never met her before, yet something in her face and gestures was familiar. He must be going crazy – he was imagining connections everywhere he turned. Ever since Magdolna had found that box of papers he hadn't been himself.

He had looked in at the Blue Heron after lunch, ostensibly for a glass of beer, but really to pump Mihály for information about the women.

'They're English, I think,' said the innkeeper, 'though they both speak fluent German and the older one speaks Hungarian.'

'That's unusual, surely?'

'True enough. The younger one is called Mrs Milburn. She paid the deposit and seems to make all the arrangements.

'What's the older one called?' István asked casually.

'Couldn't say. I think I heard the other one call her Sophy or Sofia.'

'But don't you have to check their passports when they book in?'

'Oh well,' Mihály shrugged and laughed. 'They don't look like drug smugglers, nor is this the Budapest Hilton. Mrs Milburn got out two British passports to show me, but I didn't bother to examine them. This is a free country now, István, in case you've forgotten!'

So István was no further forward. He thought he might try speaking to them at the inn, perhaps even invite them to have a drink at the house, if Magdolna and József agreed.

164

'Wow!' said András. 'I think I've got a bite!'

⍦

Kate and Sofia spent the next morning taking a walk round the village, investigating the three shops, and then wandering along some of the paths through the manor woodland. They came back, rather late and hot, to lunch under the tree in the square again. As they sat down, Kate noticed Dr Rudnay sitting at another table with three of the local farmers. He raised his hand in greeting and she smiled back.

'That's the man I met by the summer-house,' she said in a low voice to Sofia. 'The doctor from Sopron.'

Sofia looked at him discreetly over the menu.

'I see what you mean. He is much the same build and colouring as my father. No wonder you were startled, coming upon him like that.'

'Yes,' said Kate thoughtfully, and opened her mouth to say more, but thought better of it.

Because of the oppressive mid-day heat, they fell into a pattern of retiring to their rooms after lunch and resting a little where it was cool, to emerge later in the afternoon refreshed and ready for the rest of the day. At first Kate had urged this because she was afraid of tiring Sofia, but now she looked forward to the hour or two each afternoon which gave her an opportunity to be alone. She had begun to keep a journal, recording her impressions of Hungary in a hard-backed notebook with a cover patterned with vines and grapes, which she had purchased on that last day in Budapest, in Váci Utca. As she lay on her bed each afternoon she brought it up to date.

Today, their third in the village, after dutifully recording a description of their morning's walk, she paused with her pen in her hand and gazed out of the north-facing window of her room, towards the rose-coloured cottage and the Danube. Ever since she had made the decision to come to Hungary with Sofia she felt as though something within her had begun to change. It had accelerated as they arrived in Budapest, and now that they were settled in Szentmargit she found she was looking forward to each new moment with eagerness.

It is a curious thing, she wrote, *but I cannot remember the shape and layout of the rooms in Craigfast House. I close my eyes and try with my reasoned, conscious mind to imagine myself getting out of bed and walking to the window, but instead two other pictures insistently present themselves. Either I find myself in my childhood bedroom in Castle Terrace, looking out at the place where the Dun flows into the*

165

sea, or else I find myself visualising this room, which I have only known for a few short days.

Even stranger, the bedroom in London, where I rose and retired for twenty years, where my three children were conceived, is now a total blank. The most anxious and careful attempt to call up its image fails totally. My memory has become a baffling cup-shaped curve: the earlier and most recent times clear, the part in the middle dipping down into darkness. The memory plays curious tricks. Until the last few months, it was my childhood which was the book with blank pages.

She paused and looked up. The village seemed sunk in an afternoon siesta. Even the farmers were waiting before returning to the fields. There was no rumbling of tractors up the village street, or whirring of the ancient, Russian-built combine from the field away over to the right, where they had begun to harvest the wheat. She could see a goat tethered behind someone's house, nosing amongst parched grass to snatch a few mouthfuls. At the end of the garden of the Blue Heron, a lean black cat leapt on to the low wall. It walked delicately along the narrow top, picking its way over the crumbling brick, and then sprang to the roof of the pigsty in the adjacent garden. Here it stretched out in the sun, flat and motionless as child's toy. Above her head she could hear the rustling of the young birds in the heron's nest, which was immediately over her room. Every time a parent bird returned with food the rustling became more frantic, mingled with the cries of the nestlings demanding food. As the great bird landed, Kate could feel a distinct thump, and the supports of the nest-platform creaked.

Apart from the animals and birds, the village was asleep.

I love this place, she wrote. *I love the light. I love the houses with their steep roofs and their wonderful colours – lime and ochre, cinnamon and sage, wine and lemon. I love the semicircular windows in the roofs which peep out under their heavy lids of rush-thatch or wooden shingles. I love the old, counter-weighted well in the village square.*

Every house in the village has water on tap, but yesterday I saw a young man come in from the fields and strip off his shirt in the square. He was covered with little bits of chaff and straw – in his black hair, on his golden back, on his blue jeans. He dipped up a bucket of water from the well and poured it over his head. The water streamed down over him, till his hair hung down like a waterfall and his jeans were patched with wet. Two girls, going home with bread in baskets over their arms, paused and shouted something teasing at him, but he just laughed and flung back his head so that his hair spun an arc of water out across the dust of the square and spattered them where they stood.

I love the pace of life. Everyone here works hard, from early in the morning until well into the evening, yet no one seems rushed. Friends stop when they meet in the street, to talk and laugh. Women lean over the fence and chat with their neighbours. The children play for hours with simple things – a ball, a new kitten, their bicycles, or a wonderful contraption some of the boys have been making out of four ill-assorted wheels, some old beer crates begged from Mihály, and what appears to be a sort of sail, cut from someone's old sheet.

I love the chickens. They are very big and grand – copper-coloured, fat, and full of conceit. They live in special houses, little thatched cottages of their own which stand on legs in back gardens. This, I suppose, is to keep the rats away, like staddle stones on old barns. Each morning the chickens descend from these houses with mincing gravity, down sloping gangplanks. After a day spent scratching about the village, getting in the way of tractors and motorbikes, and sometimes pecking the legs of unwary children, they are summoned home in the evening by name, and ascend once again to their houses for the night.

I love the people. They are friendly, yet dignified, with a kind of old-fashioned courtesy we seem to have forgotten in England. And when you remember what the older ones have lived through, you wonder how they have managed to emerge unscathed by bitterness. Yet they do not seem bitter.

I love it here. I can't imagine ever going back to the greyness that was Dunmouth and my life before I came.

I love it here.

Kate put down her notebook and pen on the bedside table and lay back against the pillows. She closed her eyes and smiled. *I love it here.* She stretched hugely, every limb taut and then loosening, sinking down. Falling asleep.

෴

Kate came down in the mid-afternoon sunshine, bursting with energy. She felt light and free, as though weights had been removed from her limbs. She found Sofia talking to Dr Rudnay.

'Ah, Kate, my dear, Dr Rudnay has just very kindly invited us to join him and his sister for a cool drink and a cake at her house by the river. I said that I was sure we had nothing planned.'

'That would be lovely,' said Kate. 'We haven't been right down to the river yet, and we'd love to meet your sister. And your brother-in-law – I think you said he was a farmer?'

'Yes. József will probably join us later. He and Imre have been moving the sprinkler system to a new position, and that always takes quite a lot of time. The joints in the hose are not very secure, so when it is moved they leak, and everything must be carefully adjusted again.'

'When would you like us to come, Dr Rudnay?'

'Why don't you walk down with me now? And I would be honoured if you would call me István, Mrs...er?'

'Kate, please.'

'And I am afraid I did not catch your name...' he turned to Sofia.

'Sofia,' she said, extending her hand, 'will do very well.'

Kate, who knew that Sofia was not keen to reveal her surname too soon here in Szentmargit, smiled to herself.

They walked together, the three of them, down the slope from the higher part of the village, where the church, the inn and the square stood, along a dusty roadway of beaten earth between a double row of cottages, towards the half-dozen which stood beside the river itself. Kate was not surprised to see that they were heading for the rosy red cottage. To the left of it was a large barn, backing on a field of sunflowers, to the right another cottage, much smaller, painted a faded lemon colour. István's sister's house had a neat white picket fence separating it from the street, behind and through which grew enormous red poppies, spilling their petals into the dust and lifting new buds jauntily above the low fence posts. There were rows and rows of well-tended vegetables, some fruit trees, and a few flowers. It was clear that the gardener made use of almost every corner to grow practical crops, but could not resist the beauty of flowers in pots and window-boxes.

There was a balcony running around the upper floor of the house, on to which the bedroom windows opened. This was painted white and was festooned with what Kate thought, at a distance, were red streamers. As they drew nearer, however, she saw that these were strings of dozens and dozens of paprika peppers, hung up to dry in the sun, like red ribbons on a white dress. Later they would be stored for the winter's cooking.

They walked round the corner of the house and found a small area of lawn, thin and parched with the heat. A dozen bronze chickens were scratching under an apple tree, near a thatched hen coop, and the end of the garden sloped down to the river, where a small blue rowing boat was tied up to a wooden landing stage. The house door stood open and was protected from insects by a curtain of paper lace streamers, like the one they had seen in the Sterns' shop in Budapest. To the right of the door, a wooden trellis supporting a grape vine made an arbour around a window, with a bench against the wall of the house, and a table and chairs arranged in front of it.

'What a lovely house!' Kate exclaimed. 'It's so pretty – and with the view over the river – it's just perfect.'

István smiled at her a little sardonically.

'Not so good in winter, when the river freezes and the snow comes up to the windowsills. At least now we have electricity and water, not like in our childhood.'

'This was your parents' home?'

'Our grandparents' home. Our parents died when we were very young, and we were brought up here by our mother's parents.'

A woman came out of the house carrying a tray with plates and glasses, and one of the light, rich Hungarian cakes. She set it down on the table and turned to them, wiping her hands on her apron and smiling shyly.

'My sister Magdolna,' said István, switching from English to German for her benefit. 'This is Kate,' he said. 'And... Sofia.'

Magdolna shook hands with them and invited them with a gesture to sit down. She was about Kate's age, perhaps a little older, and she was unmistakably the woman Kate had seen from her bedroom window at the inn.

'It is very kind of you to invite us to your home,' said Sofia, smiling warmly and looking about her. 'Such a beautiful house, and a wonderful garden. How do you manage to grow such vegetables in the heat we have had this summer?'

'It has not been easy,' said Magdolna, unloading the tray on to the table. 'At least the river is near, so I have plenty of water. The water supply we have on tap is not always reliable. I water twice a day from the river.'

'Sofia is also a keen gardener,' said Kate. 'She is almost self-supporting. And she catches fish and shellfish from the sea where we live.'

'Really?' Magdolna smiled. 'You must meet András, my son. He too is a keen fisherman. Excuse me a moment. I will get the lemonade.'

She went back into the house, and István contemplated the two women. The thought of Sofia harvesting shellfish and growing her own vegetables did not quite fit his perception of her, and he adjusted his impressions to accommodate the idea. She was sitting very upright on the old wooden chair in a dress of pale blue linen, with a white scarf at the neck. It was impossible to imagine her netting shellfish.

'I have brought lemonade, not wine,' said Magdolna, returning, 'because it is so hot. I think one needs to drink for thirst, and wine is not refreshing enough. But we will have wine later, when József returns from the fields.'

She set down a beautiful earthenware jug on the table, and took the chair between István and Sofia. But before she could pour the lemonade into the glasses, Sofia started to her feet and picked up the jug. Her face was white.

✍

It is the height of summer and blazing hot. Sofia has taken her favourite walk through the woods, past the old summer-house and down to the edge of the village near the church. Yesterday was her tenth birthday, and she expected to feel different now that she has reached double figures, but she seems the same – taller, certainly, than she was a year ago, but still wiry and tough as a boy. Mama gave a party for her birthday, with a few guests from the other big houses in the country round about. They were not Sofia's friends, but the children of her parents' friends. They played politely with each other, the boys in long trousers and white shirts and ties, the girls in party frocks with puffed sleeves and sashes tied in big bows at the back. Sofia is glad to be back in her skimpy cotton frock and sandals, scuffing through last year's leaves in the wood, with the wolfhound Iro nosing about, looking for rabbits.

Mama has gone away to Budapest, where she will be giving a concert in two days' time, and Papa has gone with her, partly for company, partly on business. Sofia is left alone at the manor with the servants and her governess, who will be leaving soon when Sofia goes away to boarding-school in the autumn. From the edge of the wood she looks enviously at the village children playing in the square. She knows most of them by sight, but she is not supposed to play with them. Something unusual is going on.

Several of the village women are plaiting together grasses and red poppies into a kind of mat, as they sit chatting on the benches outside the village *csárda*. Children are coming in from the meadow with arms full of long grasses and more poppies. The men are standing around drinking beer and arguing about something. Sofia slips into the square so she can see better what is happening. There is another mat of plaited grass lying across one of the tables.

'It is no good,' says a thickset man, whom she recognises as the village potter. 'You cannot have the Paparuda without a gypsy girl.'

'This is the first year the gypsies have not come by in August,' says old Ágoston, taking his pipe out of his mouth and shaking his head mournfully. 'It's a bad omen. We cannot have the Paparuda, and the crops will wither for lack of rain.'

'Don't be an old misery,' cries his wife, fat kindly Ágnes, who keeps the village grocery shop, and sometimes slips a sweet into Sofia's pocket. 'We will use another child. It will be all right.'

'It is no good without a gypsy,' her husband persists stubbornly. 'It is the gypsies who have the power to bring the rain or take it away. You're all wasting your time.'

Ágnes's eye falls on Sofia. 'Hello, little countess. Have you come to join the Paparuda?'

Sofia knows now what they are preparing. Whenever there is a year when the rains are short and the crops in danger, the village holds a Paparuda to bring water back to the dry earth and make it fertile again. They capture a young gypsy girl to be the Paparuda. Sofia heard Papa say once that it must be a virgin, but when she asked him what that meant he said she would understand when she was grown-up. The villagers strip the girl naked in front of the church and dress her up in a sort of tunic made from grasses and poppies, then they walk her in procession around the village pouring jugs of Danube water over her and begging her, in song, to bring the rain. Sofia has seen the Paparuda only twice, but it was exciting and she hopes they will do it again.

The women are fastening the two mats together with shoulder straps of braided straw. The completed garment can be put over the head, hanging down at the front and back, but open at the sides. Suddenly old Ágoston taps out his pipe, and as he does so he catches sight of Sofia fingering the left-over poppies lying on the table.

'That one would do. She has gypsy blood.'

Ágnes makes a disapproving, clicking noise with her tongue and shakes her head, and several other women look shocked.

'True enough,' says the potter, looking her up and down. Sofia has always liked him, but she feels uncomfortable now and a little afraid under that speculative gaze. 'Why not?' he says.

'She is the count's daughter,' someone whispers in horror.

'She's also a gypsy,' says Ágoston authoritatively. 'She'll do.'

He gets up and takes Sofia firmly by the upper arms. She looks up at him steadily and tries not to show how frightened she is.

'Will you be our Paparuda?' he asks, not unkindly, 'and save the crop for us?'

She nods, speechless. Then, thinking that this perhaps is not enough, she says (and to her shame her voice squeaks nervously), 'I will be the Paparuda.'

The men and the boys strip off her clothes and shoes, there, standing in the square under the walnut tree before the church. The women lift the woven grass mats and lower them carefully over her head. They are a bit scratchy but quite pleasant, smelling of warm hay, and she feels cool, with the air stroking her naked skin and the bare earth under her feet. Some of the older girls weave poppies into her hair, and then they all lead her out into the sun and turn her round and round, inspecting her, until she is almost dizzy with the blazing heat on her head and the strange sick feeling of expectancy which wells up inside her.

'Fetch the water,' says Ágoston, 'and then we can begin.'

Most of the villagers hurry off down the street to the river's edge to fill their jugs from the Danube. Béla Szebani, the carpenter, fetches his old wooden flute, dark and polished with age. Sofia has never heard him play it, except for the Paparuda.

They form themselves into a procession around her, with the flute leading, playing its strange ancient melody. The first child approaches with her jug of water, a dark-haired girl of about six. Sofia is taller than she is so she kneels down in the dust and bows her head.

Paparuda, ruda, ruda

The girl lifts the jug and pours the water over Sofia's head. Blinking the water out of her eyes, Sofia gets to her feet. Her eyes meet those of the other girl, and they smile at each other, for the moment aware of no one else. Sofia licks the drops of Danube water from her lips and stands patiently as others pour their jugs over her head, and urge her on down the village street.

Paparuda, ruda, ruda
Come, give us water!
Make the rain fall,
    Oh, bring us rain in torrents:
To make the corn grow
High as the hedgerow.

She feels herself borne along by them, a crowd of strangers now, and she is alone but no longer afraid. The water has drenched her, and she feels exalted. The water runs down from the top of her head, making a river along her backbone, flooding over her ribs, forking at her crotch, like the Danube splitting into many rivers around the islands, and pouring down over her bare legs, carrying the petals of the poppies with it till her skin is sprinkled all over with scarlet stars. When she stops and lowers her head for another jugful of water, the river which embraces her runs down between her bare toes and is lost in the dust, so that Sofia and the river and the grasses and the poppies and the earth are all one.

Paparuda, ruda, ruda
Come, give us water!
Make the rain fall,
Oh, bring us rain in torrents:
To make the wheat sweet with milk,
To fill the barn for winter.

They have reached the last house in the village now, the potter's rose-red cottage down on the very edge of the Danube. The potter's little girl stoops and fills her jug from the river for the last anointing and Sofia kneels down again in front of her. The jug is fat-bellied, plain earthenware except for two dolphins glowing in white shiny glaze against its dull terracotta sides. As the sun glistens on them, and Sofia blinks through the drops of water on her eyelashes, the dolphins seem to leap and splash on the side of the jug. Juliska, daughter of the village potter, lifts the last jug of water and pours it over Sofia's head.

Sofia caressed the plump side of the jug, and the glistening dolphins slid smooth under her fingers, standing out proud from the rough terracotta. She set the jug back again on the table with trembling hands and turned from the river to Magdolna. Her eyes were wide and distant.

'Your mother, what was your mother's name?'

István looked at her, puzzled. 'Rudnay. Our parents... they were not married, so we took our mother's name.'

Sofia continued to look steadily at Magdolna.

'No. Your mother's first name.'

'It was Juliska,' said Magdolna, caressing one of the dolphins with the tip of her finger.

'Juliska,' Sofia repeated softly. 'I knew her. The potter's little girl. It was Juliska who poured the first and last jugs of Danube water at the Paparuda.'

There was a silence. Sofia sat down again. Kate looked puzzled, and Magdolna and István exchanged a glance.

'Forgive me,' said Sofia.

Magdolna silently filled their glasses with the cold lemonade in which slices of lemon and sprigs of mint floated. Kate sipped hers, watching Sofia and wondering why Magdolna and István looked as though they could only just hold back the words springing to their lips.

'Forgive me,' said Sofia again, setting down her own glass and reaching out to touch Magdolna's hand where it rested still on the handle of the jug. 'I had no right to be so secret, not here in Szentmargit. I am Sofia Niklai. Zsigmond Niklai was my father.'

৯

They had been invited to stay to dinner with the family. József had come back from the fields, hot and tired from struggling with the sprinkler system, and had gone inside to take a shower. András returned soon after, as the boys were called home by their mothers for the evening meal. Sofia said firmly that she would like to help Magdolna prepare the meal.

'We can talk gardening together. Go away, the rest of you, and come back in...?' She looked enquiringly at Magdolna.

'Half an hour. Take Kate along the river path, István. It's so cool and pleasant in the evening. You go along with them, András.'

Obediently, Kate and István rose from the table and turned towards the river.

'First,' said István, 'I want to show you something. You will understand why it was not quite a coincidence that we met in the gallery in Váci Utca.'

He led the way across to the barn, András trailing behind. Inside it was dim, but István pulled open the double doors until the sunlight filled the wide inner space. Kate saw barrels and shelves, and what looked like two big catering ovens. István beckoned her further in. On a wide table against the wall stood three clay figures, about three feet tall, waiting for firing.

'But they're...' said Kate. 'But I thought... Didn't it say "M. Buvari"?' She peered at the bases of the figures.

'Buvari is Magdolna's married name.'

'I see.'

'Whenever I am in Budapest I go into the gallery. Just to check that everything is being displayed properly. And to complain about how little they pay Magdolna!'

András was kicking a ball around the grass when they came out of the barn and closed the doors behind them.

'So you see,' said István, smiling at her, 'Sofia is not the only one who has been keeping secrets.' He led the way to the river and

174

turned on to a path which led upstream along the river's edge. There were trees here, and a pleasant dappled shade.

'When I saw you first by the summer-house, I was afraid that you were someone trying to hunt Magdolna out in her home. We try to protect her from that, because her privacy is very important to her work. Once a journalist from a German magazine found us out, and it disturbed her work for weeks.'

'I'm sorry you thought that.'

'I soon realised I was wrong. You seem to me like a person who values privacy yourself.'

She looked at him, stopping in surprise. 'I suppose I am. I've never really thought about it.' She turned away to watch the waters of the Danube lapping the bank just beyond their feet. 'I do go for long walks alone – the dog gives me the excuse for that. I find myself constantly drawn to the empty spaces of the sea. That was where I met Sofia.'

'For me, it has always been the river. When I was a child I would come this way, to escape and be on my own.'

This is the way my father would have come, he thought, if he had managed to escape. Up the river and away towards the Austrian border or downriver into the secret marshes.

They walked on a little in silence, and crossed a rickety wooden bridge where the trout stream flowed into the river. The boards were loose and Kate stumbled. István put out a hand to steady her, but she shook her head.

'I'm all right,' she said with a laugh. 'Just clumsy.'

'Uncle István,' said András, 'can we go up the stream and see if the fish are rising?'

'You go. We'll walk along here a little further and turn back in a few minutes. Mind you're not late or your mother will be cross.'

András laughed and ran off up the bank. His mother was never cross.

'When I first saw you by the summer-house,' said Kate, as they ducked under the low branches of a great willow leaning over the path towards the river, 'I thought you were Sofia's father, Zsigmond.'

'Did you really?' He looked at her curiously. 'Why did you think that?'

'Just a momentary impression. I've seen a photograph she has, of Zsigmond standing on the steps, where you were standing. Coming suddenly into the light in the clearing, I had this strange sense of stepping into the photograph, into the past. And you do look like him.'

'Do I?'

'And then you moved, and my mind snapped back into focus, and I realised where and when I was, and who you were. Or who I thought you were. From the gallery.'

They paused beside the big willow and looked across the water to the scattered islands, flat and reedy. Beyond them a large black working barge was making its way upriver against the current.

'I suppose we ought to turn back now,' said Kate reluctantly.

István looked at his watch.

'Yes, we must.'

Slowly they resumed their walk, retracing their steps along the path.

'While you are here on holiday...' said István tentatively.

'Yes?'

'I wonder if you would allow me to show you some of the countryside? I know you have a car, but if you are driving in an unfamiliar area, you miss a lot of what there is to see. And if you have only seen Budapest and Györ...'

'And Szentmargit!'

He laughed. 'Yes, of course, and Szentmargit. But Sopron and Pannonhalma are not far. And I would like to show you Mohács. I think you would be interested in Mohács.'

'What is at Mohács?'

'Come with me and you will see.'

'Do you mean...' Kate hesitated, 'both of us? I couldn't go off and leave Sofia behind.'

'Certainly,' said István courteously, 'I meant both of you.'

They dined outside, where moths came and bumped against the oil lamp in the centre of the table. Kate tried, stumblingly, to tell Magdolna how much she loved the figures and plaques she had seen in Budapest.

József patted his wife's hand as she blushed with shyness and pleasure.

'You see, it is not so terrible to be admired.'

'Your crops also,' said Kate, smiling at him, 'are to be admired.'

She had liked József at once. He said little, but what he said was shrewd and to the point. He looked at her now with sharp eyes under his bushy, greying eyebrows.

'You are interested in agriculture?'

'I am afraid I am very ignorant. I'm not even a very knowledgeable gardener. But anyone can see that your crops are sleek and healthy. I was telling...István.' She used the name awkwardly. 'Driving over from Budapest and Györ I thought the wheat and the maize looked so thin and poor, and the sunflowers could barely lift their heads.'

'We have here the central European climate, you understand,' József said. 'Very hot in the summer, very cold in the winter. Not like your England, where it rains all the time, winter and summer.'

Kate gave a protesting snort, though she saw he was teasing her.

'This year has been exceptionally hot and dry, even for Hungary, hasn't it?'

'Yes, indeed. It is causing a lot of problems. Though at least we were able to get in an excellent hay harvest. We're beginning on the rest of the harvest now, and if the weather holds like this we won't have to worry about the harvest being rained out.'

Sofia looked across at him.

'Do you still have the Paparuda?'

They glanced at each other and shook their heads.

'I remember Grandmama talking about it,' said Magdolna slowly. 'But I think many such things died out under the communists.'

'What is a Paparuda?' asked Kate.

'An old superstition,' said István. 'A ceremony to bring the rain for the crops. It would not have been approved of on the collective,' he added dryly.

As twilight slipped into darkness András was sent, protesting, to bed, and the adults sat on over their glasses of wine and a bowl of fruit Magdolna had placed in the middle of the table. Their faces, illuminated from below by the wavering light, took on dramatic highlights and shadows. Kate thought the others looked like characters in a play, and wondered whether she seemed as mysterious to them.

István was turning and turning his glass in his hand, and she watched the play of the red reflection on his fingers. They were good hands. She could imagine him as a doctor, a man his patients could confide in. A man to whom you could unburden yourself, laying your worries on his shoulders and walking away cleansed and free.

He looked up now and caught her watching him, but he simply smiled with his eyes, and then turned to Sofia.

'I was saying to Kate earlier that you were not the only one who had been keeping secrets. I did not tell her at first about Magdolna. And there is something else we need to tell you.'

Kate's eyes met Sofia's, and she knew with a sudden lurch of the heart that this was something much more significant than the identity of the artist among them.

177

'Our parents met during the war,' said István. 'No, that is not quite true. They had always been acquainted, because they both came from Szentmargit, but it was only when they joined the resistance that they truly came to know each other. Our mother was much younger than our father – she would have been eighteen then, in 1942, and he was in his mid-forties. They lived rough in the woods and operated throughout this area, over as far as Györ. Mama was the only woman in the group, and it can't have been easy – the danger, living always with death, the men away from their women. Our father – his code name was Lancelot – started by protecting her from the others. He still thought of her, I suppose, as the child he had known in the village. It ended by their falling in love and sleeping together.' He paused. 'I was the result.'

He stopped and poured himself more wine. Holding up the bottle he looked enquiringly round at them. Only József held out his glass.

'It wasn't a casual affair. I believe they loved each other deeply. That was certainly what our grandparents felt. After the war, they moved back here to live in this house, and Magdolna was born here. My father continued his fight for Hungary's independence, publishing an underground newspaper called *Freedom!* and carrying out occasional acts of sabotage against the Russian troops stationed nearby, and against the Ávó, the Hungarian communist secret police. In 1948 he was betrayed by one of the former partisans, a communist, and he was taken away to the gulags. We never saw him again. We know that he must have been tortured. We think that he probably died quite soon after he was taken.'

He stopped. The hand resting on the table was shaking. Magdolna laid her hand on top of it, and picked up the story.

'Our mother, Juliska, took over his work. She continued to publish the newspaper, and in 1956, when the uprising came and Hungary so nearly gained her freedom, she was in Budapest, in the midst of it all. When the Russian tanks moved in, mowing down civilians, killing and maiming, she was amongst a small group which managed to get away to Györ, where they carried on the struggle for some time after Budapest had fallen. In the end, of course, they were defeated. Mama was executed by firing squad in January 1957.'

They sat in silence. What can you respond to this? thought Kate. There is nothing one can possibly say.

István patted Magdolna's hand, and laid it aside. He leaned forward towards Sofia.

'There is just one thing more which must be said. Our parents did not marry because they could not. Our father was already married. He

178

had sent his wife out of the country when the Arrow Cross became powerful just before the war. He had loved her very much – this is well known. But you must understand, he loved Juliska too.'

'Who was your father?' Sofia asked.

'He was Zsigmond Niklai. Your father. We are your brother and sister.'

'I think I already knew,' said Sofia.

Chapter 10

K ate could not sleep that night.
The sky was clear and the moon bright. The thin cotton curtains in her room were no defence against its penetrating light, so in the end she got out of bed and padded across the smooth old boards, first to one window and then to the other, drawing back the curtains and letting the moon flood in. Looking down into the square she could see the inn cat, and another one she did not recognise, slipping away together behind the church.

The ancient wooden grave markers reared up in the churchyard like the carved prows of Viking ships, inclined a little forward, and from this distance by moonlight might be taken for a casual group of cloaked figures leaning into the wind. She thought about the private histories she had heard that evening. The horrors experienced by the family in the quiet cottage by the river leapt to life before her eyes, reminding her that the public history of this country was made up of thousands of individual histories, and the grief of the people, of thousands of individual griefs.

She did not have, had never had, a particularly close relationship with her own parents. Her father was a silent, reserved man. It had not prevented him from being a good teacher, since teaching did not entail close personal involvement, but he shied away from emotions within the family. And her mother had always kept Kate at arm's length. As a child she believed this was her own fault, and constantly searched her conscience for what sin she might have committed, to make her undeserving of her mother's love.

Meeting Tom, whose affection was easy-going though not passionate, had been a means of escape. Slowly gaining self-confidence during the early years of her marriage, she began to think that perhaps it was something amiss not in her but in Millicent which made their relationship so strained. Her mother was constantly critical, always eager to point out Kate's faults both in deed and in character, yet whenever her daughter tried to turn to deeper issues, a steel shutter seemed to clamp down between them.

There was an owl nesting in the walnut tree in the village square. Kate had heard it before. Now she saw it for the first time, leaving the tree on silent wings, then – as it soared towards the fields beyond the village – unable to restrain its wavering, desolate hunting cry. Kate shivered and thought of the creatures in the fields, mice and young rabbits and voles, crouching amongst the tinder-dry stems, their hearts pounding with fear. Not wanting to see the owl return clutching its prey, she padded softly across the room to the other window. It must face not due north, but north-east, she realised, for the rising moon shone in slantwise on her here, lighting up her white nightdress so that it shone spectrally. She lifted her hand and saw it blue-white, insubstantial, floating.

István and Magdolna, on the other hand, had scarcely known their parents. István said he could just remember Zsigmond Niklai, but Magdolna had been a baby when their father had been seized by the secret police and carried away to what terrible pain and death Kate could not bear to contemplate. She thought of Zsigmond in the photograph, standing on the steps of the summer-house, and her own momentary sense that she had seen him again. Of course, she could understand it now. István did look quite like his father, even though Zsigmond, in that photograph, had been no older than his late thirties while István must be near fifty. And although Magdolna had no memory of her father, she had been ten when her mother had faced the firing squad. How could you live with a memory like that? What did it do to a ten-year-old girl, or to a twelve-year-old boy?

Kate thought she could begin to understand, now, the source of the passion which vibrated in Magdolna's work. And István? She supposed his work as a doctor was a channel for the same passions. Magdolna, of course, had the support of a strong and happy marriage, and two children who were growing up in a world transformed from the world of the Rudnay children's youth. She wondered whether István had ever married.

There was no light shining in the Buvaris' house. József would rise early in the morning, like any farmer, and no doubt his family rose with him. The moon shimmered on the Danube and she could see the house as a sharp-cut silhouette standing out against the silver water. To the left she could just make out the corner of the barn, which she had previously taken to be an odd angle of the house. Now she knew it was Magdolna's studio. Once truly a barn, it had been partially converted by her grandfather, the village potter whom Sofia had known. It was this grandfather, they had learned, who had started to train Magdolna when she was a young girl, before she went to college and then on to study under the famous Margit Kovacs. When Magdolna had taken over the whole barn for her expanding needs, József had been given the use of a barn on his parents' old farm, now occupied by Imre – he of the sprinkler system and other, wilder, inventions, which they had heard about, hilariously, towards the end of the evening.

István had steered the conversation that way, Kate now realised. Once he had revealed the family relationship he had done everything he could to ease the shock for Sofia. Yet the curious thing was that Sofia did not seem shocked. She had spoken no more than the truth when she said that she had already known that István and Magdolna were her brother and sister.

'Something compelled me to come back to Szentmargit,' she said calmly. 'Do you believe in telepathy? I'm not sure that I do, but sometimes there seems to be *something*.'

'I think we all have experiences we can't explain,' said Kate. 'Sometimes I dream of a friend I haven't thought of for months, and then two or three days later I'll get a letter from her.'

'Exactly. Why should Magdolna have found the tin box of papers at much the same time as I decided I must open my mother's old trunk and force myself to confront the past? Something between us, perhaps? A telepathy between sisters? Yet although you knew of my existence, I didn't know of yours.'

'Some people would say it was predestination,' said István slowly. 'But do I believe in that? I'm not sure. A religious man would say it was the will of God.'

'Perhaps it was,' said Magdolna quietly.

'But you do not believe in God,' said István.

'Just because I don't believe in Him doesn't mean He doesn't exist,' she said serenely.

Kate smiled across the table at her. She was beginning to like Magdolna very much. She could see that, like Sofia, Magdolna combined passion with a kind of dignity and self-knowledge that Kate wished she possessed herself.

She had been nearly sleep-walking when István and József had accompanied them home to the Blue Heron, but after she had showered and changed into her nightdress she had found herself suddenly wakeful, going over and over the events of the extraordinary evening in her mind.

Zsigmond Niklai had slipped away from the manor of Szentmargit at the outset of war, abandoning his paintings, his silver, all his possessions, and joined the partisans in the forest, fighting for a Hungary free of Nazis, a Hungary where Hungarians could live in peace and democracy. Kate wished he had lived to see it achieved. It was through the spirit of men like Zsigmond that the hope had been passed down to the young people who had risen so bravely, so forlornly, for freedom, eight years after he had been taken away by night from the rose-red house beside the river.

I am ashamed, thought Kate. Sickened and ashamed that Britain and the other Western nations did nothing to support the 1956 uprising, started by students, taken up by ordinary men and women, and in the end even the army itself. In her teens she had heard the recording of those desperate appeals put out on the radio, finally falling into silence, and had felt guilty. But never before had she realised what it really meant. Young mothers like Juliska – who had been thirty-two – lined up against a wall and shot.

'They threw children into prison,' said István, 'but it was against the law to execute anyone under the age of eighteen. So the puppet government of Russia was very punctilious, very correct. They kept the children of thirteen, fourteen, fifteen in prison until they were eighteen. And then they executed them.'

How could you live with memories like that?

Kate longed to put her arms around them both, she ached so with sympathy, but they seemed to accept what had been done to them and to their parents. It was this suppressed agony of mind in herself, this yearning to touch, to embrace, out of sheer fellow human feeling, which kept her restlessly awake.

A picture kept coming back into her mind of Zsigmond and Juliska in the forest near the end of the war. Magdolna had brought out a photograph of the two of them in camouflage trousers and heavy boots, laughing under the trees, with their arms around each other. They looked radiant. Juliska was wearing a peaked cap, pushed over at a jaunty angle on her dark, unkempt curls. You would have thought they were larking about on a picnic, not living on the edge of danger, with death threatening at any moment. István said that for years he had had to keep his copy of the photograph hidden, because his parents' faces were known to the Ávó, and if he had been seen displaying it he would have fallen under suspicion. Sofia took the photograph and looked at it searchingly, then she handed it back to Magdolna, wiping her eyes.

'I am sorry,' said Magdolna, contrite. 'I have distressed you.'

'No, no. I am glad Juliska was able to give him such happiness. She was even younger than I, did you know that? And what makes me sad is that by the time that photograph was taken, they could have married. My mother died in 1944.'

Magdolna was silent, then, thinking about it.

'I don't know that it mattered very much to them,' she said at last. 'In the world in which they lived, such formalities must have seemed of small importance. We minded, István and I, when the other children called us bastards. But in the end we were accepted.'

'They had us both christened, though,' said István thoughtfully, 'so they did care for the sacraments of the Church.'

He told them of his parents' twenty-kilometre walk to the village, two days after his birth, and his secret christening by night in the Church of Szent Margit across the square from the *csárda*.

'The next night they walked back again to the partisan camp in the forest.'

'Poor little Juliska,' Sofia murmured, thinking of the black-haired child with the jug.

'No,' said István. 'She had become a very strong woman, very brave.' He took a deep breath. 'It was known amongst those of the partisans still working against the Russians after the war that my father had been betrayed by a former comrade. It was our mother who carried out the execution, in the flower market in Győr.'

Kate stared at him. She remembered the buckets of gladioli and carnations, the young man with the red roses. Magdolna was looking down, pleating the embroidered tablecloth between her fingers. István had only told her about his visit to Ferenc Kalla the evening before.

'You have to understand,' she said, clearing her throat, 'that in those times it was not possible to be an ordinary wife and mother. Not for those who believed in the struggle for freedom. Hungary always had to come first – before family, before friends, before personal wishes, before life itself. By doing what she did, she helped to start the changes which meant, in the end, that *I* could be a mother to my children, and a wife to József. That I could work in peace on my art, instead of being called upon to give my life for my principles.'

How could you live with a memory like that?

Kate shivered, standing in her thin nightdress, looking out over the silvered breadth of the Danube and the small, unpretentious house which held so much passion and pain. She climbed back into bed, huddling under the feather bed, clutching it around her for comfort, but she went on shivering.

სა

Sofia, lying quietly on her back with her hands clasped in front of her, heard Kate moving about in the room above her. The conversation of the evening played itself over in her mind, with its moments of sharp grief and regret. Yet her abiding feeling was one of calm. She had come back to Hungary partly looking for answers, partly to ease the burden of memory. She had her answers now. Her father had survived the war, only to die at the hands of the secret police some time afterwards – and she would never know exactly when. Yet she felt less grief at this than she had expected. It had been clear to her for some time now that Zsigmond must have died long ago. Otherwise, as relations between Hungary and the West improved after the end of the Stalinist regime, he would have found some way of contacting her.

His abandonment of his position as a landowner – which could have meant power and privilege under the Horthy government – seemed a natural progression in his life, starting with his liberal land reforms and gift of land to the Szentmargit peasants and continuing with his outspoken newspaper articles in the national press condemning the rise of the Arrow Cross, before censorship had silenced him. His involvement with the partisan movement was the only way he could have gone, and remained true to his principles, after Hitler had tricked and betrayed Hungary out of neutrality into the war.

It was strange to think of Juliska – whom she still thought of as the barefoot little village girl – living with Zsigmond in the rough world of the partisan camp in the forest, but oddly she did not resent it. She had spoken the simple truth when she had said that she was glad Juliska had brought him happiness. Her sense of guilt – that she had escaped and survived, while her father had been left behind to face danger and death – was a little eased by the thought of that joyous photograph of Juliska and Zsigmond, and by the existence of Magdolna and István, sprung from that love. A brother and sister – this indeed was not what she had expected to find in coming on this pilgrimage to Szentmargit.

And in thinking over her father's relationship with the village, she understood a little better her own past, and her mother's. The villagers had always looked somewhat askance at Eva. Despite her fame as a musician, despite her beauty and charm, they had resented her half-gypsy blood. A gypsy as Countess Niklai was an insult to the descendants of those who had served the ancient, aristocratic Hungarian family. She realised, now, that Eva had kept her daughter from contact with the village children as much to protect her as out of a sense of social superiority. When Sofia had been taken for the Paparuda, she had been taken as a punishment. That ceremony was an ancient survival of a ritual to propitiate the gods, and the gypsy girl was the sacrifice – made to bow her head before the will of the peasants, made to suffer so that their fields might flourish.

Sofia had never told her parents that she had been used for the Paparuda. Instinctively she must have known even then that to be stripped naked and paraded by the villagers was a humiliation of their daughter that not even her father would have tolerated from his people. Yet she had not felt humiliated. She had not felt like a victim. She closed her eyes now and summoned back the experience which had come upon her so suddenly this afternoon on seeing the dolphin jug again, made by Magdolna's grandfather, carried by Magdolna's mother. No, she remembered clearly that she had felt exalted by the experience, as if she had somehow managed to reach out and touch for a moment a secret world which she knew lay just behind the curtain of everyday life. She had run home that hot summer afternoon when she was ten, dressed again in her cotton frock but with Danube water dripping from her hair, and for the first time in her life she had tried to write a poem. She had torn it up, because it was a poor thing, but she knew now, looking back, that it was at that moment she became a poet.

Later that night, she had woken to a crash of thunder. Standing at the window of her room in the manor house she had seen lightning play about the village and heard the rain falling in torrents on the dry and thirsty earth, and she knew that it had been her doing, her gift as the Paparuda. She had broken the drought.

As they were about to leave the Buvaris' house this evening, having cleared the dishes from the table under the vine, lingering on the threshold, all of them reluctant to say good-night, Sofia had turned to István.

'When we left here, my mother and I, we had to leave my dog Bárat behind. He knew I was betraying him, and howled his heart out. I don't suppose you know what became of him? Did my – our – father keep him?'

István smiled. 'Old Bárat? He lived until I was five or six. Magdolna and I both learned to walk clutching on to his fur. Come.'

He took hold of her hand and led her, stumbling a little in the dark, to the apple tree at the edge of the garden. He guided her fingers until they touched a small wooden grave marker, a miniature of those in the churchyard.

'He is buried here. My grandfather carved the grave marker for him.'

Sofia gave a sudden dry sob as her fingers traced the carving.

'Hush,' said István, putting his arms around her and holding her. 'He had a good life, I promise you. And we loved him.'

186

'I'm sorry,' said Sofia. 'It has been a strange and wonderful evening.'

'Yes,' he said, leading her back with his arm around her shoulders. 'Strange and wonderful. Sad, but also happy.'

❧

István, unable to sleep, had gone out again after Magdolna and József had retired to bed. For a while he sat on the bench against the wall of the house and heard the soft murmuring of their voices fade away into sleep. But he was restless, and set off along the path beside the river where he had walked with Kate that afternoon. He had known it all his life and could have walked it on a moonless night without difficulty, skirting the holes where the bank had collapsed and stepping over straggling tree-roots by instinct. But tonight the moon, though not full, was clear and unclouded, and the countryside lay around him like a mysterious black and silver painting. He could hear the steady flow of the Danube at his side, a sound as familiar as the pulse of his own blood. He was aware of it only at such times as this, walking at night, undistracted by people or the busy sounds from the fields. There was a soft murmur from the branches of the willows overhead, stirring in the faint breeze, but otherwise there was silence except for the sound of an owl, hunting over the fields. The ground at his feet was dusty from the long drought, and the bushes beside the path gave off a dry, peppery scent as he brushed past them.

On the wooden bridge over the trout stream he paused, and leaned on the slender handrail, looking down at the water flowing beneath his feet. Here it met the Danube in a swirl of foam and sudden excited eddies, as if it knew it was now mingling with the great river which ran all through the heart of central Europe, to flow at last into the Black Sea. And from there, thought István, to the Mediterranean, and from the Mediterranean to the Atlantic, which mingles with the North Sea, where Kate and Sofia live beside the shore. He was taken again with that vision of his childhood, of climbing into a boat and setting sail on the Danube, on and on till the ends of the earth.

It had been, as Sofia said, a strange and wonderful evening.

He wished he had a cigarette. He had given up smoking ten years ago, and never regretted it, but now he felt he needed a cigarette.

Although he had always known of Sofia's existence, it had had no reality for him. To be confronted with the reality was deeply unsettling. It had also been a new discovery that his half-sister Sofia was Sofia Tabor, whose poetry he had read. Thinking of the poems, and

187

the woman, and the lives of all his family, he felt as though the fragments of a jigsaw, scattered and lost years ago, were beginning to come together.

And then there was Kate. Where did Kate fit into all of this? He knew hardly anything about her, yet she knew most of his history – except, perhaps, about Maria and László. She was Mrs Milburn, so she was – or had been – married, but neither she nor Sofia had mentioned a husband. Was she divorced? Widowed? All he knew about her was that she was English, she lived in a place called Dunmouth on the North Sea coast, and she was a friend of Sofia's. He turned and leaned his back on the handrail. Looking up past the fields to the higher part of the village he could see the dome of the church reflecting the moonlight and, in front of it, the shaggy silhouette of the heron's nest on the roof of the *csárda*. Below it was the room where Kate was sleeping. He wanted to know more about Kate.

God, he could do with a cigarette!

Two days later, on Friday, István took Kate on the Danube in the rowing boat. The sun continued to beat down and András (who would have preferred to fish) was helping his father and uncle with the harvest. He had been promised basic agricultural wages every time he put in a full day, and had been told that he could spend the money how he chose. József calculated that András would appreciate the coveted Reeboks more if he earned them for himself, and said that he would take him to Győr to buy them as soon as the harvest was in. András threw himself into the work with enthusiasm, reckoning that if he could get enough days' work during the harvest he might be able to start saving up for a tape recorder as well, which was his next ambition.

Sofia was feeling the effects of the relentless heat more than she liked to admit and opted to stay in the cool of the house with Magdolna who, having fired the three new figures, was taking a break from work to attend to her own harvest in the vegetable garden. Sofia offered to help with laying beans down with salt in big earthenware crocks, bottling plums, and making preserves from the sudden rush of tomatoes.

After breakfast Kate and Sofia walked down from the Blue Heron to the rose-coloured house which was beginning to feel like a second home.

'Are you sure you don't want to come?' asked Kate. 'It's bound to be cooler on the river. And Magdolna says it's very beautiful.'

'It is. Remember, I have been there often in my youth. I'll stay quietly at home and help in the kitchen.'

'I don't think that will be very restful,' said Kate stubbornly, somewhat uneasy at the thought of spending the day on the river alone with István. 'It will be hot in the kitchen, you'll be standing most of the time, and you'll be tired out by the end of the day.'

'Nonsense. I will sit outside on the bench under the vine and cut up beans in the shade. And besides,' she gave Kate a curious, secret smile, 'I want the chance to get to know my sister.'

'Of course,' said Kate, blushing. 'How stupid of me. Of course you do. I'm so sorry. I'm a blundering idiot.'

'Never that, Kate, certainly.'

So here they were, Kate and István, with a picnic basket provided by Magdolna on the bottom of the boat between them, drifting downriver. István sat at the oars, not rowing but from time to time dipping an oar in the water to guide the boat, and telling Kate the Hungarian names of the birds and trees they passed, which she tried to pronounce and immediately forgot.

'Afterwards I want to take you upstream, where we can land on one of the islands for our picnic,' said István, 'but first I wanted to come downstream, so I could show you the marshes. It's a curious area. The whole river bank along here is a network of channels running between the reed beds. In places there are tussocks and islets of solid land, but they are covered with rushes as well, so unless you know the marshes well you could be in danger there if you tried to land. For those of us born and bred in the area it is a secret kingdom.'

He turned the boat into an opening in the reeds barely wide enough to let it pass, and moved it forward by standing up beside Kate and sculling over the stern with one oar. The reeds rose high above their heads, and as soon as they had rounded the first bend the river was lost to sight. There was nothing to be seen but narrow sparkling channels, appearing and disappearing on either side, and the feathery reeds, and an occasional willow which had managed to take root on one of the muddy islets amongst the reed beds. It was warm, but not as hot as on land, and the reeds made a constant susurration in the light breeze.

'There's a heron's nest in that tree,' whispered Kate. It seemed a place for whispers.

István stopped sculling and looked in the direction of her pointing hand.

'Yes, look – it's just coming in.'

They watched as the heron soared in on huge wings, back-watered with legs dangling, and came to rest, swaying on the edge of the untidy platform of twigs. They could hear the young birds squawking greedily, and see the movement of their heads over the top of the nest.

'It's a blue heron,' István whispered. 'They're very rare. Most of our herons here are the grey ones.'

The great bird was larger than the pair nesting in the village and was tinged with cinnamon on its breast and wings.

'This must be good heron country,' said Kate.

'Famous for them. We always think of our herons as bringers of good luck. Is this true in England?'

'I'm not sure. They aren't very common, and I've never lived in an area where they nest. Do they spend the winter here?'

'Oh, no. Hungary is far too cold! When the autumn comes they fly south to Egypt and the Nile. The herons you see on ancient Egyptian paintings are the ancestors of our Szentmargit birds.'

Kate was silent, watching the great bird lift itself smoothly from the nest and go winging off with strong slow beats over the marsh. When winter came, the bird would be living near the Pyramids, fishing in the Nile. István would be here, where the waters would be frozen and the snow a high blanket over the fields. And she would be – in grey Dunmouth, in an empty house, staring out over the chilly waters of the North Sea.

István began to work the boat further along the channel and deeper into the marsh. Kate stroked the side of the boat absently. It was a sturdy fishing boat, but small enough for one man to handle, and well built, with good lines. Linda's dad would have approved of it. The inside was plain wood, varnished, but the outside was painted a soft, powder blue.

'I love the colours in Hungary,' she said. 'You make everything so beautiful. The houses, the boats, all the wonderful embroidery.'

'It is a way of saying "We are free, we will be happy, whatever you do to us",' said István with a smile. 'Like our songs, and our gypsy musicians.'

'And Magdolna's figures and plaques. There is everything there – ecstasy and grief, tenderness, agony, joy.'

'And love.'

'And love.'

They moved silently further into the marsh amongst a flock of ducks, until the boat slid through a clump of reeds and grounded with a soft bump on something more solid.

'Here is one of the little islands,' said István. 'I thought you would like to see one of the secret places of the marsh.'

He took her hand to help her out of the boat and led her in through the whispering reeds and the chirruping of invisible insects until they reached a tiny open area, no more than eight feet square, covered with rough marsh grass. A young willow had taken root, but was not yet as tall as the surrounding reeds. It was warm and very quiet.

'Sometimes the partisans hid on these islands during the war,' said István. 'Not for long, of course. But there was no way the Nazis could find them here. I think this is where my father would have come, if he could have worked the boat out of the ice before the Ávó reached our door.'

'He was that close to escaping?'

'Yes.' István turned away from her. 'But he came to kiss Magdolna and me goodbye. Can you understand this? All my life I have known that but for us our father would have escaped. I have never told Magdolna. It would have killed her.'

Kate reached up and touched his cheek.

Sofia and Magdolna sat contentedly under the vine arbour sipping home-made lemonade. Sofia was telling her sister about the tisanes she made from peppermint and other herbs. They had put up two crocks of beans and bottled a dozen jars of plums, and they were resting over lunch before tackling the pickles and other preserves.

'I am so grateful,' said Magdolna. 'You have saved me hours. It is more than twice as quick with the two of us working together, because I don't get as bored as I do on my own.'

'You don't feel you should do less of the domestic things and spend more time on your ceramics?'

'I cannot bear to waste anything!' Magdolna laughed, gesturing at the garden. 'It can be a tyrant, can't it? But I am a true peasant, hoarding everything against a snow-bound winter. And I feel so satisfied when all the shelves in my larder are packed full and there isn't a centimetre of space on the floor!'

'Yes, I know exactly how you feel.'

They smiled at each other in complete understanding.

'I am sorry I haven't met your daughter Anna,' said Sofia. 'Will she be staying in Budapest all summer?'

191

'I had a letter from her yesterday, and she has promised to come down for a few days while István is here – he's a great favourite with both the children. József is going to telephone her tonight from the inn and ask if she can come while you are here. When do you have to leave?'

'Our flight back is on the first of September, and we're booked into the hotel in Budapest for one night before that, so we will have to leave here on the thirtieth or thirty-first.'

'What day is it today? I always lose count.'

'The nineteenth, I think.'

'Of course – tomorrow is the festival. I will tell József to make sure that Anna comes at least a few days before you leave.' Magdolna looked fondly at Sofia. 'It is like a miracle, to find a sister in middle age.'

'In old age, for me,' Sofia said. 'Even more of a miracle.'

'Would you consider coming back to Hungary? Permanently, to live?'

Sofia looked out across the garden to the Danube with its familiar pattern of islands, gliding under the August heat, and she thought of her bee-filled garden where the sound of the crashing waves was a permanent accompaniment to her life.

'No.' She shook her head. 'I belong, now, to the astringent north. But part of me will stay here with you.'

István had sculled them out of the marshes, quietly, so as not to disturb the nesting birds, and was now pulling upriver. In here close to the southern shore, where the flow was broken by the islands, the current was not as strong as in the main shipping channel, cut to the north of the islands. There the river's unimpeded weight pressed on inexorably, flowing down from Germany and Austria. Along this stretch it formed the border between Hungary and Slovakia. But even here amongst the narrow channels István had to work hard. He grew red from the exertion in the midday heat.

Kate, watching him, said, 'Take off your shirt and tie.'

'You don't mind?'

'Don't be ridiculous – you look like a boiled lobster!'

He laughed and rested on his oars while he tugged at his tie, nearly losing one of the oars in the process. They began to drift downstream again.

'Wait! Let me,' said Kate, and kneeling on the bottom of the boat in front of him she untied his tie while he made half-strokes with the oars to stop them being carried away. She rolled up the tie and put it in the picnic basket, then began to unbutton his shirt.

'I can't remember when a woman last unbuttoned my shirt for me,' he said into her hair as she leaned over him, trying to remove the shirt without disturbing his rowing too much.

Kate kept her face turned away. She was already regretting her spontaneous gesture of affection and sympathy in the marsh. She folded his shirt in silence, and laid it flat on top of the basket.

'I'm sorry,' said István ruefully. 'That was unpardonable.'

'It doesn't matter.' Kate still would not look at him, so she did not see the glint of amusement and self-mockery in his eye.

They were well past Magdolna's house by now, and nearing the mouth of the trout stream with its wooden bridge. István was taking the boat between the shore and a large, flat island covered with grass and edged with reeds, shorter than those they had seen in the marshes.

'Is this the island where we're going to stop?'

'No, there's a better one a little further up.'

'You're sure you aren't getting tired?'

'Not at all. I've rowed amongst these islands all my life. It's nice to have someone to show them off to.'

'Look, there's another heron! Do you suppose he's one of our herons, from the village?'

'Watch where he goes.'

Kate shaded her eyes from the sun and saw the heron rise from the bank and circle over the river before heading back in the direction of Szentmargit.

'I think it's one of ours. Isn't it odd – he might have popped over to Slovakia just now for a spot of fishing!'

István nodded. 'When I was young and Hungary was closed in behind barriers, except where the Russians allowed us to move, I used to watch the birds and envy them. We are so close to Austria here, and Austria meant freedom. On every other side we were surrounded by communist countries.'

'It's very difficult for me to understand how it felt. I mean *really* understand. We have been so lucky in Britain – never invaded for nine hundred years – and I dare say it has made us thick-skinned and complacent.'

'You? Thick-skinned? Never. But it isn't exactly luck, is it? It comes of having the good sense to be born on an island, your demi-paradise.' He pulled hard on his right oar and back-watered with the

193

left, swinging the boat around the end of another island and into a small, sheltered bay. 'Now I am going to introduce you to *my* island.'

He jumped out into the shallow water and pulled the boat up on to a narrow beach.

'Allow me to help you ashore in my kingdom,' he said with mock solemnity, putting his hands around Kate's waist and lifting her from the boat on to the dry land.

'The picnic! Don't forget the picnic!'

'Of course I won't. You have no soul. You are supposed to be admiring my island, not worrying about your lunch.'

'I am admiring it, I do admire it. I just wouldn't want you to faint away after all that rowing.'

It took ten minutes to explore the island, which had a hill (about ten feet above river level) with two willow trees, one silver birch and a tree Kate couldn't identify. A screen of rough bushes grew around a hollow at the bottom of this hill, where a fireplace made of round stones showed that István had picnicked here before.

'I'm going to light a small fire,' he said. 'So we can make your English tea later.'

He knelt beside the hearth and swiftly assembled a neat wigwam of broken branches above a heap of leaves and twigs. The dry wood caught quickly, and he sat back on his heels in satisfaction.

There was also, as István displayed with some pride, a spring of fresh water, which bubbled up between the two willows.

'Usually there is more water than this,' he said, 'but the drought this summer has affected even the underground streams. It is beautiful water, very cold and pure.'

He held one of the glasses from the basket under the lip of rock from which the spring flowed down to spread and then lose itself in a stretch of dark green moss, which contrasted sharply with the bleached yellow-green of the grass all around. The glass filled slowly and when István was satisfied he held it up for her to see. The water did indeed look clean and pure. He offered it to her with a flourish. She hesitated.

'It is quite safe, is it? I mean, the Danube...'

'Quite safe. This comes from deep under the rocks, nothing to do with the Danube. Look, I will drink first.'

He drank deeply from the glass, then offered her the other side to drink from. The cold of it startled her. She hadn't known that water could taste like this. Thinking of the disgusting liquid, smelling of chemicals, which she had drunk for years in London, she was amazed by it. She drank it all, smiling at him over the rim of the glass.

They spread out their picnic where the trees gave some shade. Kate, with her legs curled under her, began setting out the food Magdolna had provided. István lay back with his arm across his eyes, shading them from the sun. He was, in truth, feeling tired, and was glad that the return journey would all be downstream. He was getting too old to be showing off to a girl, he thought humorously.

'What are you smiling about?'

'Nothing. Just my own foolishness. What has she given us?'

'Egg sandwiches.'

'Her own eggs,' said István.

'Tomato sandwiches.'

'Her own tomatoes.'

'Ham sandwiches.'

'Her home-cured ham.'

'Cake, fruit, lemonade.'

'Delicious.' He rolled over and sat up.

'I love your sister,' she said seriously. 'Both of your sisters.'

He realised that she truly meant this, and was touched. 'Here,' he said, urging sandwiches on her, suddenly unsure of himself. 'We must eat it all or she will be hurt.'

'Thank you.' Obediently she took one of each of the sandwiches, but then put down her plate, thinking deeply. 'I love them for the people they are, and for a wonderful quality of serenity which I envy. I wish I could attain it.'

He glanced down. Her hands were clutching each other, a gesture oddly at variance with her face, which seemed calm.

'I do understand what you mean. I don't know about Sofia, of course, but Magdolna has had that quality all her life. That's why I always come running home to her when I am distressed.'

'Despite that serenity,' Kate said, 'Sofia herself was unhappy before we came here and met you. She seems to have felt guilty ever since she left Hungary, as if she had somehow betrayed her father – I mean, your father. But he *chose* to stay behind and face the Germans. It wasn't her fault.'

'No, it wasn't her fault. But this I understand. I feel guilty about my father's death, although, as you reassured me there in the marshes, it was not literally my fault. It is the guilt of the survivor. You think – if they died, why was I spared? I am not worthy.'

They were both silent, not looking at each other.

'Your English is incredibly fluent,' said Kate abruptly. 'Why is that?'

'When I was a student in Budapest, it was forbidden to study English, unless you were a Party member in good standing, who had a valid reason for learning. This was not so many years after the '56 rising, you understand. But of course that made us all the more keen to learn it! We had secret schools in people's houses for learning English and French. You will find that many, many people in Hungary speak passable English. Probably more than would have spoken it if we *had* been encouraged to learn!'

They both laughed.

'But your German,' he said, 'that is also very fluent. Magdolna and Sofia and I were brought up bilingual in Hungarian and German, but you...?'

'I took my degree at university in French and German, and I used to teach both in a secondary school.'

'Used to?'

'Yes, I carried on after my first two children were born because we needed the money, but gave up when I was expecting my third. Then later I taught dyslexic children, till I had to give that up.'

'And why did you have to give it up?'

'My husband's job took us north to Dunmouth. I don't have a job at all now.'

There was a charged silence between them, and they picked at the sandwiches.

'Now you know about me,' she said. 'What about you? Are you married?'

But I do *not* know about you, thought István. There is something in the way you speak of the job, but not the husband...

'I used to be married,' he said.

'Divorced?'

'No.' He cleared his throat. 'My wife was killed when we were very young.'

'Oh, my God,' she cried. 'Not...?'

'No, no. Nothing like that. She was killed in a road accident on an icy day in Budapest. It was no one's fault. Luckily my son survived.'

'You have a son?'

'Yes. He's grown-up, of course. László.'

It was odd, she thought, that he had never mentioned a son. But then she had not mentioned her children either. This place seemed so distant from Dunmouth and her family that she felt like a different person, an individual with no ties and no responsibilities.

'I love your island,' she said, lying back as he had done and looking up through the leaves of the willows at the scattered fragments of blue sky.

He sat looking down at her. Neat, brown-haired, not a woman you would notice in a crowd, yet there was something compelling in her personality, which had drawn him to her as soon as he had met her.

'I had a dream when I was a child,' he said. 'I used to dream that one day I would get into a boat – perhaps this very boat, this blue boat in which we have been relaxing on the river, or perhaps some new, bigger, faster boat – and I would pull out into the main current of the Danube. And the river would take me, and the boat, and bear me away downriver. Past Budapest, past Pécs and Mohács, past Yugoslavia and the Iron Gates, through Romania, and so at last to the sea. And then I would be free. I would have escaped from this land-locked world in which I have lived all my life. Do you know, I have never seen the ocean?'

He laughed a little, ruefully.

'And now that I am a grown man, and the borders of our country are open, I am not sure whether I would dare to go, in case the reality does not live up to the dream.'

'But it never does, does it?' She looked up at him, shading her eyes with her hand. 'How strange,' she said pensively, 'that you have never seen the ocean. You look to me like a man who has the ocean in his eyes.'

She sat up and put her elbows on her knees, her chin on her hands.

'I'm haunted by the sea. When I am away from the sea I suffer a sort of claustrophobia. When we lived in London I used to go down to the river whenever I could, but the Thames is a poor thing compared with the North Sea.'

She smiled at herself.

'You'd think I would be feeling claustrophobic here, so far inland in this country of yours, but the Danube is such a mighty river it seems to compensate for the weight of all this middle Europe enclosing us and shutting us in. Didn't the Greeks and Romans regard it as the river of life? A hugely potent symbol of some great life-force? We have a river at home – the Dun. It flows into the sea where I live, and to me that has always seemed symbolic. As if by throwing yourself with abandon, without question, into the sea, you can escape from all the imprisoning walls imposed by the land and attain freedom at last.'

'And was this your dream, when you were a child?'

She lifted her head and turned to face him, looking at him steadily. 'István, I have almost no memory of my childhood. Later, yes, I have plenty of memories. But before I was about ten – nothing. When I try to force myself to recall something from that period of my life, my mind seems to shy away. A few things... A teacher at school, a few of the children I played with – I felt safe at school. A book I enjoyed – I suppose I felt safe there as well. I can call these up, but anything more profound, no.' She paused.

'I wonder, sometimes, whether I have some mental problem, to have caused this dark curtain in my memory.'

They studied each other.

'Something must have happened to you,' he said, 'when you were a child. Something which needed to be blocked out.'

'Of course, I forgot. You're a doctor.'

'I think Sofia said you lived in Dunmouth when you were a child, and only recently came back?'

'Yes.'

'And hasn't your return sparked anything from that time? Some fragment of memory?'

She looked down abruptly, blindly, at her hands.

'There is something, then,' he said gently.

'Just terrifying fragments, like a nightmare. And an overwhelming sense of guilt.'

'Guilt?'

'Yes, guilt.'

She raised her eyes to him, and they were filled with tears.

'And somehow it seems to be associated with Sofia.'

This time it was he who reached out to comfort her.

Chapter 11

Sofia, coming outside in the early evening to feed the hens for Magdolna, saw Kate and István tie up the blue boat at the landing-stage and walk up towards the house. There was, she thought, some subtle difference about them. Something had happened between them on the long boat trip, which had lasted most of the day.

'Magdolna has reminded me that tomorrow is St István's Day,' she said as they came into the kitchen together. 'And there is to be a fête in the village.'

'You won't get much sleep tonight,' István warned. 'They'll be putting up the stalls as soon as the men come in from the fields – they'll be working until midnight at least, and start again very early in the morning.'

'Does it take place in the square?' asked Kate.

Magdolna nodded. 'There are stalls all round the edge, and a platform for folk dancing and singing. People come in from the smaller villages round about, and from the farms – it's a great occasion!'

'Is it a harvest festival?' asked Kate. 'I suppose it is a bit early for that.'

'It is the festival of St István, our first Christian king,' said István. 'The twentieth of August is his day.'

'We saw his statue near the Mátyás Church in Budapest – with a crown and a halo.'

'That's him. But it's the Day of New Bread too. You will see – there will be stalls heaped high with every kind of new-baked bread for you to sample, as well as stalls for the farmers to display their produce, and perhaps one or two rides for the children, if the gypsies come.'

'They're here already,' said Magdolna. 'I saw them this morning when I went to the shop for milk.'

'Do you bake bread for the fair?' Sofia asked.

'Sometimes.'

'Of course you will,' said István.

'If I can get up early enough in the morning! We have worked very hard today, Sofia and I, while my lazy brother idled away on the river.'

'I am here on holiday,' he protested. 'I work very hard the rest of the year.'

'It was my fault,' said Kate. 'He was showing me the marsh and then the islands. It was so beautiful. I'm in love with your country.'

Magdolna smiled at her. 'Well, I hope you will still feel that way tomorrow, after a night of hammering and sawing.'

'Could I come and watch you bake bread tomorrow morning? I've never done it myself, and I'd love to learn.'

'Can you get up at four o'clock?'

'I can try!'

When Kate and Sofia walked up to the village square, everything was transformed. The front of the Blue Heron was festooned with bunting in the red, white and green of the Hungarian flag, and streamers had been looped through the branches of the walnut tree. Tractors were clattering down the road from the manor house and in from the minor lanes which radiated out from the village towards surrounding farms and hamlets. Some were towing trailers piled high with planks for stalls. Near the church a jaunty miniature roundabout had been set up, on which traditional gilded carousel horses were interspersed with hideous pink rabbits and a crude approximation to Mickey Mouse. Here and there amongst the people working in the square there were olive-skinned strangers – the men hawk-nosed, moustached, with hats of soft felt, the women imperious, wearing bold earrings and clashing bracelets. The gypsies had arrived. In amongst the piles of timber and crates and plastic drums, gypsy children with large dark eyes exchanged wary glances with the local children.

István was right about the noise. For the first time since arriving, Kate and Sofia ate their dinner in the dining room amongst the dark old furniture and heavy lace cloths, instead of outside under the tree, where the dust was stirred up by the unaccustomed traffic. Afterwards they sat for a time in the bar, which was lively with men coming in to drink a quick beer in the intervals of erecting the stalls and platform. When they retired to their rooms the banging continued, accompanied by cheerful shouts and the intermittent barking of the village dogs. There was no owl to be heard tonight, Kate thought, as she set her alarm clock for 4 a.m. and buried her head under the feather bed.

❧

As Kate walked down through the sleeping village at a quarter past four the next morning, it was not yet dawn, but there was a dawn light in the sky over to her right. No one had yet arrived to disturb the peace in the square, but she noticed lights in several houses, where the women were already busy about their bread-making. She wondered whether the competition for excellence was as fierce amongst the women of Szentmargit as it would be at a village fête in England. A sleepy cockerel crowed somewhere, and the birds in their morning chorus were singing more loudly than she had noticed since arriving in Hungary. In the oppressive heat of the day they were subdued.

When she reached Magdolna's kitchen, the first batch of dough was just being kneaded. József and András were eating their breakfast at one end of the kitchen table, but there was no sign of István.

'What a wonderful smell!' said Kate, accepting a steaming mug of coffee gratefully from József.

'It's the yeast,' said Magdolna, knocking down the dough with her strong potter's hands.

'You could get drunk on it.'

'You can get drunk on the real thing later,' József grinned, pulling on his boots. 'Good Hungarian beer. It will help you dance all the better.'

'Dance? I though that was just for the experts, on the platform.'

'Later, everyone will dance in the square,' András explained. 'There's a good gypsy band this year – we had the same one last year. I'll teach you the *csárdás*.'

'I don't think I'd be any good at it.'

He laughed. 'You can't come to the Day of New Bread and not dance the *csárdás*. You'll see, when everyone is doing it, you won't be able to stop yourself.'

An hour and a half later, when the noise from the square could be heard even in the Buvaris' house, István appeared, rubbing his eyes and yawning. Magdolna and Kate were sitting at the table, admiring the row of loaves, round and rectangular, plain and plaited, some scattered with poppy seeds, others glazed with egg so that they shone like polished wood. The smell of the new bread was intoxicating, exciting – almost primaeval, Kate thought.

'Hmm,' said István, peering at the loaves like a critical judge. 'What is this ugly, lop-sided object?'

Kate thought he was going to pick up one of her loaves, but instead he poked a finger at the one Magdolna had made with left-over scraps of dough. She had modelled it into a plaque of a woman in a long skirt and headscarf, holding up a loaf of bread. It was a comic parody of her own work.

Magdolna laughed. 'Do not listen to him. He does not have the soul of an artist. He is a grumpy bear in the morning.'

He dropped a kiss on the top of her head, touched Kate lightly on the shoulder.

'Please! It is only six o'clock in the morning! Can't a man get a cup of coffee in this terrible house?'

'A man might refill the coffee pot himself,' Magdolna suggested, 'and make coffee for the women who have been doing all the work.'

Together, the three of them sat down to breakfast while the bread cooled, then they packed the loaves into four large, flat baskets trimmed with red, white and green ribbons, and carried them up to the square. Kate noticed that István placed the bread lady on top of one basket with particular care, and that the women behind the stall set it up in the centre of the display against a brown and white checked cloth, and surrounded it with sprigs of parsley. Clearly it was not the first time Magdolna had made a bread figure for the fête.

Villagers were heading towards the church in answer to the ringing of a single bell. István, Magdolna and Kate joined them, and found Sofia already sitting near the back of the church. Kate could not understand a word of the service, but she enjoyed the chiming of the little bell, the swinging of the aspergillum, and the scent of the incense. She stood and sat and knelt, taking her cue from the rest of the congregation, and felt, as they came out of church, that she had at least paid some tribute to the great saint-king István.

'There was a large congregation,' she said to Magdolna. 'I thought perhaps, after so many years of communism...?'

'Under the communist regime,' said Magdolna, 'Christianity was tolerated, and the churches were maintained. But if you were known as a churchgoer, you would never get a good job. Mostly it was the old people who went to church. Of course, that was in the towns. It was a bit different here in the country. It was difficult enough to persuade people to stay and labour on the land. Now that we are free to worship, even the young people go to church.'

'I thought you said the other night that you didn't believe in God.'

Magdolna laughed. 'But I also said that doesn't mean He doesn't exist. Anyway, I went to the service for the sake of our good St István.'

After that, they were all caught up in the spirit of the fair and the eager, pushing crowd. Sofia joined them and they walked around admiring the stalls. Kate was intrigued by the display of apples set up by several of the local farmers. The round baskets of carefully polished fruit were placed on top of sawn-off lengths of tree-trunk, varying in height, and framed with trailing ivy. What caught her attention was the fact that all the labels were in English, or an English of sorts: Elstar, Early Glod, James Grives, Jirsey Mac.

'Why English?' she asked Magdolna.

'I suppose because we are hoping to become a member of the EU. The farmers are learning to use the European terminology. Anyway, many of the best apple varieties come from England, don't they?'

'I suppose they do. But I pity you if you become embroiled in the Common Agricultural Policy! It's a nightmare.'

'Better than having no market for our produce,' said József seriously.

The dancing displays went on intermittently all day. Groups from the various villages mounted the platform with their musicians and performed to scattered applause from the crowds strolling about the square. Kate could not appreciate the niceties of the performances, but the whirling figures of the women and the spectacular stamping and leaps of the men were full of a joyous exuberance. They wore a variety of costumes – from different regions, Sofia explained. Mostly the men wore tight black trousers, white shirts, and black waistcoats encrusted with braid and embroidery. A few, however, had high black boots with the voluminous white trousers which looked like skirts until they began to dance. The women were dressed in white blouses, skirts of red and green and blue, and long white aprons. Both their blouses and their aprons were covered in fine embroidery.

'Many of the aprons,' said Magdolna, 'are heirlooms. Probably made by their grandmothers, or their great-grandmothers. Like my linen you admired this morning. I'm afraid I am no needlewoman myself.'

In one group the women had white skirts of tiny accordion pleats, and as their partners threw them into the air the skirts opened like flowers. All through the day the dancing and the music on violin and double-bass formed a background to the fair. József was helping to man a stall displaying agricultural machinery, and Sofia and Kate were introduced to his brother Imre, a big impressive man with a flourishing moustache. Kate complimented him on the success of his irrigation system, which had made such a difference to the crops of the village.

In the afternoon, samples of the bread were free for tasting. Kate was praised for her bread, and felt she had not acquitted herself too badly. The dancing displays came to an end, and the carousel started up, instantly mobbed by the village children, who tugged at their mothers' skirts and begged for forints from their fathers. The gypsy children jumped on to the moving carousel with casual contempt, collecting fares and leaping off again gracefully as it reached full speed.

'Would you like to see the horse fair?' István asked Kate.

'I didn't realise there was one.'

'Whenever a group of gypsies gather, there will be a horse fair. It's only a small one, in the village meadow.'

They walked out of the square and beyond the last houses at the side of the village. Here the gypsies had set up their camp. Most of them, Kate saw, drove east European cars, with flashy silver caravans like the ones used by the gypsies in England. But a few still owned the traditional wooden, horse-drawn wagons. A rough enclosure had been roped off, where perhaps twenty or thirty horses were tethered to stakes hammered into the hard earth. When a potential buyer appeared, young gypsy boys, lithe and handsome, would mount the horses and ride them bareback around the makeshift ring, showing off both the horses and their own prowess. There was one girl too, a wiry little thing of nine or ten, who was displaying two of the horses – great, wild-eyed creatures which looked as though they would never tolerate a saddle.

As Kate and István strolled up – clearly not potential buyers – the girl was riding a huge black brute around the ring. It was wearing only a halter, and she was guiding it with her knees. A heavy-jowled, cruel-looking man shouted something to the child and she urged the horse to a canter, then stood up, balancing gracefully on its back. Once the horse had moved into a smooth gait she placed her hands on either side of its back and did a handstand, her cotton dress falling down over her head, showing that she was completely naked underneath. The horse-buyer leered at the gypsy, who was probably the child's father, and made some remark at which they both laughed. Kate, angry for the girl, was suddenly reminded of the child Eva, beaten if she did not practise the violin hard enough. Yet even in her nakedness there was a kind of lithe innocence about the child which should have shamed the bystanders. The gypsy girl turned a somersault, and landed on her feet with her arms outstretched, then she slid down to sit on the horse's back and slowed it to a stop. The two men were shaking hands, and wads of money were counted out. Clearly the child, like Eva, was useful to her father.

When the stranger led the horse away, the girl came up to the man and said something, holding out her hand and gesturing with her head towards the village square. He cuffed her hard on the ear, and turned on his heel, heading down towards the beer tent set up by the Blue Heron. The child ran off to the edge of the meadow, where she began to practise handstands and cartwheels, springing through the movements with such apparent ease and natural grace that it was easy to forget what hours of hard, rigorous training must lie behind such a performance.

'Why is Hungary so famous for producing acrobats and clowns? And musicians?' asked Kate. They watched the new owner lead away the black stallion, rolling its eyes, to the nearby barn which was serving as temporary stabling for the horses.

'Why do you suppose?' István threw back at her.

'Are they all gypsies? Does Hungary have a particularly large population of gypsies?'

'Many of them are gypsies. And yes, we do have many, many gypsies. There are many also in Transylvania, which used to be part of Hungary until after the first world war, when it was taken away from us and given to Romania. The gypsies have always worked with horses, and the children learn to perform circus tricks when they are very young, as you see.'

They began to walk back towards the square.

'I suppose the life of a professional acrobat, working in a circus, is a kind of extension of the nomadic life of the gypsies themselves,' said Kate.

'Yes. And for those who are successful it offers an escape from poverty. For make no mistake, the gypsies of Hungary are desperately poor, and although they form a large proportion of our population there is only one gypsy member of parliament – and to have even one is so unusual people remark upon it all the time. As for the gypsy musicians – they are a special caste, you know, and think themselves superior to the gypsies who work as brick-makers or other labourers.'

'And the clowns?'

'Ah, now,' he said, taking her arm, 'don't you think that is the most apt profession of all for a displaced and despised people? How does the aria from *I Pagliacci* go? "Ridi del duol che t'avvelena il cor!" That's something like "Laugh at grief, though it is breaking your heart." Aren't clowns said to be the saddest people on earth? Driven to create laughter to drown out the sound of a weeping heart.'

He squeezed her arm. 'I'm sorry. This is no time for such sad reflections. The band is tuning up. Didn't András say he was going to teach you the *csárdás*?'

They joined Sofia and the Buvaris and Imre at a table under the walnut tree, and drank some of the strong local beer which Imre had brought out in a jug from the inn. Dusk was falling and the strings of fairy lights slung round the square had been switched on. The carousel was still doing a brisk business, but its music was drowned out by the sound of the gypsy band, which was playing a languid, melancholy tune.

'That is the *lassu*,' András explained to Kate. 'It will be followed by the *friss*, and then comes the *csárdás*.'

Couples were getting up from the tables, and some of the older children drifted over from a stand topped by a red and white awning which bore the familiar legend 'Coca-Cola'. They began to dance, with slow, formal steps, working their way round the area near the platform which had been cleared of stalls. At the end of the hot, colourful day, the dreamy rhythm made Kate feel detached, and she sat back in the creaking wicker chair watching the dancers with her eyes half shut. The *lassu* seemed to go on for a long time, then the rhythm changed abruptly.

'That sounds like a military march,' said Kate.

'The *friss*,' Sofia answered.

More dancers joined the group in the square, and the people sitting at the tables tapped their feet in time to the strong, marching beat. Kate sat up. The music had become more compelling. András was sitting on the edge of his chair. In his embroidered waistcoat and best trousers he looked older, and Kate could see a foreshadowing of the man he would become, taller than his father, more like István in build, but with József's thick eyebrows and prominent cheekbones. His feet were beating the rhythm impatiently, and he turned and held out his hand to Kate.

'Come on!'

'I can't!' said Kate. 'I don't know the steps.'

'It doesn't matter,' said Magdolna, getting up and taking József's hand. 'Just hold on to András and do your best.'

She found herself amongst the crowd of dancers, which was growing by the moment. With András pulling her round she began to catch the general drift of the dance. Then the music changed once more. It speeded up and became wild and terrifying.

'The *csárdás*!' cried András, whirling her around until the coloured lights and the flower-covered front of the inn and the faces of the few people still sitting at the tables became a blur, one tilting, frantic, spinning mass of incomprehensible shapes. She was possessed. Her feet seemed to understand the music and carry her around with this crowd of people into which she was now absorbed, like the throbbing heart of some great beast. Was she breathing? Were her feet even touching the dusty earth?

Then gradually the music slowed, and the mass of dancers slowed, and staggered a little, like a top nearing the end of its spin, about to fall. Gradually the music released them, and they flew off the edges like drops of water, and fell, gasping, into their chairs.

Kate was gulping for air, and the table, as she clutched it, seemed to dip and sway. István laid a steadying hand on her arm.

'Breathe slowly, and do not try to speak. Did you know that it is said that a master musician of the gypsies can, if he wishes, compel people to dance the *csárdás* until they drop down dead?'

'Now,' Kate croaked, 'now you tell me. What a country! What crazy people!'

'Quite crazy.'

It was growing dark, and the band was playing Hungarian folk songs. Here and there the villagers joined in with the nasal but compelling voice of the gypsy woman singing with the band. The older people, including Sofia, drifted off to bed. Mothers began rounding up their children. Magdolna, István, József and Kate sat on at the same table under the tree, amongst the litter of empty glasses and bowls which had held *gulyás*. András had gone off somewhere with his friends. The carousel had ceased turning at last, and a pleasant somnolence drifted over the square as the staff from the Blue Heron wandered amongst the tables, gathering up dirty dishes and joking with the customers.

Suddenly someone sitting on the far side of the square near the church gave a cry. Everyone turned to look. From the direction of the meadow there came a flickering glow. Chairs were pushed back and fell with a thud on the ground. The farmers realised first what was happening. There were shouts and men running.

'What is it?' cried Kate. József had rushed off with the rest, István was on his feet.

'Fire,' said Magdolna. 'A haystack, or a barn. It's this drought... Once a spark catches...'

The crowd milled about, heading towards the glow. There was more shouting, and men came past with buckets, forming a chain from the nearest house, where the window had been flung open and women were filling the buckets and passing them out as fast as they could. Kate saw Imre and István pushing through the crowd from the far side of the square, from the direction where József and Imre had their fields. They seemed to be wreathed about by the coils of a great snake.

'Of course,' said Magdolna. 'The sprinkler system.'

The two women began to run in the direction of the meadow, and Kate lost Magdolna in the crowd. She was surrounded by strangers, all shouting to each other in Hungarian, and she found herself elbowed to the edge of the crowd.

She could see now what was on fire – it was the big old timber barn at the side of the meadow. Flames were shooting up one side in a wall of fire, and sparks were exploding from the wooden roof tiles and cascading down on to the dry grass of the meadow, where they sparked off little satellite fires.

Fire.

Kate veered off to the edge of the meadow, to come at the fire from the side. The bucket chain was working smoothly now, but it was hopeless, hopeless against this roaring, greedy monster. A group of men was struggling to set up the sprinkler, wrestling with the lengths of pipe, trying to fasten them together. There had been problems with the joints. Someone had said that. She could see István and József. András went running off down the village street waving something and calling to people in the houses.

Fire.

Then there was a scream. It sounded half human. The horses. There were horses in the barn. They screamed and no one was trying to rescue them. Kate ran on, around the edge of the meadow, and she could see only the flames and hear only the screams of the terrified animals.

Suddenly someone grabbed her and pulled her back roughly.

'The fire,' she sobbed. 'The horses.'

Her arms were pinned at her sides, but she struggled and fought, with the cries of the horses ringing around her.

'They are bringing the horses out of the other door. Around on the far side.' The voice spoke in English, but she couldn't at first understand, continuing to struggle, her face against cloth.

She was jerked around so that the blaze of the fire and its heat filled her sight, then she saw, beyond it, people leading horses, with cloths over their eyes. Incredibly the little gypsy girl was among them, leading the black stallion, without a rope, talking to him, coaxing him along.

'If I let you go, will you promise to stand still?' said the voice.

She looked round blankly, then stumbled away to the ditch at the side of the field and knelt there, swaying and retching. István knelt down beside her and put his arms around her.

'It's all right. They've managed to rescue all of the horses, and they're getting the fire under control.'

Kate began to shiver violently.

'Hush,' he said, holding her and rocking her as a mother rocks a terrified child. And Kate, whose mother had never held her, clung to him.

The shouting had died down. The hissing of the water as it met the fire drowned out the roar of the flames. The horses, still whickering in distress, were led away to the rope enclosure and tethered there. People began to drift back to the square as the flames died away and the farmers hosed down the whole of the smoking barn.

István led Kate to a fallen tree on the other side of the ditch and made her sit down. He wrapped his jacket around her and after a while the shivering became less violent.

'I'm sorry,' said Kate in a shaky voice. 'I don't know what came over me. It was the screams of the horses...'

István turned her arm so that it caught the edge of light coming from the square.

'It was a fire, wasn't it?'

She looked at him uncomprehendingly.

With the tip of his finger he traced a patch of skin on her arm which was slightly paler and shinier than the rest.

'These scars. I thought from the start they looked like burns. You have them on both arms, and on your legs. Not very noticeable, but at a certain angle to the light...'

Kate stared down at her arm. 'I've always had those...since I was a child...'

'But you don't remember when you were a small child. These were burns, Kate. At some time you've been badly burned.' His voice was gentle but firm. 'The nightmare you spoke of... is it about a fire?'

She pulled her arm away from him and buried her face in her hands.

'Yes,' she whispered. 'Some older boys and girls, dragging me along, and my own hand holding a burning bundle of sticks, and then an animal screaming – a dog, I think. But the first time I started to remember it was near Sofia's cottage.'

She took a deep breath.

'Then someone found an article from an old newspaper. I would have been about ten at the time. An outbuilding at Sofia's cottage was set on fire, and I think I must have been the one who lit it.'

'That is very easily settled. We will ask Sofia.'

'No!' she cried, grabbing him by the arm. 'No, please, no! I couldn't bear it. I've made up my mind to confront my parents when I get back to Dunmouth. I don't want anything to spoil this time in Hungary. Please don't say anything to Sofia. To anyone. I am so ashamed.' There were tears running down her face now, and he felt in his pocket for a handkerchief.

'If that is what you wish,' he promised, 'but as a doctor, not just as a friend, I think the sooner you can lay this ghost the better. If there were older children, is it likely that you were responsible? I don't think so. Be logical, Kate.'

'I am overwhelmed by guilt,' she said simply.

On Sunday Sofia declared that she was tired, and intended to spend the day reading in the back garden of the Blue Heron, perhaps snoozing a little if the mood took her.

'What will you do today, my dear?' she asked Kate.

'I think I shall go for a long walk. I don't want to hang about the village while they dismantle the fair – it's such an anticlimax.'

She did not add that she wanted to avoid István after last night's embarrassing breakdown.

'If you walk through the gardens of the manor, there used to be a lane on the other side which led south to the next village, Virgon. It isn't far – perhaps five miles? And a very pretty lane, if it is still the same – with shady trees and a small lake about halfway along.'

'That sounds perfect. If you don't mind being left alone?'

'Of course not. Why don't you ask Mihály to give you a packed lunch, and take your time about it?'

Kate followed Sofia's directions, echoed by Mihály's, and found the leafy lane which might almost have been in England, except for the dust underfoot and the hot scent floating off the fields. She dawdled by the lake, watching some brown ducks of a variety she didn't recognise, and three or four families of moorhens. The water was shallow and clean, and wonderfully cool under the shade of the trees. She took off her sandals and plunged her feet into it. The place was deserted. She had not seen a soul since she left Szentmargit. Somewhere ahead of her a church bell rang, presumably from Virgon. She picked up her sandals and waded around a curve in the lake shore. There was a little hidden bay, with more ducks, a single swan and in the distance a heron fishing.

On a sudden impulse, she put her lunch and her shoes on the bank and pulled off her clothes. The water was silky and cool on her hot, dusty skin. She slid down into it, where the bottom of smooth mud sloped away from the bank, and felt the tension which had kept her awake for most of the night melt away. She swam and floated quietly until the ducks, which had scattered at her first approach, ventured out and circled round her. One of the ducklings, bolder than the rest, made a tentative peck at her toe.

'Ow!' She rolled over and swam the full length of the little lake, then swam back again and climbed out to lie on the grass beside her clothes. The sun was so hot that she dried before she fell asleep, and dreamt of nothing but slipping through the marshes in the blue boat.

She was woken when a grasshopper landed on her nose, and came awake confused, fetching up on the shore of consciousness. She stared about her, at the water sparkling under the unclouded sun, at the heron standing motionless on one leg in the shallows, and stretched luxuriously.

That morning she had taken out her journal, not filled in for the previous day, and written firmly, *This must stop.*

Here, alone in this quiet and beautiful place, she felt in control, surer of herself than she had ever done before. István, the doctor, was probably right. Her memory of whatever had happened to her in the fire – if there had been a fire – was confused by fear, by the burning she had somehow suffered, by the distortions of childhood perception. Her sense of guilt was probably no more rational than her old sense that her mother did not love her because she was in some way sinful. It was a beautiful day, in this beautiful country, where she felt clean and new-born.

István, the man, she preferred not to think about. The two of them had been thrown into an accidental intimacy, coming together at a time when each was feeling vulnerable. They had helped each other, perhaps. It was time to step back. To be friendly and courteous to Sofia's brother, but no more.

I am a married woman, Kate told herself firmly, pulling on her clothes, which were warm from the sun. A middle-aged mother. What have I been thinking of?

She ate her lunch beside the lake, sharing the crusts from her sandwiches with the ducks and moorhens, then set off again for Virgon.

It was dusk when she returned to Szentmargit, tired with the healthy tiredness that comes from a long day of vigorous but not exhausting exercise in fresh air and sunshine. Over dinner she suggested to Sofia that they should spend a day shopping in Györ tomorrow.

'I want to buy some presents for the family, and for Linda,' she said. 'And much as I love Szentmargit, it doesn't have much to offer in the way of purchases beyond day-to-day necessities.'

'Yes, that's a good idea,' Sofia agreed. 'I should like to take something back for Chris, and you can help me choose a suitable present. I wonder...'

'Yes?'

'Why don't we invite Magdolna to go with us? I don't think she often has an opportunity to visit Györ, and when she does she is encumbered by her husband and son.'

'That's a wonderful idea. We'll have a strictly female day out.'

They walked down to the rose-coloured house after dinner to invite Magdolna, who said at first she would not be able to get away, but József and István both urged her to go.

'For one day we can manage without you,' said József. 'András can let the hens out and feed them before he comes to the fields.'

'And I will do the cooking,' István said. 'After all, I cook for myself in Sopron all the time. Off you go and enjoy yourselves. Don't spend too much money, and I'll have dinner prepared for all of us when you arrive home.'

Sofia demurred at this, insisting that she and Kate would dine at the Blue Heron, and she was so firm that it was agreed.

They had an enjoyable day in Györ. Magdolna and Sofia took Kate round some parts of the old city they had not seen on their first visit, and then they went for lunch at the Várkapu restaurant, in front of which stood a curious bronze statue of an elongated man holding what appeared to be a deer. In the afternoon Magdolna took them to the best shops. The modern shopping centre of the city had changed out of all recognition since Sofia's girlhood. Kate told Magdolna of their terrible hotel in Györ, and the noise of the lorries hitting the pot-holes in the street all through the night.

Magdolna laughed. 'It will be a long time before the streets in Hungarian cities are up to the standards of Western capitals. We say that is why east European cars are so badly made. There's no point in building good cars, because they would fall apart just as quickly as the bad ones on our terrible roads, so why bother?'

They arrived back in Szentmargit at half-past eight, laden with embroidery and books – Kate could not believe how cheap the books were. They had boxes of Hungarian chocolates and crystallised fruit, and Kate had treated herself to a piece of Herend china – a delicate little vase in the Aponyí pattern.

'A lovely, spendthrift, touristy day,' said Kate as they dropped Magdolna off at her door. 'Thank you for being such a wonderful guide.'

'Thank you,' said Magdolna. 'I cannot remember when I enjoyed a visit to town so much.'

When she entered the kitchen she found that István had prepared dinner for the family as he had promised, and András had even tidied himself up from his work in the fields and was sitting with his hands washed and his hair slicked down with water. She sometimes forgot that István had brought up his own son by himself, and was a competent cook and a parent with high standards of tidiness.

While they were eating, István said, 'I have to go to Sopron tomorrow.'

'Oh no!' cried Magdolna, dismayed. 'So soon?'

'Only for the day. Young Endre phoned the inn and left a message with Mihály. He's had a report back on some tests we had done on one of the patients and he wants me to have a look at it before we decide what to do next. I don't want to leave it till the end of my holiday. I can set out in the morning and be back by late afternoon.'

Magdolna looked at him thoughtfully. 'Why don't you take Kate with you? She gave us a lovely day today in Györ, but she hasn't seen much of the country. Sofia is happy staying here, but perhaps it is a little dull for Kate. Sopron is so pretty, I know she would enjoy it.'

'I'm not sure...'

'You won't have to spend too long at the surgery, will you?'

'No more than an hour, I suppose.'

'Well, then. You enjoy her company, don't you?'

'Magdolna,' he said uncomfortably, 'she is a married woman with three children. It is not *suitable* that I should spend so much time with her.'

'I cannot think what you mean.' Magdolna opened her eyes innocently. 'I am simply suggesting that you should show her around the old walled city, and perhaps some of the woodland walks, and then have dinner before coming back. There is no harm in that, is there?'

István sighed. 'No, there is no harm in that.'

Kate took some persuading, however, when Magdolna arrived at the inn during the evening with the suggestion of the trip to Sopron.

'You mustn't miss the chance,' said Sofia. 'Sopron is lovely.'

'Then why don't you come too?'

'Because Magdolna says it has not changed much since I saw it last, and because two long trips by car in two days is too much for me. I will rest tomorrow.'

In the end Kate felt obliged to agree, and they set off early next morning for Sopron. She was glad, later, that she had come. István drove first to the Lövér hotel, where they had coffee. Then they set off for a long walk through woods which smelled of pine needles, and were high and cool, clothing the slopes of the mountains that led up to the border with Austria.

'This is a very healthy place,' István explained. 'There are several sanatoriums here, and many people come to rest and recuperate as well as for holidays. I decided it would be a good place to bring my baby son to live.'

'How old is he now, your son?' Kate asked, as they came round the bend in the track and saw the hotel again below them.

'He's twenty-four. He lives in a village in the south, near Mohács.'

As he was unlocking the car, István paused and leaned on the roof, looking at her. 'I want to go and see László, to tell him face to face about Sofia, and all we have learned about the family. I don't want to telephone or write. I wondered whether you would both like to come with me? I thought I might drive down at the weekend and stay a couple of nights. Mohács is very interesting – I would like to take you there.'

'We'll ask Sofia when we get back, shall we?'

Kate liked István's house with its cool, lime green walls and white shutters. She had not been inside a modern Hungarian house before. Miss Huszka looked at her with speculative interest as she handed István the report he had come to read.

'I'll show you up to the flat,' he said, 'and you can relax there while I deal with this. Then we'll have some lunch and go and explore the old city.'

The big sitting room in the flat was dark, with the shutters closed against the sun, but István threw open the ones on the north side, overlooking the garden, letting in light but not too much heat.

'There are plenty of books here, some of them in English, and a cassette player. Here are my music tapes. The bathroom is through here, along the corridor past the two bedrooms, and the kitchen is the other way, opening off the sitting room. There is everything you need to make yourself coffee or tea. I phoned Miss Huszka this morning and asked her to get in milk and bread and salad, so we can make ourselves something to eat before we go out again.' He looked at her anxiously. 'Will you be all right for an hour or so?'

'I'll be fine. I'll look at your books, or just relax and admire your garden.' She smiled at him. 'Go on. Go and sort out your patient.'

When he had gone she looked about curiously, with that slight sense of intrusion which always accompanies being left alone in someone else's home. The books, she saw, were varied, from paperback thrillers to serious tomes on history and philosophy. She looked with pleasure through a big book of photographs of Hungary, and was sorry that she was not going to be able to visit the *puszta*, with its herds of horses and its horse-herdsmen in their baggy white trousers.

She visited the bathroom, noticing its spare, uncluttered look, unquestionably the bathroom of a man who lived alone, but who was neat in his habits. For a moment she plunged her face into a silk dressing-gown which hung on the back of the door. It smelled spicy and masculine, and unmistakably of István.

In the kitchen she found the coffee things and made herself a cup of instant, then, seeing by the kitchen clock that it was past twelve, she decided to make their lunch. She found the shopping the receptionist had bought, and laid out on the table bread and butter and three different kinds of cheese. She washed the lettuce and made a mixed salad, then prepared a French dressing. There was some fruit with the shopping, so she piled it up in a wooden bowl from one of the cupboards and was just wondering what István would want to drink when he walked in.

'Oh, Kate, how kind! I didn't mean you to have to do this. You are my guest.'

'It was nothing – I've only put things out on the table.'

He dropped a kiss on the top of her head, as she had so often seen him do with Magdolna.

'I wasn't sure what you would want to drink.'

'There should be wine and beer in the fridge.'

'I'm quite happy with water. I'm afraid I'm not really a beer person.'

'Then we will have wine.' He lifted out the bottle and searched for a corkscrew in a drawer. 'It is just a light Hungarian white wine. Not heavy to make us sleepy in the middle of the day so the sightseeing is too much trouble.'

They sat down to their simple meal, and Kate said, 'Did you sort matters out with your partner?'

'Yes. I think we will try physiotherapy for the patient first. There was a possibility of surgery, but I prefer to wait, and use it only as a last resort.'

After lunch they walked the short distant to the gates leading through into the old walled city. The houses here reminded Kate of the quiet roads she had explored with Sofia beyond the Mátyás Church in Budapest, but they were shabbier and looked more homely, more lived in. István pointed out the Tüztorony, the Firewatch Tower, which stood like a living monument of archaeological strata – its base a Roman watchtower, topped by a Renaissance arcaded storey, then capped by a baroque copper spire. Around the gilded Trinity column two little boys were riding races on their tricycles, and in the cobbled square opposite the museum three young mothers were sitting with pushchairs and shopping baskets full of vegetables. They looked up as Kate and István passed.

'*Jó napot*, Dr Rudnay,' they called.

'*Jó napot*. Good afternoon.' Kate had learned that much Hungarian.

István greeted them by name – clearly, from his gestures, asking after the children. She exchanged smiles with the women.

'Patients?' she asked as they walked away.

'Some of the young women who come to my mother and baby clinic.'

After they had explored the old town they went out again through the stone archway, where renovation work was in progress, then sat under a row of trees on a bench while István told Kate as much as he could remember about the history of the town.

'This area has always been half-Austrian, half-Hungarian. But when we were given a measure of independence from the Austrian empire by the Ausgleich of 1867, the people of this region chose to be part of Hungary, not Austria, and that's the way it has stayed ever since.'

They sat for a while in comfortable silence, watching people on their way home from work and mothers rounding up their children.

'You see what I mean about everything in Hungary being so pretty,' said Kate. 'Look at that.'

'What?' István asked, puzzled.

'That kiosk.'

'It's just a kiosk.'

'Yes, but *look* at it, István. You are probably so used to them you don't even see them.'

The cruciform building was made of some dark wood, with many-paned leaded windows, and a roof which was all steep angles and gables of silvery shingles. The corner of each of the four gables was ornamented with carving. István narrowed his eyes and studied it.

'Yes, I suppose you are right. I've never noticed before, but they *are* pretty.'

He turned to her and took her hand. 'You open my eyes to things I have walked past without noticing all my life.'

She dropped her eyes, then drew her hand slowly away.

'One of your patients might be passing.'

He laughed. 'Indeed, they might. Come, it's a little early, but I think we should go to the restaurant where I am going to give you dinner. We don't want to be too late starting back.'

To reach the restaurant they had only to cross the main road and walk a short way along a wide pavement.

'Look at the window!' said Kate, then laughed at herself. 'I'm sorry, I must stop this, but – look, a Venetian window, with all that fretwork like lace above it, and the curtains and lamps inside...'

He smiled and her, and took her hand again.

'You are quite right. We Hungarians and all our works, we are very beautiful.'

Kate enjoyed her meal, although she could not have said afterwards what she had eaten. István had ordered in Hungarian, assuring her that she would like it. There had been tension between them when they had set out that morning, but the discomfort had ebbed away, leaving the familiarity of old friends who can talk or be silent as the mood takes them. Somehow they had passed through several intermediate stages in acquaintanceship in quick succession. It was good to be away from Szentmargit with its intense feelings, good to be in this impersonal but charming restaurant, in a quiet corner behind oak railings, served by skilful waiters, lingering over a delicate Viennese pudding with a pink candle guttering on the table between them.

'I am glad you came with me, Kate,' said István, resting his chin on his clasped hands.

'I'm glad I came. I nearly didn't.'

'Why?'

'I think you know why. Let's not worry about that now.'

'Will you come with me to Mohács?'

'We'll ask Sofia when we get back.'

'And if Sofia does not want to make the long journey?'

'Perhaps. We'll see.'

As they walked back through the dark streets to collect István's car from his driveway, Kate felt tired, but at ease with herself and with him. There was nothing to worry about here. Sofia's brother was a charming man, someone she found she could talk to about anything, who laughed at the same things as she did.

The car purred smoothly out of Sopron on the main road to Györ, from which the road to Szentmargit turned off. Kate leaned back her head against the headrest and closed her eyes.

'Tired?'

'A bit. So many impressions. Hungary is like a piece of rich embroidery stitching itself up in my memory.'

'Rest a little. Sleep if you can.'

'Mmm.'

She had not thought she would, but the car was comfortable, the driver careful, not wanting to hurry this drive, hoping she would sleep so he could study her unobserved. He slowed down as she fell asleep, nursing the car gently round bends, easing it on to the minor road which led off the dual carriageway. Kate's head slid sideways and rested on his shoulder. He smiled to himself, but sadly. In just over a week, she would be gone.

Chapter 12

Sofia had spent the day studying the papers from the tin box Magdolna had found buried in the floor of the barn. She had brought some of the papers from Eva's trunk with her to Hungary – not the photographs, but her father's diaries and a few of the personal letters. His handwriting had changed over the years from the elegant, bold script of his youth in the letter written to Eva in Pécs shortly before their elopement, to the cramped scribble – sometimes in faded pencil – of the later notebooks which had superseded his early leather-bound diaries.

She had been puzzled and disturbed when she first read that entry which seemed to be the expression of some deep guilt. She turned it up again now.

Suppose, after all, we were to be called to account for our deeds in this world before some ultimate tribunal. The past made present, confronting us as it truly was – not as our flinching memories recall it – could prove appalling. But might there have been, even in our darkest acts, the seeds of redemption?

What if we could turn aside, walk through the unnoticed door into a hidden garden, and find there the past, ready to be lived again? Willing to be reshaped, fashioned from chaos into harmony and order? If the hurtling train of life could pause at the station, the hands of the clock stop.

If we could have another chance.

Looking back over what she knew now of his life as a whole, she thought she understood better what had troubled him. It was not a personal guilt, but guilt for his class, the guilt of having been born a semi-feudal landowner. From the time he had inherited the estate at the age of seventeen he had been trying to atone for that guilt. He had given away a large proportion of his lands to the peasants of Szentmargit, a gift which – after years of expropriation by the communist government – was benefiting them again. Had his marriage to Eva been in part a rejection of his class? It had been a profound love match, that she knew was true. But any of his ancestors would have taken Eva as a mistress, not married her, tainted – as she would have seemed to them – by her gypsy blood.

Sofia shook her head and smiled sadly. It would be difficult to imagine a more cultured, intelligent and beautiful woman than her mother, an ornament to the most elegant social occasion. But the deep-rooted nature of prejudice blinds the eye and distorts the judgement. Eva had made no secret of her part-gypsy ancestry, had indeed been proud of it. But the long contempt of the true-blooded Magyars for the gypsies must have affected her life and put her in great danger when the Nazi witch-hunts began. Curiously Sofia had never felt herself to be gypsy. Perhaps it was her upbringing in an aristocratic Hungarian milieu. Except for that one time, at the Paparuda, when the water and the poppies and the grasses had seemed to link her to the soil in some strange primaeval way.

Zsigmond's desire to expiate his own in-born guilt – as well as his principles and his belief in a free Hungary – must have driven him to join the partisans and risk death. And in his union with Juliska, a true-born Magyar peasant girl, he had come to the place he was seeking. Magdolna and István seemed to Sofia to be the true fruit of Zsigmond's blood, rather than herself. Like Eva she would always be displaced, a person outside, alien, wherever she lived. But now she was over seventy this no longer troubled her as it had done when she was young. She had learned to accept it as an intrinsic part of her own being, as Magdolna and István had learned to accept their illegitimacy.

If we could have another chance.

Her eyes met the words again. Zsigmond had made his own second chances. She had been given hers, partly as a result of his, partly through the wayward fortunes of war. She had never expected to find her mother's Guarneri violin again. Yet, because Jakob Stern had survived the camps, because the vault of the instrument shop had been safely sealed, the violin had come back to her. More important to her was the discovery of a brother and sister. She would not return to Szentmargit to live, as Magdolna had urged. She had her own home, her own responsibilities, her animals, her garden – which was an expression of herself almost as powerful as her poems. But she would come again to the village, as long as she was strong enough to make the journey. And – she thought of it for the first time, as a sparkling possibility – there was no reason, now, why they should not come to her! She thought of sitting with Magdolna and József in her garden amongst the bees and the lush green growth, so different from the parched ground around Szentmargit, watching András romp with Ákos. István she could picture striding along the beach with Kate, laughing.

No. István and Kate would not be laughing on the beach at Dunmouth together. Sofia sighed and piled up the papers again. She wondered whether she should discuss it with Magdolna.

&

Anna arrived on Wednesday, and said she could stay until the weekend. Kate was reminded forcefully of Beccy when she met her. She was not sure whether it was because of their nearness in age and circumstance – both nineteen, both just having finished their first year at university – or whether they were indeed alike in personality. Anna's attitude towards her parents combined affection and exasperation. Clearly she felt that for József to continue to work as a peasant farmer was not good enough for him (or, Kate suspected, for the father of Anna Buvari, soon to be a distinguished lawyer in Budapest). Towards her mother she was protective, like all the family, but also bracing.

'Mama, you should come to Budapest sometimes, to open your exhibitions, to be seen. It is essential if you're going to further your career in the arts, especially now that art lovers from all over the world are coming to Budapest. You need to build your network of connections in other countries.'

Magdolna smiled serenely and handed her a dish of plum pastry.

'But then I would have less time to work, Anna.'

'What I am trying to say is that you wouldn't have to work so hard. You aren't paid nearly enough for what you do. You *know* that. You could do less and still be paid more.'

'Anna,' said István, planting a firm, admonitory hand on her shoulder as he walked around the back of her chair to fetch the jug of cream from the larder, 'your mother is not interested in how much she is paid, so long as she is paid enough to provide her with clay and glazes. All she is interested in is having the time to work out her ideas, to give birth, if you like, to each of her figures clamouring to be born.'

Anna sighed exaggeratedly, ran her hands through her long, curly hair and threw it back, then laughed ruefully.

'You are hopeless, all of you. Can't you tell her, Aunt Sofia? You are an artist of international fame. Imagine! I never knew that the poet Sofia Tabor was my aunt.'

'Poetry,' said Sofia, looking at her with amusement, 'is not a highly paid profession. You get on with your career as a high-powered lawyer, as a young woman of your generation. And let your mother and me pursue our dreams in penury. We shall all rub along well enough.'

Kate liked Anna, despite this attempt to galvanise her mother into greater commercial awareness. She was a loving daughter, and had an affectionate if teasing relationship with her younger brother. She even tied back her hair and joined András and his friends in a game of football in the meadow. Not, thought Kate, quite as sophisticated as she would have us believe.

⁊

Anna's visit injected a spice into their lives, bringing as it did a whiff of the capital and the wider world into the rural simplicity and hard labour of Szentmargit. Even József delayed his start for the fields each morning. He was gruff with his daughter, but affectionate pride glowed from him as took her round the village in the evening, showing her off. The whole party of them dined twice in style at the Blue Heron so they could enjoy more time for conversation free of kitchen chores. Only Sofia seemed abstracted, disappearing to her room from time to time, where she still had all her father's papers.

'I am sorry,' she said, when chafed by Anna, 'but I am busy writing. And it is essential to seize the moment, or the idea vanishes. Your mother will understand that.'

Sofia had said at first that she would come with Kate and István to Mohács to visit this other nephew of hers, but as she became immersed in her work she grew more doubtful. István had already telephoned a *csárda* in the village outside Mohács where László lived, and booked rooms for the three of them.

'It doesn't matter,' he said. 'Kate can still use the double room. You will come, won't you, Kate?'

'Yes,' she said, not wanting to disappoint him, and curious to see his son. 'Why will you not tell me what is so special about Mohács?'

He laughed. 'You will see.'

She could have consulted her guidebook, but decided to let him keep his mystery.

Friday was Anna's last day, and she planned to spend it in the fields, helping her father and Imre with the harvest, most of which was now gathered in, thanks to the long period of exceptional sunshine combined with the successful irrigation scheme. Kate and István set out straight after breakfast.

'I am going to take you to Lake Balaton for lunch,' said István. 'We are proud of our one large lake – it is a great refreshment for the eye in our land-locked country.'

Kate had expected an unremarkable stretch of water, and was astonished when they arrived on the shores of what looked like a small sea. The clear waters stretched away into the distance, sparkling under the sun and sprinkled with the multicoloured sails of wind-surfers and sailing boats. There were holiday resorts dotted along the shore, but the Golden Cockerel, the restaurant to which István had brought her, stood on its own in wide grounds, beautifully landscaped. The building itself was a fine, rambling old house perched on a slight eminence with spectacular views over the lake.

'This was once the summer residence of one of the great aristocratic families,' said István as they sat with their drinks on the terrace, waiting for their lunch to arrive. 'Built first, very elegantly, in the eighteenth century, at the height of the Empire, then extended with less taste in the nineteenth.'

'Who owns it now?'

'It used to belong to the State – seized after the war, of course. For many years it served as a holiday hotel and sanatorium for high-ranking Party members. Then three years ago the heirs managed successfully to claim it back. They had been living in Switzerland until then, and had gone into the hotel trade.'

'Have many of the old properties been reclaimed?'

'A few. The government likes to show that it is restoring free and democratic ownership. Many of the flats in Budapest have been returned to their owners, but nobody has the money to repair them, and they had been very poorly maintained by the State.'

'Could you reclaim your father's house? The manor at Szentmargit?'

'I have no rights. I am the illegitimate son.'

He spoke abruptly. So it does still rankle, thought Kate.

'No,' he continued, 'if anyone has a claim on the estate it is Sofia, and I do not think she will take any action.'

'No, I don't think so. She has made her own little kingdom.' And Kate began to tell him about Sofia's garden, with its goat and hens and bees, and of how she had first seen her, fishing barefoot amongst the rock pools for crabs.

After lunch they drove on at a leisurely pace along the beautiful lakeside, then took the road for Mohács. They bypassed the town and reached the village of Kishíd, where László lived, and where they were to stay until Monday.

'László will not be available until Sunday,' said István, 'but we have plenty to do tomorrow. Can you get up very early? Where I want to take you is best seen early, before other people are about.'

'Didn't I get up early on the Day of New Bread? Two hours, at least, before you did.'

'Very true. We will meet by the front door of the inn at – shall we say half-past six? It will be too early for breakfast, but we will have something later.'

The inn was comfortable enough, but not as friendly as the Blue Heron, where Kate felt entirely at home now. Mihály, she realised, was responsible for much of the atmosphere there, welcoming all his guests like members of the family. Her room here, with its two single beds and a dormer window looking out over an orchard, was pleasant and unpretentious, although she did not much care for the holy picture of a bleeding heart which hung on the wall above the dressing table. Surreptitiously she took it down and rested it facing the wall behind the curtains.

After dinner they went for a short walk around Kishíd, but there was not much to see. It seemed to be partly a farming village like Szentmargit, and partly an overspill for commuters working in Mohács. It lacked the rural isolation which made Szentmargit so peaceful, if poor. Here there was a sense of being in the suburbs.

They met next morning as they had planned and let themselves out of the sleeping inn. The sun was already up, but still low, flushing the undersides of leaves pink and gilding the cross on the top of the small church which, like the Church of Szent Margit, had the characteristic onion-shaped dome. They drove a short way through the countryside, where cows stood up to their knees in mist, which would soon be burnt away as the sun climbed high.

'There are more animals here,' said Kate; 'less arable.'

'Yes, just here, perhaps. But the area for the big herds is the east of the country. Did you know that we have horseherds, cowherds, shepherds and swineherds, and the hierarchy is very strict? That is in the *puszta*, of course.'

'I've seen wonderful pictures of men herding great droves of horses.'

'I wish we had time to go there too. I wish you did not have to leave on Wednesday.'

Kate thought with a shock, *It is so soon.* She had been pushing it to the back of her mind.

'*I* wish I didn't have to leave on Wednesday.'

'You cannot stay?'

224

'No. Not possibly.'

'Perhaps next time we can visit the *puszta*.' He looked at her quizzically.

'Perhaps next time.'

They drove for a while in silence, and found themselves in the outskirts of Mohács.

'Now,' said István, 'I want you to close your eyes until I say you may open them.'

'Really?'

'Really. Do as you are told. You will not regret it.'

She obeyed, and soon the car stopped, manoeuvring into a parking place.

'Now?'

'Not yet. I will open the door for you and then lead you to where you may look.'

He took her by the hand and led her – feeling foolish – over what seemed to be gravel and grass with the hard parched feel of this summer's heat. There was the grating sound of a metal gate. Then he stopped and moved behind her, putting his hands on her shoulders.

'Now before you look, I want to tell you a story.' He paused, then continued quietly, 'In the year 1526 Suleiman the Magnificent, Sultan of Turkey, emperor of all the Ottoman lands, which then extended from Spain across north Africa to the Middle East and into Europe as far as Bulgaria, Romania and Serbia, turned his eyes at last on a small proud country called Hungary. Her king was called Lajos and he was a brave young man, just twenty, and an inspiring leader of men. He had been king since he was ten, and while he was a child he was under the control of the powerful nobles who were busy pursuing their own interests. While he was hardly more than a child he had been married to a Hapsburg princess. As he reached manhood he realised that unless the national army could be re-established, Hungary had no chance of defending herself against Suleiman's greedy reach. But he could not convince the parliament.

'His entire army of loyal followers consisted of no more than twenty thousand men, while Suleiman could put half a million into the field against Hungary alone. The forces of the Ottoman Empire were feared throughout Europe. They had a reputation for ferocious bravery and terrible cruelty to any unfortunate enough to be taken captive by them.'

Kate shivered. She could see against her eyelids the small, gallant force of Hungarians and the hordes of Turks, like a great sea rolling in from the south-east, their wicked curved swords glittering as they raised them in the sun.

'King Lajos tried everything,' István went on. 'He tried diplomatic missions to the Sultan, but his ambassadors were caught in a sticky net of honeyed words. He sent to his allies for help – to the Hapsburgs, to the king of the Poles, to every Christian king in Europe, including Francis I of France, who (unknown to Lajos) was secretly an ally of the Turks in an attempt to surround the Hapsburgs and curtail their growing power. Once again his ambassadors were turned away with smooth words. Why should these great princes endanger their armies in such a conflict? Hungary was far away, let her look after herself.'

'They didn't come?'

'They didn't come.'

'Just like 1956?'

'Exactly. Well, Lajos took to the field with his small army, knowing he had no hope, but what could he do? He was not the man to bow the knee to Suleiman without a fight. The armies met here, near Mohács.'

'Did he win after all?' Kate asked in sudden hope, although she knew the answer. She had, after all, read her Hungarian history.

'No, he was defeated. Here, on 29 August 1526. It will be the anniversary on Monday. Thousands of men died that day, but they went down fighting with honour for the freedom of Hungary against the foreign invader. Lajos himself was crossing a small stream when his horse lost its footing – it was perhaps already injured – and they fell together, the horse crushing the king under him.'

'So the Turks came to rule Hungary.' She could hear an odd tinkling noise, like a string of bells – softer and less disciplined than the mass bell in the church at St István's feast, higher and sweeter than the bells she had heard on the few bellwethers around Szentmargit.

'Well, that isn't quite the whole story. The Turks seized Budapest, as you know – you must have seen the Turkish baths and mosques there, and the Muslim prayer niche, the *mihrab*, in the Belvárosi Templom? But they did not conquer the whole country. When they were at the very height of their powers, in 1566, they over-reached themselves at the siege of Szigetvár, not far from here. Eventually they destroyed the tiny garrison, while a Hapsburg army of a hundred thousand waited in safety near Győr. But the Turks' own forces had received a mortal wound. Suleiman himself died there.'

'So the rest of Europe was saved.'

'As you say. So they were quite right, weren't they, those kings and princes? They had not lost a single soldier to the Turks, and Hungary held the line against any further Turkish attack. We were the final rock on which the wave of their advance broke.'

'May I look now?'

'In a moment. The Turks were driven out, as I am sure you know, after their attack on Vienna in 1683 – something the Hapsburgs couldn't ignore. Then in Hungary we had the Austrians instead of the Turks. Then the Germans, then the Russians. But in 1976, on the four hundred and fiftieth anniversary of the battle here at Mohács, this memorial was built.'

'To commemorate the *Turkish* victory?' Kate asked, incredulous.

'As a memorial to those who died valiantly trying to stop the Saracen advance against all odds, and to commemorate the halting of that advance at Szigetvár.' He paused. 'And of course the driving out of the Turks in the following century. You have to remember that at the time this memorial was created the 1956 uprising was twenty years behind us. We were just emerging from the dark years, on the road to the freedom which came in 1989.'

He reached up and brushed his fingertips against her closed lids.

'You may look now.'

Kate opened her eyes and blinked. Dark shapes swam in front of her eyes, and she felt momentarily dizzy. She saw a meadow dotted with strange figures which to her blurred vision seemed to sway. There was a pole with... no, it was too horrible... three severed heads hanging from it. István placed a steadying hand under her elbow and then her vision sharpened and she saw that the heads were carved from wood. The heads, she supposed, of Hungarian knights cut off by those terrible curved scimitars.

They walked amongst the figures, which were carved from some dark grey wood like the old grave markers in the churchyard at Szentmargit – oak, perhaps. They were bold and simple, sometimes almost crude, but with a terrible vigour and power. Warriors stood proudly in their pleated tunics, staring out defiantly over the field towards their certain death. Horses, beautiful even as they fell, lay around them amongst the heedless gold of sunflowers.

'This is Suleiman the Magnificent,' said István, as they stood in front of a carved head wearing an elaborate turban. The face was both cruel and complacent, the face of an implacable enemy in his moment of victory. The lips curved above a beard which jutted forward aggressively. Thin metal ornamental chains dangled from his turban, and as the breeze stirred them they rang with that sweet bell-like note

Kate had heard, an ironic counterpoint to the mad eyes and hawk-like nose. She shivered. And she understood why István had wanted to bring her here, in the quiet light of early morning, with a faint haze of dew on the grass and thrushes singing in the nearby hedgerow. This memorial at Mohács epitomised more than one gallant stand against a foreign invader. It seemed to hold the essence of all those desperate individual acts of heroism – Zsigmond amongst the partisans, Juliska and her friends defying the Russian tanks with their bare hands.

'I think,' she said humbly, slipping her arm through his, 'I *think* I am just beginning to understand Hungary.'

He pressed her arm against his side. 'Come,' he said. 'This place is beautiful but sad. We will leave it before it is spoiled for us by the tourists. We will go and find some breakfast.'

Kate did not, afterwards, remember a great deal about what she saw in the city of Mohács. There remained with her that powerful image of the battle conjured up by István, into which the wooden sculptures seemed to blend, taking on a life of their own. And she remembered conversation. All day long they seemed to be talking – over meals, sitting in a public park watching pairs of lovers and mothers with babies, and later strolling by the river. István told her about the festival of Busó, when strange figures dressed in straw robes and wearing fearful wooden masks with horns rode or drove their horses from Mohács Island into the city, making a terrible noise on drums and horns.

'It takes place on the last Sunday before Ash Wednesday, and some say that it is an ancient ceremony to drive away the winter, so that spring can come, but others claim it is a reminder of how the Turks were finally driven out of here – this place where they had won their great battle and destroyed the flower of Hungarian chivalry.'

'Perhaps it is both,' said Kate slowly. 'Perhaps there was such a ceremony, an ancient one to rid the country of the blight of winter. Might that not have been taken over to mark the departure of the Turks? After all, the Turkish rule must have been like the dead hand of winter over the country, when so many were sold into slavery.'

They walked through a grove of trees beside the river, and Kate remembered the letter Sofia had showed her, written by Zsigmond to the young Eva, an impassioned love letter that spoke of walking under trees near another city – Pécs, wasn't it?

And all I wanted to do was to walk with you in the woods of Mecsek, your hand in mine, your black hair – your glorious gypsy hair – caught back demurely in its little gold net, like a panther in a cage, or the waters of the Danube confined behind a dam, she quoted.

István looked at her curiously.

'What is that?'

'It was a letter Zsigmond wrote to Eva before they were married. Sofia translated it for me.'

Darling girl, I am in pain, just because I cannot walk with you under the trees. Will we ever win him over, this bear of a father?... I kiss your lips, my love, my Eva, my girl of the paradise from which I am banned. Your lips are as red as the paprika of Kalocsa, but as sweet as the summer apricots ripening on the trees of Kecskemét.

'They were so young,' said István. 'I can hardly bear to think of it.' He lifted her hand and kissed it. Ah, Zsigmond, my father, he thought, and what would you do in my position? Probably you would not hesitate. But then in some ways certain things were simpler for you.

&

That night Kate slept profoundly and dreamlessly in her plain, cool room in the village *csárda*. The window faced north and only the faintest light penetrated from the oblique rays of the moon. When she woke she floated up from a deeper rest than she had known for weeks, and lay under the feather bed with its cover of tiny blue and white checks feeling contented and relaxed. She looked at her arm where it lay outside the bedclothes and turned it so that she could just make out the faint pink patches which marked her skin like flattened flower petals. It had never occurred to her to wonder about these marks on her arms and legs. As far as she knew, they had always been there. If she had thought about them at all, she had simply assumed that she had been born with skin of a slightly irregular texture.

But István said they were the scars of old burns. And if the nightmare of the fire sprang from some real event in her childhood, that made sense.

'Sometimes,' he had said the evening before, as they sat in the inn garden over their simple meal, 'the mind will block out entirely an experience which is too painful to live with. I'm not a psychiatrist, but I have come across a few cases like this. It isn't unknown amongst old soldiers. And here in Hungary, people have seen things, or experienced things, during the last fifty years, which their minds prefer to forget.'

'You mean, I was burnt in a fire, and it was so frightening that I forced myself to forget?'

'It isn't always so easy to force yourself to forget. But sometimes an unconscious process can be triggered in the mind. You could call it a natural healing process, like the way the body repairs itself after an injury. And your mind may not simply have been protecting itself against fear and pain. You said you felt guilt. Even if the guilt was totally misplaced, your mind could try to heal over that, until something reopened the wound.'

She sat, turning her wine glass in her hand and thinking about guilt.

'It's one of the most destructive emotions, isn't it – guilt? Sofia has felt guilty all these years about what might have become of her father. I'm sure that contributed to the way she chose to live, shut away from everyone in her cottage. Even after the things that happened in the war – I think if she had been at ease with herself, she might have mixed more with people in Dunmouth.'

'Yes,' he said slowly, 'you may be right. You said that until you became friends, she seemed not to know anyone in your village. But perhaps it was also that she wanted tranquillity for her writing? I think she has changed, even while she has been here. Now she knows what our father achieved, she no longer feels guilt.'

'And you,' she said, looking at him penetratingly. 'You've also been carrying a burden of guilt about your father's capture. Has that crippled you? And perhaps...' She hesitated, wondering how far she dared go. 'Perhaps also guilt at the death of your wife? What you were saying before – the guilt of the survivor? "Why have I been spared?" '

A sigh rose up in István and escaped.

'Yes. You are probably right. I might have married again. Perhaps it would have been better for László to have had a stepmother – and brothers and sisters – rather than no mother at all. I sometimes think now...'

'What?'

'I tried too hard to be both father and mother to him. Was I over-protective? Probably. Certainly I am always counselling my patients to use firmness with difficult children – advice I didn't take myself.'

'Is László difficult?'

He shifted abruptly in his chair.

'Tomorrow you will be able to judge for yourself.'

She smiled at him affectionately. 'Remember, I have three teenagers. I know all about difficult children just at present.'

István had asked Kate if she would accompany him to mass in the little church in Kishíd on Sunday morning.

'I know you are not a Catholic, and I am not a practising one, not really. But I have a particular reason for asking.'

'Of course I will come,' said Kate, wondering when on Sunday the elusive László would be 'available', as István had put it, to meet his father. István had told her virtually nothing about his son, except that he was twenty-four, worked in this village, and had left home six years ago after being brought up in Sopron by his widowed father. It seemed to Kate that László was being more than difficult, to keep his father at arm's length like this. She had discovered that they had not seen each other for more than a year.

This is a poor village, she thought, looking around the church as they waited for the service to begin. The inn is much more modest than the Blue Heron, and the church is as bare as a monk's cell. Then she recalled the new, large houses she had seen, houses belonging to the commuters from Mohács, with their expensive German cars in the drives. There was money here now, but the village did not seem to have the rich cultural heritage of Szentmargit, and the new inhabitants spent their money on themselves and not on the village.

The congregation was sparse, almost entirely women. This too was different from Szentmargit, although she had only attended a service there on St István's Day, which might not have been typical. She watched the preparations for the service idly, letting her mind drift, knowing that she would be unable to understand a word of either the Hungarian or the Latin. A young priest in an austere surplice was making ready the altar, lighting candles and laying out chalice and paten, assisted by two altar boys. Kate was reminded briefly of a holiday she had once spent with a friend in Ireland, during her college days. There was a similar atmosphere here: the male ritual, the kneeling humble women – some very old, some very young – with scarves pulled forward, half concealing their faces, the smoky smell as one of the candles failed to light properly and sent a wavering plume of smoke up from the altar to hang suspended in front of the crudely painted glass window. Despite the heat of the day outside, the air in the church felt chilly and damp.

The preparations complete, the young priest and the boys genuflected and came down the aisle towards the west door. The priest walked quickly, impatiently, and the boys scuttled to keep pace with him. His face was cool, inward-looking, ascetic. He looked neither to right nor left as he passed them. István touched Kate's arm and leaned over to murmur in her ear, his lips brushing her hair.

'That is my son László.'

For a moment she was confused, thinking that he meant one of the altar boys. Then she understood, and several things clicked into place. László was a Catholic priest.

After the service they lingered until the rest of the congregation had left. László stood by the door of the church, speaking to some people, shaking others by the hand. István and Kate continued to sit in their pew, and Kate was pondering how to address this young man. 'László'? 'Father'?

When they stepped out into the sunlight again she watched incredulously as László gave his father – his *father*, whom he had not seen for over a year – the same cold handshake he had given his parishioners. Remembering the warm hugs, the touching, the kisses that were a natural part of the interchange between other members of the family, it seemed like a calculated insult. When László was introduced to her, in German, he was perfectly polite, but distant – glancing beyond her shoulder as if something more interesting was taking place behind her. Kate, who had always felt this trick showed unpardonable rudeness, experienced a stab of real anger.

Somewhat reluctantly, it seemed to Kate, László took them back to the priests' house for coffee, made by his housekeeper, a creeping mouse of a woman who looked at István and herself fearfully, and at László with something between awe and terror.

'I'm afraid I don't have much time,' said László abruptly. 'I have another service in an hour, and Father Pál is away in Budapest at the moment.'

It was disconcerting. His voice had something of the quality of István's about it, but it was so cold.

'We won't take up much of your time,' said István. 'Thank you,' he added to the housekeeper as she handed him a cup of coffee. He explained why they had come, giving a brief account of Sofia's story and the news they had exchanged about the family. László nodded, as though he was not much interested. Kate wanted to kick him. Although István was good at hiding his feelings, she could see he was hurt – hurt at his son's indifference to the reunion of the brother and sisters, and hurt at his almost palpable rudeness to Kate. It was with relief that she got up to leave, when they had barely finished their coffee.

They walked down from the priests' house to the stream beyond the village, which wound eastwards and eventually joined the Danube. With difficulty, Kate held her tongue.

'I am sorry,' said István, 'to have put you through that, but I wanted you to know everything about me, the good and the bad. You see that I failed with my son.' His voice was bleak.

Kate slipped her arm through his, defiantly hoping that they were still within sight of Father László's windows. She had read a clear message of distaste in his eyes when he heard that they had travelled together from Szentmargit and were staying at the inn.

'Why is he like that?'

István sighed. 'I don't know. As a small boy he was full of fun and charm. But after about a year at the *gymnasium* he seemed to change. He became very...thick with – is that what you say? – very thick with a boy who came from a devout Catholic family. The mother was almost obsessive, and she had vowed that her eldest son would become a priest. The boy seemed to be just as obsessed, and László fell under his influence. The more I tried to persuade him to wait till he was older, to think things through, the worse I seemed to make it and the more he turned away from me towards these people. The two boys went away to the seminary together when they were eighteen.'

He pulled her down on to a bench under the cave made by a weeping willow, which provided some shade from the intense midday sun.

'The irony of it is that after six months the other boy decided the priesthood was not for him. He had been caught misbehaving with a girl from the town and was very severely dealt with. He left the seminary at once, saying he was glad he had found out he didn't have a vocation before it was too late. In a way I think the whole episode made László even more obsessed – he felt he had to make up for his friend's backsliding. And I suspect that he found he was not altogether immune to the temptations of the flesh himself. Did you notice how he can barely touch people, even to shake hands? As a child he hugged and cuddled with such warmth and affection. Now he shuts himself inside a glass cage. So you see why I think I have failed.'

Kate leaned her head back against his shoulder.

'We can't take responsibility for our children for ever. Not when they're grown up. He has made his choice, and he'll have to work out his own destiny. But it is very hard on you. To have lost your wife, and now to have lost the normal relationship with your son.'

She fingered the fabric of his jacket.

'I'm sure it isn't too late to repair that. It's up to you, I think, to reach a hand out to him – humble yourself, even. The young are so proud and so stubborn. But we have lived long enough to know that we don't lose face by showing our love. Of course,' she said, suddenly

233

struck, for it had not occurred to her before, 'it will mean no grandchildren, no descendants.'

'A sterile withering of the line,' he said with an ironic laugh.

'At least you have Magdolna's children. And you are still young enough to marry again.'

'I wonder. I expect I am too set in my ways.'

'Not you,' she laughed. 'You are constantly full of surprises.'

And now it was the last morning of their visit to the south of the country. They had breakfast early and went for a walk out into the surrounding countryside, wanting to make the most of the time they had left together before they had to start on the long drive back to Szentmargit. There was a strange light hovering over the day, as if after the weeks of unremitting heat the sun had melted at the edges and flowed into the sky, blurring gold and blue together in a hot palette of primary colours. There was a breathless hush in the air, the leaves hung exhausted on the trees, and the dust of the lane spurted up from their feet in irritable peppery clouds.

'It will be more pleasant in the fields,' said István, pointing to a gate in the hedge ahead on their left.

They opened it and slipped through, swinging it behind them with a dull clunk of dry wood and metal. The field contained wheat, still not ready for the harvest. In fact they had seen little harvesting going on yet in this area. István pinched some grains from a head of wheat and rubbed them in his palm, then bit one. He shook his head.

'Hard as a pebble. See, it should be a little milky.'

He held out the poor dry grains for her to see.

'They need Imre's sprinkler system,' said Kate, rolling the grains with her finger in his palm, where they gritted together like gravel.

'Yes, or a Paparuda.'

At the end of the wheat field there was another hedge at right angles to the one skirting the lane, and beyond it a vast field of sunflowers which rose to the horizon, blocking out any view beyond. They managed to push through the hedge – hazels and blackthorn and brambles – and found themselves amongst the sunflowers, which were taller than Kate. She reached up and stroked the brown centre of one of the bowed heads.

'They look as though they are in mourning. Shouldn't they be turned towards the sun? "Tournesol", isn't it, in French?'

'They're exhausted, poor things,' said István. 'Too much sun even for the sunflowers.'

Amongst the sunflowers, and along the base of the trees shielding them from the lane, dozens of red poppies had seeded themselves. They, at least, seemed to enjoy the sun. They were huge and scarlet, a wonderful, flamboyant, joyous colour. István began to pick them and weave them together.

'What are you doing?' asked Kate curiously.

'Making you a crown of poppies. A Paparuda crown.'

'I thought you said that was an old superstition which had died out.'

'Ah, but I remember this from my childhood. My grandmother taught me how to do it.'

He gave the stems a final twist, tucked in the ends, and placed the garland of poppies on Kate's head. A few of the petals fell, brushing her cheeks.

'There, now you are almost a Paparuda.'

Kate laughed and looked around. 'Was that thunder?'

'Perhaps. The air does feel charged, as if a storm is coming.'

'Why "almost" a Paparuda?'

'Didn't Sofia tell you about the Paparuda?'

Kate shook her head. They continued to walk along the edge of the field till they came to a fallen hazel, where they sat down instinctively amongst the scatter of branches and nut husks.

'The villagers would capture a gypsy girl,' István explained. 'And they would strip her naked and dress her in grasses and poppies.'

'Truly?' There was another rumble of thunder, unmistakable this time.

'Truly. Do you think we will be safe here, if the storm breaks?'

'Yes, of course. Anyway, I wouldn't mind getting wet after all the unremitting sun. Go on about the Paparuda.'

'They would parade the girl through the village, pouring jugs of water from the Danube over her head – she had to kneel down in the dust – and they sang a song, begging the Paparuda to bring the rains and break the drought.'

'But I won't do for a Paparuda?'

'You haven't been stripped and dressed in grass and poppies. And you aren't a virgin.'

'No. No, I'm not a virgin.' She smiled at him. 'So I'm a very poor second best.'

'Not that. Never that.'

There was a flash of lightning, forking down the sky over towards the village, followed almost immediately by a crack of thunder which made Kate flinch.

'Do you think we are safe?' It was she who asked this time. 'The trees...'

'There are much taller ones at the beginning of the lane, and – look – up there, at those on the rising ground.'

The very air seemed to crackle. At the dusty ends of the rows of sunflowers, miniature whirlpools of grey dust were lifted by an invisible breeze, then dropped again. The whole field and the encircling hedge, the rustling rows of sunflowers and the drooping hazel trees, seemed to hold their breath. There was no sound of birdsong. A kind of creeping darkness seemed to be swallowing the world. Then the whole eastern half of the sky was lit up from end to end with a white curtain of light, followed at once by a bolt of forked lightning leaping from heaven to earth in a dazzling flash which forced Kate to close her eyes, though she could still see the jagged line on the inside of her eyelids. There was a great rushing sound like a drawn breath, and then the ground shook with the crack of thunder.

István put his arms around Kate, who was shaking, but with excitement not fear.

'It's wonderful!' she cried. 'Feel it! You can feel it on your skin. The rains are coming.'

The rush of air came again, and then the rain. It did not start gently, with a few hesitant drops. Like a dam bursting the rain fell on them, in the first few seconds starring the grey dust with exploding patches of reddish brown. The very earth was changing colour. They sprang to their feet and stood under the hazels and Kate held up her arms to the water. In moments they were drenched, their clothes clinging to them, petals from the poppies washing down Kate's face and spattering István's white shirt like drops of blood. Her hair lay on her head like seaweed, and the rain poured from it down between her breasts, and her skirt clasped her legs like a second skin, like wet leaves, and the water cascaded down to the ground so that she became a spring, a waterfall, a column of living water feeding the soil.

They clung together, exhilarated, as the rain licked their skin like wet silk, and he began to kiss her on the lips, on the eyelids, and they were covered with the petals of the poppies, and the water ran over them and down their backs, and flowed down their legs in rivers till they were standing in a sea of mud, clinging and kissing and laughing.

'I love you, Kate,' said István. 'Forgive me. Forgive me.'

She silenced him with her fingers against his mouth.

236

The journey back to Szentmargit was the strangest either of them had ever made. For a while they would drive in silence, and then – as though forced by some mutual compulsion – they would draw into a lay-by and cling to each other.

'I cannot bear you to leave,' said István again and again. 'There is only one more day. We have one more day. Please stay, beloved, I beg of you.'

And Kate, crying, said, 'I must go. I have no choice.'

'There is always a choice.'

'For you, perhaps. You are free. I am not.'

Sobered, they would drive on, only to stop again when they could no longer bear not to be holding each other. When darkness fell and they drew nearer to Szentmargit, Kate fell asleep at last, exhausted, and István cradled her against him with his right arm and tried to think.

And now it was the last evening. Magdolna and Sofia had prepared a family feast for all of them at the rose-coloured cottage standing beside the Danube. There had been rain here too in the north, though not the spectacular thunderstorm of the fields near Mohács. It had blown away now, leaving the air cooler and slightly damp, with the first hint of autumn. In two days it would be September.

They put together two tables outside on the thin lawn near Magdolna's vegetable garden, and covered them with the dowry linen made by Juliska's mother as she waited for her fiancé, the young village potter, Miklós Rudnay, to come home from the first world war. The jug with the leaping dolphins was filled now not with water from the Danube but with József's best wine.

'As fine as you would have in Gundel's restaurant in Budapest,' he promised Kate.

Anna was supposed to have returned to Budapest at the weekend, but she had telephoned a friend and made arrangements to stay until Wednesday morning, when she could be given a lift back with Sofia and Kate in the hired Peugeot. She laid the table now with the best china and glass, and István and József carried out an assortment of chairs, including some borrowed from the neighbours.

They lit candles and sat over the five courses, talking, talking. And if István and Kate were quieter than usual, no one commented, although Magdolna glanced at them from time to time, and turned away with pity.

Anna had gone into the kitchen to fetch a another bottle of wine, and Sofia and András were clearing away the worst of the dirty dishes to make room for a bowl of fruit, when Magdolna turned to Kate and touched her arm.

'Kate, while Anna is opening the wine, will you come with me a moment?'

'Of course.' Kate got up obediently and followed Magdolna to her studio. The door stood ajar and Magdolna pushed it fully open and switched on the light.

The shadowy shapes on the shelves and worktable sprang into dramatic life, and Kate saw that the three new figures Magdolna had been working on had been fired and were standing on the freshly scrubbed worktable. She thought she knew why Magdolna had brought her here.

'Would you like us to take the new figures to the gallery in Váci Utca for you? I'm sure we will have room for them.'

'No, no. The gallery sends out a regular carrier every month. I will finish some small pieces as well before they come for the next collection.'

Kate touched one of the figures, a mother and child, delicately – nervously – with one fingertip.

'They are wonderful, Magdolna. You have such vision. Such ability to see inside people.'

'I want to give you one of them. Any of the three, but in particular I would like to give you that one.'

Kate was astonished.

'Why me? They are pieces for an art gallery or a museum, not for an ordinary person like me.'

'I do not make them for art galleries or museums. I make them for people. Especially for people like you, Kate. And don't undervalue yourself. You are anything but ordinary.'

Magdolna took both of Kate's hands in hers and looked at her directly and unflinchingly. 'I know that you and István have come to love each other. For him you have been like rain after drought, and he has flowered after the dust of all these years. You will think I exaggerate to say this, but it is true. I have been watching you together. But you see I understand, as perhaps he does not, how it must be for you. Whatever you decide, I know you will try to do what is best. Remember that my thoughts will be with you.'

She stood on tiptoe, for she was a small woman – shorter than Kate and Kate was not tall – and kissed her first on one cheek and then on the other.

'Will you let me give you the figure of the mother and child?'

Carefully, Kate lifted it, finding it surprisingly heavy. The mother held the baby against her shoulder, his legs curling around her breast, her hand cupping the back of his head. Her eyes looked down at the child with anxious tenderness, and in that expression and the curve of the protecting hand, Magdolna had caught all the joy and agony of motherhood. Kate turned the figure slowly in her hands, and caught sight of the baby's face. He looked over the mother's shoulder, with a clear, innocent, perceptive gaze reaching out to the wider world.

The two women looked at each other with understanding.

'Thank you,' said Kate.

♀

And now József had escorted Sofia back to the Blue Heron, and Magdolna, Anna and András had gone to bed. A full moon was rising in a clear sky, bright with stars in this wide countryside so far from city street lamps. A few rags of cloud, the last traces of yesterday's storm, obscured a hand's breadth of sky from time to time, then drifted on.

Kate and István had walked away from the house, down to the wooden bridge over the trout stream for the last time. There was movement in the air now, and the trailing branches of the willows stirred and whispered. The stream chattered a little with the new fall of rain, and out beyond the islands the lights of a ship were moving slowly down the Danube towards Budapest, Mohács, the Iron Gates, and the sea.

They did not speak much. Everything had already been said, and tonight words would simply bring more pain. So they leaned on the handrail of the bridge where the silvered waters of the stream flowed under their feet to join the river, and István tore a leaf from the willow and set it sailing on the current. They watched it until it was taken by the stronger current of the river, spun around dizzyingly, then swept away out of sight.

'I am like that leaf, you see,' said Kate abruptly. 'I may spin here for a moment in your orbit, but there is a stronger current dragging me inexorably away.'

'Promise me,' said István, taking her by the shoulders and turning her to face him, 'promise me that you will try to see a way out of this? I know you think that I do not understand, but I do. Your husband...' he said the words with difficulty, and tried again. 'Your husband – you loved him once, deeply. I know you. It cannot have been otherwise. I loved Maria. I have never denied that. But time passes. Maria has long been lost to me and my grieving for her is part of my past, not of my present. I think your love for your husband is also part of your past.'

'I don't know,' Kate whispered, looking away from him, looking down.

'Look at me, Kate. I said I *think* your love for your husband is also part of your past. I think you do not know. I think you will not know until you confront him again. I *know* that you are in love with me. Look at me, Kate.' He tilted her chin up. 'Can you look at me and deny it?'

She looked at him. 'I cannot deny it. But my children...'

'Yes, I know.' His voice softened. 'I do understand. Your children. But they are nearly grown. Today, the children fill our lives – tomorrow they are gone, without a backward look. But you have all the rest of your life ahead of you.'

Kate sighed. 'I know. I know.'

'Promise me, *promise* me, that when you return to your grey village in the north, you will think very carefully. That you will be fair to me as well as to that husband of yours, and that you will truly listen to what your own heart tells you. Then write to me.'

She looked at him. 'I promise. I will write. I will decide, and I will write by Christmas.'

'So long?'

'By Christmas.'

Chapter 13

Both Kate and Sofia were quiet on the journey back to Britain. The Guarneri, collected from the Sterns on Wednesday after their early morning drive to Budapest, rested in the overhead compartment. It had been carefully wedged in with coats by the flight attendant, but Kate noticed that Sofia's eyes strayed anxiously upwards from time to time. They had left Anna at her student hostel before hurrying to the instrument shop.

'I'll try to come over to England next summer, Aunt Sofia,' Anna promised. 'I was going to hitch-hike to France with a friend, but now that I've got you to visit I'll see if we can come further.'

It is that generation who will keep in touch, Kate thought. Travelling casually across continents, and accepting as a right their new freedom to go wherever they wish. Unlike the young István, trapped in a country surrounded by the prison walls erected by a foreign invader. She remembered her own student days. She had not been particularly adventurous, but she had gone by bus to Greece with two friends and stayed at cheap tavernas, living off fruit, cheese and ouzo. Until these last few weeks she had forgotten how it had felt to be that carefree younger self. Briefly she had inhabited once again that former Kate, with her spontaneity and intense feelings.

But not for long, she thought grimly, leaning her head back against the seat and closing her eyes. The view outside the aircraft window today was a sombre landscape of grey clouds. They were stacked high, and the plane ploughed in and out of them. Against the windows they rubbed like wet fur.

There was a scramble again at Schipol, trying to cross the terminal from one gate to the other in ten minutes. Sofia was a seasoned traveller now, stepping on and off the moving walkway with aplomb, but Kate thought she looked tired. On the final leg of the journey, Kate refused the meal and fell asleep, waking only as they began their descent to Edinburgh airport. As usual the plane made its hair-raising turn over the Firth of Forth – enlivening things for the passengers by making them fear they were going to ditch in the cold grey water – then it swung in low over the city. Kate watched Arthur's Seat and the Castle pass by underneath, and reflected that the Festival was probably in full swing down there. And this made her think of a small carousel in a village square, and men in baggy white trousers dancing the *csárdás*, and a little gypsy girl performing handstands on a cantering horse. As the plane touched down she was not looking out at the drizzling day in Edinburgh, but at the ghostly scars on her forearms, and thinking again about the nature of guilt.

As they came out into the main concourse and headed for the baggage collection point, a familiar voice shouted, 'Mum! Over here, Mum!' It was Beccy.

'Darling!' Kate hugged her daughter with surprise and pleasure. 'Whatever are you doing here?'

'Took the bus up to Edinburgh to meet you.'

'That was terribly kind of you.' Kate looked at her keenly. 'Was there a particular reason?'

'Yes, but it will wait till we're in the car. Can I help you with that?' Beccy asked Sofia. 'Have you bought a violin in Hungary?'

'No,' said Sofia, 'just recovered one. Thank you.' She handed over the violin case and went with Kate to reclaim their luggage.

They shared the minibus this time with an elderly couple, and whatever it was Beccy wanted to tell them, she was going to wait. Given this reluctance, Kate could not believe that it was something she would want to hear. It wasn't until they had left Edinburgh behind and were heading south-east on the A1 that Kate glanced over her shoulder to Beccy, who was sitting on the back seat behind Sofia.

'Now, are you going to tell us what all this is about?'

'I'm afraid it isn't good news.'

'I didn't suppose it was. Would you like to get on with it?'

'It's Dad.'

Kate gripped the wheel and the car lurched slightly. 'Has something happened? Is he all right? Oh, Beccy...'

'He's all right,' said Beccy. 'I mean he hasn't been injured or anything. I would have let you know, but you never phoned. You promised to phone from Hungary.'

'I did try to phone, and no one answered.' But Kate remembered guiltily that after trying twice from Budapest and once from Györ she had not thought of phoning again, not after arriving in Szentmargit.

'Dad's been made redundant.'

'What!' Kate couldn't believe her ears. So soon after a major promotion – it couldn't be true.

'There's been a takeover of Crossbow Computers by an American company. Some of Dad's colleagues at head office did a secret deal – sold their bulk holdings of shares for vast profits. They've virtually become millionaires. Apparently Ted Giles – you remember Ted – tried to phone Dad and warn him, but couldn't reach him. The following day he himself went into hospital for a heart bypass operation. He's had a bad time with complications, and only phoned again a few days ago, after the takeover had happened. Dad says Ted must have rung the day the air conditioning failed and he sent everyone home. That was the only day he hasn't been in one or other of the Crossbow offices since we came up here. Do you remember?'

She remembered. They had sailed the dinghy out on to the North Sea, past the headland and the seal colony. For two hours Tom had looked almost young and happy again, explaining all those ropes to her. Now, when he had needed her most, she had not been there for him.

'I wonder...' said Kate, trying to concentrate on her driving but thinking furiously.

'What?'

'Sending Dad up to take charge of the northern half of the company – was it just to get him out of the way? Away from head office? He wouldn't have gone along with this, you know. It mattered to him that Crossbow was a British company expanding its share of the world market. Could they really have been that underhand?'

'Well, that's just what Dad thinks. And of course that makes it worse – he thinks that he was a fool, not to have guessed what was happening *And* he thinks he never deserved the promotion. And all this on top of having saved the Manchester project by taking charge himself.'

'But I do not understand,' Sofia put in hesitantly. 'Why should they make him redundant? Surely they will still need someone to do the job?'

'They always make some managers redundant,' said Kate. 'Bring in their own people, you see.'

'Yes,' said Beccy. 'Because of his known opposition, he was bound to be one of those to be axed. Some of his so-called "friends" have taken early retirement so they can go and spend their winnings in Antibes or on world cruises. Two or three have been retained in top management, to satisfy the fiction of a non-aggressive takeover.'

Kate turned on to the left fork to Charlborough, and tried to focus her mind on Tom – Tom without Crossbow, which had been his life for twenty years, to which he had given loyal, unstinting service. Crossbow had consumed Tom, destroyed his personal and private life, and now it

243

had spat him out. But despite the impact of Beccy's news, she couldn't fix Tom's face in her mind. It was blurred, and this news made it even more difficult.

'How is he taking it?'

'It's awful, Mum.' Beccy suddenly sounded young and scared. 'That's why I came up to Edinburgh. Not just so you would know before you got home, but to warn you about Dad. I think he's really cracking up. He just sits around all day, staring into space. He doesn't shave, he doesn't change his clothes – I think he even sleeps in them. He's been drinking, too, only now I think he's drunk everything there was in the house, and he won't go outside, so at least he can't buy any more.'

She gave a gulp like a dry sob. 'It's been really frightening, Mum. During the daytime he sits in the same chair all the time, but at night he goes crashing around from room to room – swearing and muttering about Crossbow and... well, about you. Why aren't you there, that kind of thing. I tried, I really did. I made him meals and put them down in front of him, but hours later they would still be there, cold and untouched. And I got so scared at night... well, I moved out.'

She leaned forward against the back of Sofia's seat. 'I'm sorry, Sofia, but I'm afraid I moved into your cottage with Chris. I didn't know where else to go. Linda offered me space on her floor, but you know how tiny the flat is for the three of them. We have separate bedrooms, Chris and me, in your cottage,' she explained earnestly. 'I wouldn't want you to think there was anything going on that you wouldn't approve of.'

That, thought Kate, is the least of our worries.

๛

That evening, exhausted, feeling remote and disorientated, Kate thought Beccy had, if anything, played down Tom's state of mind. They had dropped Sofia off at her cottage, where Beccy collected a shoulder bag stuffed with belongings. Chris was going to stay for another night or two in Sofia's spare room until he could find new digs in Dunmouth.

'I'm really sorry about Mr Milburn,' said Chris, as he opened the door of Kate's car for her. 'You know you can call on me for any help you need, if... if things get difficult.'

Violent, he means, thought Kate. If things get violent. Can it really be that bad?

244

'It does sometimes hit people very hard,' said Chris awkwardly. 'Redundancy. Men particularly, I suppose, because they see themselves as the breadwinner. And of course if you're middle-aged it's worse, because there's almost no hope of getting another job.'

'Thank you, Chris,' said Kate, pulling the car door shut.

Thank you very much, she thought, for those comforting remarks.

'Are you still working for Linda?' she asked Beccy as they drove slowly up the hill to Craigfast House, which they had passed without turning in as they came down into Dunmouth.

'Yes, and I've got quite a bit of money saved up, if it will help.'

Kate was touched. 'That's very kind, darling, but I'm sure we'll sort things out. I suppose Dad hasn't done anything about signing on or looking for another job? No, of course not.'

'I think signing on would be the ultimate humiliation. After all, he's always had a good job, hasn't he? Ever since he graduated. And your generation didn't expect to be unemployed, not like mine. I'm afraid Chris is right, you know. He probably won't find another job now.'

'He's only fifty-one!'

'That's what I mean. Nowadays, if you're over forty, or even thirty-five, they won't consider you for most things.'

Kate resolutely ignored this piece of wisdom from Beccy, but when she saw Tom, she could not imagine anyone wanting to employ him, ever again. How could someone change so much in little more than three weeks? Though she remembered how tired he had been looking before she went away. Now he was gaunt and hollow-eyed, with a dirty-looking growth of beard and his hair lank and greasy. No employer would look at him. She had seen more prepossessing tramps.

'Well, thank goodness you've seen fit to turn up at last,' he said. His eyes were cold. 'It was fine for you, wasn't it, buggering off on holiday? God knows how much money you've spent that we can't afford. You've really landed us in the shit, haven't you?'

Kate felt as though she had been struck. Tom had never sworn at her in his life before. She had intended to put her arms around him and say that they would soon sort things out, but she could not bring herself to touch this alien man, angry and ugly. She stepped back.

With fragile self-control she coped all evening. She persuaded him to take a shower and shave, and whipped his clothes away into the washing-machine. Then she prepared home-made carrot soup – one of his favourites – and they sat down on either side of the kitchen table to eat it. Beccy, seeing that Kate did not need physical protection, made some excuse and took her soup up to her bedroom.

Tom was subdued after he had eaten, no longer abusive but looking white and drawn. He would not speak to her, so Kate decided to leave matters for the moment, washing the dishes, laying the table for breakfast, transferring the washing to the tumble-drier. Doing all the routine tasks as some kind of assurance that life would continue as normal.

Now at last she was in the bathroom, having showered and washed her hair, staring at her face in the steamy mirror over the basin. The face, under the familiar twist of towel, looked the same and yet not the same. It was fuller, younger-looking, the reverse of Tom's, which looked thinner and older.

Sighing, she rubbed her hair. It sprang up, as it always did when it was wet, in tight curls, to relax into softer waves as it dried. In their bedroom Tom was already in bed, the lamp on his table switched off. She walked across to the window and opened it softly. As she went out on to the balcony the low rays of a waning moon fell across her. There were street lamps in Dunmouth. That was different from Szentmargit, which was dark after sundown. A few lights showed also from houses, and at the harbour mouth she could see the bobbing lights – red, white and green – as the fishing fleet put to sea.

She pulled the window almost closed as she stepped back into the bedroom, for it was colder here than in Hungary. She ran her fingers through her hair. Dry enough. As she climbed into bed she thought that Tom was too still, too rigid, to be asleep. She reached out and switched off her own lamp.

His arm came across her and clamped her to him. For a moment she was afraid, remembering what Beccy had said of the wandering and swearing at night. She held her breath, fear rising like sickness in the back of her throat. Then she realised he was crying – dry rasping sobs. It is terrifying to hear a man cry, she thought. Tom, self-confident, self-assured Tom, crying. His arms holding her were like a vice. She wanted to say, I can't breathe, but did not dare speak. Then he was tearing at her nightdress.

'God, I've needed you, Kate.'

They were the first words he had addressed to her since the shouting that had greeted her when she arrived.

She put her arms around him. She wanted to say, I am no longer the same. I am in love with another man. But how could she do that to him?

246

When at last she was able to curl on her side like an injured animal, she cried silently into her pillow. She was bruised, humiliated and in pain.

૭

For the next two days Kate was very cautious. When Tom sat around slumped in an armchair, she would manoeuvre him outside into the garden in the general belief that the fresh air and wider horizons must surely do him some good. The garden was rampant with neglect and demanded her attention. She was no gardener by Sofia's and Magdolna's standards, but the care of the tiny yard behind the London house had fallen to her responsibility, and she had done her best, with a climbing rose and pots of geraniums and small shrubs. The garden of Craigfast House was quite another matter, and even before she had gone away she knew she was losing the battle. While she had been in Hungary, Tom and Beccy had done nothing, not even cut the grass. Luckily the weather had been dry here too, so it had not quite become a hayfield yet. With Tom ensconced in a garden chair on the terrace she mowed the grass and dug dandelions out of the flower beds and dead-headed the roses. Tom looked a little less pale, sitting and watching her, but his eyes still had that blank dead look, which would be replaced from time to time with a glint of baffled fury.

She had made no attempt yet to discuss the situation with him. Apart from his first outburst as she walked through the door, neither of them had made even the most oblique reference to Crossbow or his present state of unemployment. Tom hardly spoke at all. Kate made one cautious phone call on her second day home to the benefit office in Charlborough, fixing an appointment for him the following week. She was doubtful whether she would be able to persuade him to keep it.

Unnervingly, he seemed to want to follow her everywhere. When he wasn't staring into space his eyes were fixed on her, but slid away whenever she looked at him. Kate began to feel a sort of claustrophobic panic. He would not even let her go out to walk Toby, who had greeted her return with relief.

'I'll just take Toby down to the beach for an hour,' she pleaded, on the second morning. A wave of fury washed over his face.

'Why can't he just run about in the garden?'

'He needs the exercise – he's a big sporting dog. It isn't good for him to be cooped up. Come with me if you like,' she added, though she would have preferred to go alone.

'Let's leave it for a bit, Kate,' he said abruptly.

247

Beccy had to do the shopping, assisted by Chris who came gravely up the hill with her and surveyed Tom out of the corner of his eye.

'Sofia has offered me lodgings with her for the moment,' he said, as they unpacked the carrier bags in the kitchen.

'That's good,' said Kate, thinking that the trip to Hungary had changed Sofia too. She was hungry for company now. 'It will be much more comfortable for you there. And it will be a help to have you around, in case she needs a hand with any heavy jobs. Tell her,' she added, 'that I'll be down to see her as soon as... as soon as it's possible.'

'Of course.' He nodded.

This narrow existence, shut up in the house and garden with a husband who looked as though he might as any moment break down entirely, set Kate's teeth on edge. At times his intense stare, fixed on her, was frightening. Even the views from the house only served to mock her. She was reminded of István as a child, dreaming of escape down the Danube on a boat to the sea, away from his imprisoned country. For the first time in her life even the nearness of the sea could not comfort her.

Roz was due back on the Sunday after Kate's return, Stephen on the following Friday. Every time Kate passed the telephone table in the hall, her eyes were drawn to two official-looking envelopes – the GCSE and A-Level results. She would not open them, of course, but she was tempted to hold Stephen's letter up to a strong light, to see if she could make anything out. Suppose he hadn't gained the necessary grades? It would be yet another complication in what was becoming the tangle of confusion in their lives. She didn't even know what redundancy payment Tom would receive for twenty years' service. Nothing had been paid into the bank account yet, apart from his final salary at the end of August. Presumably these things took time.

Kate's virtual imprisonment in the house meant, however, that she could postpone confronting her parents about the events of the past. She kept them at bay with phone calls, listening to Millicent's brisk advice and Howard's sympathy with equal meekness. She arranged for Angie's mother to collect Roz from the coach which would bring the music students back from camp and deliver them to the school playground in Charlborough.

'My husband isn't very well,' she said down the phone, truthfully enough. 'Could you possibly drop Roz off here? I'd be really grateful.'

But she was growing angry with Tom, demanding all her attention like a spoilt child. And there was his physical violence towards her at night. Every evening she postponed going to bed, filled with a sick dread. Now Roz was coming home in triumph, and they should both be there to meet her. It would be an anticlimax to be ferried home by Angie's mother.

In the event there was a last-minute change of plan. Beccy and Chris took Kate's car and went to meet Roz, so they could forewarn her about Tom. At half-past eight on Sunday evening the Peugeot drew up in the drive and Kate ran out and hugged Roz as she tumbled out of the car.

'Here you are!' she cried. 'Isn't it marvellous! I want to hear everything about the music college offer, and how the concert went in Aberystwyth. Were you the sensation of the evening?'

'Of course!' Roz giggled. 'Everyone queuing up for my autograph!' She was fizzing with excitement and swung Kate around on the gravel. 'Seriously, Mum, I can't *wait*. This is just going to be so marvellous – to get real, intensive teaching from the very best people. And not have to wait another two years before I can go.'

Kate suddenly remembered the matter of fees and living expenses. She would have to talk to Mr Elliot, now that he was back from Wales, and find out about scholarships. But she wouldn't say anything to dampen Roz's exultation. Time enough to worry later. As they all processed into the house with Roz's luggage – which seemed to have expanded while she was away – she realised that Beccy too was a problem. She had been receiving her fees at university, but no maintenance grant because Tom's income had been too high. Kate would have to do something about that quickly. And for Stephen too. Somehow the whole family was going to have to plan, and it was impossible to do that until they knew where they stood financially. Tom must have been told something by Crossbow. He must have something in writing. He would have to be made to confront matters soon.

Supper that evening was the least dismal meal since Kate had come home. Chris stayed to eat with them, so five of them sat down at the kitchen table to Beccy's omelettes and Kate's salads and a rather squashed cheesecake Roz had bought at a wonderful place in Wales and carried all the way home on the bus. Tom did not speak throughout the meal, but Kate hardly noticed, because everyone else was talking so much. It was as though Roz's return had burst a membrane of tension which had been stretched around them.

Later, after Chris had gone and Roz was unpacking in her room to the sound of Holst's 'Hymn of Jesus' played at full blast, Kate and Beccy tackled the washing-up together.

'We've got to think about the coming academic year,' said Kate, squirting washing-up liquid into the bowl and dumping in a handful of cutlery.

'Have a heart, Mum – I haven't even had a holiday yet!'

'Sorry, darling, I know. You've been marvellous this summer. But I was wondering how we go about reapplying for a grant. Surely you'll be entitled to some maintenance now that Dad's unemployed?'

'You're right,' said Beccy, stacking dirty dishes on the draining board. 'I'm sure there was something in the notes with the grant form. You were to let them know if your parents' financial circumstances changed. I'll look out my file tonight and ring from the bookshop tomorrow, after the grant office opens.'

'Wonderful. You are a tower of strength these days.'

'Well, some of us have to be, don't we? Just how bad is the financial situation?'

'I haven't dared ask. What I do know is that buying this house and doing it up cleaned us out of any savings. We've nothing to fall back on.'

There was a noise behind them, from the open door of the kitchen. As they turned, they saw Tom, with his shoulders hunched and his hands in his pockets, turning away.

'Oh, dear,' said Beccy, letting out her breath in a gasp. 'How much of that did he hear?'

'I don't know.' Kate was partly sorry, but perhaps it would galvanise Tom into some sort of action.

The following day, the atmosphere in the house did seem to have changed, but Kate was not sure that it had improved. Roz banged about, rearranging all the furniture in her room and putting in four hours' violin practice, so it was not as quiet as it had been. She had not bothered to open her GCSE results until that morning. They were satisfactory, but not exceptional.

Tom, instead of following Kate about, now seemed to be avoiding her, and when she did speak to him he looked away and would not meet her eyes.

That evening Beccy said she had phoned the grant office, who would send a form so they could set out the change in the family's finances. Kate wondered with dread whether Tom would have to fill it in, and if so whether he could be persuaded to do it. Writing the facts down on paper would give the whole nightmare episode a reality which he seemed to be trying to avoid. Well, he was going to have to face it sooner or later.

Mr Elliot was sympathetic when she telephoned him, and said briskly that he would contact the music college at once about financial assistance for Roz.

'She is too late to try for one of the regular scholarships, of course. Those will have been awarded before the summer vacation. But there is a Benefactors' Fund which the Principal can use at his discretion, as well as some small bursaries which can be awarded after she arrives and takes the bursary exam. Please don't worry, Mrs Milburn. We'll sort something out. And please tell your husband how sorry I am. Nobody's job seems safe these days, does it? However good you are at it.'

Kate began to feel a little better. It looked as though Beccy and Roz would be all right for the next year. There was nothing she could do about Stephen until he arrived home and they found out whether his A-Level results would gain him a place at one of the universities he had applied to. Otherwise they would have to start the mad dash of shopping around for a course through clearing. There would be his grant to sort out as well.

One thing at a time, she thought. If I can make sure things are settled for all three children for next year, then after that I will tackle Tom about what we are going to do ourselves.

On Thursday, two things happened. The first was a visit from Sofia. Roz had taken the bus into Charlborough to see Angie and go to the cinema in the evening. She was planning to stay overnight and come back the following morning. Beccy was at work in the bookshop. Kate still hadn't seen Linda since she had arrived home, and was waiting to give her the book of photographs of Hungary she had brought as a present. Tom was somewhere about the house, but still avoiding her.

'I've decided I'm not going to take a holiday, Mum,' Beccy had said at breakfast. 'I think I'd better stash my money away for emergencies.'

'Don't you think you need a break before term starts?'

'Not really. It's not tiring at the bookshop, except when we check the stock, and I really enjoy it. I'll go back to Uni reasonably refreshed – and much richer!'

'What about, er...Jerry?'

'Jerry? Oh... Jerry! That's all over with. It was pretty cooled off before I came home.'

Kate was thinking about this exchange as she came in from walking Toby on the rough ground at the top of the hill beyond the garden. As she hung up her coat she saw Sofia through the kitchen window, approaching the back door.

'How lovely!' said Kate, throwing the door open. 'I'm longing for company and you're just in time for a cup of tea.'

She ushered Sofia in and sat her down at the table. Then she noticed she was carrying Eva's violin.

'Heavens, Sofia, have you carried that all the way up the hill? It's bad enough if you're unencumbered.'

Sofia was a little breathless, but she smiled. 'It must keep you fit, going up and down that hill all the time.'

'I haven't been doing much of that since we got back,' said Kate, putting the mugs of tea and a plate of biscuits down on the table. 'Not at all, in fact.'

'Yes, Beccy and Chris explained. I'm so sorry.' Sofia looked around. 'Is your husband at home?'

'He's somewhere about. I'm afraid he's brooding a good deal at the moment.' It came to Kate suddenly that Sofia and Tom had never met. After the disaster of the dinner party she had not tried again to bring them together.

'Roz is back from her music camp, full of excitement at going off to college when term starts. Stephen gets back tomorrow – at least that was the original plan. We've had no news since he went to France except one postcard from Avignon posted nearly two weeks ago.'

'You'll be glad to have them back.'

'Yes,' said Kate simply. 'Yes, I will. But it won't be for long. Now that this offer has been made to Roz, all three of them will be going away from home in a few weeks. It's a bit of a shock, really. And with Tom not working, everything will be very strange. But we'll sort something out. I'll try to get a job.'

'What I particularly wanted to see you about, Kate, was Roz.'

'Roz?' Kate was surprised. Sofia had met Roz a few times, but did not know her as well as she knew Beccy.

'I want her to have the Guarneri.'

Kate stared at her, dumbfounded.

'But, Sofia, you can't possibly! I've no idea what it is worth, but it must be... tens of thousands? Hundreds of thousands? I haven't a clue. Anyway, we couldn't possibly accept.'

'Kate, I do not play the violin. My mother would have wanted it to go to someone who will love it and play it and care for it.'

'If you sold it, the money would keep you for years.'

'I don't want to sell it. I want to give it to your daughter, who is a talented violinist. Perhaps, some day, even a great one. And I would never have recovered the violin if you hadn't taken me to Hungary.'

'But it is far too valuable for us to accept. You must see that.'

Sofia looked at Kate. There were tears in her eyes. 'I was alone, without family or friends. You brought me both. Now, I feel as though your family is also my family. In families, such things are perfectly possible.'

Kate leaned across the table and took both Sofia's hands in hers. 'Yes, I feel the same. I have a family, but I was very lonely. Now I have you, and... all the others in Hungary.' She did not want to say their names. 'I know what we will do – and this, too, is perfectly acceptable in a family. The Guarneri will remain your property, but you will lend it to Roz to play. We must have it valued, and make sure it is properly insured. Is that a solution?'

'That is a perfect solution.'

After Sofia had gone back to her cottage, Kate took the violin up to Roz's bedroom and laid it on the chest of drawers. She noticed that the room was much tidier since Roz had come home. Either the camp had forced habits of tidiness on her, or she was growing up enough to value it for herself.

And then the second unusual thing happened. Kate heard the front door close and, looking out of Roz's window, saw Tom walking across to the garage and getting his car out. He swung the car round with a violent crunching of the gravel and she heard it turning out of the drive in the direction of the main road to Charlborough.

It was a good sign, she thought. It was the first time he had gone out of doors of his own volition since she had come home, and the first time he had gone away from the house since he had come back from Banford the day he was made redundant, two weeks ago now. She sighed with relief. She would leave it till the weekend, after Stephen was home, and then she would make Tom sit down and discuss the future.

Roz came back from Charlborough by the lunchtime bus on Friday, and Kate told her about the Guarneri. At first Roz went pale, then red, and she raced up to her bedroom. By the time Kate caught up with her she had the violin on her lap, stroking it like a cat.

'Isn't it beautiful, Mum? Oh, I can't believe it!'

253

'It's amazing. Let me tell you the whole story of where it has been all this time.'

'Just a minute.' Roz flipped through her collection of CDs and selected one. The sound of the Bruch violin concerto poured out. Eva, playing the Guarneri. Kate turned away, thinking of Eva and Zsigmond, of Jakob Stern and his family driven away on the death march, of Zsigmond and Juliska with the patriots in the forest, of István watching the secret police taking his father away, of Juliska and the firing squad, of Magdolna and the figure of the mother and child.

'Mum, what's the matter?'

'Nothing,' said Kate. 'I'm just so glad we were able to recover the violin.' And she told her the story they had heard in Budapest.

'Of course, I can't play like Eva Tabor,' said Roz, 'but shall I play something for you?'

'Can you play the Bruch?'

'It's not the same without an orchestra.' Reverently Roz picked up the violin, tightened the bow and began to tune the strings. Then she tucked it under her chin and started to play the violin part from the first movement. The rich lyrical melody sang out, filling the bedroom. They were so engrossed that they did not hear the back door open and close, and only when his feet clattered up the stairs and he appeared in the doorway did they realise that Stephen was home.

He looked magnificent. He was as bronzed as an Australian surfer and his hair was bleached fair with the sun. Kate thought he looked heavier, too. Not fat, but as though his body, which had been gangling and adolescent when he had gone away, had somehow solidified into adult male flesh. He looked like a man, and her heart gave a jerk that was somehow pity.

'Where on earth did you get that violin?' was the first thing he said. Even he could recognise the difference.

'And hello to you too,' said Kate.

'Hi, Mum.' He submitted to being kissed.

In a cascade of speech, both of them talking at once, they told him about Roz's success at the music camp, about the offer of a place at college, about the recovery of the famous violin in Budapest, about Sofia's loan to Roz of the Guarneri.

'That's great,' he said kindly. 'Looks as though you've really fallen on your feet, Rozie. Mum, I'm absolutely starving – is there any lunch going?'

'We were just going to have some. Come down to the kitchen and tell us about your holiday while I make us something.'

As they went down the stairs, Kate thought: Not one of them has asked me about my trip to Hungary, not even Beccy. It's almost as if it never happened. Of course, Roz and Stephen left while I was still here, and have come back to find me here again, so to them I might never have been away. But neither Beccy nor Tom has so much as mentioned it. The whole journey seems as insubstantial as an illusion. Yet István has changed me, altered the very essence of me. And they see nothing.

Stephen was giving them a day-by-day account of his journey and a series of hair-raising adventures involving lost wallets, a tumble into a canal, and an encounter with a frisky bull.

'We found this really fantastic place called Villevent, not far from Avignon, and stayed there most of the time. Camped in this farmer's field, who was really great. They gave us eggs and melons and vegetables, and we also went into Villevent for meals at the *bar-tabac*.'

'How's your French now?' asked Roz.

'Brilliant,' said Stephen, modestly. 'Mick absolutely refused to speak it, so I had to do all the talking. I can understand just about everything now, and at least I can make myself understood when I speak.' He laughed. 'I've probably picked up a Provençal accent.'

'We all went there on holiday once when you were quite small,' said Kate, 'but I don't suppose you remember. When we went to Brittany we tried to persuade you to speak French, but you never would – at least nothing beyond "une glace, s'il vous plaît".'

'It's much easier when you have to speak it, in order to survive.'

'So it is.'

'I mean, we'd have starved in Villevent if I hadn't been able to go into the village shop and ask for things. There wasn't a supermarket where you could help yourself, and nobody spoke English – or only a little.'

He started to describe the breathless journey back, rushing to catch the ferry, when he suddenly stopped in the middle of a sentence with his mouth open.

'I've just thought – have my A-Level results come?'

'The letter is in the hall, on the telephone table,' said Kate, who had heated up soup and was making sandwiches. 'But why not have your lunch first?'

He ignored her, running out of the kitchen and down the hall.

There was a long silence, in which Roz and Kate looked at each other apprehensively. Then Stephen gave a howl and they heard the front door slamming shut.

'Oh, no,' said Kate.

'Watch out, Mum, the soup's going to boil over.'

Kate grabbed the pan and pulled it to the side of the stove. Through the window she saw Stephen running out of the garden and up the hill into the rough turf and scrub which lay beyond Craigfast House. She thought, sickeningly, of the outcrop of rock up there, which ended in a sheer cliff overhanging Castle Terrace, two hundred feet below.

Things like exam results can be so devastating when you are young.

'You have your lunch,' she urged Roz. 'I'm going after him.'

'Shall I come too?'

'No, better not. We don't want to smother him.'

Kate went out of the back door from the kitchen and began to scramble up the hill behind the house as fast as she could go. At first she could not see him, then she caught sight of his red sweatshirt ahead of her. He was still running, but not so fast. As she watched, he flung himself down behind a clump of gorse, a place where he had sometimes taken his books when he was studying for his exams. She slowed her pace, and came up with him quietly, sitting down beside him on the tussocked grass. He did not look at her, but thrust out the sheet of paper in his hand, crumpled where his fist had been closed over it: Mathematics C, Physics F, Chemistry F.

She could not believe it. He had worked so hard. Surely there must be some mistake? Then she remembered his unease after the exams, his worries about whether he would be good enough. And her own doubts when he decided to switch from arts to science subjects.

'I'm sorry, Mum,' he said tightly. 'I'm sorry, I'm sorry. I've let you down.'

'Don't be ridiculous.' She put her arm round his shoulder, laying the paper on the ground and weighting it down with a small stone.

'I tried, I really tried. I worked as hard as I possibly could.'

'I know that. We all know that. I was worried you were working too hard. Nobody could have worked harder.'

'Then why?' He gave a rasping sob. 'What have I done to deserve this?' He choked, and the tears began to fall. Kate put her arms around him, and he stopped trying to be brave. His arms and shoulders were hard and muscular, and she thought, This is a man, this is a grown man now. But he cried as he had done when Benjy died, when he was only ten.

ೲ

Tom did not come home until half-past eight, chewed his dinner in silence and then shut himself in the little back room they had assigned

256

as his study, but which he had never made use of since they had moved to Craigfast House. Kate badly wanted to talk to him about Stephen, who had gone to bed straight after dinner with a headache. She had spoken briefly to Beccy, who was going out to the pub after dinner with Chris. Beccy, though sympathetic, was not able to offer much help. She had gained straight As in her exams the previous year, and been accepted by the university of her choice. Like Kate she was baffled by Stephen's results, and suggested tentatively to him at dinner that he should appeal.

'No!' he shouted. 'Obviously it's all I'm worth, isn't it? I'm a failure, a total failure. I'd better see if I can get a job at the chicken factory. Slaughtering and plucking chickens, that's about all I'm good for.'

Roz looked sick at this, cutting up her veggie cheeseburger. Tom stared at him blankly. Kate suspected that he had not even taken in what they were talking about.

Tension in the house, which had eased briefly when Roz arrived home, built up with a vengeance. Stephen veered from refusing to talk about his results to pacing back and forth wherever Kate happened to be, talking and talking. One moment he would be going over what he knew he had done right on the papers, which *proved* he should have had better marks; the next he was kicking the furniture, saying again that he was useless and ought to go job hunting at the chicken factory.

One day he started to sound quite serious about this, instead of just blustering, and Kate said briskly, 'Come on, we are going to talk about this sensibly.'

She sat him down on the terrace, where the wind was blowing off the sea with the first chill of autumn in it. The cries of seagulls circling the harbour floated up to them.

'Now,' she said firmly, 'point one: you are not going to start looking for a job. You know how difficult it is even for people with degrees to get jobs.'

'I don't mind what I do. With Dad out of work, we need anything I can contribute.'

'Not regardless of the cost to your future.'

Tom had still said nothing about his redundancy money, and no money had appeared in the account. The bank balance was diminishing with frightening rapidity. Kate was being very careful about household expenses and thought with relief that the large fuel bills would not come until after Christmas.

'I've already made enquiries about a teaching job. I might at least get some supply work. That will help.'

'I want to be some help too.' He sat with his hands clasped loosely between his knees. She looked at the strong knuckles and the tanned skin. It seemed only a short time ago that those hands had been small and plump, clutching her skirt.

'Of course you do, and I'm quite happy for you to get a holiday or weekend job like Beccy. But you know perfectly well that to have got this far, and to throw it all away, is just stupid.'

He said nothing, staring out at an oil rig support vessel heading out to sea. They were sitting so still that a large herring gull, crying raucously, flew into the garden and settled on a stone urn still filled with scrawny wallflowers Kate had forgotten to root out in the early summer.

'I had a word with Mr Ramage,' she said carefully. She had, somewhat guiltily, phoned the headmaster at his home. 'He thinks you should go back to school for another year.'

'I don't want to go back. I'd feel such a fool.'

'Apparently there are a few others going back – some to do resits, some to take extra A Levels. He's planning to form a small third-year sixth.'

Stephen clenched his hands, then sighed. 'I don't think I really want to resit the same subjects. I don't think I have the right kind of brain for science.'

'We always did think you were going to take arts subjects – English and history...'

'Last year I thought I'd switch to science because the job prospects were better. And I thought I could do something useful in the world. I loved the arts subjects, but I thought it was a bit immoral, just sitting around reading books and enjoying yourself.'

Kate smiled. 'Better to take subjects you enjoy, and do well in them, than to suffer, studying something you hate. Anyway, I was reading an article in the paper on Sunday that said graduates with arts degrees were just as likely, and possibly more likely, to find employment. They're seen by employers as more flexible, while scientists are perceived to be specialists. That may all be nonsense, of course, but it's worth taking into consideration.'

'I'd quite like to do French,' he said hesitantly, 'but I couldn't possibly catch up, could I? In just one year?'

'I could help. You'd probably only need to take two subjects, wouldn't you? If you could get good marks in two, then with the C in maths...'

'Maybe I could do French and English. I've read most of the English set books that were on the syllabus for this year.'

'Let's go and see Mr Ramage,' said Kate, giving his shoulder a squeeze. 'And see what he thinks.'

Lying awake that night, as she did so often these days, Kate felt as though she was convalescing from some severe illness. She was drained. At least Stephen had been safely steered in the right direction. She had been afraid he would not listen to her, and she thought of István with his son at much the same age. Like her, he had not been able to share the problem with another parent. Thinking of his tragedy, with his young wife killed when László was just a baby, she felt that Tom's problems shrank into insignificance.

He was lying beside her now, breathing deeply, but holding himself apart even in sleep. The new mood of withdrawal was some relief to her, after his violence, but his hostility and furtiveness were chilling. Whatever it was that he was up to, it had shaken him out of that nearly catatonic state which had so frightened both Beccy and herself. She had told him about the appointment with the benefits office, but did not know if he had kept it. At the moment she did not care what had galvanised him – it might even be a woman, for all she knew. Examining the thought as she watched the rectangle of the window grow pale with the rising moon, she found she felt nothing.

She turned on her side and closed her eyes so that she could see again the wide cool room, reaching the full width of István's flat in Sopron, with its shuttered window overlooking the garden. It would be an hour later there, even nearer the middle of the night. Was István asleep, or was he working? Certainly he would be back in Sopron by now, away from Szentmargit with all its powerful memories.

Thinking of him, she fell asleep.

Carefully István turned his wrist so that he could see his watch: 3 a.m. Old Lanja's breathing had been rasping for hours, but there was a difference now. Her frail hand, spotted with age, lay in his like a bundle of fragile twigs, apparently lifeless. The change in her breathing would mark the change in her condition. They had not called him soon enough, her good-for-nothing son and his wife, and the antibiotics might have come too late to relieve the congestion in her lungs.

Lanja took a few shallow breaths. Too shallow, like some small, dying animal. Then she drew a deep shuddering breath.

'Easy, my dear,' said István, leaning over her. 'Breathe slowly, now. Think of the scent of lilacs in the spring. Take a slow, deep breath. Can you smell them?'

He did not know if she could hear him, but the breathing slowed, deepened, took on a regular rhythm. Her eyelids flickered briefly, and he caught a gleam from her eyes. He smiled at her, in case she could see him.

'There now, well done.'

She relaxed, and the breathing became the steady rhythm of sleep. István, exhausted after a long day, leaned his head back against the wall beside the bed, still holding the old woman's hand, and closed his eyes.

Kate, he thought. Oh, Kate.

Chapter 14

The walnuts on the old tree in the square had ripened. The village boys picked those they could reach by climbing, and knocked others down by throwing sticks up into the branches, but a few continued to cling on tenaciously at the very top of the tree. Most houses in the village now had a store of walnuts in a pot high on a shelf. Magdolna still used a crock her grandfather had made as a young man, soon after he came back to the village after the first world war and set up as village potter in succession to his father.

István had come home to Szentmargit for a weekend and was sitting under the walnut tree with a group of other men on the Friday evening. Soon it would be too cold to sit out here, and the favourite places in the Blue Heron would be those near the big hearth with its glowing fire of logs gathered from the estate forest. István picked up a fallen walnut from the table and turned it in his fingers, thinking of the contorted pattern of the nut inside the hard shell. Like the complications of our inner lives, he thought, protected inside a carapace which presents a smooth, hard surface to the world.

The others were discussing the latest plans for the manor house.

'I think this idea to turn it into a school of agriculture is a good one,' said Imre. The others accorded him respectful attention. Since the dramatic effect of Imre's irrigation system on the harvest, he was regarded as one of the thinkers of the village.

'See,' he went on, 'it will bring some employment – they'll want staff to maintain a big place like that – the house and the garden and the greenhouses. And then the pupils and teachers will want to shop in the village. That will improve business all round. It could make it easier for us to get hold of new agricultural machinery and better seed corn. We might even get the road into the village repaired, for the first time in thirty years!'

István listened to him without comment. He was inclined to agree with Imre. It would mean change, of course, and the village would seem less of a secret place, a peaceful retreat for him in times of stress. But he had the luxury of a solid profession and a steady income. He could not begrudge a little more financial security for the villagers.

'Who's to pay for it, though?' József asked the world at large. 'Seems to me the government doesn't have the money.' He jerked back from his beer glass as a walnut fell into it, splashing him. 'Damn – will you look at that?' He fished the nut out of his glass, licking the beer off his fingers.

'You ought to take the house over, István,' said Mihály. 'As the son of the last count.'

'It's not mine to claim,' said István calmly. They had been through all this before. 'And I'd have no use for it. Can you imagine what it would cost to heat?'

They all thought about this, with the winter snows not far away now. The older men remembered the powerful black cars ploughing through snowdrifts on the long driveway in wartime, with SS officers sitting inside in their fur-lined jackets. And the people of the village shivering and dying, huddled together over the few fires lit with illicit wood filched from the forest. István recalled the great stoves in the manor, with their network of secret corridors, and thought it unlikely anyone would ever attempt to use the house in wintertime again. Last week it had been closed to visitors until next Easter.

'Come on,' said Imre, picking up his half-empty beer glass. 'It's getting too cold out here. Let's move inside.'

Stephen had gone back to school. It turned out that Mick's results, though slightly better than Stephen's, were not good enough for the university course he had set his heart on, so he had decided to retake the same subjects in the hope of getting better grades.

And then Chris had said, on hearing Stephen's depressing news, 'I failed my A Levels first time round, you know. But it didn't matter in the long run. Only held me back a year, and I think I got more out of university, being a year older and really knowing my subjects better.'

Stephen probably paid more heed, Kate thought, to Mick and Chris than to anything she herself could say, but she didn't mind. So long as he could see some goals ahead and feel he was moving forward. She went with him to see the headmaster and the head of the French department, who was pleased with Stephen's fluency and gave him an armload of books to start reading. It was agreed that he would take just French and English at A Level this year, and combine these with his existing maths result for entry to university next year.

Beccy and Roz went off together, two weeks after Stephen started back at school. Kate still felt that sixteen was too young to be starting alone at a college in London. She had wanted to take Roz to college, but conceded that she was needed more at home. Beccy would see Roz settled, spend the night with one of her old school friends in London, and then travel up to East Anglia the next day. She telephoned from her flat to say that all was well with Roz.

'She's in a super new hall of residence – only built last year. It makes this place look really grotty. We met two of the other freshers who seemed very friendly and nice, and she was happily going off with them to explore when I left. The Principal is keeping the Guarneri in the safe in the main teaching building, so Roz has to collect it and return it there whenever she wants to use it. He said he couldn't be responsible for its safety if it went out of the building.'

'Fair enough,' said Kate, thinking of the years the violin had spent sealed in the cellar under the shop in Budapest.

On Saturday, when Stephen came down for breakfast, she had the local paper spread out on the table. He had settled down apparently quite calmly at school, but she thought he still looked depressed.

'I've had an idea,' she said, pushing the boxes of cereal towards him.

'Mmm?' Stephen was not at his best in the morning.

She tapped the paper on the section headed 'Pets'.

'As you are going to be at home for another year, I thought we'd get you a dog of your own.'

'Really?' He looked pleased. 'You don't think Toby would mind?'

They both looked at Toby, who was sprawled in a patch of sunlight on the floor, chasing rabbits in his sleep.

'Not at all. You know how gregarious he is. He'll love having another dog to play with. Mark you, I expect you to train and clean up after this puppy yourself. Promise?'

'Yes, yes.' Stephen turned the paper round so he could see it, and began running his finger down the column. 'I quite fancy a Labrador, don't you? Like Sofia's Ákos.'

'I'm not sure he's pure Labrador. He was a stray she took in – she thinks someone abandoned him on the beach when they found how large he was getting.'

'It's awful when people do that, isn't it?' He looked at her bleakly. 'You shouldn't abandon your dog any more than you should your child.'

263

They spent a happy day together going round a short-list of kennels, but Kate knew Stephen had made up his mind at the second one they visited. They came back to it towards the end of the afternoon with Stephen sitting on the edge of his seat, saying, 'Hurry, hurry. What if they've sold her already?'

He had fallen for a golden Labrador bitch, all big feet and gangling frame. Kate was surprised. She thought he would want a dog.

'No,' he said firmly, 'a bitch is better. Toby might feel ousted by a dog, especially as the Lab will end up bigger than he is.'

The puppy took to Stephen at once, and when the purchase had been safely made she sat on his lap all the way back to Dunmouth, alternately looking curiously out of the window and licking his chin.

Toby accepted the new puppy calmly, taking a proprietorial interest in her and inspecting her from head to tail. Stephen christened her Sarah, because, he said obscurely, she looked like a Sarah. Despite Toby's affability, Kate decided to give him a long walk on his own on Monday, so he would know that he was still her particular companion. Because of the difficulties at home, they had not been for one of their walks beside the sea since Kate had come back from Hungary. Also, she thought she might call in at the bookshop to see Linda. Apart from telephone calls and one visit by Linda to Craigfast House, they had hardly spoken.

Kate took Toby along the sandy beach from the castle, where she was less likely to be spotted from her parents' house in Castle Terrace. After they had passed the last house in the row, she clambered up a breakwater, and over the tussocked dunes, both of which helped to keep the sea from nibbling the beach away. Then she crossed the road and began to search for the gap in the embankment which would allow them into the hidden valley where the old railway line had once run.

It was Toby who found it, disappearing completely from sight through a dense thicket of broom. Kate pushed after him, and the dried seed pods on the broom bushes rattled about her ears and popped seeds down the back of her sweatshirt. It was much warmer in here than on the beach. The embankment provided shelter from the east wind coming off the sea – a small wind as yet, an autumn wind, not a winter one, but it had a cold edge to it. They found the traces of a path which led from one end to the other of the valley, with branches wandering off here and there, penetrating the undergrowth. Everything seemed larger and more vigorous than it had when she had last explored here in the spring. From the state of the path, she thought that few people had been here since then, though there were animal tracks to be seen. Toby found plenty of rabbits to chase. They had made a network of warrens in the embankment and in the rising ground on the opposite edge of the valley, where there were sandy slopes at the foot of the steep cliff leading up to the houses which stood out of sight beyond the top of the high ground, on the main Charlborough road.

Walking on they found a small muddy stream, and there were more animal tracks here, which might have been a dog's, but from Toby's intense and quivering interest Kate guessed they belonged to a fox. Great rampant briar roses hung over the stream, studded with clusters of bright scarlet rose-hips the size of plums. A blue tit, perched between the vicious thorns on one of these branches, swayed up and down gently as it preened itself. It cocked its head at Toby, passing underneath, and fixed Kate with a beady eye, but did not take fright. She passed within two feet of it.

Kate found a hump of rock sticking up through the damp, overgrown grass and the spikes of dying willow-herb, and sat on it while Toby ranged around her, following interesting smells into the bushes. Drifts of willow-herb seed-heads, soft as silk, floated past her as he disturbed them. All this tumultuous growth and wild profusion reminded her in some indefinable way of the secret waterways through the marshes at Szentmargit, where the boat had slipped under the waving heads of the reeds. Reminded her, too, of the ragged hedge at the side of the field of sunflowers, where the thunderstorm had caught them.

Every other inch of ground in Dunmouth, she thought, even Sofia's garden, is planned and disciplined. Only here do things grow unchained, according to their own natures. In less than thirty years, since the railway line was dismantled, this place has changed from the bare cindery area of a man-made track to something belonging entirely to nature, and not to man at all. The flowers and bushes and trees had to compete with each other, but they have found a modus vivendi. Over those years a balance has been struck, so no one species has dominated and driven out the others. Standing up at last, she reached over to a hazel tree and picked a handful of nuts. They were ripe and sweet, and she munched them as she followed a different path back to the gap behind the thicket of broom.

Her first weeks back in Dunmouth had plunged her into frantic activity, but now she had a sense of being sucked back into that dark isolation which had clouded her first months at Craigfast House. All that vitality which had flowed into her in Hungary – from the people, from the countryside, from Magdolna, from István – had seeped away. She was exhausted. She felt dispossessed. The busyness she tried to create in her life seemed a sham, and she saw herself like one of the last lingering fishermen of Dunmouth, casting and casting a net into the sea, but always hauling it up empty.

She would visit Linda. Time in her company would bring some comfort, but she could not speak to Linda about the things that were really troubling her, or about the wordless debate which raged continuously inside her.

Kate felt disreputable as she walked into Harbour Steps Books. There were twigs and leaves in her hair and seeds of willow-herb and cleavers attached to her skirt, but luckily Linda had no customers. Toby sat down in the middle of the floor and panted meaningfully.

'Hello, stranger,' said Linda. 'How did you know I was just going to put the kettle on? Yes, Toby, you can have a bowl of water and a biscuit.'

'You're going to have another dog to spoil soon,' said Kate, following her into the big kitchen built on to the back of the cottage. 'Can I nip into your bathroom and tidy up? I feel like the Guy Fawkes bonfire they used to build on the pebble beach.'

'They still do. Not long now till Bonfire Night. What other dog?'

'Tell you in a minute,' said Kate, climbing the stairs and shutting herself into Linda's elegant new bathroom.

Over tea and shortbread, Kate explained about Stephen's puppy.

'What a good idea,' Linda said. 'With both girls away at college it will give him something positive to enjoy.'

'That's what I thought. And training the puppy will stop him becoming too obsessed with his exams.'

'And how are you?'

'All right, I suppose. I'm still not sure where we stand financially.' Kate had told Linda a little, cautiously, about Tom's redundancy and his difficult behaviour. She felt she could speak openly to Linda, who had been through a similar experience with her father – though Dan Wilson had come out fighting.

'You're going to have to sit down and work things out soon, you know. You say Tom is at least going out of the house now, instead of hiding. Perhaps he's ready to cope with plans.'

'Yes. I'm a coward. I've always hated confrontation and I've kept putting it off. But today I've been trying to get my courage up. I'm going to try to tackle him this evening.'

'If you were out all day on Saturday puppy-hunting, I suppose you missed the excitement.'

'What excitement?'

'A little boy of eight – he's in Lucy's class at school – was swept out to sea. I can't think what his parents were thinking of, letting him play on the estuary in one of those inflatable boats that are meant for swimming pools. The tide was on the ebb, and you know what it's like, with the river current and the tide both running. In minutes he was swept right out beyond the mouth of the river and into the shipping channel.'

'What happened?'

'They launched the lifeboat, of course, but before they had it manned and under way, that chap from the water sports centre, Harry Stannard, got on one of those awful jet bikes and reached the child first. I must say I've always disliked jet bikes in the past, with the noise they make, but I feel differently about them now.'

'The little boy – he was all right?'

'Fine. A bit cold and frightened, though not as frightened as his parents. The odd thing was that it should have been Harry Stannard.'

Kate looked at her enquiringly.

'Didn't you know?' said Linda. 'He's the son of Eddie Stannard, who was coxswain of the lifeboat which was lost with all hands in '78. Grandson of that old devil who lives in Barometer Cottage. Odd sort of family. Dad used to say that they always had to be leaders of the pack amongst the lads in Dunmouth – always a bit wild, but brave as well.'

'I've met the old man. I didn't realise Harry was his grandson.'

'Ed Stannard brought Harry up after his father was drowned. His mother had gone off with a lorry driver from one of the seafood wholesalers, when Harry was two. Ed's a difficult man. He's always had a chip on his shoulder because he was declared unfit to serve in the navy during the war. He'd had rheumatic fever, I think. Dad said he went a bit daft afterwards.'

Linda sipped her tea thoughtfully, and fed Toby another biscuit.

'Ever since Chris came up with those newspaper cuttings, I've been wondering... I bet Ed was behind those attacks on Sofia's cottage during the war. It would be just like him to jump to the conclusion that they were German spies. He's paranoid about foreigners.'

Kate was staring at her. Things seemed to be clicking together in her head.

'Ed Stannard would be about the same age as our parents, wouldn't he?'

'Yes, or a bit older.'

'So Eddie Stannard was our age?'

267

Linda looked at her curiously. 'Surely you remember Eddie Stannard? He was the ringleader of that gang of older boys and girls who used to bully you. Do you really not remember?'

A face swam into Kate's memory. Was it Eddie? Or was she remembering Harry, from the sports centre?

'And he was drowned, going out in that terrible storm, to save people from a ship drifting in the North Sea?'

'Yes.' Linda looked at her in concern. 'Are you all right? You've gone as white as paper. Have some more tea.'

Kate accepted the mug absently. 'I was just remembering something.'

But it wasn't a memory, not really, she thought. Just images floating in her head.

Three customers came into the shop then, and Kate slipped away, leaving Linda to attend to them. She walked along the harbour front and paused to look at the lifeboat station and Barometer Cottage, with the fishermen's church just beyond. Was there some clue here to her nightmares? Her mother must have been about nineteen when the first attacks on Sofia's cottage took place. Ed Stannard, the old man in Barometer Cottage, must have been older. He was already a married man with a son. How had Millicent come to be involved with what Howard had called the 'bad business' at the cottage? She didn't come from one of the fisher families, but from snobbish, middle-class Castle Terrace, and in the Dunmouth of those days the social dividing lines were much more rigid than they were now. If Millicent had been caught up – accidentally or otherwise – in the tormenting of the Hungarians which had ended in Eva's death, it would explain her anxiety ever since to dissociate herself from Ed Stannard and his like. Probably they had never seriously meant to hurt the women. If Eva had not already been ill, the blow on the head might not have killed her.

Kate walked on, and paused again in front of the plaque on the side of the lifeboat station. It was difficult to sort out her own jumble of feelings. If Eddie Stannard was the boy who had been forcing Kate along with her arm twisted up her back on that night – that night which came back to haunt her with the smell of burning and the howls of the trapped dog – could he really be the coxswain who drowned twenty years later?

She would have to face her parents. For too long she had been running away from the past. Millicent must be made to explain the events at the cottage in 1944. And surely they must know something about what had happened to Kate in her childhood? Had she managed to hide the terrors of that night successfully from them even then? As she now seemed to have buried the memory so deep that she could not recapture it without help? She needed someone who had been an adult at the time.

Tonight she would tackle Tom about their future. Later, when she felt strong enough, she would tackle her parents.

She had reached the three Georgian houses at the end of Harbour Walk. Toby sat down heavily on the pavement and scratched his ear, looking at her to detect where their walk was going from here. The largest house, she saw, was still for sale. The board was leaning over even further now, and was so swathed with weeds and stained with rain that it was almost illegible. She heaved the sign up out of the tangled growth and made out the name of a local Dunmouth solicitor, located in St Magnus Street, who was acting for the owners. Dunmouth had no estate agent.

'I wonder,' said Kate to herself, gazing up at the house. It was comfortable-looking but shabby, badly in need of affection and brisk care. 'I wonder.'

Mr Tarbert, in the solicitor's office, was busy but obliging. He knew Kate's family. He was quite happy to give her the keys of the house and let her go off to examine it on her own.

'It's been standing empty for nearly two years,' he said frankly, 'and it needs a lot of decorating. But you'll find that the essentials are sound – the roof, the wiring and plumbing. And to be honest, Mrs Milburn, I think you'll find my clients will accept any reasonable offer. They had to move to Bristol two years ago and they've been paying two mortgages all that time. I'm sure we could come to some satisfactory arrangement.'

He did not, Kate noticed, show any sign of surprise that the new owners of Craigfast House should be showing an interest in a much less desirable property. As she had known all her life, it was difficult to keep a secret in Dunmouth. The entire village had probably heard about Tom's redundancy before she had even arrived home from Hungary.

She walked back along the seafront to the house. Toby sniffed with interest at the door frame as she turned the key in the lock and stood for a moment with her hand on the handle. Under the weather-beaten paint was a solid six-panelled door. It moved smoothly on its original hinges, and admitted her to the central hall of the house. Toby followed her inside, his nails clicking on the bare boards. The layout was very simple. On the ground floor were four rooms leading off the hall, one in each corner of the house. Behind the back room on the right a passage led to a collection of small rooms which would once have been pantries and larders but which appeared to have been used in recent years as junk rooms, not cleared out by the previous owners. From the hall a broad staircase led up to an identical arrangement of rooms above, with four bedrooms leading off the landing and a bathroom – plain but modern – located over the pantries. A narrow staircase behind a door led up to the top floor, which held two attic rooms with dormer windows. The house was more roomy than it appeared from the outside.

Kate stood at the window of one of the front rooms upstairs and looked out at the river. The harbour was to her left, and beyond it she could see the castle on the promontory which formed one wing of the harbour. To the right past this last house in Harbour Walk the road petered out into a grassy track which served as a foot-path and cycle track along the edge of the river. She could hear the raucous calls of the gulls, and straight in front of the house half a dozen swans were clustered in a curve of the shore. The house smelled empty, but not damp, and it seemed to be waiting, with breath held, for her to pass judgement. She turned around and smiled at the room. She knew this would be a friendly house.

Out at the back of the house was a jungle. There might have been a garden once, but now it seemed to have become a communal rubbish tip for Dunmouth. Looking down from one of the back bedrooms she could see rusty tins and bicycle wheels, plastic bottles, broken pieces of concrete slabs and torn carrier bags. The wall on to Fish Lane at the back was low, and it was clear that many people found it convenient to toss their rubbish over into the garden of the empty house. Still, a skip and a few days' hard work would take care of that.

Suddenly there rose before her eyes a picture of Szentmargit, a village much poorer than Dunmouth, without a scrap of rubbish in sight. Why have we become so dirty in our habits in this country? she wondered. Is it because we are always expecting someone else to come along and clean up after us? Szentmargit was immaculate, apart from the dust blowing from the unmade streets. But at least that was just earth, not this kind of litter. In Budapest, she remembered, there had been an army of old men sweeping the streets and pavements with old-fashioned whisk brooms and capturing any stray scraps in long-handled dustpans. They moved with dignity about the city, taking a pride in keeping it clean.

As she pulled the front door of the house closed behind her, and checked that the lock had engaged, she gave the handle a surreptitious pat. 'I'll be back,' she promised.

❧

'I've bought a boat.' Tom was staring at her defiantly, like a guilty child caught in a misdemeanour.

His words made no sense. They were sitting in the drawing room of Craigfast House beside the first open fire of the autumn. Toby and Sarah lay sprawled in front of it, warming their stomachs. Stephen had gone out with Mick to a football match, so Kate had judged that it was at last time to have matters out with Tom. No money had been paid into the bank account since the last salary payment at the end of August, more than two months ago. Kate had just explained to him that she had received a phone call during the afternoon with an offer of two days' language teaching a week at Charlborough High, standing in for the regular teacher during maternity leave. She would start at the beginning of December and continue until Easter. It wouldn't mean a lot of money, but it was something. Whenever, during recent weeks, she had asked Tom if he had sorted out the matter of unemployment benefit, he avoided her eye and changed the subject. She had thought he was still too ashamed to talk about it – but now he confronted her with this.

'What do you mean, a boat? A dinghy? How can we afford it?'

'I used my redundancy money. And it isn't a dinghy, it's a thirty-foot sloop. I'm going to sail it round from the marina at Charlborough Bay next week.'

She was aghast. 'But we need the redundancy money to live off until you get another job, or start drawing benefits. Have you done *anything* about either? Oh, my God, Tom, have you gone completely crazy?'

He smiled complacently to himself. 'Thought you'd be surprised. I'm not going crawling on my hands and knees to some arrogant clerk wanting to know all my personal business. I've been enquiring about the grants and loans available for setting up your own business. Once I've been unemployed for six months I'll be eligible for several things.'

'What are you talking about? What business?' Kate felt her grip on reality was slipping.

'I'm going to run fishing trips in the estuary, and sailing trips for those who aren't interested in fishing. Advertise in the posh magazines and Sunday supplements. I've been looking into it. You can charge a fortune. We've plenty of room here, we can provide accommodation for parties of up to six.'

Kate felt herself flushing as her anger mounted. 'What about me?' she shouted. 'Why haven't you discussed any of this with me? Where do I fit into all of this?'

He shrugged. 'I thought you'd be glad I was doing something positive. If you're only going to be teaching two days a week, you should have plenty of time for a bit of cooking and bed-making. It won't mean a lot of work.'

'Tom,' she said, trying to keep her voice steady, 'have you really thought this all through?'

Wasn't he the one who was supposed to know about business plans and financial forecasting?

'It's almost winter. You can't run these trips in winter – the estuary is terribly dangerous during the winter storms. You wouldn't be able to start until the spring. What are we going to live off in the meantime? There are three of us to feed, clothe and keep warm in this great house for the best part of six months – and the girls as well during the holidays. It just won't work.'

'We'll have your teaching salary. And I might get a start-up grant. I can set the business up, even if I don't start running the trips till later.'

With a sigh Kate fetched her folder of household bills and her calculator from her desk in the corner. She started estimating as best she could what their running expenses would be during the winter, but this was difficult without a previous year's figures for Craigfast House. However optimistic her calculations, the columns of figures she passed over to Tom always ended up negative.

She could understand his need to manage his own life and make his own decisions about a job, better perhaps than she would have done a year ago.

'I just don't see why you have been so secretive,' she said. 'We could have talked it over, worked things out.'

He looked at her and then his eyes slid away. 'You've been pretty secretive yourself since you came home.'

She could find no answer to that, but instead told him what she had been thinking about when she looked over the house in Harbour Walk that morning.

'If we sold Craigfast House, which we own outright, and bought this other house, we'd have money left over which we could put in an interest-bearing account. It would be a cushion against disaster. We'd get the house for a very reasonable price – the owners are desperate to sell. And Mr Tarbert said Craigfast would sell like a shot. There's a company wanting to develop the land at the top of a hill as a golf course. They've got planning permission, and he thinks they'd like to get their hands on this as a club-house.'

272

Kate wondered why she felt no emotion at the thought of parting with the house, which was beautiful and had such wonderful views. But she had not been happy here. The house made her think of loneliness and the slow deterioration of her marriage. She felt no warmth towards it.

'I bought this house because I thought you'd like it,' said Tom bitterly, 'but I never seem to have been given credit for that.'

'I know, I know, I'm sorry. The months since we moved here have been so stressful. But this house in Harbour Walk, Tom – I'm sure you'll love it. It's right by the harbour, so it would only take you five minutes to get to the boat. There are six bedrooms, if we use the attic. In fact one of the ground-floor rooms could be a bedroom too. And the garden is much smaller. It's a tip at the moment, but once it's tidied up it won't need much looking after.'

It might be possible for them to mend their life together, after all. If she was prepared to spend all her free time catering and cleaning. Don't think about that for the moment. Take some action, she thought, so at least we can survive the winter.

'Come on,' she said. 'Let's go and look at the house. I know it's dark, but you can see what it's like from the outside – there's a street lamp in front of the house next door.'

❧

If they had been lucky with little else recently, they were lucky in the matter of buying and selling the houses. The company developing the golf course was keen to have immediate possession, so they would have time to convert the building ready for the scheduled opening of the course in June. They were prepared to pay a little over the odds in order to settle matters quickly. And the owners of 24 Harbour Walk accepted £20,000 less than the official asking price. By the third week in November Kate, Tom, Stephen and the two dogs found themselves camping out in the new house. The survey had been cautiously approving and they decided to do nothing to the house apart from putting in some inexpensive DIY kitchen units and redecorating the main rooms.

Stephen was enthusiastic about the move. His new bedroom was smaller but warmer than the room he had occupied in Craigfast House, and the proximity to the middle of the village – with its fish and chip shop only five minutes' walk away – was a clear advantage. The Harp and Anchor pub in St Magnus Street had recently acquired a snooker table which was proving an irresistible attraction on Friday evenings.

Beccy and Roz, busy with their lives elsewhere, had shown little interest when Kate phoned to tell them of the decision to move to Harbour Walk.

'It's fine by me,' Beccy said cheerfully. 'After all, you don't need such a big house now that we've left home. And Stephen will be gone soon.'

Kate felt chilled by such finality. Did they really no longer feel that home was with the family? Beccy's tone was not consciously cruel, but it cut deep.

Unable to do much to further his planned business venture, Tom was prepared to spend some of his time, when he could be prised away from his boat, helping Kate paper and paint. At the weekends she had enthusiastic if messy assistance from Stephen and his friend Mick, whose mother was a busy freelance accountant with little time to cook. Mick regarded substantial meals as adequate payment for his decorating efforts. The furniture which had seemed sparse and inadequate in Craigfast House filled the new rooms satisfactorily, and curtains stored after the move from London could be taken out and rehung. After three weeks the house was beginning to look as Kate had hoped it might, and when she arrived home in the dark from her teaching days in Charlborough, the house glowed welcomingly.

Tom was less welcoming. His thoughts were absorbed in the new sloop and the fishing gear he was buying. The only times he spoke to Kate, it seemed, were to issue instructions about how the future clients were to be looked after. That brief period, after she had first come back from Hungary, when he had needed her physically and intimately, might never have been. Nowadays they never touched, and in bed kept a distance between them. Kate could not decide what her feelings were about this. In one corner of her mind she was angry that, after such pressure had been put on her, she was now cast aside and unwanted. But for the most part she was filled with the same dull indifference as she had felt when she had locked the door of Craigfast House for the last time and handed over the keys to the representative of the new owners.

She said nothing of these things to either Linda or Sofia, though both of them were more solicitous than usual. Infrequent letters from Beccy and Roz showed that they were busy and contented, and that was some consolation. Above all, Stephen seemed to have come to terms with his situation. He was deputy head boy now, and in the end-of-term exams he came top in French and fourth in English. It was evident from his cheerful demeanour that he was enjoying school far more than he had done for the previous two years, and Kate began to feel that the disaster of his A-Level results in science might prove a blessing in the long run.

Roz had written to say that she was to perform a solo on the Guarneri in the college's Christmas concert, and she was anxious for them all to go. Kate thought Tom might refuse, but he seemed willing enough.

'If Beccy comes down to the concert from university,' Kate suggested, 'then we could drive both of them home for Christmas. What we save on their train fares will pay for the petrol.'

Tom had sold his BMW and bought a second-hand Volvo estate, a little battered but built like a tank. It would be more practical for his future needs, he said, and would be the kind of vehicle to appeal to his customers. At any rate, Kate thought, it would hold all five of them and their luggage for the drive back from London to Dunmouth. Howard and Millicent had decided they could not manage the journey in the unreliable December weather; Howard's arthritic hip made long car trips a painful ordeal. Kate promised to buy them a copy of the concert tape the college was making. She had seen very little of her parents since she had come back to Dunmouth. The problems of her husband and children, she persuaded herself, were occupying too much of her time. But she knew that she must confront them about the events from the past which still troubled her sleep. She would do it before Christmas, because Christmas was when she had promised to write to István. And Christmas was only a week away.

Several of the students were featured as soloists in the college concert, but it was clear to Kate as soon as she examined the programme that Roz and a pianist called Richard Verdhun were the principal soloists – they were each playing a full concerto, while the others had short pieces or single movements. The pianist played in the first half. He was twenty-one and in his last year at the college. Evidently he was accustomed to the concert platform; he took his seat on the piano stool calmly and professionally. He performed Rachmaninov's second piano concerto with great technical panache, and Kate began to ache for Roz, who could not possibly match his experience. In the interval she left the rest of the family having refreshments in the refectory and wandered about the grey stone corridors of the college, reading the notices pinned on the boards and thinking the grim institutional place an odd nursery for so much bright young artistic talent.

Roz was to play near the end of the second half of the concert, followed only by the senior choir singing a medley of Christmas carols arranged by one of the college staff. When it came to Roz's turn, Kate found she was gripping her hands together so tightly that her knuckles were white.

As Roz came on stage carrying the Guarneri, she stumbled. It was nothing, just a misjudging of the top step, and she did not drop the violin, but Kate's stomach lurched, and she saw that Roz was a ghastly yellow white. She is going to have to overcome her nerves, thought Kate, or she will never be able to have a concert career.

Roz was playing the Elgar violin concerto. During the long opening passage played by the orchestra the soloist must stand and wait. From where she was sitting in the third row, Kate could see that Roz's right hand, holding the bow, was trembling. When at last she lifted the violin and began to play, the first three or four notes sounded uncertain, even to Kate's inexperienced ears. But the colour was coming back into Roz's cheeks, and suddenly the notes became confident and the violin began to sing, gravely, seriously, as the orchestra drew back leaving the violin to its deep contemplation.

Kate closed her eyes to listen. She was thinking of Roz, but she was also remembering Eva, the little half-gypsy girl, forced to practise until her fingers bled. She thought of Eva running away with Zsigmond after her concert in Pécs, and of how beautiful she had been in that photograph of Sofia's, holding the violin and with red roses in her hair. She thought of the escape down the Danube, and the violin left lying in the vaults, silent for all those years, then rescued and cared for by Jakob Stern, when he returned from concentration camp, the sole survivor of his family. All of these people, all of these scenes, were interwoven with the music, but when she opened her eyes as the last notes were dying away she remembered that this was her daughter, this was Roz who was playing – and she was very good indeed.

She realised that other people in the audience had been anticipating this performance. Of course the college had probably advertised the fact that Roz would be playing the missing Guarneri. But there was something extra in the applause which greeted a flushed and smiling Roz. She's never going to be my child again, thought Kate sadly, clapping and cheering with the rest. She's public property now.

Roz played some quick, clever little piece as an encore, and the concert finished on a seasonal note with the choir. At the party after the concert for the performers and their families, Roz was besieged. Her family found it difficult to fight their way through the crowd to reach her, and Kate was worried until she saw how poised and capable Roz seemed. One term at music college had changed her.

On the long drive north the next day, Roz slept most of the way, slumped against Beccy's shoulder.

'Delayed shock,' Kate whispered, grinning over into the back seat as Beccy rolled her eyes and groaned quietly about the weight of her sister's head.

'Just so long as she doesn't get too stuck up,' muttered Stephen. 'It's an awful squash in here, Mum, with these two fat females taking up all the room.'

๛

A steely winter light filled the bedroom, reflected upwards from the surface of the harbour. Kate was safely out of the way, shopping in Charlborough for last-minute Christmas supplies. In a patch of the silver light Toby lay stretched out at the foot of the bed watching Tom as he laid his hand on the top of Kate's dressing table. Tom felt one brief qualm as he pulled open the drawer where Kate kept her personal papers. At the top, with no attempt at concealment, was a stiff envelope with YOUR PHOTOGRAPHS printed across it. He drew it out and began to lay out the photographs along the dressing table in front of the piece of pottery Kate had put there.

The first pictures showed buildings and well-known landmarks from Budapest. Then the photographs of people began. He swept the earlier photographs back into the envelope and laid out the later ones in their place like a hand of cards. He raised each one to his face in turn, tilted it towards the light and scrutinised it closely. A kind of excitement seized him, tightening in his chest till he thought his heart would stop beating. The last photograph. He held it for a long time close to the window. The sense of relief which flooded through him set his heart racing again, and he felt his hands grow damp with sweat. He wiped them on his trousers, then carefully stacked the photographs together.

He had known he was right. Everything was easy now. For the first time in weeks he felt the band of pain in his head loosen and melt away. He smiled.

Chapter 15

On Christmas Eve there was the first hard frost of the winter. Kate got out of bed in the front room upstairs at 24 Harbour Walk, and looked out over the river. She had woken late, after hours of frantic cooking and parcel-wrapping the day before, and it was already light. The pebbles on the foreshore glinted in their casings of ice, and as she opened the window and leaned out to smell the air, which she liked to do every morning in this house, she could hear the ice-sheathed rigging tinkling like a chime of bells from the fishing boats in the harbour.

Tom had not come home last night. He said he was staying the night in Charlborough Bay. He had gone, he claimed, on business. Something to do with gear for the boat. But he never looked Kate in the eye these days, and she knew he was deceiving her. Had he found some other woman during those weeks when he had gone off alone, ostensibly searching for a boat? A woman who would not judge him a failure, as he accused Kate of doing? Or had he simply gone off drinking?

She thought it might be a woman, but found she no longer cared. Her emotions seemed as frozen as the thin grass in the front garden. Apart from her children and the secret thought of István, nothing moved her deeply any more. And her children needed her less and less. She felt she was standing marooned on shore while the children flew away from her, impelled by some inexorable centrifugal force. Shivering in the cold wind off the river, she pulled down the window and went over to her dressing table, where Magdolna's figure stood. She lifted it and turned it in her hands, as she had once done in Magdolna's studio. Mother and child were both intensely absorbed – the mother in the child she was holding, the child in the fascinating world opening up behind his mother's shoulder. Kate laid her cheek lightly against the cool ceramic hair of the mother and thought of Magdolna's insistence that she should take this particular figure. Magdolna was right, of course. We are so wrapped up in our children we cannot see that even in infancy they are reaching beyond us. Put down that baby, Kate told the mother, and he will toddle away from you.

She breakfasted alone. Beccy, Stephen and Roz had come in late last night from a party Chris had given before going home to his parents' farm for Christmas. They would probably sleep till midday. She took the stuffings, made last week, out of the freezer to thaw, checked that the door of the odd little larder was locked, so the dogs could not get at the turkey, and surveyed her preparations. Apart from cleaning the vegetables and stuffing the turkey this evening, everything was ready. There would be eight of them for Christmas lunch. Her parents and Sofia were spending the whole day with them. She wondered how Millicent would react to Sofia. Well, she would be able to judge better after this morning. Tomorrow evening, Linda and her two girls were coming for Christmas tea, which would bring them up to eleven. A number easily accommodated in Craigfast House, but it would be a tight squeeze here.

She called Toby and Sarah and let herself out of the back door.

The road was slippery along the harbour. An onshore wind had thrown spray up over the pavement and roadway when the tide was in, and during the night it had frozen. It was Sarah's first experience of ice, and she slithered about alarmingly, but decided this was some new game. Ed Stannard came out of his cottage as Kate drew level, and tapped the barometer, wiping his nose and eyes with a large spotted handkerchief.

'Good morning, Mr Stannard,' said Kate. He was so bent and wizened, crouched against the cold wind, that she felt a surge of pity. She could not think of him as a vicious gang leader, a murderer even.

He looked up, startled. 'Morning,' he said gruffly, then – as Sarah slid past on her backside and splayed front paws – he gave a rusty bark of laughter. 'Look at that then! New to ice, is she?'

'Yes, she's only a few months old,' said Kate, smiling. 'You watch yourself, it's treacherous underfoot. The sea has been over the wall.'

'Aye, well.' He paused. 'Merry Christmas to you, missus.'

'And to you, Mr Stannard.'

જી

There was a strong east wind blowing, but Tom stood well out from the land, reaching northwards up the coast in the sloop *Lorelei*. He had sailed her up to Charlborough Bay yesterday morning and taken the bus home, congratulating himself on his stratagem. His family wouldn't

279

even notice that *Lorelei* was gone from Dunmouth harbour. None of them was interested in his plans.

In the evening he had driven back to Charlborough Bay, leaving the Volvo hidden away in a back street where it wouldn't be found too soon. He had told Kate he would be staying overnight and only returning late on Christmas Eve. That had given him a twenty-four-hour start.

He had left before dawn. Now he was past Berwick and lying off the Scottish coast. Would he be able to reach Leith before it grew too dark?

She was a beauty, the *Lorelei*. She moved soft and smooth beneath him, carrying him on, carrying him away from Kate. *Lorelei* wouldn't deceive him as Kate had. He'd done everything for Kate and the children. More than twenty years of his life he had sacrificed to them, and they simply turned away from him now, looking as though he embarrassed them.

He hugged his arms around himself, whistling a tuneless air.

That would teach Kate. And he would not come back. He had had enough of bearing responsibility for other people.

He pulled the wad of photographs out of his pocket. He had not bothered to bring the pictures of buildings and scenery, only the pictures of people. The same people again and again. A middle-aged couple – the man in overalls, the woman square and plain. Sometimes a gangly boy with them. A tall angular woman he had seen Kate talking to in Dunmouth. And a tall man with greying hair at his temples, looking humorously at the camera, as though he was about to spring out of the picture. And one picture of the same man with Kate. They were not looking into the camera but towards each other, and the man's hand rested lightly on Kate's shoulder.

Slowly and methodically, Tom tore the photographs into tiny fragments and dribbled them from his fingers into the sea.

Last of all, he drew a studio photograph of Kate out of his wallet. It had been taken shortly after their marriage. She looked so young. Untainted by childbirth and motherhood. His only. Viciously he tore the photograph across the face and threw it after the others.

The scraps of pictures spun and swooped on the waves like coloured bubbles, then floated away astern in the foaming wake of the *Lorelei*. Tom felt a sharp clean pain in his chest. He was free now.

How long would it take him to reach Orkney?

ॐ

Kate's parents were surprised to see her. They were just putting away the breakfast dishes, but offered her tea from the remains in the pot. They all sat down in the prim sitting room, screened – by the private road, by the Terrace private garden, and by the fence – from any view of the sea. Only up on the first floor, where Kate had once had her bedroom, could you see into the distance.

The dogs were banned to the kitchen.

'I'll not have them in here,' said Millicent, 'with their dirty paws all over my clean carpets.'

Kate made a token protest, pointing out that the ground was frozen and the dogs' feet were no dirtier than her own shoes, but she did it more because it was expected of her than because she hoped to be listened to.

Over their tea they talked about Roz's concert and the arrangements for the next day, and then Kate put down her empty cup.

'Sofia Niklai will also be coming to us for Christmas,' she said.

There was a sudden, palpable silence in the room. Millicent, who was sitting beside Kate on the sofa, turned towards Howard where he sat in an armchair by the fire, as if she expected him to field this disconcerting remark, but he said nothing.

'As you know,' Kate went on carefully, 'Sofia and I went together to Hungary in the summer.'

Millicent opened her mouth and Kate knew she was going to make some superficial critical remark. She held up a beseeching hand.

'Just a minute. Before we went, Chris Harding discovered some stories in the *Dunmouth Herald*'s archives about disturbing events that happened at Sofia's cottage during the war. Linda also told me one or two things her father had mentioned. I haven't felt up to talking to you about this before, but I think we need to clear the air before you spend Christmas Day in my house with my friend Sofia.'

They were listening to her intently now. Millicent was twisting a fine lawn handkerchief into a tight coil between her fingers.

'As I understand it, Sofia and her mother were taunted and attacked on several occasions after they came to live in the cottage. They were accused of being Nazi spies. They were, of course, Hungarian refugees from Nazi persecution. In 1944, when Sofia was trying to get out of the cottage to fetch a doctor for her sick mother, a stone was thrown which struck her mother on the head, and she died shortly afterwards in Charlborough Hospital.'

Kate paused.

'Her mother was the world-famous violinist Eva Tabor, whose Guarneri violin Roz played at the concert last week.'

Still they said nothing.

'At that time Ed Stannard, who was a young fisherman, had been rejected by the navy on health grounds. He was bitter and resentful, and he was looking for someone to take out his anger on. Perhaps he really did believe they were Nazi spies, and that he was being a hero. I don't know. But someone threw that stone. There was murder done at that cottage, and I believe you were there.'

Tears were running down Millicent's face. Her head was bowed, and Kate could see the pink skin of her scalp shining pitifully through the carefully permed white hair. Like Ed Stannard, she looked old and vulnerable, and Kate wondered at the way age can appear and disappear in the human form – Sofia looking younger and younger, Millicent ageing visibly.

'I was there,' Millicent whispered at last. 'It all started as a bit of a silly game, I suppose. I don't know whether we really believed Ed when he said they were Nazis. But everyone was very nervous about invasion all up this coast. There were concrete posts put up as barriers against landing craft along the beach, and some of the pillboxes on the headlands are still there. We half believed him, I think. Someone had thrown a stone before and had hit the girl on the forehead – she was a little older than I was, and she wasn't really hurt. I swear I never threw anything. I just tagged along. I wasn't supposed to have anything to do with that lot – my parents would have been horrified – but I was bored, and Ed was quite a handsome young man, very persuasive in his way. That grandson is very like him.'

The words were tumbling over each other, as though – having decided to talk about it – Millicent could not get the words out fast enough.

'Ed threw the stone that night. The girl opened the door when he had just picked up a heavy piece of stone to throw at the door. The light flowed out, and he threw it anyway, into the light. He can't have aimed at anything. We didn't know till later that the old lady was hit.'

'She wasn't an old lady.' A great depression settled over Kate as her suspicions were confirmed. 'She was only forty-two.'

Millicent was sobbing now, an ugly, dry, rasping sound that shook Kate more profoundly than a lifetime of harsh criticisms. 'I never meant any harm,' she said pleadingly. 'I never had anything to do with Ed and those others again, but I've never forgotten it. Then after the war your father and I got married, and I thought it was all behind me. But I still dream about it – the shouting, the path of lamplight as the door opened, the awful thud of the stone hitting something inside the cottage.'

She laid her hand tentatively on Kate's arm. 'I'll understand if you don't want us to come tomorrow.'

Kate put her arms awkwardly round her mother, something she had never done before. 'Of course I want you to come. It's Christmas.'

Millicent clung to her briefly, then pulled away, wiping her eyes and blowing her nose. 'I'm sorry. But perhaps it's best to have it out in the open after all these years.'

Kate took a deep breath to steady herself.

'There's something else. Fourteen years later, in 1958, there was another attack on the cottage. There was a fire. I think Eddie Stannard, Ed's son, was probably the instigator on that occasion. I have almost no memories of the first ten years of my life, but I think I remember something about that fire. I keep having nightmares about it. You must know. Was I somehow implicated?'

Her parents looked at each other, then Millicent said in a strangled voice, 'No, I don't think I can talk any more,' and she got up and went out of the room. They could hear her climbing the stairs. Kate and Howard sat in silence. Toby had heard Millicent leave the sitting room, and he came ingratiatingly in, nosing the door open and followed by Sarah. They lay down at Kate's feet.

'Dad,' said Kate, 'I need to know. Whatever it was, it's better to know the facts than to go on like this.'

Howard cleared his throat. 'Yes, I do understand. We tried to shield you, of course, when you were a child. And then your mind seemed to have wiped out any memory of it, so we left well alone. As for facts – well, I don't know the facts. It's mostly guesswork.'

'Tell me the guesswork, then.'

'It was a November evening, so of course it was dark quite early. The week after Guy Fawkes, and I think that was partly the trouble. Some of those big boys – Eddie and his friends – had made a huge bonfire, and they were all still a bit fire-crazy, I think.'

'But they were all much older than I was. Why was I there?'

'They'd been bullying you for years. We didn't realise, of course, or we'd have done something about it. In fact it was that very day, when I was out looking for you to call you in for your tea, that Dan Wilson mentioned Linda had let something drop. He was afraid they had been making your life a misery. Why didn't you say something?'

'I don't know. I can't remember.'

'Afterwards, of course, we sent you away to boarding-school as soon as possible.' He paused, looking out at the bare trees in the long formal rectangle of the Terrace's private garden.

'I was coming back along Castle Terrace from the middle of Dunmouth, where I'd run into Dan, when I saw flames suddenly shoot up into the sky from the direction of the cottage on the headland. I didn't know what to think. It might just have been the boys with another bonfire, or it might have been the cottage. I called out to Bill Herward, who kept the Castle Bar – where the Castle Café is now – to phone for the fire brigade, and I started running. By the time I got to the cottage I could see that the shed was well alight, and there was a gaunt woman I'd never seen before dowsing it with buckets of water. I helped, and so did Bill when he arrived, and between us we managed to put it out, though the building was destroyed. By the time the fire brigade arrived, all they had to do was make sure the fire was really out and the house wasn't in danger.'

'Was anyone else about, on the headland? Eddie and the others?'

'Nobody. But I recalled seeing a crowd of them running along the beach back to Dunmouth as I turned into Castle Terrace. It wasn't until we'd put the fire out that I remembered I was supposed to be looking for you. I found you eventually, not far away. You were chest deep in the sea, and your clothes were burned to tatters. You kept babbling something about lighting the fire. I carried you home, and as soon as I had you in the light I could see that your arms and legs were covered with burns – great patches as red as poppies.'

Kate pushed up her sleeve and tilted her arm wonderingly, looking at those silvery shadows on her skin.

'You were very ill for a time, in hospital. You had to have some skin grafts in a couple of places – one on your back and one behind your right knee. And as a result of wandering in the November sea – we don't know how long – you developed pneumonia.'

'I don't remember anything about it.' But Kate wondered whether her lingering discomfort around hospitals had started then.

'You never spoke of it, except when I first found you. None of the older children seemed to have a mark on them, so we were afraid – your mother and I,' he cleared his throat again. 'We were afraid you were the one who started the fire.'

❧

The gate in the wall round Sofia's garden was unlocked when Kate arrived at dusk. She had been walking for hours with the dogs in the secret valley behind the embankment, ever since she had left her parents' house at the end of the morning. With part of her mind Kate knew that the valley was beautiful – the lace of fallen leaves trimmed

284

with frost, the berries on the rowans scarlet as blood. But most of the time she simply sat on a log near the stream with her arms wrapped around herself, so still that once a squirrel ventured within a yard of her.

Sofia's garden was still beautiful, but sad, like a lovely woman grown old and fragile, clinging on to her dignity. The bees were hibernating, the hens were shut up, even the goat was in her stall. One last red rose bloomed on a bush by the seat where they had sat in the summer, drinking tea amid all the busy life.

Sofia took one look at Kate, with her mud-stained skirt and lips blue with cold, and at the tired dogs with burrs in their coats, and shooed her into the sitting room where a driftwood fire burned on the hearth. Kate flopped into one of the old, shawl-covered chairs without a word, and she heard Sofia feeding the dogs in the kitchen. Ákos, who had returned to his spot by the fire, raised his head at the sound of his dishes being used, but he had already eaten, and lay down again with his head on Kate's shoe. The house was filled with the smell of cinnamon and when she closed her eyes she felt as though she was back in Magdolna's kitchen.

Preceded by the dogs, Sofia came in carrying a tray with a bottle and glasses, and a plate of little cakes.

'I thought this would be better than coffee,' she said, drawing the cork. 'It is the bottle of his Tokay that József gave me when we came home. I thought we would open it in honour of Christmas.'

'You may not want to drink with me, Sofia,' said Kate, 'when you hear what I have to tell you.'

Sofia looked surprised, but she filled the glasses and waited. Kate told her of the nightmares, and of István's theory about her mind blanking out some terrible event of her childhood. She held up her arms and showed the pale skin, which he had said was the mark of old burns. Then she began to explain what Howard had told her that morning.

As she was speaking, Sofia carried over a glass of wine and placed it beside her, with some of the little cakes on a plate. Then she took her own wine to the other chair and listened in silence until Kate had finished.

'So you see,' said Kate, 'I will quite understand if you do not want me for a friend. A vicious little arsonist, who tried to burn your house down.'

Sofia raised her glass to Kate, then took a sip.

'My dear Kate,' she said, 'I have always known who you were, from the time we met by the rock pool, back in May.'

'You *knew*!'

'Of course. I thought at first that you did also, but then I came to see that you had truly forgotten, and I did not want to waken painful memories.'

'But, Sofia...'

'Listen. Your father is right about the things he saw – the fire and how he helped me put it out, the crowd of older boys and girls running away. But he is wrong about the things he did not see.'

She paused, sipped her wine again, and Kate, without noticing, drank some of hers and bit into a cake. She realised suddenly that she had eaten nothing since early morning.

'I was upstairs changing my clothes. I'd soaked my skirt fishing for crabs, so I didn't see the crowd of you arrive. Then I heard a noise and I looked out of the window. The biggest boy had you in an arm lock, and he was waving a crude torch of twigs in your face, trying to force you to set fire to the shed with it. You were fighting him like a wild-cat, I may say. I saw you bite him. I flung up the window and shouted at them, and that must have made him give up the attempt to force you. He dropped you on the ground and pushed the torch under a broken plank in the side of the shed.'

Sofia closed her eyes, remembering.

'It was a dry frosty night, like tonight, and the wood caught immediately. The rest of them ran off at once, and I rushed down the stairs and out into the garden, because my dog was shut in the shed. I had a bitch then, with young puppies, and I hadn't wanted them to follow me down on to the beach when it was getting dark. Honey was howling in terror at the fire, and with fear for the pups, and there you were. You hadn't run away with the rest of them – you were tearing at the burning planks, trying to get to the dog. I pulled you away, but your clothes were already on fire, so I rolled you up in some old sacks to try to put the flames out.'

'The dog,' said Kate, anguished, 'I can still hear the dog.'

'She was fine. I unlocked the door of the shed – which was on the side away from the fire – and got her and the puppies out safely. I don't know why you hadn't opened the door yourself – the key was in the lock – but you were only a child and I think you were half crazy with fear and pain by then.'

Kate stared at Sofia. Tears of relief were pouring unnoticed down her face.

'Once the dogs were out, I went back to where I'd left you, but you'd disappeared. From what you've just told me I realise that you must have run into the sea to ease the burning. Then your father arrived, and another man, and we put out the fire between us. I didn't know then that he was your father, or that he was looking for you. Since my mother's death I hadn't mixed much with the people of Dunmouth. And I assumed you had just run off home when you saw the dogs were safe. I had no idea you had been so ill.'

For a long time they sat in silence. Kate thought about the events of that night, which had remained in her memory as a blur of pain and guilt and fear, while Sofia had always known the true story. At last Sofia leaned forward and took both of Kate's hands in hers.

'I am so sorry, my dear. I would have told you long ago if I had realised you didn't understand what happened.'

'I've felt so guilty,' said Kate. 'I knew there was something here I should be ashamed of, but it was all confused in my mind.'

'You had nothing to be guilty of. Quite the reverse, in fact. You risked your life to save my dogs. And that boy, Eddie Stannard, he more than compensated for it later, when the lifeboat was lost.'

'Yes.'

Sofia turned and reached down beside her chair, where Zsigmond Niklai's leather-bound diaries were piled.

'I don't think I've ever shown you this, Kate. It was the passage in my father's diary which most set me wondering what had become of him. I felt guilt too, guilt at being the one who had survived, when my mother was dead and my father left behind. But you will see, he felt guilt too. Guilt simply to have been born who he was – privileged, wealthy, when people in his country were poor and starving.'

She began to turn over the pages, looking for the passage.

'István felt guilt,' said Kate slowly. 'The guilt of the survivor, he said. He believed that if Zsigmond had gone without saying goodbye to him and Magdolna, he might have escaped.'

Sofia said nothing, but touched her hand gently.

'Here it is,' she said, holding the open book out to her and translating aloud.

Suppose, after all, we were to be called to account for our deeds in this world before some ultimate tribunal. The past made present, confronting us as it truly was – not as our flinching memories recall it – could prove appalling. But might there have been, even in our darkest acts, the seeds of redemption?

What if we could turn aside, walk through the unnoticed door into a hidden garden, and find there the past, ready to be lived again? Willing to be reshaped, fashioned from chaos into harmony and order? If the hurtling train of life could pause at the station, the hands of the clock stop.

If we could have another chance.

István had come home for Christmas. Anna was back from Budapest, András was on holiday from school, and the house was full of the spicy smells of festive cooking. And, remarkably, László would soon be here. Over the months since his visit to his son with Kate in the summer, István had travelled south three times to see László, acting on Kate's suggestion that the rift between them might be bridgeable. He had tried to show his son that he had accepted his vocation to the priesthood, that it need not stand between them. Gradually, László was thawing towards his father. Last week he had telephoned István before he left Sopron for Szentmargit and said that he would join the rest of the family at Magdolna's house two days after Christmas. He could not come for the festival itself as he was needed in his parish, but he had arranged with Father Pál to take a week's holiday afterwards, his first since he had taken up his ministry.

István reflected, as he walked along the river path in the dusk, that his son's intense commitment to his vocation for the last six years had probably contributed to the division between them. László had been determined to excel in his studies, and had thrown himself into his ministry with impassioned zeal, as the new freedom in Hungary resulted in more and more people turning to the Church – not just the old, who had retained their faith from pre-communist days, but the young, born under communism, and new to Christianity.

He needs a holiday, thought István. Some quiet time here in Szentmargit will do him good, and help us to get to know each other again.

László had not been in the village since his mid-teens, had lost touch with his cousins. In the past Anna had been an adoring shadow, András just a toddler. Their bright young company would help László ease off that stern armour he had adopted.

István's feet crunched over the snow. No one had walked here since it had fallen a few days ago, and this evening's hard frost had crusted it over so that it had the texture of cake icing on the surface, but where his boots broke through into the softer snow beneath they squeaked against it, compressing it into deeper hollows where his footsteps fell.

He reached the bridge and leaned in his favourite place on the handrail, which was sheathed in ice. The trout stream below his feet was frozen, but deeper down beneath the locked ice he could make out the secret, constant movement of the stream. The Danube itself was frozen, here among the small islands. He could have walked across the water to the island where he had taken Kate for a picnic. The cold ashes of their fire would be lying under a foot of snow. The moon was rising now, over to his right, where the marsh was a forest of frozen reeds, standing clustered in silhouette like the spears of the silent wooden warriors he had seen with Kate at Mohács.

The herons had gone, the grey herons from their nest on the roof of the *csárda*, the rare blue herons from the marsh – flown away to the warmth of the Nile and its papyrus beds. Even the hunting owls were silent. Everything, on this bitter Christmas Eve, was frozen and still.

Kate had not written. She had promised to write by Christmas with her decision, but he remembered – as he counted the last days – that she had not said whether she meant she would send the letter by Christmas, or he would receive it by then. He might allow himself a few more days to hope.

The bell from the Church of Szent Margit began to ring out for the Christmas Eve family service. The air was so still that it sounded as clearly to him here on the bridge as it would have under the bare branches of the walnut tree, where the leaves and nuts of the coming year were already forming in some hidden part of the old tree's being. István gripped the icy rail of the bridge, feeling the cold flow into his hands and the warmth of his own blood melt the ice and reveal the rough wood beneath.

'I haven't given up hope, Kate,' he said.

When Kate left Sofia's cottage it was getting dark. Soon she must go back to the house on Harbour Walk and cook dinner, and make the final preparations for Christmas. But first she walked out along the rocky headland which projected beyond the cottage into the sea. The dogs, puzzled but game, followed her – ranging about, sniffing at interesting deposits left by the sea, peering into rock pools where reflected stars swam amongst the sea anemones. Out towards the end of the point the going became more difficult, and Kate had to crouch and use her hands to scramble over the broken rocks, which were coated with treacherous, half-frozen seaweed and a slick covering of ice.

At the very end of the headland she stopped. Here a huge flat rock almost as large as the cottage had been deposited millennia ago. It dropped like a cliff into the sea and its lower reaches, washed by the waves, were studded with barnacles and gripped by seaweed. Its top surface had been smoothed by the breaking waves of storm seas until it looked polished, with a few hollows like giant thumbprints which always held water.

Kate balanced here, standing upright now, and looked out to sea. In the pocket of her coat there was a five-forint coin, which she carried for comfort. She ran her fingers over it, tracing the faint outline of the heron amongst the reed beds.

When she had arrived at the cottage she had been exhausted, drained of energy and emotion. But Sofia's revelations had lifted a black burden from her, and she understood now how much it had weighed upon her over the months and years. She felt liberated, light-headed.

'You are guilty of nothing,' said Sofia, 'except risking your life to save my dogs. All this time you have been trying to bear someone else's responsibility.'

And then she had read that passage from Zsigmond's diary, reflecting his guilt about the compromises made by his country's government, about his inherited crime of having been born to wealth and ease. Zsigmond, certainly, had more than appeased that guilt. But he had said more.

What if we could turn aside, walk through the unnoticed door into a hidden garden, and find there the past, ready to be lived again? Willing to be reshaped, fashioned from chaos into harmony and order? If the hurtling train of life could pause at the station, the hands of the clock stop.

If we could have another chance.

Kate, perhaps, had opened such a door, could have another chance.

She breathed deeply, filling her lungs with the sharp, cold, salty air. Once, she had lived closed in by the darkness of her shadowed past. Then remembered guilt had pierced it like a sharp knife, but even as it had cut, it had let in the light. Somewhere out there, a different future might be waiting. She could perceive distances now.

The moon was rising over the sea ahead of her, and as it lifted clear of the waves it laid a silver, trembling path across the water to the foot of the boulder on which she stood. As a child she had always been filled with wonder at the path of moonlight on the sea, and had imagined she could step on to it and walk away from Dunmouth, into those mysterious distances.

Something was moving out there in the water, causing the moonlit path to break and shiver and close again. A seal? No, this was larger, more vigorous. Then as she stared out, half dazzled by the moon, it rose again in a perfect leaping curve. A dolphin. They were rare on this coast, but sometimes a solitary dolphin passed, searching perhaps for its lost companions. It leapt again, the moonlight turning its powerful sides and the cascading water to silver. Then it was gone, slipping away to the open sea.

Kate began to write her letter in her head.

My darling István, when do the herons of Szentmargit fly home from the winter grounds of the Nile?

The wind off the sea was cold on her cheeks, but the coin lay warm in her hand, deep in her pocket.

Look for me when the herons return.

THE AUTHOR

Ann Swinfen spent her childhood partly in England and partly on the east coast of America. She read Classics and Mathematics at Oxford, where she married a fellow undergraduate, the historian David Swinfen. While bringing up their five children and studying for an MSc in Mathematics and a BA and PhD in English Literature, she had a variety of jobs, including university lecturer, translator, freelance journalist and software designer. She served for nine years on the governing council of the Open University and for five years worked as a manager and editor in the technical author division of an international computer company, but gave up her full-time job to concentrate on her writing, while continuing part-time university teaching.

In 1995 she founded Dundee Book Events, a voluntary organisation promoting books and authors to the general public. Her first three novels, *The Anniversary*, *The Travellers*, and *A Running Tide*, all with a contemporary setting but also an historical resonance, were published by Random House, with translations into Dutch and German. *The Testament of Mariam* marks something of a departure. Set in the first century, it recounts, from an unusual perspective, one of the most famous and yet ambiguous stories in human history. At the same time it explores life under a foreign occupying force, in lands still torn by conflict to this day. Her latest novel, *Flood*, is set in the fenlands of East Anglia during the seventeenth century, where the local people fight desperately to save their land from greedy and unscrupulous speculators.

Currently she is working on a series set in late sixteenth century London, featuring a young Marrano physician who is recruited as a code-breaker and spy in Walsingham's secret service. The first book in the series is *The Secret World of Christoval Alvarez*. She now lives on the northeast coast of Scotland, with her husband (formerly vice-principal of the University of Dundee), a cocker spaniel and two Maine Coon cats.

www.annswinfen.com

Printed in Great Britain
by Amazon